Ronen Lalena

SHIMON ADAF

ONE MILE AND TWO DAYS BEFORE SUNSET

Translated by Yardenne Greenspan

Shimon Adaf was born in Sderot, Israel, and now lives in Holon. A poet, novelist, and musician, Adaf worked for several years as a literary editor at Keter Publishing House and has also been a writer-in-residence at the University of Iowa. He leads the creative writing program and lectures on Hebrew literature at Ben-Gurion University of the Negev. Adaf received the Yehuda Amichai Prize for Hebrew Poetry (2010) for the collection *Aviva-No*; the Sapir Prize (2012) for the novel *Mox Nox*, the English translation of which, by Philip Simpson, won the Jewish Book Council's 2020 Paper Brigade Award for New Israeli Fiction in Honor of Jane Weitzman; and the I. and B. Neuman Prize for Hebrew Literature (2017).

Yardenne Greenspan is a writer and Hebrew translator born in Tel Aviv and based in New York. Her translations have been published by Restless Books, St. Martin's Press, Akashic Books, Syracuse University Press, New Vessel Press, Amazon Crossing, and Farrar, Straus and Giroux. Her translation of Yishai Sarid's novel *The Memory Monster* was selected as one of *The New York Times* 100 Notable Books of 2020. Greenspan's writing and translations have appeared in *The New Yorker*, *Haaretz*, *Guernica*, *Literary Hub*, *Blunderbuss Magazine*, *Apogee*, *The Massachusetts Review*, *Asymptote*, and *Words Without Borders*, among other publications. She has an MFA from Columbia University and is a regular contributor to *Ploughshares*.

By

SHIMON ADAF

The Lost Detective Trilogy

Book 1: *One Mile and Two Days Before Sunset*

Book 2: *A Detective's Complaint*

Book 3: *Take Up and Read*

Aviva-No

One Mile and Two Days Before Sunset

One Mile and Two Days Before Sunset

Translated from the Hebrew
by Yardenne Greenspan

Shimon Adaf

Picador | New York

Picador
120 Broadway, New York 10271

Printed in the United States of America
Originally published in Hebrew in 2004 by Keter, Israel, as
קילומטר ויומיים לפני השקיעה (*Kilometer Ve-Yomayim Lifnei Ha-Shkia*)
English translation published in the United States by Picador
First American edition, 2022

Library of Congress Cataloging-in-Publication Data
Names: Adaf, Shimon, author. | Greenspan, Yardenne, translator.
Title: One mile and two days before sunset / Shimon Adaf ; translated from
the Hebrew by Yardenne Greenspan.
Other titles: Ḳilomeṭer ṿe-yomayim li-fene ha-sheḳi'ah. English
Description: First American edition. | New York : Picador, 2022.
Identifiers: LCCN 2021060836 | ISBN 9780374227036 (paperback)
Subjects: LCGFT: Detective and mystery fiction. | Novels.
Classification: LCC PJ5055.2.D44 K5513 2022 | DDC 892.43/7–dc23/
eng/20211217
LC record available at https://lccn.loc.gov/2021060836

Designed by Janet Evans-Scanlon

Our books may be purchased in bulk for promotional, educational, or
business use. Please contact your local bookseller or the Macmillan
Corporate and Premium Sales Department at 1-800-221-7945, extension 5442,
or by email at MacmillanSpecialMarkets@macmillan.com.

For book club information, please visit facebook.com/picadorbookclub or
email marketing@picadorusa.com.

picadorusa.com • instagram.com/picador
twitter.com/picadorusa • facebook.com/picadorusa

10 9 8 7 6 5 4 3 2 1

And an entire mythology
Is gathering
Beneath my fingernails

When I see people
Their darkness approaching
It's a pain I
Can no longer resist

—"Before Everything," Blasé et Sans Lumière,
from *One Mile and Two Days Before Sunset*

PROLOGUE

1

There was a moment when it seemed to Dalia that summer might just be bearable, though she knew it would linger for a long time yet over the Tel Aviv buildings. The unappeasable light would scowl; many pounds of indignation would blow across the tops of the dusty trees on Gordon Street, down which she was now walking, plastic grocery store bag sweating in the palm of her hand. Evening had slowly conquered the street, and she could feel it breathing down her neck, inching after her, flowing down from the sea to dim the brief, too brief past, stretching between her and the supermarket on the corner of Ben Yehuda Street. She was already waiting at the light on the corner of Dizengoff when the summer dark, the weight and heat of which were indistinguishable from the weight and heat of daytime, caught up with her, grazing her back. In a flash of befuddlement, she turned toward it. A light breeze blew, caressing her face. The street held its breath, a rare strip of time in which the silences and spaces contained in every motion, in every movement, occurred at once. For a fraction of a moment, creation ceased, and human deeds, their loosening ticking, filled the land with their disruption—no one started an engine, no one parked a car, the sliding doors of the drugstore froze, the sycamores paused in their rustling, the fruit bats avoided dropping their feces on the cars waiting at the light from north to south, Gordon Street was desolate from east to west, girls obliterated their giggles, boys hid away the growl of their broken voices, the beggar with the amputated leg gathered in his murmurs, the espresso makers of coffee shops fell silent.

When was the last time she felt such glory, the absence of the extant beating on? When? The grocery store bag tapped the sidewalk, Tel Aviv's smoke-stinking blood renewed its flow down asphalt veins, and Dalia reached out her hand to grab hold of the traffic light pole. Seven years had gone by since she descended from the number 5 minibus on this corner.

"Ask the driver to let you off on the corner of Gordon, turn right, and walk about three hundred feet. Make the first right, onto Israëls Street. I live at number seventeen, first floor on pillars. The buzzer doesn't work, so if the front door looks closed, just give it a little push. Go up the stairs. It's the first door you'll see. Don't ring the bell, it stopped working about a week ago. Just knock hard, because sometimes I'm deeper in the apartment and I can't hear it. Come after four o'clock." Ronnit had sounded out of breath on the phone, and not very inviting, but Dalia had taken so long just to muster up the courage and call her cousin, the only person she knew in Tel Aviv.

From the ages of five to eight they sat together, wide-eyed, watching *The Smurfs*, *Belle and Sebastian*, *The Little Lulu Show*, and *Maya the Honey Bee*, scampering around Dalia's yard, scribbling on the walls of her bedroom, being scolded, looking forlornly through Ronnit's bedroom window at the gray skies of Sderot, or through the third floor balcony at the lawns, throwing carefully cut pieces of paper on the head of the Romanian's son, the one with the training wheels on his bicycle, who made fun of them, calling them the two fat-asses. And when summer soared, the intoxicating fragrance of those red flowers—hibiscus, said Ronnit's mother, who was a teacher at the same elementary school where Ronnit's father was principal—and the public pool, the sweetness of chlorine, the bothersome odor of the skin after swimming and basking in the sun, which years later she learned to equate with the odor of semen, and the time spilling in abundance around them. And winter again. The town of Sderot skipped over autumn and into a sudden cloudiness, puddles formed by sparse rain between thickets of dandelions and beds of stork's-bills, but Sderot never rested in its race to the gold and the next brightening of weather, an explosion of chrysanthemums in the small valley on the way to Dalia's house, Passover on the horizon, and the two of them gathered one mum after another, tying heavy floral bracelets around their wrists, one year and then the next, until Ronnit's father was transferred—so pronounced Ronnit, with a stern expression, glowing in her gravity: "My father is being transferred to Beersheba." And that was that.

No, that wasn't that, because Dalia saw Ronnit one more time. Six years later, on a school trip. Dalia hated organized school events—field trips, Holocaust Remembrance Days, Jerusalem Days, educational outings. But that day, she couldn't find a way out. That rolling laughter, growing until the breath caught, replaced with brief wheezing, rang in her ears as soon as she set foot on the steps outside the Museum of the Jewish People, and she followed it, bewitched, knowing she was being pulled by a sound she'd heard before, but unable to place its source among her many memories. When she reached the tall, skinny girl who had emitted it, she paused, flummoxed. Something about the facial features looked vaguely familiar, but only in the way that a stranger might resemble a forgotten friend. The girl who turned to her cheerfully, saying, "Dalia, you haven't changed a bit," was indeed a stranger. She wasn't joyful Ronnit, easily enticed by any childhood mischief. The time that had melted her fat had also imbued her every movement with steel, replacing her natural friendliness with reserved conceit. Dalia didn't understand this right away. For hours, she dragged behind Ronnit and her friends, enduring their biting comments. Only after a long period—too long—did she learn that "you haven't changed a bit" was, in Ronnit's new and sophisticated lingo, an insult.

It stung even five years later. Dalia's mother called Ronnit's mother. "Dalia is having trouble finding her path lately . . .

no, she didn't enlist . . . really? Intelligence corps? An officer? Wonderful . . . Yes, I know she's renting a place in Tel Aviv. That's actually why I'm calling . . . She'd like that? They haven't seen each other in so long . . . I know, they used to be so sweet together . . ."

Dalia stopped eavesdropping and returned the receiver of her bedroom phone to its cradle, using a maneuver she was well-versed in, dropping a heavy book—Samuel Delany's *Dhalgren*—from her shelf to the floor to camouflage the hushed click of her hanging up.

"Dalia, how many times do I have to tell you? Be careful with the books you borrow from the library. You don't own them," her mother called from the living room, then lowered her voice once more to continue her conversation.

On the Seventeenth of Tammuz, Sderot put Dalia under siege. On the Third of Heshvan the wall fell. Winter began. Life with her parents became unbearable. If she had to sit for whole days, waiting for the rain to stop just so she could step out onto the streets of Sderot, where every crack sprouted a memory, where every turn offered up the same convergence of sight and smell, eucalyptuses and moist pines, glistening thatched-roof houses and loose dirt and ozone, she would lose her mind.

She made the call, packed her things, and left. When she got on the number 5 minibus, she lost herself so deeply in her Walkman that she didn't hear the driver calling, "Who wanted Gordon Street?" and rode on to the end of Dizengoff Street, where she stood up, startled, approached him, and whispered, "Excuse me, driver, have you passed Gordon yet?"

He showed her where to catch the minibus going the other way. This time, she sat at attention. She got off at the light, dragging her bag behind her, letting it drop to the sidewalk, reaching a hand to grab the traffic light pole, breathing a sigh of relief. Then the world stopped turning in the wintry air, bathed in thick amber light.

Two weeks later, she and Ronnit parted ways with a fight that shook both houses, the House of Shushan and the House of Abraham, reopening some old wounds. Dalia found an apartment with roommates in the Florentin neighborhood of Tel Aviv, but a year later, passing through Dizengoff, she saw a notice attached to a tree: "1.5 bedrooms for rent on a quiet street in central Tel Aviv." The woman who answered the phone gave her the details: 17 Israëls Street, first floor on pillars. She was filled with victorious glee. Though she was unemployed and could just barely scrape together a deposit, she signed the lease and never moved out.

Now she crossed the street heavily. Light signals of distress lurked on the edge of her consciousness. Seven years earlier, Ronnit had waited for her with pursed lips, skinnier than Dalia had remembered. Even though Dalia was late, and according to her calculations Ronnit must have been waiting for at least an hour, she was still wearing her officer's uniform. Well, sure, thought Dalia, Ronnit would never miss an opportunity to show what she's worth.

"What's up, baby?" Ronnit asked, smiling with satisfaction. "Did you miss the bus?"

Yes, Dalia wanted to say, just like you made me miss the school bus back from the museum on that field trip. But she was too tired to talk. Besides, she'd been feeding off of that memory for much too long for her to waste it right away.

"Why don't you take a nap, and then we can go out tonight? You're going to love Tel Aviv."

Dalia remained silent.

"All right, well, I've made up the office for you. Maybe you'll want to go out tomorrow night, once you've had a chance to walk around a little and get to know the city."

Why not? Ronnit had lived there for six months and already Tel Aviv was "the city." Her city. With whose permission? With the permission she was brave enough to demand. There's an age, sometime before the end of adolescence, which is crucial. If by that point you haven't gained the courage to formulate your desires as a list of demands, you're done for. Men are primed for this, but women? If you miss that train, you'll spend eternity trying to appease life.

"I'm sorry," Dalia muttered and walked past Ronnit, into the room that was prepared for her.

What's going to welcome me this time? Dalia wondered. I'm going to sacrifice the first creature to walk toward me out of the building to the gods of Tel Aviv. The thought amused her and she straightened her back, as she always did when she was expectant. Eran, the officer from the second floor, came down the stairs with that signature bouncy gait of his. She would have been happy to sacrifice him, but somehow she didn't think he'd make a proper offering. "And a happy day of mourning to you too," he greeted her with a chipper sneer.

The signals she'd so successfully ignored now became a burning flame. Every step in the short flight of stairs leading to her apartment was harder than the one before, more bitter, a step toward the gallows, toward a date she'd tried to suppress, because it reminded her of him. It never ended. She slammed the door behind her and tossed the bag into the middle of the living room. Then she walked from the living room to the balcony, crossing the distance with long strides. Peeking out at the sky. The Ninth of Av was already descending fully on the outside. She could see the evening.

Dalia plopped down into the armchair and thought of the last time she'd seen him. That meeting she'd so been looking forward to. Her body was scarred with longing for his touch, any kind of touch. For a week her flesh had been wanting, but he had avoided any physical proximity, inching away as she moved closer. She grabbed the notebook from the living room table and wrote feverishly, more an etching than a composition, stopping occasionally to pierce the paper with circular motions of her pen in an effort to conquer the emptiness washing over her, roiling up her bloodstream, approaching her heart, gripping, sentence by sentence. Dalia felt like she was drowning. She closed the notebook and threw it at the television.

"Enough," she said out loud. "Stop it, stop it, stop it," her voice grew louder. "God, if you save me now, I, I . . ." she gasped. "Stop it, stop it." She felt her voice attempting to rip open the boundaries of her throat, climbing up into a scream. "Stop it!" She shoved her right hand into her mouth and bit down on it. A thin stream of clarity appeared along with the pain. A breach was opened inside the blackening air.

To her, crying was a shock that had hardly any physical manifestation. Even as a little girl, she cried like a fossil. Her tears streamed down, unhindered by expression. Her facial muscles thawed from their tension, their effort to delineate an emotion. She got up and went to the bathroom to wash her face.

Her crying bout was brief but to the point. True relief did not spread through her body, but the heaviness in her limbs, that made her move like her bones were shattered, shrunk and drained into her chest. She leaned over the sink, getting closer to the mirror, examining her face, the blood-drenched vessels. The fluorescent light spread a sickly hue, pushing away any illusion of wholeness or softness, gaping open every blemish on the skin, highlighting the small pimples, revealing webs of wrinkles and pockmarks.

A branch from the mighty ficus out in the yard banged against the bathroom window, getting tangled in the bars. Wind, again? The Ninth of Av was losing steam early this year. Oh, well, she thought, I haven't done this in a long time, not since I was fifteen. What was the point in trying to control the season if you couldn't even control your own heart?

She stepped into the bathtub, reached out, and collected a dry leaf from the windowsill. She ran a hand through her hair and tore one single, short, black hair from her scalp. From the kitchen cupboard she pulled out a candle and a saucer. She lit the candle and dripped a circle of wax onto the saucer. Then she tied the hair around the leaf, wrapped it with a piece of paper, and placed it in the center of the circle. She walked out onto the balcony, placed the saucer on the plastic table, lit the ball of paper on fire, and said, "I, Dalia, daughter of Esther Shushan, on this eve of the Ninth of Av, command summer to die."

2

Rami Amzaleg was angry. Everything he tried the past week had gone wrong. And now the fucking sampler wouldn't turn on. He was hot. The angrier he got, the more his sweat levels rose. His black T-shirt, with the words "Wired is the Lord" smeared across the chest, weighed on him with its dampness. He'd bought it at the designers' market on Shenkin Street and couldn't remember if the designer with the pierced lip had promised that each printed statement was unique. At any rate, he'd never seen anyone wearing a similar shirt. The bad noontime of Tel Aviv boiled and boiled. He took off his shirt and ran it over his shaved head, feeling the film of sweat thicken and irritate. The bad noontime of late August scorched and sizzled. He didn't know whether to crack a window and let the tumult of Herzl Street in along with a random gust of wind, or continue to assume that the closed windows were helping to preserve some kind of shaded, nocturnal chill. It must have been even more hellish outside.

He thought if he could work for a spell he might relax, but that fucking sampler wouldn't turn on. It was the heat. Had to be. That sampler was only a year old. The human body has its own built-in cooling system and yet even it could barely take this heat, this humidity, this fucking Tel Aviv humidity. How much? Eighty percent humidity? You could swim through the fucking air.

These past few months, he'd made a habit of shoving the word "fucking" into every turn of phrase. He thought he'd tapped a way of refreshing clichés, rescuing them from their fucking cheesiness. Nicole laughed with contempt whenever she heard him use the word. Maybe that had been the last straw. No, it had been the last fucking straw. "If you're going to insert that word into every other sentence, you need the skills to back it up," she said.

Nicole and that mouth of hers. For six months that mouth worked overtime while he listened, enchanted. It was her idea to move to southern Tel Aviv. "Look at these gorgeous floor tiles," she said. "And the ceilings! So high! It's going to be nice and cool here in summer. We won't need AC. And listen to this," she said, opening the windows–the street emitted honking horns and spurting engines–"you can totally feel Tel Aviv." And he, like an idiot, was deeply moved by her enthusiasm for the real Tel Aviv, the city hidden within the city. He sampled the racket of the spice market. The monotonous din of the textile factories. The flatulence of buses. He woke up at five thirty to stake out trucks, drivers fighting over parking spots; he hid beneath the balconies of Lewinsky Street apartments where greedy contractors had squeezed ten Thai migrant workers into a single room, recording their excited evening chatter; he visited the makeshift churches of Nigerian laborers on Sundays, stopped house cleaners from Ghana on the street and asked them to shout something in their native language into his microphone. He even considered going to one of the massage parlors on Ha'aliyah Street and wearing a wire to smuggle out recordings of fake Russian moans, but the idea angered Nicole, and he had to let her moan into the sampler instead. He downloaded this cacophony onto his computer, put together beats made up entirely of the ruckus of the corner of Herzl and Lewinsky, layered them with atonal melodies, roars and rattles, curse words and arguments, the Mediterranean basin meets Generation X. "It's amazing," he'd tell anyone willing to listen, "a brand new urban sound. Pure Tel Aviv, none of that German industrial nonsense." Once, under the influence of a combination of Jägermeister and some exceptional weed, he got lyrical: "If only I could capture the sound of soot and cumin." Dalia wrote a song based on that statement that he planned to include in his instrumental album.

And after all her gushing about the terrific location, and how fun it was to use a sun heater rather than an electric, Nicole left, leaving him there, in that microwave of an apartment. No high ceilings and no nothing. The greenhouse effect. There was a considerable piece of the ozone layer missing over Herzl Street. Well, sure there was, with all those Persians with their third-rate textile stores and all the dust those fabrics collected. But the truth was–for brief moments he was able to admit it to himself–that he'd left her first. He had abandoned her.

One night, they were sitting at the Pill. Everyone he knew left before midnight. There was a concert at the Barbie–three pretentious kids making noise. They probably went by the name Avant-Garde, or Lipless Faucets or some other self-important shit. "I'm so fucking tired of all these promising young musicians," he told Dalia. "Makes me miss the old fogies like Shalom fucking Hanoch."

"I can't take the way you talk," she said, taking advantage of a brief pause–Nicole had gone to the bathroom. "You and that cow you're about to marry are competing over who can give vulgarity a worse name. Besides, you're drunk." She dropped a fifty shekel note on the table and left.

When Nicole returned from the bathroom, he told her, "I think Dalia went to the Barbie, too. I'm so fucking tired of all these promising young musicians. Makes me miss the old fogies like Shalom fucking Hanoch."

Nicole gave him a withering stare and said that thing about his skills in the bedroom. And he stopped hearing her.

She tried to wake him up before dawn, because she couldn't sleep. She may have tried to apologize in her clumsy way, but he'd stopped hearing her. He mumbled something and went back to sleep. She must have yammered on for a good three hours longer.

Dalia kept claiming that he was an enigma. That it was strange how a person with such underdeveloped self-awareness and a million crude layers of defense could be so brilliant. He didn't know if he was brilliant. It was a fact that he lasted no longer than a year as a philosophy major at Tel Aviv University—the department with the lowest possible intellectual requirements. He had a good sense of structure. That he did. Whenever they worked on composing a song she brought in, he knew exactly what the structure should be, where they needed a C part, how to break the harmony in order to surprise the listener, where the melody should relent, how many times the chorus should be repeated without getting tired. It wasn't a musical gift. He didn't hear it, he saw it. When he told Dalia, she said, "Who says there's no evolution in the art world? Have you ever considered what people who make interactive art or installations did five hundred years ago? It's like every invention of the artistic medium bends human development, forcing it to make that famous evolutionary leap. You're the perfect musician for this era. Who needs to hear music these days when you can see it on a computer screen in living color?"

The year he'd spent at the Philosophy Department, where he met Nicole, prevented him from writing off Dalia's argument. She might have been the most intelligent person he'd ever met. He decided to put off thinking it over till later. In those moments, he couldn't afford to lose himself in thought. Instead, he would open a new Pro Tools file, lay down a basic drum track, and improvise on the guitar.

Come to think of it, there was not a single moment when he did allow himself to sink into thought. He barely felt Nicole's absence. One morning she simply wasn't there anymore. If she hadn't taken the portable AC unit with her, her disappearance would have become just another unimportant fact in the general mayhem of his life. Over the phone, Dalia told him, "I wonder what needs to happen to shake you out of your numbness," and he'd said, "Another bottle of arak, that's what. Let her rot in hell. That whore."

He giggled when he recalled that childish curse, and thought that he was losing his cool. Becoming hysterical. That the computer would crash too from the heat if he tried to turn it on. That he had to leave that fucking sauna and go someplace with air-conditioning.

3

Dalia sat in the corner farthest from the door, wearing sunglasses. That girl is going through something rough again, that much is for sure, Rami thought as he walked into the Espresso Bar on Herzl Street. And what's she even doing here? The cold air enveloped him like a cloud, kissing his face but not yet osmosing into him, under his skin, into his blood. He was sweating harder than he had at home. He waved at Dalia and went to the bathroom to stick his head under the faucet. What was she doing there? He pulled out paper towels from the dispenser on the wall, using too much force. At least half of the towels fell out. Not that Dalia's presence bothered him; on the contrary, he'd been missing her the past month. They barely talked, and when they did it was purely technical. "Can you burn Smog's *Wild Love* for me again? I think I lost it." That kind of thing. But other times, Dalia demanded absolute, devoted attentiveness, and judging by the way she looked now, like a ghost from a third-rate television production—Israeli television, no less, the Kids' Channel or some such bullshit—this was definitely one of those times. Not that he minded listening to her and not talking about himself. Dalia was the only person he was willing to do that for, but the timing was bad.

On his way to the café, he'd kept wondering what he'd do if his sampler really was broken. Where did he put that warranty? He would probably have to call Nicole and ask if she accidentally took it along with her files and folders. And how would he ever get the money to buy an air conditioner, because fans gave him a cold? Her timing really sucked. At least the heat, which he'd never been able to cope with, had retreated. He wiped his face. The aroma within the café, deep and rich, was a panacea.

"Hey Dal, what brings you down south?"

"To Eilat, to Eilat," she sang, playing along with a regular joke of theirs. Her voice was cracked. "I was waiting for you. What took you so long?"

"I was trying to work. How'd you know I'd be here?"

"There aren't that many places in Tel Aviv where you're allowed to smoke in the AC. Nicole took your unit. You live like three hundred feet away. It's noon. Things are simple when you look closely."

"If my sampler turned on you'd be left to wait here for another two hours. Why didn't you call?"

"It's fine, I've been here since this morning. I think the server is sick of me already."

"The day after a double terror attack at the old bus terminal, and you're spending the whole day at a busy café?"

"Somehow all the truly interesting events always pass me by." She raised her chin. The server's shadow fell over Rami. He turned around. What was with the sunny demeanor first thing in the morning?

"Let me guess, a latte with no foam and a glass of water." The server was seventeen or eighteen years old, all supreme happiness, dark skin—a soft, natural tone, not an aggressive tan. The embodiment of joy.

"Allow me to surprise you. Um . . . let me think," he made her linger. Her body was hesitant, fighting off youthful leftovers, the dimples deepening. What a body it was going to be. "Let's go for something a little different. Something like a no-foam latte and a glass of water. What do you say?"

She smiled with pleasure. Such joie de vivre. "And for you?" The glow on her face now changed course toward Dalia. "Another coffee? Or something else?"

"No thanks." Dalia smiled briefly. Rami's eyes were fixed on the server's back, her ass, as she walked away. "Men," Dalia muttered.

"What? What? I'm not allowed to look?"

"I'm so lucky I gave up on all that. Sometimes I walk behind girls like her on the street, behind the women they grow to become, who look and dress like a storehouse of seduction. I catch the glances slicing through her and I tear apart, every time. I don't know what I'd rather be feeling–despair because that kind of glance will never be directed at me, or relief. There's such power in being desired; such horror."

"Stop it. You're making me feel bad about myself. You really know how to push all the fucking buttons. Sorry, just 'the buttons,' I forgot you don't like–"

"Forget it, forget it," she said, cutting him off. Her sunglasses turned to face Rothschild Boulevard. What was the deal with those glasses?

"So what's new?" In all the years they'd known each other he'd never been able to ask how she was doing directly. Direct approaches always accomplished the opposite result, even when she looked eager to speak openly. She scared easy, closed up easy. He softened his voice. "What's up, Dalia?"

"Not good, Rami. I'm finished with Tel Aviv. That's it, I'm leaving. I've already called the movers, I've notified my landlord, I even called my mother and told her I was coming home. Tomorrow. What can I tell you, I'm overjoyed." Dalia had impressive dramatic tendencies and excellent timing. The server trotted into their conversation with Rami's coffee.

"What are you going to do there? You aren't only going back to your parents' home. You're going back to Sderot. Have you gone mad? They'll eat you alive down there. Besides, there's missiles there."

"I'll finally have the chance to see a bombed city. I won't be in Tel Aviv for the next war, either."

"Listen, Dalia, are you nuts? What's this nonsense? You can't even say 'I'm going back to Sderot.' You're only saying, 'I'm leaving Tel Aviv.'"

"I'm going back to Sderot. Moving back in with my parents. I haven't slept all night. I'm so tired, of this city, of the expectations, of the never-ending traffic. Malkieli called me two days ago to ask if I've got anything new. I told her I have twenty finished songs on an acoustic guitar, and that I was going to start working on a demo. My father promised to get me a computer, so I think I'll do all the work down there. I definitely won't be leaving the house. You know what my mom said when I called her this morning? I called her early. I had to call someone, and she's always awake at dawn. I started telling her some boring story. What's this got to do with her? I asked myself in the middle. Why am I telling her this? She obviously doesn't care. So then I paused my story and said, 'Mom, I'm thinking of coming back to Sderot,' and she said, 'If that's what you want, *ya binti*, I'm not going to interfere with your life.' You get it?"

"You're working on a solo album?"

That wasn't the correct response. He was having a really shitty day. He was supposed to be glad she was finally leaving the apartment, attempting to talk to someone, getting some distance from the city. He'd often thought that would be the best solution for her problem. He was supposed to support her. It wasn't a coincidence that the fucking sampler wouldn't turn on, it was a sign. To hell with friendship, he couldn't take offense, but—"Is that what you're saying? That you're going solo?"

"No." Dalia paused. "That's exactly why I'm leaving." The cracks in her voice had widened to the point of hoarseness, and she took a sip of his water. "Because not everything in my life has to do with my art. I want to live first. I'm not living, I'm creating."

"How are you going to live in Sderot? And when did you write all these songs, anyway? I spoke to you a month ago, and other than throwing shade at the tracks I played for you—throwing shade? What am I saying? You destroyed them—anyway, other than doing that, you didn't say anything about writing new material. I thought you were blocked and that you were coming down on me out of frustration."

"Forget it, Rami. Blasé is dead, we haven't been Blasé et Sans Lumière for two years. I'm writing because I can't *not* write, but it's got nothing to do with Blasé. And I wasn't coming down on you. I told you that you were too talented to start marketing house and trance music as an art form. You make those tracks in a second. The thing that takes all those poor DJs weeks or even months, you create in a single afternoon. You want to sell your music? Sell it, make some money, I'm the last person who'll stop you. But don't expect me to buy the aesthetic philosophy behind the club music industry. It's just drum and bass. Big deal."

"You're exaggerating. I've never treated anything I make like art, except for our Blasé stuff. Well, I guess I flirted here and there with what you called 'the urban beat,' but even then you were part of it, you were involved—"

"Rami, do you want to be a part of every single event in my life?"

"No, I want us to keep creating together. I want you to feel good, to be happy, even though that word is a little much for you. When's the last time I asked you about your private life? After you dated that son of a bitch, the one whose name you didn't even want to tell me, who ended up dumping you, I stopped asking. But I want us to make at least two more albums together."

"I need time to redefine the space in which I create. To shrink it so it doesn't take over my entire life. The demo is nothing. It's only meant to get Malkieli off my back. I'm having a hard time, don't you get it? Not everyone takes things as easily as you."

Space, shmace. Dalia had been using that same excuse for the past three years, and in the meantime she'd written twenty songs, and who knew how many others she'd already tossed out or forgotten. Enough with the lies. But she never lied to him. She simply maneuvered him. He didn't like fighting with her. The result was the same every time. He was deeply hurt, though he knew he shouldn't be. The intensity of insult in his body was stronger than that knowledge, but the knowledge wouldn't relent either, not allowing him to give himself over to insult, to let it wash over him.

"We haven't made much progress since last time," he said, trying to speak thoughtfully. "How am I supposed to forgive you? You keep making me mad, then making me feel guilty for being mad." He banged on the table. The water glass tipped over, spilling over his pants. The smiling server hurried over. It's all right, he signaled to her. "Well, thanks for taking over my neighborhood café."

4

Everything was poison. Dalia looked at her hands. The veins had begun to mark their way through her skin, bluish paths beneath a translucent cover. The light in the bedroom was too bright. Everything was poison, the reddening August skies, the pale wind, as shallow as the breathing of a passed-out girl, the five hundred books she had to pack, the naked CDs piled up in the living room, which still had to each be matched to their boxes, the dishes in the kitchen, the smell of cardboard and tape mixing in with the rustle of the air conditioner, the Dizengoff backyards that her bedroom window gaped at, everything was poison, the air, every object in this apartment that had been brushed by a word he'd said to her, which he'd soured by force of his touch, by the hand that pushed her against the wall, by the force of the mouth huffing with lust, the body pinning her to the floor, skin under skin, the slow, sleepless nights in this room, it was all poison.

Dalia opened the doors of her closet and dropped her clothes into a suitcase without any particular order. Her mother would wash and iron them all over again anyway. Her hand lingered on a cashmere knit, rubbing it. How necessary were these winter clothes? Her bones told her this heat wave would not be waning, and the cashmere made her eyes burn. Recently, small things had been breaking her spirit. She didn't tell Rami the right story. How could he understand? Only women can love like that, with such intensity, so attuned to another, until their sorrow, and their beauty, and their powers of observation are constructed through him. The middle of the night finds them awake, no angel bothering to show his face, and they can do no more than keep losing to themselves. Why were there hours in which the whole world was nothing more than an interpretation of her mental state? Every book she cracked open reminded her of what she was fleeing from. Every poem.

And in the morning, with the ashes of an entire night on her tongue, with all her words and her pleas dried up, she made some coffee, discovering, too late, that the milk had spoiled, and she watched with wonder, with confusion, as the small lumps spread through the dark liquid, as if she was witnessing a breach of a basic law of nature, watching white planets spinning in the dimness of the cup like a nebula being born, and she called her mother. Rather than tell her about the iron prison around her flesh, lowering her voice to a whisper, she told her about the milk, and her mother said, "Maybe you need a new fridge."

"But, Mom, I want to tell you something else. Something different."

"What, *ya binti?*"

"Maybe I should come back to Sderot?"

"If that's what you want, *ya binti*, I'm not going to interfere with your life."

You get it, Rami? My device is finally getting reception, like you always like to say. This complete acceptance—I had been wrong to interpret it as neglect. It's time for me to go home.

Once the rest of the clothes had been quickly tossed into suitcases, Dalia turned to the real challenge—her books. She considered leaving some of them, but that would have required her to sort through them, open some, perforating more tunnels into her memories, which were all wrapped around him, drenched with him. He dumped her, is that what Rami said? He must have thought she thought he didn't know. Rami was so naïve. She let out a long sigh and began to put together the boxes the guy from the moving company had brought over, hoping she'd be able to squeeze all her books into twenty boxes. "Twenty-five books per box, okay? I don't want my guys breaking their backs or tearing the boxes in the middle of the street, you got that, lady?" A weak sound broke through the *vvvvvt* of the packing tape. She paused to listen. She thought she heard somebody knocking at the door.

PART ONE

AN ENTIRE MYTHOLOGY

1

Ahem, in fact, to start summarizing the relation between serial killers and poets, the similarities between these groups, one might discuss the purpose apparent in their compulsion. Both poet and serial killer try to create a scene, or an arena, made up entirely of a system of symbols, but the experience re-created there, over and over again, is found outside of said arena. The experience is almost always pain, heartbreak, loss, hurt. I imagine stronger words are called for here, because the results—at least when it comes to the murderer—are horrendous. But words are not where power is found, but rather the emotional world, where it seems that hurt and pain are echoed so loudly that they no longer have any connection to the mundane meaning of the word. I know I'm making a stretch when I say that, even for poets, words are not where power lies, meaning . . ."

Elish was losing his words. He could tell his explanations were growing convoluted, even to his own ears. He sneaked a glance at his watch. It had only been an hour. When he'd prepared this lecture, the central idea was so clear: to talk about poetry and serial murder as scrupulous and impossible rituals, because they have two conflicting goals—creating a whole product that speaks for itself, and retracing an ancient, exterior pattern that imbues the creation with its meaning. What could be simpler? Then why couldn't he be eloquent? Why couldn't he express himself as clearly as usual?

He cleared his throat and slowed down his pace: "I want to repeat my point. The repetition you can find throughout a poet's work, the recurring fixation on certain subjects, is often articulated only on a metaphorical level, and yet it can still be viewed as parallel to the repetition demonstrated by serial killers. If you will, a poet has only one poem in their heart, and a serial murderer has only one murder in their head, and everything they do is merely rehearsal in preparation for a perfect show. But because they are human, perfection is never at hand . . ."

What was he doing there? What was he rambling on about? The hall in which he was teaching was unwisely facing northwest. The five o'clock light floating through the windows, the setting October sun just managing to redeem itself from the measured clouded sky of pre-winter, emphasized his final sentence, the last thing he needed. He already felt he was toeing the edges of pathos, and that snaking, splendid light dressed his words with the cloak of revelation. He glanced at his watch again, nervously. He should buy a digital. The analogue hands moved too slowly. If he asked someone to draw the curtains, there would be a small commotion, killing five minutes. Not worth it. Thank God he brought films. He raised the glass of water resting on the desk to his right, brought it to his mouth, and found it empty. He felt a sudden hankering for cigarettes, though their smell typically made him feel sick. It was odd, how the memory of nicotine burned, the rough flavor of smoke, and how it could–though he was already accustomed to the phantom sensations of smoking–shake the body. He twisted his right ankle, perhaps crushing an imaginary butt or perhaps feigning embarrassment, then looked up, focusing his eyes far off into the light.

EITAN WAS THE ONLY REASON HE HAD AGREED TO COME, EVEN though he'd promised himself he'd reduce his public presence to the bare minimum. Eitan had called him two months earlier. He was what you might call "a college friend," even though Eitan had already been a master's student at the time, and even though they'd spent more time at the Humanities cafeteria than in class. Elish hated sitting on the lawn like the other students. He said he hadn't been born after so many years of evolution only to go back to grazing and ruminating. But no one got the joke, not even when he explained drily that the lawns were the result of a secret organization's scheme to turn all students into vegetarians. The cafeteria hours were the only time he recalled fondly from his university days.

"Elish?"

He recognized Eitan's voice right away, and his directness. No "hello," no "May I speak with," just "Elish." He was glad about that. Most of his human connections did not survive the breaking of daily contact. As long as they lasted, they involved honesty, affection, and support, but when they evaporated just as quickly as they'd formed, they left no feelings of camaraderie on either end.

"Hey, Eitan, how's it going?"

"That was quick. Listen, Elish, I need a favor."

"It's been two years and that's how you start? 'I need a favor'? How about 'How are you? What's new?' Where are your manners?"

"How are you? What's new?"

"Not bad. Still at the university?"

"Are you serious? The last time we spoke you told me I was only born so that I could be buried on the third floor of Gilman Hall, between the watercooler and the photocopier."

"Well, you were getting on my nerves. You've finished your doctorate, then. Dr. Eitan Peretz. Has a nice ring to it. How can I help you?"

"So here's the thing. I'm in charge of the class Literature and Other Arts. It's a panoramic lecture series presenting a different speaker each week. Today the lecturer of the third class left me in the lurch. I've got to finalize the syllabus tomorrow and I need a substitute, quick. Then I remembered that series of essays you had in the *Haaretz* literary supplement, 'Literary Portraits of Serial Killers,' and I thought you might want to teach a class on serial murder and literature. Something along the lines of De Quincey, you know, 'On Murder Considered as One of the Fine Arts.' The truth is, I want it to be the first class. This is my first year designing this class, and I want to revive it a little."

Elish considered this. Eitan had no idea that, for the past eighteen months, Elish had been running an investigation agency. That would have made this lecture idea even more glamorous. Elish had already managed to forget those essays. From a two-year distance, he remembered them dripping with childishness, a futile attempt to adopt a different personality. "Hang on," he said, "are you trying to tell me you want to make this class cool?"

"No, no, just attractive. Last year we only had fifteen students enrolled."

"I don't know. Murder and literature? That's kind of corny."

"Not for first-year students. And you'll have two months to prepare."

"It was kind of you not to ask me to teach about poetry and rock music, and I do owe you a favor or two."

"Yup, that's true. So what do you say?"

"Remember that time my mother came to visit the campus with my sister?"

"Don't remind me." Eitan lowered his voice. "I still have a burn mark on my heart. Is your sister still married to that guy with the funny name?"

"Bobby? Yes. May he live long and prosper. Anyway, my mom told me to watch out for you. She thought you were going to drag me down. It's been five years and you haven't changed a bit."

But Eitan *had* changed, and Elish could hear it in his voice. He wasn't disappointed two months later, when he knocked on the door of Eitan's office on the third floor of Gilman Hall, between that eternal, rusty watercooler and a state-of-the-art photocopier. Eitan looked just as he'd expected. He'd lost some hair. Gained some weight. Gotten married too.

"BUT I DON'T UNDERSTAND," SAID THE CHUBBY STUDENT IN THE first row, with the red hair she'd put up at least five times in the last hour, before each question she asked, pen in mouth, twisting the too-straight hair quickly with her right hand, her left hand stretching the hair tie, pulling out the pen and holding it up as she raised her hand, her fervor making her levitate a little in her chair, the urgency of her movements making the hairdo fall apart, bits of it falling against her eyes, bits that she quickly pushed away with sharp motions as she spoke. Her voice was excited yet firm. He was supposed to hate her. There was a student like her in every class—energetic, demanding. He used to loathe the type when he was a student himself, but in these moments she was his only lifesaver.

"I don't understand," she complained again. "For example, in *Crime and Punishment*, Raskolnikov's crime is imperfect because he feels remorse, and what you're saying is that people can't perform a perfect murder or write a perfect poem because there's something about them that makes them human?"

She looked behind her to register the impression left by her question. His eyes followed hers, falling on a skinny student with a shaved head he'd noted as soon as he walked into the room. There was something familiar about his face, beyond the expression and position of his body, something upsettingly familiar. Not the expression. The expression was easily decipherable. Elish had an eye for types. A skill earned through years of practice. He thought part of him was always busy involuntarily mapping the people around him, an urge that was stronger than him, a defense mechanism that never relented. There's one of them in every classroom, reclining in their seat, casting bored looks all around, occasionally mumbling something to themselves and sighing, then after more than an hour had elapsed, raising their hand and asking a sophisticated question they'd been formulating since the beginning of class under the guise of demonstrable boredom. He knew this type well. He *was* that type.

"No," Elish answered the redhead patiently. "Raskolnikov is not a serial killer. His psychological profile, if you will, is different."

A cigarette. A cigarette. This lecture wasn't going anywhere. He reached out for the glass again, without glancing to see if Eitan had refilled it. There was no doubt in his mind that he had. Even at the cafeteria, Eitan would get up without prior warning and return a few seconds later with napkins or sugar. Not out of a desire to please. Eitan was one of the most self-assured people Elish had ever met. The comfort of the people around him mattered to him, and maintaining it came naturally to him. Comfort was a subject that had been honored in many of their cafeteria conversations. Sometimes they reached the conclusion that their attitude about comfort was what shaped their respective worldviews. "Comfort numbs you," Elish always said. "You're only human when you're awake." A violent cloud must have trapped the sun. The light was now running out of the windows swiftly, like blood draining out of a dead body.

Three, two, one, he counted backward silently as he pulled his eyes away from the earthly, sealed windows back to the classroom, recognizing the consolidation of determination on the aloof male student's face. Why did the bothersome students always sit to the left of the teacher? he wondered with amusement. *Here it comes.*

"So how is the poet and the serial killer's obsession different than any other obsession? And why poetry, out of all art forms? I can't think of any art medium whose initial patterns cannot be described using the word 'obsession.'"

A well-worded question, accurately aimed to collapse his premise. He expected nothing less. This was the exact question he himself would have asked five or six years earlier, then leaned back in his chair, watching the lecturer twist themselves into a knot or stutter some clumsy explanation. The truly well-oiled lecturers directed him to an impossible reading list, asking with a curious and condescending tone if he'd read this or that thinker, since the question he'd raised had already been discussed over so many podiums that honoring it with an answer would be redundant. The student leaned back, resting his arm over the back of the empty seat to his left. Elish assumed his eyes were narrowed with concentration in spite of the casualness projected by his body.

"Very good question," he began after a long sip from his glass, swishing the water around in his mouth. He wondered if anyone in the room was able to appreciate the irony–nay, the self-directed humor–embodied in his last sentence. He couldn't see it from this distance, but he had no doubt that momentary suspicion was narrowing the student's eyes even further. The dark, still mass of fifty-some students crowding inside the classroom was at alert, sloughing off its indifference.

"Both poetry and serial murder aspire to reach creation, yes, creation. There is no other appropriate word for describing the result of the effort made by both arts." He felt a certain urgency sneaking into his voice, just as had happened to him many times before. The wording took on a life of its own, and he had nothing more to do but listen to himself and wonder at his word choice. "A creation in which every element is both symbolic and standalone, being the thing itself, you see? A poem, a murder, are both deeds in and of themselves and objects in the world, a totally closed system that has a separate meaning in addition to a profound re-creation of an experience, a pattern implemented into the creator's soul. The right of existence of each part, the logic of choosing that part, exist beyond it. But within the system of a poem or a murder, it functions as the thing itself. To put this argument differently, every component of the poem or the serial murder is twofold. The tree appearing in the poem is a tree, the raised knife is a knife, and the wound is a wound. But the tree and the knife and wound inherit their meaning from a source existing outside of the poem and the ritual."

"So what are you saying?" another student spoke up. "That obsession has no meaning or rationale? That in music things don't stand alone? Or in prose? Or film?"

"That's exactly my point. Obsession has only exterior meaning. The meaning of the actions of obsessive people are forced on them from the outside. The role of obsession in order, in repetition, is to anesthetize existential dread, the fear of chaos. Poetry and serial murder, on the other hand, are an attempt to devise a formula of sorcery." He was becoming too abstract. When his explanations slipped out of his control he always got too abstract. "Look, an obsessive person, someone who has OCD, for instance, is . . . they might clean incessantly or hide food around the house or count the steps in every flight of stairs they ever take. But the action is not performed with an independent purpose. The counting in itself is meaningless. But, um, ahem, when Anne Carson writes, 'Something black and heavy dropped between them like a smell of velvet,' she means specifically the physical image her words portray, but also something else."

"You mean like in Song of Songs, where there's a ton of fucking but it's actually supposed to symbolize the relationship between God and the Israelites?" the chubby student cut him off.

"Yes." He ignored the vulgarity of her word choice, which was merely a protest over having the attention taken away from her. "But it's wrong to say 'it's actually supposed to symbolize,' because both planes exist at the same time, and not only them, but every comma and letter constituting them. No, no, not every comma and letter, because then there would be such a thing as a perfect poem. A perfect murder. Yes?" Elish's eyes rested on her, and she seemed to have cooled off, lowering her eyes to conceal an embarrassment he could not read.

"Now," he carried on, "obsession. I prefer to say 'a measure of compulsion,' because I don't think pathological people can create, and that is the major difference between the serial killer and the poet. At any rate, a measure of compulsion is indeed necessary for any creation. But the aspiration in other art forms is not to make a piece that is utterly symbolic and interior but still has exterior sources upon which it supposedly does not depend. The relationship between inside and out is momentary, not absolute . . . Music, for instance, is only the thing itself, though you could depict it using similes–"

"Then what's the difference between a serial murderer and a plain murderer, like Raskolnikov, who was mentioned earlier?"

"Raskolnikov murders out of the desire to test a moral issue with metaphysical elements. There is no ritual, no creation around the act of murder. Even if he killed a thousand old ladies, the murder itself would not be charged with private meaning. It would still merely be a byproduct of the moral experiment. A phantom. When it comes to other murderers, most of them act out of panic. I imagine about ninety-eight percent, if they had the choice, would have chosen not to commit these murders. Moreover, when you look at Dostoyevsky's biography–"

"Excuse me, excuse me," he heard a student calling excitedly from the back of the room. When he looked over, he was surprised to find her standing on her chair and waving her arms. "I've been raising my hand for like five minutes," she said. "I wanted to ask if you could repeat everything you said after 'they might clean incessantly,' because my pen fell and I couldn't catch up. But now I have a different question. Is Dostoyevsky in the course reading list?"

He looked at Eitan imploringly.

"No," Eitan said, turning toward her. "Is there a problem?"

"If he isn't on the reading list, why is he talking about him so much?"

"All right." Elish smiled. "I don't want to shake up your

organized world. Luckily for you, I've brought a few films that are considered serial killer classics. *Psycho*, *The Silence of the Lambs*, *Seven*. I hope for all of our sakes that this is the closest we ever get to any kind of murder. I want you to pay special attention, in the scenes we're about to watch, to the connection between the psychological background and the ritualistic structure that the murder takes . . ."

The air in the room was electrified at once. The utter silence accompanying his words had come to an end. He let his words die out.

2

Mr. Ben Zaken! Mr. Ben Zaken!" And when no answer came: "Elish! Elish!"

Elish was on his way to the cafeteria. He was relieved when Eitan asked the students to hang back in the classroom for a few more minutes and discuss their assignments for the following week. The lecture had gone horrendously, and he had no desire to speak to any of the students. His urge for a cigarette had evaporated, replaced by a need for coffee, any kind of coffee, even the murky brown liquid served at the Gilman cafeteria. Flavor and scent, Elish thought when he heard her calling him. Words and sounds existing only in the present, temporary, not sending roots back, while the actuality of the past, everything he wished to detach from, roared at him with flavors and scents, ripping him away from the brief control the words had offered him for a thrust of minutes, days sometimes, because they could not be translated—especially not the scents—could not be converted, as solid as old injuries.

He turned his head. The redheaded student was waving at him with broad motions, a woolen cardigan tied around her waist, her bag flapping against the side of her body, bouncing hurriedly toward him. He stopped to wait for her. She was holding her notebook against her chest, gripping it firmly with both hands. Her hair spilled down her face and she blew it away. "That was an incredible lecture, Mr. Ben Zaken, really, I wanted to tell you that, and also—"

"You didn't stay back in the room to hear the assignments?" His voice was dry, impatient, like a bark. "You can call me Elish."

"Gila, nice to meet you." She tightened her arms further around the notebook, crushing her breasts. "I'm not enrolled in the class, I'm just auditing it. I came to the lecture because of you."

"I'm flattered." He tried, but his tone was still rough. "Listen, I need coffee, so if–"

"No problem." Gila heard this as an invitation and started walking toward the cafeteria. Elish remained planted in place. She paused when she sensed his absence beside her and turned toward him. Her eyes filled with understanding. He could hear the blood rushing to her face. At another time he may have regretted his curtness, but not right then. Flushed, she said, "That's fine, absolutely fine, but would you mind signing my copy of your book?"

She released one arm from her notebook clench and pulled out a well-worn copy from her bag. The blue cover was stained by the letters of the title, black letters smeared at the edges–"The feeling of tar," he'd told the cover designer at the time, "of something sticky, like a swamp"–*The Sky Is Dust: The Rise and Fall of Israeli Rock Music.*

It had only been two years since its publication, and Elish already viewed this book as a piece of far-off childhood mischief. Or, more accurately, he preferred to think about the book in those terms than as an art piece from which he was forced to alienate himself. Signing it, taking ownership of it, seemed like cheating, but what business was that of hers, really? He could say no, of course, but restraining himself would be easier. "Sure," he said, "no problem." He took the pen she offered him and scribbled, "To Gila, who knows how to listen, Elish."

"Lovely, lovely." She closed the book, pleased. "Have a good day."

SIX YEARS HAD CHANGED A THING OR TWO ABOUT THE GILMAN cafeteria. The entire sound system had been replaced. New speakers dangled from the ceiling, playing Madonna's "Ray of Light," which made it hard for him to determine if they'd finally appointed—as he'd jokingly suggested to the manager back in the day—a person in charge of the playlist. "It can be the limping busboy or the panini girl," he said at the time. "Doesn't matter who, it'll still be an improvement." It was either that, or the radio could have, as usual, been tuned to the pop station operated by the IDF. They'd also introduced a new coffeemaker. He could smell the blend, inhale it. When he was seven years old, he cut his finger on a utility knife he'd been playing with in spite of his father's threats, peeling off a piece of flesh from his left middle finger. No matter how much pressure his mother applied with an alcohol-laden cotton ball, the finger wouldn't stop bleeding. Panicked, his mother had torn open a bag of Turkish coffee grounds, spilled some on the exposed flesh, and covered it with a cotton ball, squeezing. "Hold tight," she said, placing his right hand over the wound. "I'll go get a bandage." She kissed him, one tender kiss over each eye, wiped away his tears, and ruffled his hair. "Come on, baby, stop crying. Your dad's about to get home from work. Be a big boy." A tingle spread through the tip of his finger, like swarming ants but not as sharp and painful as the burn of the alcohol. But itchy. He removed the cotton ball. The blood and the coffee grounds had merged to form a black, viscous, intoxicating film.

"Double espresso, milk on the side." This request seemed inappropriate for the ambience of a kibbutz mess hall that even the coffeemaker and the speakers could not banish.

"Mr. Ben Zaken." A hand was placed on his shoulder. "You got a minute for me, bud?"

Bud? He didn't know anyone who used that word. The face of the man who had addressed him was vaguely familiar, perhaps from a television or newspaper image. The man removed his hand from Elish's shoulder and offered it for a shake. "Nice to meet you. Manny Lahav."

Elish ignored the offered hand. Manny Lahav smiled with pleasure, as if he only ever offered his hand with the hope of being turned down. "Large latte for me," he called out. Like his body, his voice was expansive, booming. "Hell of a lecture you gave there. So what do you say?" he asked Elish. "Shall we sit?"

"No, we won't sit, Mr. Lahav. If you don't mind, I'm a little tired right now, and I'm waiting on a friend."

"No biggie, I can take a hint." He ran a large palm over his thinning, graying hair, a habitual gesture that flattened his hair, concealing the balding recessions. His green eyes glowed with curiosity, focused. "Can I book an appointment, then? Tomorrow afternoon, say five o'clock, your office?"

Elish nodded. "If it's that kind of appointment, of course we can do it tomorrow. Call my office in the morning, speak with Lilian. I'm almost certain I'm free during that time, but she'll be able to tell you for sure."

"Elish," Eitan called to him from the entrance to the cafeteria. "Order me an espresso. I'm grabbing a table outside."

As Elish walked outside, carefully balancing the two cups of coffee, Manny Lahav winked at him from his table.

BACK IN HIS APARTMENT, AFTER FIVE PAGES OF NEAL STEPHENson's *Cryptonomicon*, he realized just how tiresome his lecture had been. His thoughts wandered from the pages in front of him to the words he'd said, his brain re-creating the moments in which he'd phrased himself crudely; made generalized, baseless arguments; allowed himself to speak with uninhibited enthusiasm. No, not the lecture itself, but something that happened during it, scratching the edges of his consciousness, unresolved. Oh, damn it. The windows were open, the fridge empty, the living room large enough to walk in circles. He returned to the sofa, battling Stephenson's words, advancing and retreating. Eight p.m. Barbunia was open but wouldn't be too busy. The drunks and weirdos that contributed the lion's share to the bar's vibe had probably begun gathering. Yes, a beer wouldn't hurt.

Ben Yehuda Street was charged with growing energy; distilled force. Tel Aviv lived in reverse, awakening from its summer slumber, a mighty being, ageless, stretching its limbs, relieving the poplar trees from their load. He almost felt some sorrow at abandoning the street for the wood-coated interior of Barbunia, but that was where warmth and joy were, and the banished world. Oh, to be a wanderer, a momentary visitor.

He took a seat at one of the tables. "Leffe Blonde. And, yeah, get me the shrimp and calamari mix." The owner walked by and patted his shoulder. Someone he didn't know offered him a joint. No thanks, a beer would be enough, its heaviness spreading slowly, the warmth and the floating sensation. The day was gradually forgotten, peeling away, the juiciness of the seafood between his teeth, teasing his palate, the speakers playing one hit song after the other, eighties music, ridiculous electronic drums, melancholy cheerfulness.

Even within the formless mélange of human music at Barbunia, he still got chills upon hearing the opening chords. The choice of song was supposed to be unexpected, but within the spectrum, the space he now inhabited, its very bearable loneliness was obvious. Dalia Shushan's voice emerged from the speakers, cracking at the edges of the high range, scattering in the low range, but always clear, a voice whose youth was cruelly cut short, that's how he remembered describing it in the article he sent to *Everything Tel Aviv.* He closed his eyes and listened. "Sometimes I forget to breathe, like I'm underwater, no, I tell myself, the stories of sailors, human memory, are nothing, only the shadow of fear, whatever the sea takes is given to it willfully."

At the end of the singing part an instrumental segment erupted, horns spinning into each other, swallowing the flute and violin that had been playing throughout. It hypnotized him each time anew. How appropriate, hearing Dalia Shushan singing on the first wintry night of the year. *It's been two months.* Whenever he recalled her murder, which had been extensively reported in the media, he was shocked all over again. A gunshot in each temple and one in the heart. She'd refused to be interviewed for his book, as she had for newspapers. Actually, after he left her four unanswered messages, he'd gotten a call from Debbie Malkieli, her agent, who suggested he speak with Rami Amzaleg, her partner in the duo Blasé et Sans Lumière. He asked Rami about the Sderot music scene, and Rami said that as far as Blasé was concerned, the Sderot music scene could go fuck itself, and that he'd already consulted with Dalia about what he should say, and had no intention of discussing Blasé's place in local rock history. Instead, he would only be willing to talk about . . .

Of course, of course, he could be such an idiot sometimes. The face of the bored-looking student with the difficult questions flashed through his mind. Of course. He'd shaved his head and lost some weight, but his expression revealed his identity. Rami Amzaleg, he told himself, without a sense of contentment or self-satisfaction, more like relief for things taking their normal course, as if a grain of sand that had been poking his eyeball had been removed. Cleanliness.

3

Manny Lahav filled the office with his presence. He was wearing a similar shirt to the one he'd worn the previous day, surely one of an endless series of shirts of a blue so light it bordered on white, which were meant to imbue him with a unifying, unchanging, steady appearance. This shirt, like the previous one, stretched tightly against his gut. Manny Lahav arrived at five o'clock sharp.

"I didn't properly introduce myself yesterday," he said. "Chief Superintendent Menachem Lahav, head of investigations for the Yarkon Police Precinct."

Elish gave him a once over. Manny dropped a sealed brown envelope onto the desk, sprawled out on the chair without being invited to, without offering his hand to be shaken, his face large, smile-ready, but expressionless in that moment, trained on Elish.

"So how can I help?" Elish asked. "I hope this isn't about the lecture I gave yesterday."

"No, not at all. Did you attend Tel Aviv University?"

"Uh-huh. For about two years, philosophy and computer science."

"Did you know Dr. Yehuda Menuhin? Did you take any of his classes?"

"'Knew him' is too strong. I knew of him, and I sat in on one of his classes. Only the first week, though. I didn't come back."

"May I ask why?"

"Hang on, is this an official investigation? Is this meeting about my work or what? I don't understand where this is going."

"Relax, bud, I'll explain in a minute."

It seemed to Elish that Manny's face was proficient in the expression of friendliness. The wrinkles of laughter and time were poised, just beneath the skin, to slip into it. But the timing with which he presented it was unusual. He seemed to enjoy causing others momentary distress. And again with that word, "Bud." Where does he think he is? His pupils were hard, untouched by his smiles. Of course Elish had known Dr. Yehuda Menuhin, just like anybody else who'd passed through the Tel Aviv University Philosophy Department in the past ten years. He was infamous, the topic of gossip. "Was" being the operative word. He'd killed himself just two and a half weeks earlier. "Clearly his bitterness and cold could only stem from an oversized self-hatred," Eitan had said just the day before, then adding with contempt, "Good riddance."

"You must know he was found dead in his home two and a half weeks ago. His brother found him in the evening after Yehuda had missed their appointment. They'd had lunch plans. Yehuda didn't show up and didn't call. He was too busy shooting himself in the head."

"Yes, I know. I read all about it in the newspaper. His brother is one of those new members of parliament, from the Shinui party, right? What's his name, Gideon Menuhin."

"Actually he's a deputy minister. And a good friend of mine, just so you know, before you bad-mouth him. The truth is, when the head of my special investigations team told me the identity of the body, I went to the scene myself and became more involved than I usually do."

"I can't bad-mouth him. I barely know anything about him. He's not one of those members of parliament who have a love affair with the media. I hardly even read anything he had to say about his brother. Not that the suicide was that widely reported, but still, I have to admit he's unique."

"That's true, he hardly gives interviews at all. Anyway, I don't believe his brother committed suicide. Gideon says he isn't the type."

"Well, who is?" asked Elish. Then, after a brief pause, he added, "Look, I still don't understand where all this is going."

Manny leaned back, crossing his legs, linking his fingers behind his neck and watching Elish with curiosity, but not just that—his face projected something else, perhaps amusement at the man's resistance, another shadow of his smile of pleasure from the previous day. "I'm here in service of a friend. It's a pretty simple deal. I want you to investigate the circumstances of Yehuda Menuhin's suicide. I don't want to know too much about the progress of the investigation. The less I know, the better. When you have results, I'll set a meeting for you and Gideon, and you can talk about it all you like. I don't want to be involved any more than that."

"That makes two of us."

Manny leaned in, focused, the fingers of his bearish hands intertwined under his chin. "Can you explain why?"

"Not before you explain to me why you came to EE Investigations of all places."

"This job requires someone with an academic background, who understands the inner code of the university. Someone sensitive to this field. I came across your name in the Dalia Shushan file. The head of the special investigations team updated me on the progress of that investigation every few hours, and I looked over all investigation materials with him. So I read what you wrote in the press about her music. You could say I know you a little bit. You seem to have sound judgment. EE Investigations—especially in the last two years—has gained a reputation for professional discretion. And honestly, I've crossed paths with your partner in the past, when I was still a detective, and I always respected her, even if I wasn't always satisfied with her results. Actually, she and her ex-husband helped another friend of mine, though it was unintentional. This friend's wife, who'd hired them, was really a whore straight out of hell, if you'll pardon my French." He laughed—an open laugh, his entire body trembling in participation, a laugh that Elish, though he scowled, couldn't help but think of as "warmhearted."

Elish drummed the fingers of his left hand against the desk. Whenever he was nervous or concentrating hard, the pain in the tip of his middle finger came back, and tapping a hard surface sent electric currents to the base of his hand, a rhythmic beating of life. He floated his gaze over the office. Normally, he was able to see it through the eyes of his clients, who ran their eyes over the walls, because their stories always involved an element of embarrassment or discomfort, causing them to move their eyes away from his face and onto an invisible spot on the wall. When Elish adopted their point of view, he'd spot stains, new cracks, a crookedly hanging picture, blinding lights, dust on the shutters. Manny, on the other hand, had fixed his eyes on Elish from the moment he walked in, which made Elish feel restless. He must have been an excellent detective. His heavy body translated into the burden of an accusatory yet amicable look, waiting forgivingly for his counterpart to confess their sins, or, at the very least, to not let him down, to meet his expectations.

Suddenly, Manny got up with a start, as if lack of movement or action was unbearable to him. He patted the envelope he'd tossed on the desk when he'd walked in. "This is the police file for the Menuhin case. Read it. I expect to get it back within two days. I'll say it again—I want you to run this investigation exclusively. No partners."

Elish pushed away the envelope. "Sorry, but no. I'm sure you'll be able to find a decent investigator to take this on, but it just doesn't comply with the type of work this agency does."

"Gideon is willing to pay handsomely, with a generous expense account, anything you want."

"It isn't about money. Again, I apologize."

"I'm not often wrong about people, and I was convinced you'd pounce at this. I'll tell you what: Keep this envelope for now, think it over, and if you don't change your mind in two days you can give it back and we'll call it a day." He didn't give Elish time to consider this. Instead, he offered his hand. Elish gave his hand back, almost by instinct. Once more, Manny's face was flooded with that pleasurable smile. "Later, gator," he rhymed in parting.

"LILIAN," SAID ELISH. MANNY HAD LEFT THE DOOR TO ELISH'S office open. The stench of smoke flowing in from reception made Elish's stomach turn.

"What, hon?"

"How many times did I tell you not to smoke in the office?" He opened the southern facing window and rolled up the shutters. Evenings at the beach contained a chill, the promise of winter, but the air was heavy with rust and urine. He looked at the breakwater, the dilapidated harbor. When he was a child back in Ashkelon, the sea was a natural part of the city, but in Tel Aviv the sea was a threatening boundary preventing the town from expanding and overpopulating. It cut off the urban mayhem. If it weren't for this view, he would have talked Eliya into moving EE Investigations to a different location—some industrial park, half ruins and half glass and metal laden skyscrapers, the kind that prevailed all over Tel Aviv, bringing together schnitzel shops, bakeries, garages, and other small businesses in daytime and brothels and casinos at night, a landscape more accurately reflecting the nature of this agency. Though Atarim Square, their current location, projected its own unique, less prevalent brand of cheapness: the cheapness of rotting Tel Aviv with its made-up past and the shards of its ridiculous desire to be a proper city. With time, he'd learned to like the delusion of Atarim Square, a remnant of a magnificent past that never was, as if the bohemian revolution of the sixties, the wild and free sex roar of the seventies, and the dark glamour assault of the eighties truly had erupted over Tel Aviv like mighty water, leaving behind nothing but rubble. And this crooked, beaten square–a lone survivor.

The first time he came here to meet Eliya, one of the two previous owners of EE Investigations, the appearance and smell of the place made him want to turn around and go home. Though he knew the square and had passed through it countless times since moving to Tel Aviv, the idea that he would willingly spend his days in this decrepit hybrid of hotel and dying shopping center disgusted him. But his meeting with Eliya Avital–previously Abutbul–had convinced him to stay. Eliya was in debt. She and Eric, her ex–firmly believing that their own business would be a portal to the kingdom of heaven–had made that common Israeli blunder of mixing their private wealth with their business capital, and found out five years too late that even the savviest of accountants had their limitations, that money was fickle, and that much like with other members of the middle class–which had begun its deterioration–things for them were worse than they'd realized. "Going bankrupt is one thing," she told him, "but I panicked when I realized it was more than that. We're on the verge of hunger."

Her relationship with her husband was no longer forged from the burning love of their younger days, and the financial crisis drove them even farther apart. Drained from the divorce process, Eliya was unwilling to part ways with the only certainty she still had left–EE Investigations, which she'd started with the encouragement of her husband. It wasn't the first agency Elish had looked into. Every weekend, he would circle want ads along the lines of "A veteran, licensed investigation agency owner from central Israel looking for young hires with means and connections." Meaning, PI with experience looking for an investor. When he joined EE, he bought out Eric, who was glad to get away from Eliya. "And anyway," Eric had told him, "this business was Eliya's idea. My heart was never really in it."

Six months after buying Eric's share of the business, renovating Eric's office and settling in, he figured out what the agency's problem had been in its previous incarnation. Eliya was a top-notch investigator—he learned that the hard way when she had to step in and rescue him during his early and not-too-successful investigations—but a bad manager. He hired Lilian and took over running the office. The name of the agency—which remained EE: Eliya and Elish—gained fame. Business was booming.

"WHAT?" LILIAN BLEATED. "BUT I THOUGHT IT ONLY BOTHERED Eliya," she said, pointing at the latter's darkened office, "and she went home thirty minutes ago."

He placed the sealed envelope on her desk. "I need you to mail this to the address on this card."

"Yarkon Police Precinct, yowza," she said. "Oh, is this the same Manny Lahav who came to see you? Since when are we in business with them? It's after five now so I can't get a messenger. I'll do it tomorrow morning. Is it urgent? I've got to run in a minute. You don't have any more meetings today." She glanced into a compact mirror, fixing her lipstick.

"Got a date?"

"Uh-huh. Someone from OkCupid. Looks super cute. Say, does six o'clock seem like a legit time for a blind date?"

"How should I know? I guess it depends on what you're after."

"Okay. So good night, hon, I'll see you tomorrow."

ELISH TOOK A SEAT IN LILIAN'S CHAIR. IT WAS TOO EARLY TO GO home. The truth was, though he refused to admit it even to himself, he was riled up from his meeting with Manny. He felt that same hint of excitement that had shot through him when he decided to buy this agency; the kind of excitement he knew he could not share with a single soul–not with his mother or his sister, not with Eliya–who had wondered out loud when they first met about his desire to buy out her husband's share of the agency–nor with Eitan, whom he was able to tell the day before, sitting at the darkening, emptying Gilman cafeteria, "I want to be a clerk of small human sins. That's the only kind of investigation I'm willing to take on. Not tracking down missing persons, not locating stolen vehicles, not industrial spying. Only infidelity, corruption, frauds. And that's the kind of cases we get anyway."

He was alone with his excitement, just as he'd been twenty-one years earlier, when he opened the first volume of the Encyclopedia Brown series and read thirstily about how Leroy Brown (nicknamed "Encyclopedia" by his friends) wrote on the lid of a shoebox "No questions without answers," and hung it up on the door to his parents' garage. It was childish, and thinking about it was pointless. But here, his excitement signaled to him, was a tangle; a thicket of facts that did not sit together; open questions. He had to sort them out, position them alongside each other, and untangle. Seek out the motivation, he told himself. Uncover the power structure. If there ever was a method, that was it.

"The obvious problem is," he thought out loud, "if I were a deputy minister whose brother the police determined had committed suicide, but I didn't believe it, I would have raised hell. I would have accused the Israel Police of not doing its job. I would have confronted the minister of interior in the hallways of the Knesset with a journalist alongside me and demanded that he have the case reopened."

He was intimately familiar with the rumors about Yehuda Menuhin that had spread through the hallways of Gilman while he was a student there. Sexual harassment, sexual extortion, female students receiving grades in accordance with their responsiveness to his advances. Once, during a cafeteria conversation, a student joined their table and told them he'd been sitting outside of Yehuda Menuhin's office one day, waiting for an appointment with the professor, when he overheard the man having erotic conversations during office hours. Elish could never quite believe gossip. At a young age he'd given up on the attempt to decipher the logic of it. Do some qualities make certain people more convenient or interesting objects for gossip, or was it just a random pattern? And what was the correlation between the intensity of the gossip, its relation to the facts, and the personality of its object? No one is ever clean. Everyone lies in the dark, crying about their sins. Why then, are the sins of specific members of the human race deemed more unforgivable? He had even more trouble believing the gossip about Menuhin. The man looked like a monk–dry, shriveled, desire-less. But still, a media-heavy investigation would have opened his can of worms. Even if ultimately it would turn out that the rumors were baseless, it would be difficult to clear his name, so it made sense that his brother didn't go to the media.

His thoughts arranged one at a time, organizing into an argument that he himself had no way of defining when he'd started the process. The fingers of his left hand kept drumming the entire time.

Gideon Menuhin wanted an investigation, that much was clear. But he didn't want to be connected to it. He wanted it to be done discreetly and for the findings to be directly reported to him. He could of course go straight to Chief Superintendent Menahem Lahav and asked him to personally open the file. Had Manny agreed–Elish was convinced the two had discussed this possibility–the story would have leaked to the press within two days, tops. The head of the special investigations team answering to Manny had himself closed the case, and opening it again without any further information would have raised questions. And with every crime reporter lurking at police stations, just waiting to get their hands on a juicy story to jump-start their career, a media storm would have quickly ensued. Something along the lines of, "A Deputy Minister Abuses Private Connections and Public Funds," "Corruption at the Top," "A Disruption Among Public Officials," etc. In light of the many scandals of recent years, and the common belief that every Israeli with authority was abusing their power and influence, investigative reporting was enjoying its golden age. Opening the case again without any new evidence could mark the end of both men's public careers. And how did Manny Lahav fit into this story, anyway? If Gideon was pressuring him, it meant the investigation had closed to his dissatisfaction, or–stranger still–that his interest in reopening the case was only piqued after his brother's death was determined a suicide.

There was one possibility. Gideon Menuhin, to judge by his very prominent absence from the media, was terrified of the spotlight, to the point of paranoia. And like any true paranoid, he assumed the world was obsessed with him and waiting breathlessly for his every move. He couldn't very well afford to walk into a private investigation agency without a gossip item appearing online that night, and in a national newspaper the following day. Or so he imagined. So instead he turned to his good friend, Chief Superintendent Menachem Lahav, and asked him for a little favor.

And there was another possibility. Gideon Menuhin was a very skilled politician. The paranoia he'd manifested to Manny may have served him well, diverting Manny's attention from what he was actually asking him for. He could promote his political career with baby steps, a proposition here, an early-morning-show interview there, a little television, some criticism of the financial plan, a discussion of Israel's military activity in the occupied territories, slowly trickling into the public's consciousness. Or he could make it blossom at once, avoiding interviews until he got his hands on real journalistic dynamite. That way, he'd be mining for political gold without putting himself at risk. Elish wondered if, in this case, Manny Lahav grasped the ramifications of the investigation he'd just ordered. If Elish found anything non-kosher about Yehuda Menuhin's suicide and could provide evidence, Gideon might very well publicly crucify Manny, accusing his precinct of negligence. What a cliché. Gideon would become a momentary media hero, appearing on talk shows–the politician who followed his sound logic and sense of justice, never backing down. But if the investigation awakened any demons, he'd pay Elish off, bury the findings, and stake out his next opportunity.

Elish chuckled. None of these theories were especially convincing. There was too much missing information. For instance, what did Manny Lahav have to gain from all this? Let's assume there was something suspect about Yehuda Menuhin's suicide, he thought. Could Manny Lahav have come to see me under duress from Gideon because he thought I was too much of an idiot or a rookie to catch on?

ELISH HELD THE ENVELOPE MANNY HAD GIVEN HIM UNDER A lamp. That last thought had made his blood boil. It was enough to make him decide to peek at the contents of the envelope. But opening it would be a kind of submission. The light could not break through the brown paper. He hadn't expected it to. Lilian and her little niece looked back at him, embracing, from the heart-shape picture frame on her desk. He cursed her. She was too efficient. A less efficient secretary would have worked harder to find a messenger. To please him. To rid him of this envelope Manny had left him. But not Lilian. She knew the working hours of every service provider they used by heart. Her world was organized, decisive. He cursed again as he carefully stripped away the envelope tab and pulled out a binder and another plump envelope with the word "Archive" scrawled across it.

He leafed quickly through the file. Case opening report, a photocopy of a gun license under the name of the deceased, an autopsy report (male, Caucasian, forty-four years of age, excellent health, point blank gunshot in right temple, traces of gunpowder on right hand, a few lines he thought he understood, though he still had to look into them) followed by a ballistic test report (the bullet found in the deceased's skull matched the diameter of the barrel of the gun in his hand, a perfect match), a photocopy of the death certificate, and the case closing report with the findings of the autopsy matching those of the police investigation: unequivocal suicide, above the swirling signature of Chief Superintendent Menachem Lahav.

He turned his attention to the archive envelope, which he also opened carefully, as if neutralizing explosives, before scattering its contents over the desk. It contained newspaper clippings. He rummaged through them. The bulk comprised a supplement piece about a libel suit made by Menuhin against his university colleagues for their public criticism of the moral foundation of his philosophy, which he claimed was accompanied by personal slander and the besmirching of his reputation. Elish read carefully. The Philosophy Department faculty members had lined up, each waiting his or her turn to make their claim against Dr. Yehuda Menuhin, a forceful man who made use of the absolute, staunchly defended freedom of expression promoted by the university to preach destruction, teaching ignorance. Many of them addressed the preface of Menuhin's book, which had caused an outcry at the time, and rang a vague bell in Elish's head: "These days, every average dump contains the raw materials necessary for producing a lethal bomb. The only two things preventing it from being produced are knowledge and morals. We've got too little of the former and too much of the latter."

"How dare he speak like that at a time like this," protested one of his colleagues, another philosophy professor who, not long before, in the same newspaper, had criticized the government for being too soft on the Palestinians. "Language has the power to shape reality, and Menuhin's language could drag Israel to the edge of an abyss." There was no shortage of this kind of harsh commentary, each person expressing it according to his or her own views and the political and social initiative they wished to promote. But harshest of all was Professor Ora Anatot, head of the Philosophy Department at Tel Aviv University, who determined he was "a thinker who would not be suited to any philosophy department in the world."

Yehuda Menuhin had responded: "At first look, it appears that the enemy of philosophy is the layperson, who acts according to emotions. But the truth is, the worst enemy of philosophy is the lowly clerk holding a key position in academia." It isn't easy being detested, Elish thought, smiling bitterly with unexpected camaraderie. Welcome to the club.

The clippings contained additional references to the libel suit, a long piece about the court ruling that obligated Menuhin to pay legal expenses, a small piece about his book of essays being translated into French, and, at the bottom, a small excerpt from an interview with certain lines highlighted: "Shushan is a second-year student in the interdisciplinary program . . . Dr. Yehuda Menuhin was so impressed with her entry exam that he asked her to be his teaching assistant in the Philosophy Department as early as her first year." At the top of the page was a handwritten title: "From an interview with Dalia Shushan, *The Heart of the South*, October '98."

Elish held his breath. October '98. The month when Blasé's first song came out. His first thought was: How the hell did I miss this article? Well, a southern local newspaper must not have appeared at the central Tel Aviv library. When he realized just how out of context this thought was, his other thoughts scattered to the wind, a pack of rabid dogs. This variable didn't fit into any of the formulas he'd just finished outlining. He opened Lilian's desk drawer, where he knew she kept an extra pack. The elegant, fragile rectangle of the cigarette pack froze in his left hand. He was so close to bringing it to his mouth, tearing the reflective plastic wrapping with a violent bite, but then felt nauseous when he pictured the smoke rising and swirling helplessly to the ceiling, diving into his lungs, legions of loneliness and soot hardening his blood.

He closed his eyes and watched all his theories collapse. What were the goddamn odds? He'd heard a Blasé song just the previous night, and now Dalia Shushan's name was being flaunted in his face. Manny's answer to the question of why he'd come to him was far from satisfactory, and now these highlighted newspaper lines ignited the question even more. There was no doubt that Chief Superintendent Lahav was anything but naïve, and that he was playing his own complex game, which Elish still did not have the tools to decode. Why did he come to him? No. No, he couldn't allow this suspicious attitude to wash over him. It was all so baseless. He paced the reception room nervously. As far as he could discern, Lahav was a friendly older man, a tired and lackluster police officer, not a brilliant mastermind. The whole story was ridiculous. There had to be a logical explanation. No, no, why him? Why him, of all people?

The nervous, stimulating pacing slowly calmed him. A pleasant tension coursed through him, that same old hint of excitement forced alive. No questions without answers, he thought. In the pit of his stomach, the tension brewed into a small storm. He preferred Edgar Allan Poe's phrasing, which he'd discovered at some point and assumed was the source of Encyclopedia Brown's slogan: "It may well be doubted whether human ingenuity can construct an enigma of the kind which human ingenuity may not resolve." "It may well be doubted whether human ingenuity can construct an enigma of the kind which human ingenuity may not resolve," he whispered to the walls in the empty office, and they echoed back the dull, rolling sound of Mediterranean waves.

4

It took Manny two hours to get back to him. In the era of cellular communication and the internet, this was too long, Elish thought. He'd left Manny a voice-mail message at ten in the morning. "Manny, it's Elish. I read the material. Let's talk. I'll be in the office until the afternoon."

He put the phone down and yawned. The previous night had been long, overladen with thoughts, sleepless. And the morning, after two cups of coffee, seemed impossible, an illuminated, viscous fog inside which words and figures moved with unbearable slowness.

When it was past midnight and Elish began counting the hours of the new day, he knew he was staring with horror once more into the gaping maw of the night. Xanax, Klonopin, Oxazepam, valerian extract, what difference did it make? Sleep had become a magical creature, evading the body's reach. Just as a man in the depths of his disease is gripped by the certainty that there is no resurrection for him, that he will never be able to move his limbs freely, without pain and the struggle for health, Elish was chilled with the realization that he'd never fall asleep again.

He got out of bed, boiled some milk, and went up to the roof, where he'd arranged planters rooted with herbs: mint, tree wormwood, rosemary, verbena, a few miniature trees, and some flowers the names of which he could not recall but which he saw as a kind of tribute to the flower garden his mother had attempted to nurture ever since the time of his bar mitzvah, only for them to fail miserably once and again. Even he could not produce such orderly, wilting rows, in spite of the knack for dysfunctional gardening he'd inherited from her. There was something poetic about the dereliction she'd sowed. Cracked roses like hers, laden with parasites, wild pansies perforated from the wind, withering and wilderness, no, not even Elish, with the curse of death moving through his bones, could bring nature to create such a wretched garden.

The heart of Tel Aviv sprawled before him from his position on the roof. The still Tel Hai Street and the ones surrounding it: King Solomon, Zamenhoff, Ein Harod, their dimness broken by streetlamps and the flight of fruit bats. Stars did not pierce through the clouds, nor did the waning moon of Tishrei, the only whispered sketching of light Elish could spot, an ember in the night sky. On a similar night, from the other side of winter, in the month of Shvat, when the force of the sun had dipped beyond its lowest point and begun to grow again, four and a half years earlier, he'd seen Dalia Shushan performing for the first time. He'd gone to the Logos to see a show by a band named Dildo Express, most of whose members he'd known from other bands with better names that he'd written about when he was a student working as an art critic for the culture section of *Everything Tel Aviv*.

At the Logos, where there was nothing but words and sounds, he almost felt at home, safely ensconced in the main artery of Israeli rock, smiling in all directions, the eye-stinging smoke—monstrous product of dozens of lungs—and smell of alcohol-drenched bodies were not revolting, but rather friendlier than usual. He knew everyone he needed to know. The rivalries and romances reported in gossip columns became family mythologies at the Logos. The beloved bassist of one band leaned in to chat with the front man of another; an adored radio DJ whispered with a no-less-adored drummer; others chattered excitedly, demonstrating guitar sounds for each other; female rockers with low voices sat at the bar, running their hands through their hair, laughing together; an artist who had just won eternal fame leaned back, passing a cigarette to the person beside them; a rising star argued with the bouncer, his arm around the shoulders of the hottest model of the moment, bypassing the line of kids crowding at the entrance, tapping the glass to signal to the owner. Elish never saw the Dildo Express show. He'd lost any interest in it as soon as, running into Debbie Malkieli, the band's manager, at the entrance, he asked about the meaning of the ridiculous name, and she answered with an enthusiastic smile that "Dildo" was an acronym for the first letters of the band members' names: David, Ilay, Lior, Danny, and Orna—wasn't that great? Wasn't that the most brilliant thing he'd ever heard?

Dildo's warmup was a duo with the bizarre name of Blasé et Sans Lumière—a guitarist plugged into a computer and keyboard and a singer who looked like a roadie, or, at best, a ticket scalper. He knew her, though his memory refused to share where from, and only the lump in his chest signaled the truth. From the first note the guitarist strummed, it was clear to Elish this was a brand-new sound. After three songs and a tornado of applause, he stepped outside, dazed from the monotonousness of the music, the symmetry of the parts that was broken in a manner that sounded random, spontaneous, but in fact was the embodiment of complex pattern, and awed by the way the melodies merged and by the voice of the singer, Dalia Shushan. That was the night he decided to write a book about Israeli rock, for the simple reason that that was the night when he realized that Israeli rock was drawing its final breaths.

Now he shifted uncomfortably. He was getting cold in the sneaky October air that had slipped through his polyester cover while he was drinking his milk. He was wearing boxer shorts and a T-shirt. He walked back inside and over to the bookcase, which stretched across an entire wall of his study. He had three copies of *The Sky Is Dust*, two of which he'd never cracked open.

A wave of disgust washed over him as he pulled out one of these untouched copies and flipped through it. Every sentence read like an accusation. *Traitor, villain, son of a bitch asshole, you and whoever created you*, the lines screamed.

The penultimate chapter, "Ousted Angels Staking their Sleep," which discussed the question of the future of Israeli rock, was mostly devoted to Blasé et Sans Lumière. Dalia refused to be interviewed and asked Rami not to talk about her hometown of Sderot or her relationship with other musicians who hailed from there. Rami obeyed. He spoke about the founding of Blasé from his own point of view. Elish edited and cut down, making Rami's bouncy speech, which was peppered with childish profanities, more eloquent. Perhaps that was a mistake. At any rate, that was his only sin–not all that nonsense he was accused of by his former colleagues, critics and musicians who bad-mouthed him, showering him with evil. He'd simply created flow in his interviewees' words, and perhaps imbued them with some misplaced poeticism, but that was his only sin, he kept repeating to himself, though without much conviction, in the months after the book came out, when one concert after the next was closed off to him. It was hard to read the text, but he forced himself to.

"I MET DALIA IN COLLEGE, IN YEHUDA MENUHIN'S INTRODUCtion to Contemporary Philosophy. Her name rang a bell, and so did her face, but I didn't put the two together. I'd seen her at a few shows. Actually, she was a regular at Logos and Twelfth Night, and so was I. From the moment I arrived in Tel Aviv, six months before I started school, I spent every free hour there. I noticed she always stayed back after each show to talk to the bands. At first I despised her a little. She looked like a pathetic groupie. She wasn't even pretty. I stuck around after the shows, watching musicians put away their gear, staking out an opportunity, hoping to stumble into a conversation with one of them, or even one of their managers, and slip the demo I was always carrying around into their hands. But the more I watched Dalia, the more I realized she was anything but a groupie. It seemed like the musicians were the ones who actually wanted to talk to her, and especially the lead singer for Dildo Express. I wondered who she was, but I didn't know anyone who could tell me. Once, I even tried asking someone who was standing beside me at the bar at a Dildo concert: what's the deal with that uggo hanging around Lior Levitan? Did she really think he gave a damn about her? But the guy just looked at me angrily and muttered, 'What an idiot.' Then Lior Levitan invited Sammy Lalo, an old friend and the best guitarist he knew, to come up onstage and play a song with them, and it turned out to be the same guy from the bar.

"I knew her name because I'm a credit freak. The acknowledgments are the first thing I look at when I buy a new CD. The Dildo album included a special thanks to Dalia. When the attendance list was passed around during that first philosophy class, I saw her name, and during the break between classes I asked some people if they knew who she was and someone pointed her out. I couldn't believe it. Shushan was that ugly girl from Logos whom, in the six months before the beginning of the school year, I'd already become obsessed with.

"I went over. She looked lonely against the backdrop of Gilman Hall. We couldn't really talk, but I insisted and kept trying, and I never regretted it. She was on another level: brilliant, sharp, but quiet. She had a talent to move people. Some people are like that. They have unbelievable emotional intensity, and every little thing they do projects it.

"I came up to her at the end of the semester and told her I didn't usually do this, and that I wouldn't be asking if I didn't admire her so much, and that I would be thrilled if she listened to the demo I made at home and give me notes. She just smiled. A few days later, I went to a Fortis concert, even though it was finals season. I thought I might see her there and I was right. She was glad to see me and said she'd been meaning to call me and tell me she thought my demo was problematic. On the one hand, the playbacks were very good, but on the other hand, the lyrics and music still needed work. At any rate, she thought I should keep trying different things, because she liked the general feel of the arrangements. I told her I had a ton of playbacks without music over them and that I'd love it if she could help me sort out the best ones for me to start playing around with. She agreed, and we made plans for the following week.

"She came over and I played her some stuff. After a few playbacks she didn't like, I played her one of the first ones I'd ever written, and she asked to hear it again. I had an acoustic guitar. She picked it up and quickly found the chord progression it was based on. She asked me to put the playback on a loop and played along with it three times in a row. The fourth time, she added lyrics. It was amazing. Her performance was a little hesitant, but the song was gorgeous, and she sang it with such feeling, so much lonesomeness in her voice . . . I remember thinking, why am I not recording this? But at the same time I sensed that every move I made would break the spell of that moment. But as soon as the playback started over again she repeated the song, over and over again, with slight changes, until she reached a final version. Later, after we'd been working together for a few months, I learned that it was a special moment for her too, that she felt the same, that this was it, the real thing. Even though we wrote all of our songs in a similar fashion, this was the only song that ended up in our album exactly as we created it—four-track playback, acoustic guitar, and voice. I'm talking about 'Night,' the song that closes out our first album ('I don't want to stay alone tonight / but the city is built around me like a maze / carefully designed to prevent me / from going outside and meeting.' E.B.Z.).

"We met up regularly to write songs. Meaning, Dalia wrote

them while I experimented with a drum machine and different sounds. My idea was to create a world of sounds that would reflect the lyrics Dalia wrote or inspire her to write new ones. At some point, Shushan's musician friends started showing up, and they were blown away too. Lior Levitan was the most enthusiastic. He wanted to bring over his manager to meet us. After some consultation we decided we didn't want to play our stuff for his manager, but we did agree to open for his band at their upcoming concert. Our first performance was electric. Unbelievable. I knew the songs and Dalia's depths, but the concert still exceeded my expectations. She showed up in the simplest dress, sat on a chair in the center of the stage, and stayed there for the course of the show. Thinking back, I should have been worried. The audience came to see a high energy concert, but instead got some depressing singer doing slow songs. But even I was trapped in Dalia's mesmerizing voice, and I didn't think about anything. I was swept away in spite of myself. We did three songs while the audience sat quietly, listening in. Then Dalia thanked them, and they went wild. And the rest, I think, is history."

Alongside Amzaleg's interview, the book featured a section from Elish's review that he'd sent the morning after that first show to *Everything Tel Aviv*. The magazine's culture editor had given him a standing invitation for new pieces. He was proud to have been the first one to recognize the duo's potential, the first one to have put Blasé on the map. The words contained a double estrangement—their presence in the book and the thin veil of time—which turned them into the words of another, and thus susceptible to judgement, guilty of floweriness: "Occasionally, a person might come across a vision or an experience that makes existence in this world bearable. The transparency of rusty air in evening, the deep aroma of the sea at high tide, or Dalia Shushan's voice—the voice of a siren with a corpse in each chamber of her heart. At the Dildo Express concert, I heard the next big thing—their opening act, Blasé et Sans Lumière. A two-person band, Dalia Shushan and Rami Amzaleg, which proved to me that rock could tear open the gates of heaven and hell. I didn't stay for the Dildo concert. After listening to Blasé (and let's be honest—nobody, not even the most devoted radio DJ, and I believe there are many, will refer to this duo by its full name, so for the benefit of the immense amount of ink that will be spilled over them, let's just agree to call them Blasé, a name that does not match their spirit at all), I had to leave for fear that the memory of the songs would fade when touched by a different music."

He closed the book. This really was too much. After his review was published he walked around tense for three days, jumping at every knock on the door, every ringing of the phone, telling himself, Now it's time for the flesh to speak, burning hieroglyphs of sudden kingdoms, emerging with a touch, collapsing with legions of distance; he recalled how, in an interview on the occasion of an album release, Phil Collins was asked why he thanked Winona Ryder in the liner notes, and Collins replied that he was hoping Winona Ryder would call to ask the same question. Was it tension that had him flinching? He waved away the thought. Dalia had touched him, deep in his being. She was the paralyzing power of the past, the mystery of the future, if that was something that could even be said. She expressed things he'd never dared put into words. But it wasn't just her voice, her lyrics, her performance. It was something else. And her death, her murder, a newspaper headline—"Rock Singer Murdered by Gunshot"—and below that, "Three gunshots put an end to the life of singer Dalia Shushan. 'A horrible murder,' says police spokesperson."

FOR TWENTY YEARS, ELISH'S MEMORY HAD BEEN DECEIVING him, concealing things from him, emerging in all the wrong places. He spent the rest of the night lying in bed with his eyes open, groggy and defeated enough to remember what he'd already managed to successfully block out. I could feel memory coming, he thought now. It had remained deeply numb throughout all the Blasé concerts, all the times I listened to their albums, but her death cracked all of my careful defenses, and the animal of the past began scratching the walls of my innards, and I could feel the waves of pain that had sunk its talons into my flesh, but I didn't dare reveal its source to myself. And just as had happened in the past, the memory that hadn't existed just a moment before finally hit him with full clarity, detailed to the point of nausea—flavor, smell, lighting.

She looked about fifteen years old. Her dark hair fell on her face as she strummed the guitar with hesitation. Her movements were clumsy; the clothes she was wearing were intended—not all too successfully—to hide her plump body. The year was approaching April, the purity of the sky and the scent of dusty eucalyptus trees that had started burning through the air. She was sitting beneath them, at a wooden table on the lawn of Sapir College in the Negev Desert. An older boy stood beside her, watching her hands carefully. "Not like that, Dalia," he said, "you're missing the beat."

She paused.

"Listen," he said, tapping his thigh. "One, two, three, four. Emphasis on the one, this is where the count starts."

She began to strum again, occasionally matching his metronome beats before evading them again.

"That's better," he said. "The problem is that you're listening to the outside beat I'm giving you but you aren't flowing. You only need to listen to the first few bars and then get the beat into your body. You see? The beat is in the body."

She nodded vigorously.

Elish walked closer. He was curious about this girl and he followed her music.

"Good," said the boy, "you're catching on." He stopped tapping.

The girl lost herself in her strumming, raising her face, her eyes closed. She isn't pretty, Elish thought, but she's got strength.

"Now try changing chords," said the boy.

Her fingers got tangled, and she paused again and opened her eyes. Elish was locked inside her gaze, seeing himself, at seventeen, his limbs already fully developed, tall, his eyes blinking in the sun. "You're starting to look like a man," his mother had told him two days before his bar mitzvah. He hadn't liked that assertion, hadn't liked the way he looked. His body was bigger than he wanted, evading his authority, elongating and thickening, raising muscles and stretching skin. But in this girl's gaze he saw his body differently. As whole.

"Listen, Dalia, I've got to run. You're getting better with every lesson. The problem is you don't practice. Get yourself a guitar already." With that, the boy took his guitar back and walked away. Elish was outside her line of vision now. She waved goodbye to the boy and picked up the book that was lying beside her. A book Elish would have spotted had he not lost himself in her image. A small, rectangular book, wrapped in plastic, new, which didn't quite sit with the short red strip on its spine, signaling that it had been borrowed from a public library. The image of the golden Buddha on the backdrop of clouds and lightning bolts stared at him from the cover. *Lord of Light.*

"You're reading Roger Zelazny?" Elish gasped.

"It would be more surprising if I wasn't," she smiled.

At another time he would have thought she was being smart and turned away. But since when did girls read science fiction? Certainly not any girl in his class. Not that he ever spoke to them and not that they ever noticed him. Her eyes nailed him down, and through them he felt once more the weight of the body that had grown around him, the legs that grew a little longer each morning, causing him to feel dizzy when he got out of bed, learning his new height, and the biceps, whose hardness still surprised him, and the armpit hair, which he had been afraid of revealing until he was fourteen, walking with his arms crossed, making sure never to raise them whenever he wore short sleeves, and the baby mustache and the stubble. That whole horror of the body. That whole horror of the body was suddenly forgivable.

"This book." Why did he even open his mouth? "When I read it, it was like . . . I don't know."

She looked at him expectantly.

He erupted, "Maybe it was like the first time I heard Eurythmics' 'Here Comes the Rain Again,' those opening organ notes, and my heart jumped. I knew nothing would be as it once was." Then he fell silent just as quickly. Nothing would be as it once was? He didn't talk to people about this stuff. Why was he telling her?

"Talk to me like lovers do," she quoted drily. Her eyes let go of his, and she looked ahead to the horizon, looking over his shoulder, ponderous, chewing on her bottom lip.

He'd never imagined how much he was like the other boys in his class who celebrated their limbs–comparing dribbling skills and passing drills on the basketball court, sweating, undressing in the gym, peeing in the urinals together, coming up to the girls during recess with a knowledgeable expression, covering the embarrassment that aroused them to whisper and chuckle amongst themselves. He grew apart from them as soon as he'd returned from summer vacation between fourth and fifth grades, and by the time puberty struck out of nowhere, and with it the clumsy industry of courtship, he already was, he believed, an outside onlooker. But he was wrong. His senses were ahead of him, smarter than him, already in the midst of courtship without his knowledge, the eyes consuming and the nostrils flaring and the mouth gaping without his permission. The flesh was too strong. Nothing could prepare him for this moment, none of the books he read, none of the songs whose lyrics he'd followed with a shiver. No, untrue. Some songs did prepare him. There was that Nick Cave album, *From Her to Eternity*, in which the rhythm of every song reminded him of the different ways in which his body had learned to act when images from the books he read in hiding and the movies he watched floated into his mind at night.

Dalia returned her gaze to him. "Have you ever heard Nick Cave's *From Her to Eternity*?"

That was the moment he knew. Knew what? Nothing that could be procured. Just that there was something worthy of knowing, that it was close and tangible, the comfort that certainty existed, that it was before him. No, no, this was a later phrasing that had nothing to do with the excitement and reeling, the phrasing of men lying alone in bed. And no, no, not excitement and reeling. Not words in any language that could be spoken. The standing on end of hair, the engorging, expanding blood vessels, the flesh becoming an echo chamber for a single beat, arriving beyond the crudeness of time, from the depths of the oceans, even this stuttered breath was merely a translation of it, a shadow.

"Elish," he muttered with difficulty, taking a seat beside her.

"Dalia. But you already knew that," she said, not even pausing to ask, like others did the first time they heard his name, "What did you say your name was?"

"So what do you think of the book?"

"Messy. I prefer *The Chronicles of Amber*."

He'd forgotten about his private math lesson, forgotten about how anxious his mother became when he came home late without letting her know. His mouth easily shattered all the prohibitions applied to him. Dalia, who seemed unaccustomed to conversation, also spoke, her voice shaking with effort.

When did his consciousness escape the spell that had been cast upon him? When he noticed that all the while the air was crowded with senseless sounds, that there was no importance in the words exchanged, only in their ceaseless movement, hours on end. The gangly-bright afternoon of near Passover evaporated at its own time, unaware of the wonders it offered. He put his hand on hers. She said, "*The Head on the Door*, what a perfect album. Robert Smith is a god. What do you think of Echo and the Bunnymen?" Her voice was low, on the verge of purring, their hands studying each other, the fingers soft, revealing. The electricity, the electricity.

"That's a strange thing to ask. The Smiths are obviously better," he choked.

"I have to show you something." She released her fingers from his.

They walked out through the college gates to the shoulder of the road leading to Sderot, passing by the gas station, the eucalyptuses that darkened as they walked, a long walk whose length was meaningless, talking. Streetlamps turned on, he stopped, she stopped, her breathing was choppy, perhaps from the walk, her face offered. He held onto her shoulders and lowered his head, lips on lips, how sloppy, the tongue, what to do with the tongue, the teeth knocking against each other, beyond the barrier of the mouth. "It's soon," she said.

Intoxicated, he said, "I don't know, this place is starting to give me the chills." Sderot was behind them, an invisible shadow of the dark path they were swallowed in, cypress trees standing sentinel on both sides.

After they walked a little farther, she laughed and spread her arms, look it, look it, and spun in place cheerfully. Elish looked. They were surrounded by tombstones, their feet stepping on the dirt of a cemetery.

"Isn't this the most magical place on earth?" she cried.

"Dalia, let's get out of here."

The moon yellowed and silvered in the cloudless sky, climbing to illuminate the cemetery. Dalia fled with a squeal of joy.

"Dalia!" Elish called after her. "What are you doing?"

Dalia's arm waved and her voice led him. "Catch me! Over here, I'm here!"

Elish scampered awkwardly among the tombstones, recoiling whenever his foot hit a wreath, hopping.

"Over here," Dalia's voice urged.

He finally reached her. She was standing there, flushed, beaming. "You're nuts," he said. "Couldn't you have warned me earlier? What if I were a descendant of the temple priests?"

"It's a shame you aren't." She reached out her hands.

He ignored them and approached her expectant, raised face, wrapping his arms around her body, and kissing her. The tongue was adjusting, investigating the inside of her mouth. After an eternity went by, he detached his mouth and looked around. "You could have warned me," he chuckled. Her eyes were still closed, concentrating. He felt the blood running out of his face, a shiver trickling, his eyes fixed on the words on the tombstone, reading them but refusing to focus: "Dalia Shushan, May She Rest in Peace."

He walked backward. Dalia Shushan was standing before him, on the backdrop of her own tombstone. "What do you want from me?" In movies, protagonists would cross themselves right now. But he was Jewish. Perhaps he should sketch the shape of a Star of David through the air. And he could see her in sunlight. How was that possible? "Are you a ghost?" The words sounded hysterical and idiotic in his own ears.

Dalia widened her eyes. "Don't be stupid."

He started running, drawing away from her, panicked.

"It's my grandmother's grave. I'm named after her. Don't be an idiot. Elish! Elish, come back!" she shouted, but the sights and sounds were already getting muddled in his mind, uninterpreted, the world pounding against him.

He couldn't remember exactly how he got home. He knew he hitchhiked. The face of the driver who picked him up was blurry. The driver must have felt sorry for the dumbstruck boy who only mumbled, "Ashkelon." He dropped him off on the outskirts of town, from where he must have walked for an hour and a half to get home, his head full of lead. His mother yelled at him, how she yelled at him, and Yaffa was pale with tears. "We didn't know where you were. We were scared something might have happened to you or that you'd hurt yourself! You weren't at math class. Where did you disappear to? Zalman wanted us to call the police. You almost killed us!"

He walked into his bedroom. "I have a fever," he told his mother.

"But the doctor said it was over, that the fever attacks wouldn't come back. Tell me what happened," she pled as she followed him into his bedroom. He spent the next three days in bed, suffering his final fever attack. He never told a soul about that day.

AT DAWN, HE FELL INTO THE KIND OF SLUMBER THAT DID NOT offer remedy, no dreams to liberate the consciousness from the splint of reason, whose cogs kept turning all the while in suspended wakefulness. At ten in the morning he left Manny a message. At noon he was shaken by the ringing of his office telephone. His head was resting in his arms, which were crossed on the desk. Drool dripped from the corner of his mouth, pooling on the wooden surface. It was Manny.

"Elish? It's Manny. What's up?"

"Okay, look, you were right." He was exhausted and afraid he might lose his thread, so he clung to an informative, impersonal tone. "I really am interested in this case."

"I'm glad. Say, are you all right? You don't sound good."

"I'm fine," he said tentatively—had he recognized signs of concern for his well-being in Manny's voice?—"just a little tired."

"Up all night partying, huh?"

"No, I just couldn't sleep." He was being dragged into a conversation he didn't want to have, but there was nothing crude about Manny's sudden intrusiveness, only honest curiosity Elish wondered what the man wanted.

"Try Calmanervin. Ever since our two daughters left home, my wife's had trouble falling asleep. Calmanervin really helps."

"I'm way beyond that, believe me." He felt a bit of pride for what he was about to say, like a kid boasting about his booboos. "I've been living in the trippy world of sleep chemicals for a long time now."

Manny laughed heartily, and Elish was gripped by moderate fear. He wasn't joking.

"Look." Elish went back to business. "I've got one condition. I want to meet Gideon Menuhin."

Manny fell silent. Elish could hear him taking a breath before he answered, "No, out of the question. I already told you the terms. You get results, the two of you meet. I don't want to play mediator too much, and if I know Gideon . . ." He fell silent again.

Elish was too curious, though his common sense roared at him behind the haze of fatigue: Drop it! What do you need this for? He was stubborn. Always had been. From the moment a desire or interest aroused in him, he became fervent, refusing to delay gratification. Reality was merely an obstacle to be removed. "Fine," he said, "I might need a few other things later on."

"So bye for now, Elish."

5

"Eliya, can you come in here for a second?" Elish yawned again, a chain of yawns that fed into each other, threatening to swallow the world.

"Didn't anyone ever tell you it's rude to yawn in public?" Eliya scolded as she closed the door behind her. "Not to mention unhealthy. What did you need?"

He handed her a document. "Tell me what you think." Earlier he'd photocopied the pathologist's report from Yehuda Menuhin's file and removed every identifying detail. Eliya was reading the autopsy report of an anonymous person, and he looked her over carefully as she did. Behind her boyish appearance—the high, prominent, sharply contoured cheekbones, a pair of eyes watching the world through rectangular, intellectual-looking glasses, a short haircut, very black hair, probably dyed, that highlighted the paleness of her naked face—was an iron cast. She shook her head and looked up at him. "So what's the question?"

"I need an objective opinion. What do you see here?"

"It's an autopsy report for a man who killed himself."

"You don't see anything strange? Unusual?"

She shook her head sharply.

"The substance found in his stomach?"

"What about it? Alprazolam. It's the active ingredient in some sedatives or common antidepressants. Lots of people take them as often as sleeping pills. They make you sleepy."

"Yes, I know. I'm familiar with the subject. But according to the report, the deceased," he was both delighted and repelled by the dryness of the word, "took the pill about thirty minutes before killing himself, along with a glass of wine."

"That only proves the fact that he was trying to harm himself."

"Why would someone who wants to kill himself and has a gun take a sleeping pill with wine?"

"Maybe he was in emotional turmoil or deep depression. You know, it takes more than a glass of wine and a sleeping pill to kill yourself."

"I know that from personal experience too. The combination has a numbing effect. It clears you of all feeling. But the next day you're sorry you were born."

"Maybe the depression was so severe that the combination didn't work, and that's when the gun came in. What's this about? Are we investigating a suicide? If you insist on finding something wrong, you'd better look elsewhere, because right now what you've got," she shifted her eyes, which had been turned aside while she talked, her neck craning to the right, to meet his, "is pretty weak."

He was angry, but she was right. The bullet that ended the life of Yehuda Menuhin was shot by a gun registered to his name. So why was his brother insisting on this? "You're right. I'm just doing somebody a favor."

"Who? That cop?"

He looked at her quizzically.

"Last night as I was leaving the office I saw Manny Lahav walking into the building, and you just handed me an autopsy report, so . . ." When he smiled, she added, "If you ask me, that cop has too many friends."

He knew that this was Eliya's reserved way of expressing severe criticism. She didn't tend to comment, positively or negatively, about investigations in which she was not involved, but from the moment she became involved, she grew judgmental and sharp. She adjusted her glasses. "We ran into him, Eric and I, a few times in the past, during our own investigations. He has a tendency to interfere and interpret the law in his own favor."

"Meaning?"

"He asks for favors–very sympathetically, mind you–but there's always an authority to his request. He asks you to understand him, to understand that no harm was caused to anyone, so no one needs to know the results of any surveillance. For instance, I had this one case, about three years ago. A woman hired me to find out what her husband, who'd become a workaholic one fine day, was up to when he told her he was working late. A few days later, the mighty chief superintendent showed up here and tried to convince me that perhaps, for the sake of marital harmony, I ought to destroy some of my findings–rolls of films and recordings."

"Yes, he told me some of that story from his own point of view. It turns out that friend of his benefited from your investigation, so you're actually in his good graces because of that. Do you have any idea what's going on in his precinct right now?"

"I do, actually. I have information-sharing agreements with some cops. Let's say this past year was not kind to the heads of the different departments at the Yarkon Precinct. Ever since the underworld assassination wars began. Shooting on King Solomon Street, a bomb on HaMasger Street, a car bomb on the border with Jaffa–you know. The inspector general is just waiting to lop off some heads. If terror attacks aren't enough, now he's got these people settling accounts and mostly hurting innocent bystanders. I'd say, because of the department Manny Lahav is leading, he's been in the precinct commander's sights. And it's a shame, a real shame, because up until a year ago, everyone was convinced that head of investigations was not the last stop in his career. He's considered a very good politician. A guy who understands people. The kind who knows exactly who's on his side and who isn't, and how to take advantage of it."

Manny Lahav's determined declaration, "I'm not often wrong about people," which Elish thought at the time was a ridiculous affectation, floated into his head. "Give me an example," he told Eliya.

"All right. About a year ago he insisted on making a specific detective, Binyamini, the head of his special investigations team, even though there was no shortage of reservations regarding Binyamini's skills as a detective—still might be, actually. But I assume that with that promotion he acquired an important ally in the precinct."

Seek out the motivation, the line buzzed in Elish's mind. Uncover the power structure. But what did that actually mean? "Eliya, I want you to prepare a file for Gideon Menuhin, the member of parliament. I want to know everything I can about him, as soon as possible."

Eliya whacked her right hand with the document in her left. "Oh." She tilted her neck again, her lips rounding. "I see." She waited, watching Elish with curiosity.

"I know I don't need to ask you to be discreet, but still—not a word to anyone."

"Of course. What do you want to know?"

"Everything there is to know. His past. The skeletons in his closet. His relationship with his brother. His connection to Manny Lahav."

"All right. I'll talk to you on Monday."

ELISH LINKED THE FINGERS OF HIS HANDS, TURNED HIS PALMS outward, and stretched. Yes, Eliya was right, of course. There was nothing out of the ordinary about the conclusion that Yehuda had committed suicide, and as far as he could discern, it had occurred just as the police had deduced. It was the motivation for suicide that needed to be investigated. Why would a doctor of philosophy kill himself? He almost laughed when the thought sounded in his mind. It required an existential interrogation. What a bore. The reasons had to be entirely worldly, and Elish had no doubt that they had to do with the fact that Gideon Menuhin wanted to remain in the shadows in all manners related to the investigation he ordered. His thoughts swirled in his mind. He needed sleep, even for an hour. But first he had to make a phone call.

Eitan was home. In the background Elish heard the crying of a child and the sounds of children's songs. "He's teething," Eitan explained.

"It must be torture, feeling something sharp slowly cutting through your flesh," said Elish. "Sorry, I'm making it sound monstrous."

"No, not at all," Eitan reassured him. "I've been thinking the same thing whenever he cries, how pain is an inseparable part of human existence."

"Yes, those are the first times you experience yourself as a body, flesh and blood. Through pain."

Eitan sighed. The crying in the background grew louder. "I can't talk for long."

"I need a little information," said Elish, "about the Philosophy Department. About Yehuda Menuhin."

"Thank God you didn't add 'may he rest in peace.' I won't ask why you want to know."

"Good, don't."

"So let's see. You know the usual stuff. He was a doctor of philosophy for fourteen years, and though his class was popular, and though he acquired the status of a cultural figure outside of academia, he never made full professor. The official reason was always that he didn't have scientific publications in foreign languages, most importantly in English. His book of essays was translated into French and received rave reviews. I heard he was even invited to the École des hautes études as a visiting professor last year, but turned it down. At any rate, that French translation wasn't considered a scientific publication, because it wasn't published as part of a university press."

"Okay, I do know part of that story."

"You must have heard about the libel suit."

"Uh-huh, yeah. But about that promotion, you said the official reason was lack of publications?"

"Rumor has it that Ora Anatot personally prevented his promotion. She's been the head of the department for the past five years, which means she's also on the appointment committee. She vehemently refused to give him full professorship. She couldn't stand him on a personal level, and couldn't stand his brand of philosophy. He was considered an innovator, and she's old school. But again, their relationship was definitely more than just an ideological rivalry. Besides, she's a bulldozer, you know that."

"You think the libel suit was his way of putting pressure on the department?"

The baby started crying again. The sound of a baby crying is heartbreaking, Elish thought. "Do you want me to call you back later?"

"It won't make much of a difference," Eitan said. "It's going to take him weeks to cut these teeth. If Menuhin thought he was going to put pressure on the department through the libel suit, he was a moron. Which reminds me, during the summer break, things between him and Ora Anatot really came to a head. Not that before that they would greet each other in the hallway, but over the summer there was actually shouting in her office, and Menuhin stormed out. Ora's department secretary gossiped with our department's secretary: 'Ora and Yehuda really aren't getting along lately.' That's what our secretary told me."

"Why didn't she fire him?"

"She couldn't. He had tenure. Dismissal would require him to be impeached, and I think he would have to commit ethical or criminal offenses for that to happen."

"He had a few ethical offenses under his belt, if memory serves."

"I don't think she could have proven them."

"Is there anything else that might help me?"

"Let me think. The last scandal Menuhin was involved in happened about a year ago. The custodian hated him and would delay all his orders—you know, like a DVD player and a slide projector. The story was that Menuhin had harassed a cafeteria worker, a relative of the custodian's, and caused her to be fired. He complained about her to the administration."

"Do you remember her name?"

"No, I need to check . . ." Eitan began.

The baby sobbed in the background and Elish cut him off. "I understand you have to go, but promise me that if anything new comes up, any rumor about Menuhin at the university, you'll let me know."

MAYBE THIS WASN'T MY LAST PHONE CALL, HE THOUGHT. ONE conversation led to another. Goddamn human communication.

"Hello, Philosophy Department," someone said nasally within a racket of enthusiastic voices.

"Hello, can I please speak to Professor Ora Anatot?"

"Ora isn't here today. Call back on Sunday."

"Could you tell me what time? Or take a message?"

"Sir, I have about a million students here waiting to alter their course registration, so if you don't mind, please call back on Sunday." Miss Nasal hung up.

Elish kept the phone to his ear for a few moments longer, listening to the broken, urgent sound from the earpiece. Bitch. This was a sign—he definitely had to start the weekend as soon as possible. He had to go to Ashkelon tomorrow. Yaffa, his sister, was out of town with her husband and their daughter, and she had asked him not to leave their mother alone on Friday night.

He took his jacket off the hanger. He planned to walk down the boardwalk, at a safe distance from the water, all the way to Frischmann Street, then toward Tel Hai in the chilly air. But when he crossed the threshold of his office on the way out, Lilian called after him: "Elish, phone call." He thought it was Eitan, recalling some important detail, but only when he put his hand on the phone did it occur to him that Eitan didn't have his office number. He was thinking slower than usual. He was so tired he could die.

"Elish," Manny's voice assaulted him with amiability. "Got a minute?"

Would he ever start a conversation differently? The fraction of thought broke through the wooly cloud around his brain. "Not really, I'm just heading out."

"Look, I'd like to correct the impression you may have gotten before. Regarding my refusal to let you meet Gideon Menuhin."

"What impression was I supposed to get?"

"I don't know, like maybe I'm somehow sabotaging your case."

"I thought you didn't want to be involved."

"I don't. That's the thing. That's why . . . it's important that you understand that . . . listen, maybe we can meet this afternoon. I'd like to clarify a few things."

"Sorry, I can't. Can we talk on Sunday?"

"Sure, no problem. Take care."

The sea air, thought Elish. Then sleep.

6

The road to Ashkelon was open, the traffic light, dusk illumination hovering over the Tel Aviv–Ashdod highway. Darkness hadn't descended yet, turning driving into a careful crawl through dim tunnels. The front windows were almost completely closed, and through the remaining cracks, the interior was assaulted by the wind, the rattling of the engine, and autumn, which carried the persistent, inexpungible scent of guavas and the dampness of the asphalt. Driving with the land sprawled out before you to the horizon, when you knew the way, surprised only by its minute oddities: a chopped tree, a building that had sprouted an additional floor, changes in weather—in October one could see God's fingers of light spreading the clouds wide, like a child hurriedly undoing the crinkly wrapper of a candy—and when the right music emerged, filling your ears . . . this kind of driving could be bearable. Elish hated driving. He couldn't accept the existence of traffic jams and was nervous from the moment he got into the car to the moment he got out, craning his neck involuntarily to expand his field of vision and check for cars slowing down in the distance. If the jams were the results of car crashes or slow trucks blocking whole lanes, that would be one thing. But inexplicable traffic, an accumulation of vehicles at some random point along the road without any apparent reason, drove him insane. He would spit a curse word whenever he had to hit the brakes and sigh with relief whenever the cars started moving normally again. Particularly long jams made use of his entire arsenal of swear words, leaving him breathless.

Elish wondered if God, some supreme wisdom from outer space, or another outside observer, watching the overarching scheme known as "Elish's life" with pleasure from the comfort of its home, could find some kind of pattern or meaning in the chain of curses and sighs he released into the air. Maybe the entire world was nothing more than a calculation unit; a function in a program intended to process a series of data, digesting them, and outputting the coded results with a highly sophisticated vocal cipher. In that case, Elish had no doubt that he was one of the central output units. Otherwise, what would be the point of arranging unreasonable traffic jams whose entire apparent purpose was to cheat him out of sounds and rustles?

Or perhaps the motorized world was nothing more than a faulty version of hell, arranged in circles, starting with a slowing of traffic on the Ayalon Highway in the evening and ending with a full stop on the Jerusalem inclines in the morning—he knew the latter well from those unfortunate days when he had to follow a subject to the holy city. A full stop that gave him an idea of what perfect hell would be like—the Jerusalem inclines drew on forever through summer mornings, just a crude threat of heat. Trucks crawled along the right lane, a car was on fire in the left lane, and the middle lane was motionless. Unmoving, unmoving.

Elish shook himself. He was daydreaming. He tried to remember what he'd been thinking about, but was met with nothing but empty space. Maybe because he hadn't brought any CDs with him. Music had that blessed quality of scattering his thoughts, which tended to develop a forgettable, tasteless point, inspiring in him an indifferent, meaningless anger.

His CD collection mostly included Israeli music he could no longer listen to after having published *The Sky Is Dust.* The Decemberists, Neutral Milk Hotel, the Magnetic Fields, Circulatory System, 16 Horsepower, Papa M, Smog, and the older generation—the Cure, the Smiths, Nick Cave, Pixies, Television, Pearls Before Swine, Leonard Cohen, the Jesus and Mary Chain,

Jane's Addiction—back home he flipped through them with growing exhaustion, intentionally ignoring the two Blasé albums winking at him; he'd abandoned them from the moment Dalia Shushan was murdered. Elish turned on the radio, flipping quickly through stations. Nothing, nothing, jazz, nothing, classical music, jingles. He paused. Until the songs came back on, commercial jingles would at least fill the space.

The jingles died at the Ashdod intersection light, and from within the static emerged Haim Moshe's song "Pireas's Voices." A Mizrahi music station—or Mediterranean music, as it was now more politically correctly referred to. Shitty Israeli music. He was better off listening to nothing. His mother loved Haim Moshe. From the day the radio started playing hours upon hours of Mizrahi music in different stations, she clung devotedly to the little clock radio he bought her, and which until that time she'd used only as an alarm clock. She moved the radio into the kitchen, where it played ceaselessly from the moment she woke up until the moment she went to bed at night. Elish assumed she was captivated by the songs because they tirelessly dealt with the loss or elusiveness of love, just like years ago, when he and Yaffa were just children, she was addicted to the Turkish films shown on pirated cable channels every Wednesday night.

His mother would sit in the dark living room, bawling, emerging later with red eyes, wiping away her tears. It seemed that Orhan, Cüneyt Arkın, and Fatma Girik, her three favorite movie stars, had signed a contract obligating them to torture her. Every week, like clockwork, one of them died on-screen at the end of a film—a terrible, torturous death, their heart smashed to pieces. One week, one of them lost all of his children in a series of horrendous accidents. The next, another waited for her forbidden lover until her hair turned white, watching as her family fell apart in a series of fights, tragedies, and revenges, all because of her waiting.

Yaffa would wait for their mother in the kitchen, as early as age eight, a smile across her face, comforting her softly, "Mama, come on, what are you crying about? They aren't really dead. Once the movie is over they get up and get their salary from the producer. They'll be back next Wednesday. Am I right?"

His mother would say, "No, you're wrong, Yaffa. I'm not crying for them."

And Yaffa would serve her the cup of tea she'd prepared in advance.

Until last Rosh Hashanah, Elish had thought Turkish films were still one of his mother's few pleasures. In a moment of inspiration, he bought her copies of every Turkish film he could find in the old central bus terminal and was planning on giving them to her as a holiday gift, along with the gift cards he bought her for every special occasion. His mother was in the shower when he showed up, and Yaffa stepped out of the kitchen to open the door. She offered her cheek for a kiss, as cold as she'd been over the past fifteen years, while she wiped her hands on the apron around her waist, and took the package in her moist hands. "What have we got here?"

"Nothing, just ten Turkish films I found at the bus terminal. There are even two with Cüneyt Arkın when he was young. One of them, you wouldn't believe it, has Orhan, Cüneyt Arkın, and Fatma Girik—all together. Did you know the three of them did a movie together?"

"Oh, come on, it's their most famous one. You mean when Cüneyt Arkın and Fatma Girik are husband and wife, right? Mom's seen it at least four times."

"So now she can see it again."

"I don't think so. She hasn't watched Turkish films in a while. She's addicted to telenovelas like *Muñeca Brava*, and to AXN shows—especially *Walker, Texas Ranger*. I don't know what she sees in Chuck Norris. But she also watches *Viper* and *MacGuyver*. You'd know if you listened to her every once in a while."

"I do listen to her," he lied quickly, "but what's wrong with a little nostalgia?"

Yaffa gave him her tired look, the one reserved only for him since adolescence, a look that, in addition to a silent plea not to burden her with his crude existence, contained a subtle measure of accusation. "You and your nonsense. Besides, her VCR broke two days ago. Tahel shoved a coin inside of it. It was terrifying. Thank God she shoved it into the VCR and not her mouth."

Elish didn't ask why nobody took the VCR to be fixed. He and Yaffa had an agreement, according to which she took care of their mother, keeping her company, and he was in charge of all renovations and payments. He knew Yaffa would not have parted with their mother even if she were asked to, and still he wouldn't want to trade places with her. He recalled Yaffa's face at age eight, on the beach, burying her small head in the summery, floral fabric of their mother's skirt, her hands in fists. He remembered her at age ten, getting off the bus that had pulled up with a screech under their building. Their mother was hanging laundry and startled when she saw Yaffa's teacher waving her arms and shouting for her to come downstairs. Elish was at her side, plagued by one of his fever attacks–one of the worst ones, which had him in bed for two full days–and was just recovering. He also felt his knees buckling when he ran downstairs with his mother and saw Yaffa getting off the bus, crying, blubbering, her nose dripping, gasping for air, her limbs trembling. "What happened? What happened?" Zehava had asked the teacher urgently, though she could see clearly that, in spite of her dramatic crying, Yaffa was alive and well.

"I don't know," said the teacher. "She's been like this from the moment she came to school today."

That day, Yaffa was supposed to go on her first overnight school trip. She stood there, wiping her nose on her T-shirt, staining the print of Farrah Fawcett's face. Elish looked beyond her. The bus was filled with children making faces and cracking up. One of them pointed at Yaffa. Another put his finger to his temple and twisted it from side to side. If it were not for the weakness that had taken over Elish's body, he would have pushed past his mother and the teacher, who were still whispering, run into the bus, and dragged that little punk by the ear, forcing him to apologize to Yaffa. Instead, he put his arm around her shoulder and walked her toward the building. "Mama, we're going upstairs," he called over his shoulder, and to Yaffa, who had shaken off his protective arm, he said, "You don't need them. We can have fun at home. They'll never understand you."

No, he would not want to trade places with Yaffa. Their silent agreement was simply a reflection of their roles since childhood. Yaffa needed to be close to their mother in order to feel safe. He needed someone he could give to freely, without keeping score, just to feel like he existed.

HE PARKED UNDER HIS MOTHER'S BUILDING. THERE WAS NEVER any shortage of parking spaces around the southern Ashkelon projects. There were other issues. He pulled the CD player from the dashboard, inserted it into its black leather case, and glanced around. The street was empty. The neighborhood residents were watching television or at synagogue. Good, no one saw. He shoved the leather case into the glove compartment and closed it. So far, his car had never been broken into. Maybe, he thought toxically, because he only came to Ashkelon on Fridays, and those who spent all week long smashing the windows of parked vehicles were now probably atoning for their sins with song at the synagogue.

Elish pulled out the puzzle he planned on leaving as a surprise for Tahel, and a new VCR in a cardboard box. That was the problem with electronics made in China or Taiwan—as soon as they broke, it was cheaper to buy new ones than fix the old. He looked up, examining the window and balcony of the apartment he'd grown up in. Things had changed. Things always changed. His mother had given up her attempts of forcing the balcony to become a garden and left it to be inherited by the two lawn chairs. So many times he'd tried to persuade her to leave the ugly, gray project building with the laundry decorating the balconies, the lousy acoustics, the yelling of neighbors filtering in, the hysterical volume of the television, the sound of water trickling down the pipes, the bad insulation, almost canceling out the power of the AC he'd installed for her, the cheap tarring of the roof–every winter there were leaks, which caused mold, which forced Elish to repaint every Passover, making the smell of whitewash synonymous with the smell of spring, and causing every wind to shake the antenna and ruin reception until legal cable was finally introduced–how many times?

"All my friends are here," she told him. "All my memories. Besides, the new buildings are all by the sea, and I don't want to live by the sea. I want to stay here." When he tried to get Yaffa to convince her, his sister told him off: "Stop assuming you know what's best, and stop trying to compensate everybody. Mama's an adult, she knows what she wants. You think a better home would make her happy? This is how she's wired."

The light rectangles on the wall facing the street were empty of human traffic. His mother must have been in the kitchen, which boded well. If he saw her silhouette scampering restlessly, he would have been worried, because he planned to tell her as soon as he walked in that he wouldn't be staying long. His heart wouldn't have allowed him to leave her alone had she been in one of her torrential Friday night moods, and he would have had to stay longer, bearing her looks with silence, hating himself for sitting across from her, and knowing that nothing he could tell her would change anything. He would not be involving her in his world the way he wanted her to be involved. He wouldn't make her read his book. What did she care about Israeli rock? What did it have to do with her, if that rock once knew glory for reasons not directly related to the quality of its musicians? "Why don't you write songs for Aviva Avidan or Ron Shoval?" she once asked him over the phone when he was a student, after he told her he was making some money writing music reviews.

"They write their own songs. They don't need me," he muttered, hurrying to end the conversation, which embarrassed him.

ELISH HELD THE PACKAGE IN BOTH HANDS, BENT HIS RIGHT shoulder, and pressed the buzzer. He was surprised when Yaffa opened the door, leaning down toward Tahel, who was grabbing onto the ends of her pants, and pinching her cheeks. "Such hearing my daughter has! I love you so much I could die, *capara*." She picked her up and kissed her, making sucking noises. Before Elish could ask what she was doing there—wasn't she supposed to be in Eilat? Or at least to let him know that she was staying in Ashkelon?—Yaffa handed over her daughter: "Kiss Uncle Elish, Lelush!"

Tahel spread her chubby arms. "Eyish! Eyish!" she cried joyfully, rubbing his cheeks.

Elish walked inside. "Where's Mama?"

"Where? In the kitchen. Where else could she be?"

"I bought her a new VCR. The installation is pretty easy. Super easy, just two cables. So easy that Bobby can do it himself after Shabbat."

"Very funny," said Yaffa, who'd followed him through the dining corner into the living room, which used to be a bedroom—the wall where the door used to be had been removed, but the two spaces were still disconnected. "And would you start calling him Zalman like everyone else, damn you?" She leaned Tahel's head on her shoulder. Tahel stared at him, wide-eyed, her thumb in her mouth. He was still struck by her beauty. When Yaffa came back from her ultrasound and called to tell him she was having a girl, she said she hoped her daughter would turn out smart, like him. Elish said if that's what she wished upon her daughter, she shouldn't have married Bobby. He also said he thought it was more important that she be pretty. Everything comes more easily to beautiful children.

"Elish," their mother said, stepping out of the kitchen and taking Tahel in her arms, "this girl adores you. She recognized the sound of your car downstairs. She stared shouting 'Eyish' five minutes ago, didn't you, *zhin*?"

Poor kid, Elish thought when his mother also assaulted Tahel's cheek.

"She couldn't have heard it from that far away."

"A fact's a fact," his mother said, gluing another kiss onto that cheek while Tahel pulled the thumb out of her mouth and reinforced his mother's argument with another cheerful "Eyish!"

"So what's the deal?" He turned to Yaffa. "Why didn't you go to Eilat?"

"Mama, are the salads ready?" Yaffa ignored him, and when his mother shook her head, she went into the kitchen, not before telling Elish, "And don't you even think of getting out of it today—it's your turn to do the dishes."

"Bobby?" Elish asked his mother.

She nodded.

Yaffa stepped out of the kitchen. "Zalman, his name is Zalman."

"What happened this time?"

His mother whispered, "He welded without a mask on. Spent all day yesterday in bed with teabags over his eyes. They had to cancel the hotel reservation. Yaffa's pissed. Don't say anything when he gets here."

"YOU SEE, THIS PART GOES HERE." HE HELD ONTO TAHEL'S FIST, which was wet with saliva and closed around a purple, eggplant-shaped puzzle piece, and led it to the appropriate spot on the board. He was sitting on the living room sofa, its back to the dining corner, Tahel on his lap. She tried to shove the puzzle piece into place, paused, her blue eyes watching him imploringly, or perhaps proudly, because she returned her face to the puzzle piece, examined it for three seconds, turned it over, and slipped it easily into place.

"This kid is getting smarter every day," he called to his mother, who he knew was watching Tahel from the living room doorway. Ever since she was born, without verbally formulating a plan, Yaffa, Bobby, and his mother had taken shifts, keeping an eye on him as he played with Tahel, protecting her from the curse of death contained in his bones. Bobby's thick, crass voice rose in answer behind him, singing, "Welcome angels of peace, angels of above."

Zehava joined him, "Stand before the king of kings, the god almighty." Her warm voice emphasized his off-key singing.

A raging, painful swell of gold drowned Elish's brain, a gold the nature or origin of which he did not know—the force of light at the height of summer? The circle of sun losing its shape in the waters of the Sea of Galilee the one time they went to Tiberias and he woke up early, alone—or so he thought—sinking excitedly in the glitter on the water's surface, and only noticing his mother in his father's arms, her face hidden in his, when he awoke from the magic spell and turned his head? Or perhaps something else. The wedding ring on his father's finger, how the man always twisted it while singing "Angels of Peace" on Friday when he and Elish returned from synagogue, twisting it and watching Zehava, who came out of the dining corner and into the hall to join the singing? What? Don't push. Leave it, Elish.

"STAND BEFORE THE KING OF KINGS, THE GOD ALMIGHTY . . ." His mother's voice was drowned out as Bobby's grew louder. When they reached the end of the song, Bobby stood up in the doorway to the living room. He was wearing a bright, white, ironed shirt and a festive white yarmulke decorated with silver embroidery on his head. What a moron. He never understood the minutia of different symbols. His eyes were still slightly red and squinting. He snatched Tahel from Elish's lap, and she said, very clearly, "Da-da."

"So what's new, Five-O? Who'd you snitch on this week?" Bobby asked mockingly. Ever since Elish bought his share of the investigations agency, Bobby kept calling him "Five-O" and "the heat," in accordance with the tradition of the neighborhood, which nurtured a hatred of law enforcement and anyone who was perceived as a collaborator, no matter the genre.

"Zalman, don't start," said Yaffa.

But Bobby was absorbed in Tahel, raising her into the sky with sharp motions, shaking her, bringing her closer, covering her with kisses. "I'll eat you up, *capara*."

Tahel squealed with joy. "More, Da-da!"

"Not Da-da," Elish corrected. "Say Bobby. Bo-bby."

"Da-da," Tahel answered him. "Da-da."

"Damn it," Bobby muttered, shooting Yaffa an angry look.

Elish turned to her as well. "Hey, now, he started it."

"Two idiot children," Yaffa said, taking Tahel. "I'm going to give her a bath. Try not to fight."

On the first day of summer vacation after third grade, a year before that summer of age ten, all the children went directly from school to the beach.

"Look at me!" cried young Bobby, who was then still known as Zalman Danino, "I'm diving like the Man from Atlantis!" He emerged a few seconds later, coughing and spewing water.

"Barf me out," said one of the other kids, emphasizing his own use of a slangy phrase that had come and gone without anyone mourning its loss. "What can I say, exactly like the man from Atlantis."

Nobody could remember the name of the Man from Atlantis,

only that the guy who played him was the same guy who played Bobby on *Dallas*, and from then on "Bobby" became synonymous with Zalman, who, unfortunately, was Yaffa's first boyfriend, starting in eighth grade. And even though they broke up several times, with anger and yelling and insults, Yaffa had been happier since the day they got together, and had announced immediately to all of her friends that he would be her husband.

"So," Bobby asked clumsily, "how's work?"

"You already asked me that."

"Fine," Bobby said angrily. "Don't do me any favors, narc."

"Elish, Zalman, come to the table," came Zehava's voice from the dining corner.

THE STATION HIS RADIO WAS SET TO HAD FINISHED ITS BROADcast for the day. Kind of early, Elish thought. It was only eleven o'clock. He was on his way back to Tel Aviv. The road was empty. The strong flavors of his mother's food rested upon his tongue. He ran his tongue over his teeth, seeking little mementos; every crumb, like a DNA segment, containing the qualities of the whole from which it had been derived. Elish was no longer used to shoveling in large quantities of food the way he once had, but he'd been enticed by his mother's cooking. He was in for a long night of slow digestion. He racked his memory, wondering if he'd bought Pepto Bismol or some other digestive medication. His tongue touched the crumbs, one by one, like a skilled archeologist, counting the contents of the near past, every crumb inviting the flavor and aroma of the original into the space of his mouth. It was almost a ritual, perhaps the only one he devoted himself to wholeheartedly, a crumb of hummus from the harira soup, a crumb of gray mullet, the heat of the chili peppers in which it was cooked, deep and refusing to dissemble, a crumb from the stuffed cigar's greasy puff pastry, a crumb from the lung and brain stew, which had disgusted his sister ever since the summer when he was ten and she was eight, but which made his mouth water. And the different salads were also to be found on the tip of his investigative tongue—the matbukha, which his mother called "cooked salad," the coleslaw, the green salad, the many versions of eggplant: fried, roasted, baked, smashed in mayo; the egg salad and the potato salad.

Tahel went to bed quickly after her bath. Bobby was unusually quiet. He'd rushed through the Kiddush prayer, not insisting on singing parts of it with his thick, party-pooping voice, nor had he attempted to badger Elish with one of his extreme political statements, like the plan he came up with when the Second Intifada broke, to annihilate the Palestinians with cruise missiles, an operation he estimated the IDF could complete within twenty-four hours, before the leaders of the Arab world could respond, since all of them, every last one, were hypocrites, and as soon as Israel did them a favor and got rid of those belligerent Palestinians (whom they all hated), they'd make real peace. Instead, he persisted in his blessed silence. After he mopped up the fish sauce with the soft insides of the challah, leaving his plate clean, his eyes started to close. Perhaps the pain had returned to them due to exhaustion and the spiciness of the fish. He'd been a metalworker for twelve years and he still hadn't figured out that his eyes couldn't tan like skin or develop immunity to the radiation of the welding? Elish was mad at the man's selfishness. He knew very well how much Yaffa had been looking forward to this weekend, and Bobby had spoiled it with his utter thoughtlessness, just because he was too lazy to walk all the way to the other side of the shop and get a mask from the hook in the tool room. The first time he visited their home with his new status as Yaffa's boyfriend, their mother told Elish with sad resignation, "She ended up with a hick."

Elish flipped through radio stations. He passed by a familiar sound, but by the time he found the station again the song had faded, and the DJ's low and indulgent voice melted away with the end of the song: "... tomorrow at ten o'clock at the Barbie, we're going to be broadcasting live from the concert. In the meantime, stay tuned." Then the opening notes of the Beach Boys' "I Wasn't Made for This Time" overtook her voice. Tel Aviv rushed toward Elish on the dulcet tones of Brian Wilson. He got off the highway at Hashalom intersection, the Azrieli Towers revealing themselves, laughing, careless. It's easy to imagine what the end of Tel Aviv would look like, he thought. All one needs is to picture every possible disaster. One of them is sure to take place.

When he walked into building number three on Tel Hai Street, he noticed a letter in his mailbox. Hadn't he emptied it last night? Hadn't he checked it this morning? He was tired, and his stomach was bothering him. He pulled the envelope out. His name and address were printed on it. It contained an invitation in the form of a blurry black-and-white image of Dalia Shushan covered with loud fonts: "An Entire Mythology Underneath My Fingernails–in Memory of Dalia Shushan." He looked at the date–tomorrow night? At the Barbie?–and examined the list of participating artists, still holding onto the envelope in his left hand. A yellow note fell out. Round, black letters read: "Elish, I'd love for you to come. I'll leave you two tickets out front. Malkieli."

The light in the stairwell went out. He stood, petrified. No, he was wrong. Nobody could ever be totally prepared, with all scheming thoughts, with all the atrocities the human imagination could conjure, it was simply impossible to be prepared. Just like back then, during that summer of age ten; just like that night, years later.

That rare night. The dying blossom in the dimness had calmed. Only a faint perfume wrapped itself around the air instead of an assault of sweetness. He was sitting on his roof, taking pleasure in the mere act of sitting. He was not plagued by insomnia. Even the tiny pains, signaling constantly to his body during daytime hours, had been expunged or fallen beneath the threshold of consciousness. The moon was a moon. No image of a weapon popped into his mind as he watched it. In his distraction, his entire system of imagery had fallen away, and he remained defenseless before the world. He was not afraid. He felt the breath of Tel Aviv, on all its summer, gradually coming to a halt. The waiting stretched through it during the day was rebuilding. He wasn't afraid. He waited with the rest of the city for Friday morning. A heavy sun climbed, beginning to melt the sky. The phone rang.

"Elish?" said Eliya. "I just called to see if you're okay."

"Yeah, why wouldn't I be?" he'd said languidly. Then, recognizing the urgency in her voice, he sat up, alert. "Was there another suicide bombing or something?"

"No, no. You really haven't heard? It's all over the news. Dalia Shushan was murdered."

7

He saw them coming, congregating on the edge of the inner alley, which was covered with galvanized sheet metal, escaping the first rain, which had begun trickling down in the afternoon, exacerbating with evening. He saw them shoving their hands in their jacket pockets—tattered leather jackets, worn-out denim jackets, felt jackets with the moldy quality of clubs and long nights deeply woven into the fabric. He saw the female counterparts adjusting scarves, tightening their coats with pale fingers, running hands through their hair, whipping it this way and that to rescue it from the dampness. The wind hit them; lightning spread veins and arteries of light above them. He saw them rubbing their hands and blowing fog, inhaling bluish smoke from a never-ending cigarette. He saw them gathering, a silly herd, feeding on the remains of a pleasure left behind by a generation already gone, their eyes gleaming, burning at the darkness as they had four years earlier, with unshaken faith that the present was possible, that it was a time and place in and of itself, that the night could rebirth them, stretching a misleading flesh over their bones, dripping with alcohol and disorientation, sex and dreams. He saw them, their limbs filling with electricity and animal wakefulness, smiling at the bouncer and waving their tickets, old friends and new enemies, ancient allies and new-found haters. He saw them coming to the Barbie gates to bestow a final honor upon Dalia Shushan, who had never performed in that club.

Elish stood on Kibbutz Galuyot Street, watching them, lowering his umbrella to shade his face. When he'd arrived there, he thought of waiting for the entire audience to walk in, but the flow of arrivals did not wane, and soon they would not be selling tickets anymore. He closed his umbrella. With all due respect to rain, he thought as he left his apartment, I'm going to a rock concert, not the philharmonic. Bringing an umbrella would be ridiculous. But halfway down the stairs he turned around, went back up, and grabbed one from the hook. I'm getting old. Whatever. He crossed the street.

Seven or eight years ago, things were simpler. It was easy to slide, with intentional thoughtlessness, into that world of shadows, an additional layer of unconscious with which Tel Aviv cloaked itself at night: a layer of urgently whispered urges, blow jobs at the Logos bathroom, lines of cocaine in front of the mirror, throwing up into sinks. Of the two, what was the true illusion—that faraway existence, when he spent his days studying philosophy and computer science, his nights at rock clubs, drinking his thoughts to death? Or the painful sobriety of the present, with the hours of darkness stretching onward as he stared at a graying Tel Aviv from his perch on the couch, trying to wade through the words of Neal Stephenson or Cordwainer Smith, occasionally turning on the television and smiling at *Scooby-Doo* on Cartoon Network?

Things were simpler even two years earlier, when they were already in the midst of crumbling, and Elish was not yet required to judge. And that was when he wrote the book.

The idea for the book had fermented inside of him for about a year, during which he hung around clubs, watching them emptying out, losing their charm, shutting down due to the threat of suicide bombings or another reason he thought he knew. He watched the rock girls that had once filled the Logos with their black outfits as they transitioned from night into day, switching to coffee shops, their bellies swelling, beginning their unavoidable journey toward bourgeois life. He eyed the void they left behind, realizing with astonishment that something other than time was at work here, because others did not take their place. He watched the wild boys, the ones who used to slam their tumblers on the table to ask for an encore, as they lost their hair and accepted the fact that they would remain messengers and delivery guys forever.

He prefaced his book with a historical sketch of the early days of rock and roll—a kind of rebellion against the establishment, but one designed in advance to create a new establishment, a sound more appropriate for the beautiful Israelis, the ones fighting with all their might to keep from going home and listening to old-timers screeching over the radio. The times necessitated a rough, spurning sound. Elish was working with clichés—Shalom Hanoch, Arik Einstein, that lot. From there, he moved on to the decades that truly interested him: the 1980s and 1990s. He sat at the library and university archives, reading every interview ever given by Israeli rockers, news items about concerts, and reviews, the patriotic enthusiasm at play when Israeli bands succeeded abroad—a list which included only two bands, Minimal Compact and Foreign Affair, both of which were made up of more or less the same musicians—the realization that it was an escape from familiar language and place, and the renewed excitement when these musicians returned to a local career in Hebrew.

In his writing, he described how the media began speaking the language of the margins and had transformed, near the end of the eighties, the edge of rock music into the main cultural event of the early nineties. He traveled through Israeli cities, speaking to club owners, interviewing rock musicians both major and minor, listening to their complaints, their stories about performances in remote hellholes, their moments of greatness. Historical anecdotes, private jokes, rambling speeches about the moments when certain songs were born, those who believed in them and those who did not, their relationships with their agents, their fans, dreams that came true, and dreams that were shattered. And Elish went to see said agents, the musical editors of radio stations, rock reviewers, and they shared with him the moments of revelation they experienced upon hearing certain songs, when they realized things were changing, how they could tell in advance who was going to become a star, and how they recognized from the very first listen who was destined for failure, their hand in the matter, their surprise when some people succeeded against their instincts and vice versa, who sold out, who made strategic blunders, who devised tremendous public images, and who fell apart because they hadn't.

Gradually, an insight built up in Elish's mind. There was a scheme underneath the surface, a silent understanding that was formulated in those years. Elish's thesis was simple: the young audience that had tired of the bothersome norms of mainstream music, wishing for new self-definitions, had joined the magazines of local culture, which wished to deal only with itself and the world of its writers, requiring an exterior engine that would allow it to act. So it hitched its star to rock music. This impure contract, Elish argued, created a cultural gap that allowed for the avant-garde, a true rebellion against conventions. In the space that was created, any music that deviated from the dominant sound of Shalom Hanoch, Shlomo Artzi, Gali Atari, and their counterparts was received with enthusiasm. So, in fact, there was no direct and essential connection between the artists working on the scene and the amount of influence the scene had on culture at large. The fact was, as he'd proved beyond any reasonable doubt, that the inertia of the unwritten contract had worn itself out in the first six years of the 1990s, a new identity had not been created, and those who craved the experience of masses unifying into one body, a thousand throats singing a single tune, sought it out elsewhere—on the dance floor, at trance clubs and acid raves. The rest were content with listening to the repetitive military-run radio station playlist.

The book was published. Every once in a while a marginal

guitarist from a forgettable band stopped him on the street to rebuke his failure to mention said band's enormous contribution to the development of the local rock scene. Sometimes they cursed him out. A legendary radio DJ, considered the godfather of Israeli rock, came up to him at some concert, wrapped an arm around Elish's shoulders, and said, "Gotta admire your courage." But that was it. Nothing out of the ordinary, except for that one time when a drummer–who, to add insult to injury, was now newly religious–chucked an empty glass at him at Freeland, or that time when Lior Levitan from Dildo Express pulled up next to him on Allenby Street and yelled, "Fuck you, Ben Zaken, fuck your limping whore of a mother."

But the book did exceedingly well, and Elish was invited to television panels to discuss dying youth culture and give speeches on the weakening of the Israeli spirit. Then the trouble started. Success is one of the worst crimes a person can commit against their friends. Someone must have said that before. Too many musicians misinterpreted his claims, which he himself did not view as judgmental, and concluded that he was accusing them of opportunism, imitation, exploitation, and irresponsibility, which ultimately rendered them irrelevant.

Four months after the book had appeared on both the *Haaretz* and *Yediot Ahronot* bestseller lists, an article appeared in the "Seven Nights" supplement. The toxic tone of the writer and the interviewees stunned him. The reporter included every kind of quote, from relevant accusations–including an attack on Elish's imprecise interpretations of historical fact–the likes of which Elish could handle, to malicious gossip and unfounded rumors. Anyone who'd ever been part of the rock scene became, in this article, someone who'd shared their darkest secrets with Elish Ben Zaken. One woman said he was a frustrated rocker himself, like all critics. Another claimed that Elish's reviews were ingratiating, and his bandmate added that in his reviews he always tore apart the weaker links while kissing the strongest links' asses.

Another woman said he was impotent, and that the book was his means of acquiring power, and one critic, a former colleague, contributed the article's entire tone—and headline—when he said, "Enough with the games. We all know where he's from. He's just an *ars* from Ashkelon pretending to be an intellectual."

The wild allegations were like lead needles under Elish's skin, invisibly accompanying his every move. Elish Ben Zaken had become an opponent of Israeli rock. A pariah. Two years of exile, he thought. Just two, and already redemption is striding nearer in all its filthy glory. Shushan's murder must have been a harbinger of the messiah, for here he was, entering the hall with the rest of his generation, to gnaw on the bones of Israeli rock.

ELISH PUSHED HIS WAY AMONG THE MASS OF BODIES GATHered at the Barbie, their combined body heat driving away the chill of materializing October. The three hundred sets of smoking lungs mussed up the air, but Elish felt nothing but a light tingle on his skin, because inside of him arose an answer to the storm formed by the bodies. Once again, he experienced the pagan power inherent in crowding, as well as insight into how this same power had caused the dwindling of the rock scene. Someone waved at him, and this time he recognized the man right away. Rami Amzaleg was standing at the corner of the bar, near the stairs leading to the balcony, hidden in the shadows, taking turns nursing his bottle of Carlsberg and puffing on his cigarette. Elish leaned against the bar beside him. "Screwdriver, Absolut," he told the bartender.

"Welcome to the leper colony," said Rami. "So what brings you to the shittiest freak show in the Middle East?"

"An invitation."

"You know what the problem is with former journalists? Even after they stop writing, they never get rid of their freeloading habit. Invitations here, free CDs there."

"Yes, I get it. Except I'm here on a job. I'm working on a piece for the *Haaretz* supplement on Dalia Shushan."

"Really?" Rami said incredulously. "So that the elderly that still read that paper can discuss contemporary culture at their stuffy cocktail parties? You'd best write about something the bourgeoisie can enjoy too, like, I don't know, Radiohead, or an irrelevant group of academics that's established a subversive publishing imprint."

"You know what the problem is with young people who are past their prime?"

"Why don't you tell me? You've got plenty of experience."

"So what were you doing at my lecture?"

"I was wondering if you recognized me, seeing how seriously you answered my question."

"Wasn't it meant to be taken seriously?"

"Are you kidding? It took me thirty minutes to phrase it so it sounded like something a student would ask. I'm rusty. It was a great lecture."

"You haven't answered my question."

"I've been a fan of yours ever since the first time you wrote about Blasé. Dalia always said you were the only critic who truly understood what Blasé was trying to achieve."

Elish's heart screeched and stuttered. Rami stared at him, lighting a cigarette. "Look at them," he said, sweeping his arm to refer to the entire audience. "Just fucking look at them. Doesn't it make you want to cry? Remember that disturbed kid who used to shout 'Let's go Morocco' at Knesiyat Hasekhel concerts at the Logos? The one people say died in a military training accident? I'm sure I saw him wandering around here. Remember the bald server from the Bonham? I saw her locking her eternal bicycle by the parking lot. And watch this, they're coming back, all the black-clothes girls of the eighties and early nineties. Someone has to die for the scene to be revived, huh? Night of the living dead. Night of the fucking living dead."

Elish said nothing. Instead, he listened to his heart laboring to release its grip and return to working order.

"GOOD EVENING, AND WELCOME TO AN ENTIRE MYTHOLOGY Underneath my Fingernails, a rock marathon in memory of Dalia Shushan," a young voice spoke from the stage, and the racket that had before been made up of broken conversations and hugs and pats on backs and cries of surprise–Years! I haven't seen you in years! I'm so glad you're here!–became one unified roar of excitement.

"Who is that?" Elish asked, leaning closer to Rami to better hear his response.

"Another one of those scavengers that Malkieli surrounds herself with. It used to be the case that every Israeli singer wanted to be PJ Harvey or fucking Celine Dion. Now they all want to be Dalia Shushan."

The singer, a young woman dressed in white, accompanied herself with acoustic guitar. It was clear to Elish she was inexperienced, because she kept her mouth too close to the microphone and the sound was smeared, but he could still capture the words:

Literature is a metaphor
So stifling and meager
For the world.
And still, if you could
Just imagine
What a sad song
Your back traces
As you walk away from me.

"What is that song?" he asked Rami. "I don't know it. It sounds like a Dalia Shushan song. I mean, the words and the music."

"It's a new song. Malkieli received a copy of Dalia's last demo. She was going to make a solo album and had recorded like twenty songs on an acoustic. That's why this girl is just using an acoustic. It's not like someone had some spark of genius arrangement, it's because there's no artistic production to speak of here. They have no source to steal an arrangement from, so they just kept the acoustic. Assholes."

"Dalia recorded a demo before she was murdered?"

"Uh-huh. But let me listen. I only heard Dalia perform it once."

> I don't want to wake up tomorrow,
> I know each wrinkle on morning's face,
> I know each crease of light.
>
> I don't want to get up tomorrow,
> I know the ragged street like the back of my hand,
> Which now carries for both of us
> A redundant eternity.

Rami wasn't the only one concentrating on the song. It had been so long since Elish had last seen such a mass of mortals all behaving the same. He'd missed it so much. When the song was over, the crowd went wild. Rami yelled, "Ruining Dalia's song like that? That's ass-backwards. Fuck her. Fucking Memorial Day adaptation." Then he tossed his cigarette butt and crushed it with an angry foot.

"Uh-huh." Elish's initial instinct was to respond like Rami, with irritation and swear words. But he suppressed the urge, saying, "She totally missed the sliding of Dalia's voice. I can imagine how Dalia would have performed it. So, how come you're not participating? How come they didn't get you to be the artistic director?"

Rami either didn't hear, or chose to ignore the question. He was focused on Lior Levitan, who had come up onstage and turned to face the crowd, beaming. "Thank you all for coming to pay this final respect to Dalia Shushan, an artist we all revered, not only for her talent, not only for the incredible, moving songs she left us, but for the wonderful person she was."

"Son of a bitch," Rami muttered, slamming his beer bottle against the bar. "Son of a thousand bitches."

"I'd like to read one of Dalia's favorite poems, by the American poet William Carlos Williams. Dalia even translated it into Hebrew. It's a little long, and I know you're here for the music, but please bear with me."

"He thinks just because he dated her for a year he's got ownership of her cultural world. Dalia would die before she let him read a poem she loved. Oh, wait, she did die." Rami cracked up. He was already tickling the threshold of drunkenness.

Lior and Dalia were a couple? Elish was surprised.

"All women are fated similarly, facing men, and there's always another, such as I, who loves them, loves all women." Levitan's voice rose with pathos.

"Yeah, right," Rami murmured, giggling, "try to keep a relationship going with a girl who doesn't cheat on you for over a year, I dare you. Oh, if you trash-talk fate it'll grab you by the balls."

Rami was completely drunk. He giggled again, lit another cigarette, and blew the smoke in Elish's face. The combination of nicotine and alcohol fumes made Elish feel queasy. He opened his mouth for some air, but the oxygen was equally filthy wherever he turned, stained with lichens of smog. He'd worked so hard to calm himself that evening before going out, running his mantra against the effects of cigarette smoking, the haze of nicotine webbing through his lungs, through his mind. It used to work like a charm—his inner persuasion affording him the ability to enjoy another concert, rewarding him with a sense of uplifting, another victory of human will power. But he'd made a mistake earlier, taking a stroll along the beach. These were the hours when the universe reversed its polarity, the aroma of the sea pounced, the weight of salt scorched his nostrils and swirled his innards. He'd held his breath, closing his eyes to defend himself against the wind, the dizziness of waves, the aura of water, and then he stumbled backward and threw up.

He had no idea how long he stood there, calming his body. The music came from outside his bubble in waves, and the human weight, sweating and cheering. Rami was still at his side, smoking and drinking casually. Elish repeated his previous question: "So why aren't you part of this evening?"

"I'm in a dispute with Malkieli, that bitch. It's in her interest to keep me out of anything to do with Dalia."

"Meaning?"

"Meaning that whore screwed us over five years ago, making a bundle off of us, and now she's going to make another bundle off of Dalia's demo." He used his empty bottle to signal to the bartender that he wanted another beer. "It's pretty confidential, the whole affair, but five years ago Malkieli signed me and Dalia, separately, on a three-album deal. We were glad at first. We thought it meant she believed in us. Then, when the first Blasé album came out, we realized what we'd done. That bitch had us sign a publishing contract. Do you know what that means?"

"It means a percentage of the royalties from record sales and song plays goes to her, right? That she gets a percentage of copyrights."

"Yes, it's not that unusual, but typically the percentage is low. But she had us sign an equal partnership agreement. Do you understand what that means? It's as if she wrote the songs together with us. Our first album sold seventy thousand copies, the songs were played on the radio a million times, but we got less than a quarter of the earnings. Luckily, our concerts were always sold out and we could live off of that profit. The rest went to Malkieli. When we discovered what she'd done, things exploded. We haven't really talked since. Besides, my ex-girlfriend works for Malkieli, and she's running the show tonight, so I'm sure she doesn't feel like watching me onstage, either." For a moment, Rami sounded exhausted. He fell silent, taking small sips from his bottle.

"Can you smell that?" Elish asked indifferently. "That's nano gas. They spray it in massive gatherings. An American corporate development. The tiny robots you're breathing settle onto your nervous system, causing you to prefer certain brands over others."

Rami glanced at him briefly, but kept silent. By this point, the fourth song had started playing, and the crowd whooped. "Now it's time for the flesh to speak," someone Elish didn't know crooned off-key. "Burning hieroglyphs of sudden kingdoms, emerging with touch, collapsing with legions of distance."

Rami sighed.

"This evening is getting pathetic," Elish remarked.

Rami smiled. "Speak of the bitch." He pointed. Nicole, her face glowing with glitter makeup, her blond hair swooped atop her head, was making her way over, waving. "I've had enough. I'm out of here. See you around," Rami said half-mockingly before being swallowed by the crowd.

"Where's Rami Amzaleg?" Nicole shouted into Elish's ear. "He was just standing next to you." She was wearing an unflattering sparkling silver dress.

"Nice to meet you, I'm Elish Ben Zaken."

"I know, we met once at a Blasé show." Nicole glanced around her, trying to pin down Rami. "Did he tell you where he was going?"

"No, only that he'd had enough."

"Motherfucker."

"Look," Elish leaned in, "this might not be the best time, but Rami told me I ought to talk to you."

"About what?"

"About Dalia Shushan's demo. I'm about to write a piece about her myth and legacy. I was wondering if we could set a time to talk."

"You need to speak to Malkieli, but you won't be able to get ahold of her tonight."

"I hear the demo showed up in your office after she died."

Nicole turned toward him sharply. Finally, he'd caught her attention. "You really do have to speak to Malkieli. It's an unbelievable story, just amazing. Malkieli was broken up about the whole thing. You know, the murder and all that. Someone woke her up in the middle of the night to let her know and she couldn't stop crying. I came in late the next day and checked the mailbox. There was a package for Malkieli. It must have been delivered the day before, but the messenger couldn't find anyone at the office to give it to. So I walked inside with the package, opened it in the stairwell, and suddenly I'm holding a CD with the words 'Dalia Shushan–Demo' on it. I was trembling from the coincidence. Malkieli was sitting by the phone, crying, and I handed her the package, stunned, but I mean really stunned, and she opened the CD and started crying even harder, saying 'It's like Dalia knew she was going to die. Poor girl.' She kept repeating herself like a broken record. 'It's like Dalia knew she was going to die.' I've heard people say that artists are semiprophets. That their guts work overtime. But not like that, that was really scary, I'm telling you, but I mean really, really scary–"

"What, what was it?" Elish couldn't be bothered to listen to her yammering any longer. He preferred her terse, apathetic answers to this deluge of words. Her tone was screechy, and that irritated him.

"The CD itself had the word 'Menuha' written on it with marker. You know, Menuha, as in rest, like final rest. Maybe it was plural, 'Menuhot.' No, no, let me try to get this right. That's it, it said 'Menuhin.' Isn't that frightening, for her to call her demo CD that?"

No, it isn't frightening at all, thought Elish. It just makes things that much more complicated.

8

Something that had been said, or not said, helped him sleep. A moment before sleep conquered him; in the gap of twilight, memory emerged, carried on a wave of fatigue. The spells of slumber he had cast over so many events in his past weakened as reality demanded its place, and the memory of Menuhin, which was contained someplace deeper, beneath a film of oblivion, banged and tossed in the moldy caves in which it had often lain in recent days, finally rising, erupting from the abyss of Elish's dearest friend—the unconscious. He recalled how arrogant Yehuda Menuhin had been when Elish came to see him after class, the hoarse dread of adrenaline making him weak in the knees, turning the interior of his mouth sour. As a soldier, he used to read *Lampoons* stealthily during guard duty. The sentences pounded him with force. He carried the book among his personal effects from one guard post to the next, from the mosquito-laden entry point guard post at Kzi'ot to the dull rectangular structure in Qalqilya, a former house that the IDF had appropriated and filled with bleary-eyed armored corps soldiers who paced the elegant living room, making pointless dirty jokes to shoo away the ghosts of the owners who had been forcibly removed from their home. He carried that book from Sasa in the Upper Galilee to the Jordan Valley, reading and rereading, marking down the statements that shook him up the most, but which had faded from his mind until they were nothing more than an echo, like most of his early childhood memories, the moment Yehuda Menuhin told him in his dry, reserved manner, "With all due respect to your curiosity, I'd rather you get out of my sight." The strong, infuriating lines, and the places, the sleepless map he'd sketched over guard posts in the last two years of his military service, with the help of *Lampoons*, returned to him as if he'd never erased them from his mind.

His sleep was heavy, dreamless, as opaque as velvet. That was the first thought he had upon rising, a line from a Blasé song. He hummed the song. His entire body was prepared for the new week. His head was clear in spite of the three vodkas he'd poured into himself the previous night, or perhaps because of them. Dizengoff, Ben Gurion Boulevard, winter was shrinking. Not the wind, but the mark it left on trees, the shifting of branches, a mysterious language, the air it raised at him, pure and purifying. Tel Aviv was the right city. Elish walked into his office.

Dalia Shushan had been Yehuda Menuhin's teaching assistant. Dalia Shushan had sent a demo to her manager with the word "Menuhin" on it. These two facts chased each other up and down the neuron paths in his mind. Why did he feel that Dalia's spirit was haunting anything he touched lately? Elish wasn't a man of faith, but the schemes and conspiracies he saw in every corner often mimicked the work of faith. He wondered if somebody was trying to tell him something, and if so, what. He still couldn't figure out his role in the grand pattern. These new discoveries insinuated additional coding, archived games. Thin wires, too thin for him to guess their placements, hidden from sight, were stretched before him. If he stepped on one of them, an enormous ax would be released, slicing through the air, or a barrage of poisonous arrows would fly at him from out of nowhere.

He asked Lilian if Eliya had looked for him, and Lilian said between two phone rings that Eliya would be out all day, doing fieldwork, and that her phone would be turned off, but that she'd check her voice mail every hour on the hour.

"Then it can wait till tomorrow," he said, taking off his jacket and making himself some coffee.

"Hello, Tel Aviv University Philosophy Department," that same nasal voice answered, annoyed at being disturbed from its idleness.

"May I please speak to Professor Ora Anatot?"

"Sure," said the secretary, and Elish heard her shouting, "Ora, it's for you. Line two."

"Hello?" Professor Ora Anatot's voice was soft, as if she were terribly far away, murmuring words from within a dream.

"Hello, my name is Elish Ben Zaken—"

"Hello," she cut him off, suddenly enlivened. "That name sounds familiar. Don't you teach at Ben Gurion University?"

"Unfortunately not. But that's actually the reason I'm calling. I'd like to offer a lecture series to the Philosophy Department."

"Meaning?"

He lingered. He'd weighed a few possible plans before making the call, and this one had been the best, even though it required him to improvise in a lingo in which he was no longer fluent. "I want to teach, that's the long and short of it. But, with your permission, I'll say a little more. I'm thinking about broad platforms"—good word, "platforms"—"such as the Tel Aviv University Philosophy Department, upon which the philosophical discourse can be opened up to discussion, through which one could redefine the boundaries between disciplines." What was he saying? "Because, between you and me, we both know the worst thing that has happened to contemporary philosophy is the absolute breach, the legitimacy afforded to every deconstructive discussion of basic concepts, turning philosophical discussions essentially parodic, and mostly charlatanic." He chuckled knowingly, a lingering chuckle, buying some time. "Not that I'm saying that the discussion itself is bad, God forbid, but when it ends with destruction rather than rebuilding, when it doesn't validate the mere necessity of basic concepts or the concepts themselves, it feels somewhat like, how should I put it . . . *unheimlich.*" He rolled the last word expertly over his tongue.

"That's certainly a refreshing approach," said Ora.

Bingo. Elish smiled into the space of the office. Eitan had been right. Old school. Ora Anatot was one of those professors who was fed up with the new generation of academics: students who'd read two pages of Nietzsche, three pages of Foucault, and one paper on Derrida before scampering from one conference to the next, heatedly lecturing on the death of absolute truth, the fickleness of meaning, and the way in which any argument that did not support this claim served systems of knowledge and power designed to oppress the Other. The problem with this generalization, which was mostly fair, thought Elish, was that it also silenced some rare, interesting voices.

"Perhaps we can meet and talk more?" he asked, taking advantage of his momentum.

"Look, it's hard for me to imagine a scenario in which I allow an outside hire to teach a class." Her voice filled with that distance again. Perhaps she was browsing the internet or playing Solitaire.

"Would you at least give me a chance?"

"I can't make any promises. I'm free on Thursday between ten and ten thirty, if you want to come by then."

"Great, so Thursday. I take it your office is located next to the department secretary's?"

"Yes," she laughed. "Next to the secretary's office."

HE WAITED TWO HOURS BEFORE CALLING LIOR LEVITAN, WITH whom he'd been eager to speak since the previous night, and not because of his bad rendition—perhaps the worst one of the evening—of the title track from Blasé's first album, "One Mile and Two Days Before Sunset." Dalia used to sing it softly, but with great determination. Rami Amzaleg had engineered, in his typical way, a brilliant playback that captured the tension in her singing–aggressive drum and bass lines he'd borrowed from the techno world, airy wind instruments–flute, recorder, clarinet, saxophone–that hovered over the industrial rhythm. The playback wanted to sound like one thing, but ended up sounding like something completely different. Dalia's singing contributed to the chaos of sounds by not matching the beat, always too early or too late. Before Elish heard her performing the song live–"Singing on the beat like a goddamn jazz guitarist," a critic standing beside him muttered–he'd been convinced that the rhythmic games had been constructed in a moment of inspiration, through artificial means, by a venerable studio technician. Lior Levitan, on the other hand, screamed it out, bringing in the crushing typhoon of the original orchestration, turning it into hard rock, a repugnant anthem. When Levitan's throat gave out in the shouting of the chorus: "I woke up upside-down again, finding shards of dreams in my apartment, where am I going, one mile and two days before sunset," Elish knew for certain that Dalia Shushan shared nothing with Lior Levitan, neither emotionally nor intellectually. The man was worthy of nothing but contempt. An aging rock cliché. How did she spend an entire year with him?

"Yeah," Lior Levitan's sleepy voice emerged over the phone.

"Lior? Hi, this is Elish Ben Zaken. I–"

"Elish Ben Zaken?" Lior's voice rose. "What is this, a joke? Am I being pranked?"

"No, it's really me. How are you? I'm working on an article about Dalia Shushan, and I wanted to–"

"I'll show you where to go, you motherfucking assclown," Lior yelled into the phone before hanging up.

Well, the years have brought no improvement in the originality scale, Elish remarked to himself. The fingers of his left hand began drumming of their own accord, the sharp pain piercing the serenity of the arm. He had to find another way to reach him, maybe through Malkieli. He checked his voice mail. Eitan had left a message in a tired voice: "Hey, the name of the cafeteria worker that was fired is Levana Hacham."

Why had Menuhin plotted against a cafeteria worker? If Elish had correctly assessed Menuhin's worldview based on their brief acquaintance, the man saw all service providers as belonging to a shadow world with no identities, faces, human thoughts, or sorrow. No, a shadow world in which there was nothing but roles and tasks. Did he intentionally abuse her, or did she just happen to be there? And either way, what were the repercussions?

Elish's thoughts did not have a chance to wander far. The phone rang, and Lilian's voice intoned in a whisper, "Elish, honey, you've got a call from someone named Manny. Should I tell him you're here?"

"Yes, patch him through." Then, a moment later, "Manny, how are you?"

"Excellent. How about you, bud?"

"The usual."

"So you want to meet up later."

"I still don't understand what this is about."

"Like I said on Thursday, I just want to make myself clear."

"In that case, I have a condition."

"Name it."

"I need you to bring Dalia Shushan's case with you. I want to take a look at it."

On the other end there was silence, a sigh, more silence, then heavy breathing. "It isn't that simple."

"Why isn't it that simple? You're a police officer. This case belongs to your department."

"I'm telling you it's complicated. Believe me."

"Give me one reason why I should. So far, you've turned down every request I've made."

A brief silence. “Okay, let me see what I can do. I'll be free around seven thirty. Let me know when and where.”

“Barbunia. The bar, not the restaurant. On the eastern side of Ben Yehuda Street. Say, eight o'clock?”

“I'll see you there.”

“HELLO, MAY I PLEASE SPEAK TO LEVANA HACHAM?” ELISH spoke gently, carefully, even though he was somewhat upset. Lilian had tracked down the woman's address and phone number within seconds and had them written down on a note she placed on his desk. The name of the street where she lived in Jaffa was too familiar. He pulled the copy of Yehuda Menuhin's case from his drawer, and his suspicions were verified: Levana Hacham and her husband lived in the same building where Menuhin had lived.

“Speaking.” The voice on the other end was unnecessarily crass.

“Good afternoon, Mrs. Hacham. My name is Elish Ben Zaken and I'm a law PhD student. I'm writing my dissertation about the ethical norms of informal courts, such as interior ethics committees. Closed societies that form independent courts. One of my chapters discusses the–”

“I don't understand that shit. Talk straight,” Levana cut him off. “What do you want?”

Elish let out a blast of patronizing laughter. “Mrs. Hacham, I understand you've been wronged. You were unjustifiably dismissed from the university merely on the basis of a staff member's complaint, which was not thoroughly investigated. Well, it turns out you aren't the only one. All over the country, academic establishments employ the same arbitrary methods.”

“Oh. Now you're making sense. Those pieces of shit fired me just because this one professor, a dried-up prune, complained,” she muttered. Elish could feel the spraying spit splashing against the receiver with the force of the words.

"That's exactly what I was saying. The chapter I'm writing discusses the dissonance in the heart of an establishment experienced in producing ethical norms—"

"Again with this bullshit? Didn't they teach you how to speak like a normal person at that university?"

"Do you think we could meet for an interview? I'm very interested in your story."

"Am I going to see any money out of this?"

"Excuse me?"

"Money. Shekels. If we sue the university—because that dirtbag who told them to fire me is already dead, shot himself in the head—will I see any money out of it?"

"Listen, Mrs. Hacham, I deal with the academic side of things. I imagine if you devote your time to this work, I could pay you by the hour."

"No, that wouldn't amount to anything. I want the compensation I deserve."

"Maybe we should meet. I can stop by today—"

"No, no," she cut him off too quickly, almost defensively. "I have a doctor's appointment tomorrow morning in Tel Aviv. Zamenhoff Clinic. I'll be finished by eleven. Can we meet in Tel Aviv?"

"Of course. How about Giglio? Corner of King George Street?"

"I'll see you there."

ELISH WALKED SOUTH ALONG THE BOARDWALK, HEADING HOME at a safe distance from the sea. The seagulls screamed. All birds looked the same to Elish. The warblers and sparrows the neighborhood children giddily shot down with their cap guns; the rare birds that welcomed summer vacation mornings with their clear song; the hummingbirds among the jasmine thickets he watched one summer in the synagogue yard as they fluttered quickly from one tiny flower sepal to the next, the speed of their wings inconceivable; the late fruit bats of Tel Aviv; the storks up north on a school trip; the parrots at the petting zoo—they were all to him that same pigeon Yaffa had found on the kitchen windowsill the autumn when he was nine, right after the High Holy Days, when the July of his tenth year was already a storm brewing in the distance. Yaffa had dragged a chair over to the wall, climbed up, and reached her fingers toward the eggs in the nest. The pigeon that had laid them flew away with panic. Elish stopped her. "If you touch the eggs, the mother will never come back, and the eggs won't hatch."

"But I want an egg."

"What would you rather have, an egg or a baby bird?"

"The pigeon," Yaffa laughed.

"Stupid, the baby birds will grow up to become pigeons."

"Today?"

"No." He put his arm around her shoulders, helping her down from the chair. "A long time from now."

That night, when their father came home from work, Yaffa took him by the hand and showed him the nest. The pigeon was napping on her eggs. "I want them," Yaffa whispered indulgently, "but Elish won't let me."

Prosper smiled. "Elish is right. When the baby birds hatch, we'll remove the mother and keep the babies to ourselves."

"Tomorrow morning?" Yaffa asked.

A week later, Elish recalled tenderly, Prosper lifted Yaffa to the windowsill. The baby birds chirped. "Go away," said Yaffa, waving her hand at the mother pigeon. "Shoo, the baby birds are ours. Go away already, go lay new eggs."

The memory in all its clarity exploded in Elish's head and chest. On Frischmann Street, the sea's force grew stronger. Seagulls pierced the skies, the ancient gold of five o'clock faulted and frayed, the waves broke harshly against the beach, whacking and slapping it, a wild gust of wind laden with foam spray polished his face. No, it wasn't that pigeon that contained every bird in the world, but rather the smell of the kitchen where they stood, night after night, for an entire week, Yaffa's hand in their father's, silhouetted against the window, watching and waiting. So much water and salt swelled in Elish's nasal passages and airways, just like on the day of his bar mitzvah. Prosper's brother had come all the way from Kiryat Shmona to accompany him to the synagogue and had found the boy in bed, burning with fever, his mother cooling his forehead with a damp towel.

"ELISH."

"Yeah, Mom?"

"What's new with you all?" She always asked in plural form, as if using the singular would break some rule, creating a misplaced intimacy. He'd heard the phone ringing from the stairwell and had run into his apartment.

"We're all fine," he replied in turn. "How about you?"

"Well, as you can tell, still alive. Have you talked to Yaffa?"

"What would I talk to her about? You see her more often than I do. Unless something's wrong."

"No, no, nothing's wrong. I think she's been angry with you since Friday, because of Zalman. You've got to be more gentle with him."

"You mean he's got to be more gentle with me. Besides, I behaved the way I did because of her. She wanted to go on vacation. But you know very well that, just like you, she hasn't been angry with me only since Friday."

"Why do you say that? I'm not angry at you, Elish. I'm . . . well, what difference does it make? I just want the two of you to get along."

"Mom, if only all siblings got along like Yaffa and I do." He knew this was an empty statement, one that used to be true before Yaffa went into puberty and slowly detached from him, constant suspicion sneaking into all of her expressions and responses, as if she'd finally processed that summer when she was eight and he was ten. But why did his mother have to always remind him? Did she think he was so lonely that he had nobody but his sister?

When he was in seventh grade the other kids thought Yaffa was his girlfriend. She came with him to the school's Purim party. They didn't wear proper costumes, instead only switching one shoe. She wore his right shoe—a black Chuck Taylor—and he wore her right shoe—a white Chuck Taylor. "The checkers twins," they told anyone who asked what they were supposed to be. When he told the kids in his class that she was his sister, they all wanted him to ask her if she'd be their girlfriend, delivering notes through him. Yaffa would make nasty comments: "This one never showers, and that one, does he ever change his shirt? Tell your friend he needs a haircut. And that other one, I've heard of him, he's my friend's brother, and she told me he asks every girl he sees to be his girlfriend. This one looks cheap, and that one? Look how many spelling mistakes! Must be a slacker."

Elish couldn't understand how within six months of starting fifth grade, Yaffa had become an authority on matters of fashion and social norms, but he laughed at all her comments. Yaffa grew from an obedient child into a young woman with a sharp sense of criticism. Looking back, Elish could admit he'd been worried about her, afraid she was too good for the world in which they lived, that she would be vulnerable to lies and abuse, though he'd never put those insights into words. His mother, on the other hand, saw the change in her differently. "Well, princess, it isn't like your parents are anything special. You're being too picky," she'd say. "I feel sorry for the poor guy who ends up married to you."

Then Bobby showed up and changed their mother's mind.

Now she paused for a long time on the other end of the line. "Don't be angry," she finally said.

"I'm not angry. Why do we keep talking about anger? I'm glad you called."

"No, it isn't that. Don't be angry, because someone called this afternoon and asked for your phone number. Said he was looking for you."

"I hope you didn't give him my home number."

"No, just your work number. He wanted the address too."

"Did you give it to him?"

"Yes. Then I told Yaffa, and she said that was going to bother you."

"Well, Yaffa was right. Did he say what he wanted?"

"He wanted to mail something to you and talk to you."

"Well, so far no one's called. How's the VCR working out for you?"

"It works well, but it's a little complicated. Zalman showed me how to use it. The remote control is different than what I'm used to."

"Watch the movies I brought."

"I will, when I have some time."

She has all the time in the world, he thought. How much more time did she need? "Is everything good otherwise? Do you need anything?"

"Everything's fine. I don't need anything. Will you come on Friday, God willing?"

"No, I think I'll stay in Tel Aviv. I have a few things I need to do."

"Suit yourself."

"Bye, Mom."

9

When they sat down, Manny said, "May I ask you a question that's been on my mind since the first time I came across your name? What kind of name is Elish?"

"Elish, Belish, Bom," the girls used to joke in first grade, swapping his name into a popular gibberish nursery rhyme. "What kind of name is Elish?" they teased.

"Elish is short for Elisha," he said then and now, to the girls with wounded pride, and to Manny with submissiveness.

They were sitting at Barbunia. Manny had squeezed his large frame into the narrow space between the table and the chair. "Nice place," he remarked, "great atmosphere."

"My parents were obsessed with the Book of Kings and wanted to be original, so they named me Elisha after the prophet. Only when I turned one, my mother says, after so many people kept telling them, 'Poor kid, how can you let him walk around with that name?' did they decide to give me the odd nickname Elish. They thought 'Eli' was too common, and that 'She'i' was as bad as Elisha. You could say my name's been Elish since I can remember. When my sister was born they decided not to take any chances and gave her a simple name: Yaffa."

"So what's good here?"

"The fish is terrific. The shellfish too."

"What kind of bourbon do you have?" he asked the server. "Jack Daniel's? Can I have one, on the rocks?" Then he turned to Elish: "Get yourself something to eat. On me."

"That's fine, I can pay for my own food."

"Don't worry about it," Manny said with a wave, his hand accidentally slamming the table. "Get us a nice platter," he told the server. "Shrimp, calamari, mullet fish, whatever you've got."

The server picked up the menus. Manny ran his hand through his hair and examined Elish, who'd gone quiet. "I can't get your lecture out of my head. Thinking of poetry and murder as forms of ritual. It's deep . . ."

"That's not accurate. What I was trying to say was that the ritualistic logic can be a good tool for analyzing the work of a poet or a serial killer. And I'm referring to serial killers as they are portrayed in literature and film. It's tricky, finding a serial killer in Israel. You know that better than anyone. The country isn't crowded enough or large enough, and the social integration systems are very pushy, so the level of alienation and anonymity is lower."

"Uh-huh. Well, I'm not as eloquent as you are. I tried to explain to my wife what you were talking about, but I wasn't able to re-create it. I think your conviction affected me without me completely understanding the contents."

"Is that a compliment?"

"Absolutely. But something's still bothering me. Do you even feel like talking about this?"

"Of course. I'm interested in your thoughts."

"Have you ever seen a dead body?"

So that's what this is about, thought Elish. Never hurt a man's professional pride. Wounded pride is hard to appease. Appease? Did he want to appease Manny?

Manny did not wait for an answer. Instead, he sank deeper into his attack. "I've seen dozens of bodies in every possible formation. In heaps of garbage, covered with flies. On the beach. Dissected bodies, severed bodies, naked bodies without a hint of respect, inside of homes, covered with knife marks. Junkie bodies, eyes open, staring at you as if the last thing they saw in their lives was God. Believe me, there's nothing aesthetic about it.

Dealing with murder as if it's art seems . . ." He paused, searching for the appropriate word.

"Twisted?" Elish offered.

"Yes, twisted."

"No argument here."

"So?"

"So, about my lecture? Let me clarify two things. First, I think murder is deplorable. Second, my investigation agency, like I mentioned the first time we spoke, does not deal with this kind of thing. I enjoy thinking about serial killers because they're easy to deal with. It's like an exercise. There are no moral dilemmas. I mean, in terms of pathology, the question of morals is not appealing. All that is left is the complexity of the killer's performance and talent. And those, if you ask me, are relevant to art, as well. Now, murder–simple, random murder, not preconceived, makes me shudder, but not because of the things you mentioned. Not because of the cruelty or the fact that the murderer removes themselves and their victim from the rest of humanity, but because, to me at least, it brings up moral questions that I can't handle."

"What kind of questions?" Manny was giving Elish his undivided attention, and it weighed heavily on Elish.

"I don't have good examples, just theory. Look, I believe human beings are stupid, selfish, obtuse, and unable to appreciate what others give them. To me, that is the amalgam of characteristics that produces evil. Pure, satanic, malicious evil, whose sole purpose is to ruin and destroy and bring about chaos, is a ridiculous invention made up by slow, scared brains to whom the world appears to be an inexplicable, dark place. That is the reason for my agency's policy. I can cast judgment in cases where the evil stemming from human qualities is in its raw state. A husband cheating on his wife, a wife stealing from her husband, or vice versa. You know, people trying to betray others." His conversation with Eitan came to mind again: "I want to be a clerk of small human sins."

"I don't get what this has to do with murder or morality."

"I'm getting to that. Random murder raises intense moral questions, because I don't believe I can judge cases in which someone acts as a vigilante because of a sense that the familiar justice systems are collapsing or powerless. Hang on, that sounds bad. Maybe I should clarify that it's about a sense the perpetrator cannot formulate: rage, or entrapment, not a philosophical conclusion. I don't think there's room to have a philosophical discussion about murder. As far as I'm concerned, you can tie Camus's *The Rebel* and Dostoyevsky's *Crime and Punishment* to a rock and drown them. Anyway, how did we get into this heavy stuff? And, while we're on the subject of murder, did you bring what I asked for?"

Manny bit his lower lip. He may have been unhappy with the dead end their conversation had reached, or perhaps he was subconsciously expressing the uneasiness he felt regarding Elish's request. He pulled out a brown manila envelope from his leather briefcase. "This is the Dalia Shushan file. Are you sure you know what you're doing?"

"Trust me." Elish reached out his hand.

Manny pulled back the envelope. "Listen, I took this out when I left the station, and I want to bring it back when I come in tomorrow, so I need to have it back by eight a.m. Is that clear?"

"No problem," Elish said, snatching the envelope. "My nights tend to be long recently."

"Still having trouble falling asleep?"

"One night I do, the next I don't. I'm not too concerned about it. Was there something you wanted to tell me?"

"Oh, yes. If it were only up to me, I would have stayed out of this Menuhin brothers' debacle. It's none of my business. I have full faith in Binyamini, my head of special investigations, and he closed the case. I have no interest in reopening it. But, and this is a big but . . ." He fell silent as the server approached with their food.

"Gideon Menuhin is your friend and you can't say no to him. We've been over this. Why did he come to you only after the investigation was complete? Why not sooner?"

"It ended very quickly. The guy shot himself in the head with his own registered gun. I gave you the autopsy report, so this is not new information. They found traces of sedatives and alcohol in his stomach. He was trying to self-harm before he even used the gun."

"Maybe Gideon got some new information?"

"I doubt it. It's more likely that grief has made him lose his mind, as well as the guilt that always comes up in these moments. Stupid guilt for not having rescued his brother in time. It's easier for Gideon to believe that something else happened. Understand, as far as I'm concerned, you're providing a psychological service, not an investigative one."

"The truth is I still don't understand what you're hoping to achieve by bringing me into this."

Manny looked truly embarrassed. "I'm not sure what you're asking me." He lowered his eyes toward the steaming platter with its fumes of garlic and olive oil. "Tempting, but I need to stay on track with my diet." He ran a hand down his chest. "My wife is being hard on me. Maybe just a little bit of tahini. I can't resist tahini." He dipped a piece of bread into the paste.

Elish said blandly, "I don't know why they even keep serving tahini. Don't they know that every hundred grams of tahini take one point off your I.Q.? It's a Middle Eastern conspiracy to bring down the rest of the world into eternal ignorance and idiocy."

Manny choked on his food and let out a cough that gradually turned into laughter. "Is everything okay with you?" he asked Elish.

"I'm fine. You were in the middle of talking."

Manny opened his mouth to say something, then paused, thought better of it, and instead said, "Gideon and I have been friends since we were fifteen. We went to high school together. And the military. I owe him this favor. There are things I can't share with you. They don't pertain directly to Menuhin's case. I need you to believe me when I tell you I have no intention of sabotaging your investigation, that I don't . . . that I'm on your side, I mean; that as far as you're concerned . . ."

"In other words you're asking me to trust you without having a special reason to."

"Yes. I'm asking you to trust me with a grain of salt. I don't want to stop you from exercising your judgment."

"Don't worry, I exercise it all the time." Elish's eyes grew misty, the left corner of his mouth bending into a smile.

"Why are you being like that?"

"Like what?"

"You know, defensive."

"I'm being defensive?" A rebellious tone of anger entered Elish's voice. He said nothing. Manny is too easily insulted by me. How did this happen? It was easier for Elish to stay quiet around other people, but Manny, he was learning, was different. The urge to say something to alleviate the man's anger–as brief and nearly undetectable as it was–was strong. Could he be feeling remorse? No, that was nonsense. He forced his eyes to wander over the display of bottles on the bar, dipping a pink shrimp in the garlic and olive oil sauce and slipping it into his mouth.

"I read your book," said Manny. "I may have accidentally made certain assumptions about you. I apologize."

Elish's mouth lingered on the intense, juicy flavor of the shrimp. He wanted to ask what Manny thought of the book, and what it was about the book that insinuated defensiveness. That was a topic he'd never considered before. But why did he care about Manny's opinion?

"Speaking of which, it's an excellent book." Manny's voice

crept into the tension weaved through the air. "Not that I know anything about Israeli rock. I'm a relic of the time when Uri Zohar was peeping on girls in changing rooms at the beach." He laughed an open, healthy laugh. "I'm part of the Israel of–what did you call it? Israel of the national lie."

"Thanks." Manny's laughter had melted away some of Elish's hostility. He thought of that laughter, trying to figure out why it had that effect on him.

"Don't thank me, you're the one who wrote it. What I was actually trying to say was that even though I didn't know half of the musicians you mention in the book, I got the feeling of what they did. I was fascinated. Now my wife wants to meet you." He smiled fondly. "She's been trying to get me to read for years. She reads everything, every new Israeli book. When our girls still lived at home she would constantly shove books into their hands: 'This book is great, you have to read it.' Or, 'I saw this writer on television and heard that one on the radio.' But now that they're out of the house, all her efforts are concentrated on me. Who has the energy to read? But I bought your book on a Thursday and spent the entire weekend reading it. My wife couldn't believe it when she saw me reading something other than the paper. I told her I was going to meet you, and she said, 'If this book made you read, I've got to meet him too.' She's reading it now. I'll let you know what she thinks."

Elish signaled to the server. He promised himself he wouldn't drink. He wanted to stay sober. But one beer wouldn't hurt. He couldn't explain what had happened. The more Manny talked to him, the more Elish liked him. There was an integrity about him. Yes, integrity, that's what it was, and an openness, which Elish was more and more convinced were not a put-on but a manifestation of a warm and honest personality. No, no, Manny was evading his questions. There was something misleading about him. It was easy to be fooled by human warmth. People like Manny, who are naturals at human relationships, discover the power of openness at a young age; the ease with which they impress the people around them with their simplicity and the amiability they exude. All people become dependent on their most prominent qualities—at worst, converting them into weapons, and, at best, using them as a means of procuring love.

ELISH THOUGHT ABOUT BEN YEHUDA STREET, HOW THE WIND blowing through it promised nothing, and neither did the smoke from the Reading Power Station disappearing into the sky, or its colorful neon rings, cut straight from a Hong Kong dream, but which, suddenly, if one walked south long enough, were found to twist toward the sea. The legs never tired from wandering down the maze known as Tel Aviv. The story Manny told him scratched the edge of his consciousness, which was only made sharper by the single beer he'd consumed. Manny went on and on about his two daughters, with pride, asking Elish if he thought he'd done the right thing, applying a curfew when they were teenagers, or preaching to them so much—the normal hesitations every parent feels—gently probing Elish to find out if he had a similar relationship with his own parents. Elish evaded the questions, talked a bit about his mother, Yaffa, Bobby, and Tahel, offering nothing from his own life experience. Even the question about his father, whom Elish had not mentioned, was delicately deviated. Rather than answering, he just stared at Manny as if the man had asked the most unrelated question imaginable. He had the impression that Manny was doing everything he could to prove how honest he was being, the extent to which that eloquent simplicity was his true nature. He seemed to be aware of Elish's natural suspicion, the reservations he exuded, and was trying to skillfully disarm him, honoring Elish's deterrence of a question even before he was finished asking it. They spoke of insipid things, fragments of life that seemed to be invented for the sole purpose of tying together mundane chatter. Manny discussed the tensions between his wife and their daughters, who, as his wife affectionately teased him about on occasion, he doted on, while she'd always fantasized about having a boy.

Elish ignored the comment about yearning for a son, but Manny was already caught up in the heat of his own story. Between the births of the two girls, Manny's wife was pregnant, and insisted she was carrying a baby boy. "I don't know what came over her. She acted strange, scaring me. She planned little outfits for him, and what toys she would buy. She didn't show at all until she was three months along, and I couldn't shake off the feeling that even though the doctors had confirmed it, this was a false pregnancy. One day I was in the interrogation room. Noga called to tell me she was heading to the hospital. She was having contractions. Contractions at five months along? I panicked, but not so much about the timing. Her independence scared me, I can't explain why. I drove to the hospital as fast as I could. Noga was already in surgery and the nurse wouldn't let me in. I waited out in the hallway for two hours, with no idea who to call, who to talk to. Galit, my eldest, was at my mother's. I was all alone. I paced like a madman. I walked over to the door every minute to check if anyone was coming out, even though I could have done the same thing from my seat. I remember how, the more time went on without anyone coming out, the more anxious I became. I was thinking about how I'd never felt so alone, and that I didn't know how to be alone. Two hours later, the doctor came to find me. The fetus had died. I went into the room to see her. She was lying there, staring at the ceiling, wrapping her arms around herself. The nurse told me, 'Just be yourself. She needs somebody right now.'"

When Manny became captivated by his own story, his voice filling with a tone Elish had not heard from him before, Elish felt an impulse to get up and leave. It was hard for him not to like

Manny, but developing empathy toward him meant letting go of all his defenses.

When Manny finished speaking—his face turning red, taking another sip from his second Jack Daniel's, his gaze scattered, seeking commiseration, painfully human—all Elish said was, "It's obvious to me why you were scared when you heard she was going by herself. It sounds like she really wanted that child, but people should never want something that badly."

10

It isn't easy to find Dalia Shushan's apartment. In spite of the instructions she gave me, I found myself lost in the small alleys near Dizengoff. When I finally made it, a handsome woman with shy eyes opened the door and invited me inside warmly."

Elish sighed. He didn't expect much from a local newspaper, but to call Dalia handsome? The picture that accompanied the article certainly did nothing to support the writer's claim. The caption below read, "Shushan. Listening beyond sounds." He read eagerly through Dalia Shushan's case. He'd assumed he'd read every news clipping regarding Blasé while doing research for his book. They were mostly reviews and concert listings, because Dalia refused to give interviews. But the *Everything Tel Aviv* archive was more thorough than the central library's. Those were the first materials he looked at. He knew all the clippings, including his own, on the margins of which someone had scrawled, "Elish Ben Zaken, now the owner of EE Investigations." But he'd never seen this short piece from the *Heart of the South* local paper, the tone of which seemed lifted straight from a high school informational pamphlet and was in keeping with the headline: "One of Ours." He read on:

> Shushan lives in a cute, bedraggled student apartment. Piles of books on the floor, a small CD player, and beanbags in the living room. Dalia Shushan (22) is one of ours. She was born in 1975 to Yossef and Esther Shushan, and was raised in Sderot. When I ask her what that was like, she

smiles and says, "What's there to say? Have you ever been to Sderot? Living in Sderot is like living in a town where time doesn't exist, only place. Neglect upon neglect upon neglect."

There's something sad about Shushan and the way she speaks. She took a guitar class as part of her theater studies at Sapir College. The class was canceled after only two weeks, but in that brief duration Shushan realized music was her calling. "The first day," she says, "I heard somebody playing. Normally I don't dare speak to boys I don't know, but the playing drew me in so much that I approached him and asked if he gave private lessons. And that was it. He taught me the basic chords, and I took it from there."

In spite of her young age, Shushan has a few achievements to her name. She was accepted to the Tel Aviv University Interdisciplinary Program for Outstanding Students, a prestigious program accepting only fifteen of the hundreds that apply every year. Shushan is a second-year student in the program, and studies different topics, from psychology to history and film. Dr. Yehuda Menuhin was so impressed with her entry exam that he asked her to be his teaching assistant in the Philosophy Department as early as her first year. This week, Dalia's band released their debut single, "Before Everything." Dalia refuses to explain the band's unusual name, Blasé et Sans Lumière.

Shushan has extraordinary opinions about everything to do with the different aspects of her life. She moved to Tel Aviv at age twenty. She forewent military service and recommends that all girls do the same. Regarding the political situation, she remarks, "Nothing can be resolved between us and the Palestinians as long as both sides have to choose their own policies. We're like two quarreling children, except these children spill blood and their toys die for real. We need an adult to separate us; international intervention." When asked about the Sderot music scene, she says, "I don't feel like I'm a part of it. I don't think all the bands hailing from Sderot have anything in common. I know that in the past some people have claimed that there's a kind of Sderot sound, a meeting of east and west, but I think Knesiyat Hasekhel has more in common with Hachaverim Shel Natasha than with Teapacks."

HEART OF THE SOUTH: Do you know the musicians in those bands? Do you have a good relationship with them? Do you have any plans to collaborate with them?

DALIA SHUSHAN: I know some of them. Regarding collaboration—no, no such plans. I'm not trying to hurt anyone, because I have a lot of respect for those of them that I know. But unfortunately, rockers are the worst chauvinists, no matter what part of the country they come from.

HS: Do you define yourself as a feminist?

DS: I define myself as a woman. Freud said anatomy is fate. I tend to agree.

HS: How do your parents feel about your success in Tel Aviv?

DS: I wouldn't call myself successful. This is only Blasé's first single, and we don't even know if it's going to be played. Anyway, they accept me the way they always have—with open arms.

HS: What do your parents do?

DS: They're both factory workers. My mother works at a local chicken nugget factory, and my father worked for most of his life in frozen carrot and garlic production. Last year he went on early retirement.

HS: So it sounds like you've gone a different way.

DS: Parents and children always speak different languages. The trick is to listen beyond the sounds of the language and find the places it comes from. In those places, the words are all intelligible. No translation necessary.

HS: Do you ever write poetry?

DS: No, I don't believe in written poetry, only in sung lyrics. Because of the voice of Hebrew. On first listen, this statement might sound unfounded. After all, Hebrew has been a written language for so long. Its entire history is pages in books and ink on paper. But that's precisely why I think it's time that Hebrew be heard, celebrating itself, its throat and lungs. I want to feel Hebrew all over my body—from the tips of my toes to the roots of my hair. Now it's time for the flesh to speak.

HS: So what are your plans for the future?

DS: It's a little early for me to discuss them. I'm at the age when the future is still happening to me.

I tell Shushan how much I loved her song, especially the lines: "When I see people, their darkness approaching," and ask her if they're about love. "Love?" She smiles. "What is love, anyway?"

The first document in the case was a report signed by Detective Pinto and Detective Elimelech. Pinto and Elimelech had been sitting in a squad car parked on Dizengoff Street when they spotted a suspicious man carrying a large bag and limping southward. The suspect was familiar to them: Ezra Buhbut, a junkie from Jaffa who'd served time for some random burglaries. They drove toward him. When Buhbut spotted the squad car he dropped the bag and broke into a run. Detective Pinto chased him while Detective Elimelech opened the bag and found a silver Panasonic mini-disk set. Pinto returned a few moments later with Buhbut, who had put up a fight, in a grip. Buhbut refused to answer the officers' questions and was cuffed and put in the squad car. Elimelech contacted the dispatcher over the radio to ask if anyone had reported a break-in around Dizengoff and was told that no one had. On their way to the Yarkon Precinct, a message came in over the radio that a man living at 17 Israëls Street called the police to report a suspicious person fleeing the building with a bag. They turned the car around. When they entered Israëls Street the suspect began to go wild again, and when they tried to get him out of the car he cursed, spat, and even tried to bite Detective Pinto's hand. Eran, a military officer and building tenant, met them outside of the building and pointed at the door of the parlor floor apartment, which was ajar. Buhbut was asked if this was the apartment he'd broken into, and in response shouted "It wasn't me!," cursing all the while. Detectives Pinto and Elimelech carried him into the apartment, and the man turned violent. Pinto had to subdue him again. Inside the apartment they found the body of a young woman. The detectives called for backup.

Elish moved on to the next documents, the odd case of Dalia Shushan's murder re-created before his eyes. Shushan's body was found in a puddle of blood, her arms spread beside her. Her death had been immediate. The autopsy report stated that the cause of death was three gunshots–one in the right temple, one in the left temple, and one in the chest, piercing her heart. Traces of gunpowder, a spray of bodily tissue, and crumbs of soot were found in the center of both her palms, on the sides of both wrists, and around her ankles. On her face were bruises formed close to the time of death, sometime between 8:00 and 8:15 p.m.

When Eliya called him that morning to tell him about the murder, Elish rushed to the nearest kiosk on Dizengoff and bought every daily paper. Though Eliya had told him the police had already arrested a suspect, the papers made it real. That

Friday morning—the day after the Ninth of Av and two days after a double suicide bombing at the old Tel Aviv bus terminal, which had killed mostly migrant workers, making it less appealing to the media—presented a surprising break in the sequence of Israeli disasters, and the only heartbreaking news fighting Dalia's murder for attention had to do with the lethal car crash that killed a bride and groom on the way to their own wedding. And so the newspapers ended up describing the shocking murder in detail that Elish found excessive. They quoted the police spokesperson's description. Shushan was supposed to move that day. Half of the contents of her apartment were packed up, and the intruder, Buhbut, had scattered the contents of the boxes searching for something worth stealing. People lamented the cruelty of coincidence—"If she'd only moved a day earlier!"—but, like Elish, they found some comfort in knowing the perpetrator had been captured.

Further details leaked in the two days that followed. The man's shirt and pants had blood stains matching Shushan's blood type. Dalia's body, contrary to what certain twisted minds suggested, had not been defiled. But the bruises on her face added to the general sense of horror. Buhbut's fingerprints were not found in her bedroom, but the estimated time of death matched the time when Buhbut was in her apartment, and a pair of gunpowder-stained socks was found in her living room. "This is a familiar pattern," one police officer told the press, "among random intruders. They pull a pair of socks from the closet and use them as gloves so as not to leave incriminating fingerprints."

Buhbut's trial was swift, both in courts and in the media. "A heinous murder," pronounced the united voices of judges and reporters. "What's most horrific," it was stated over and over again in the crime sections, as well as in conversations in living rooms and office hallways all over the country, "is that Buhbut not only murdered Dalia Shushan for a mini-disk set, but tampered with her body with sadistic calm. Why not make do with one gunshot? Why three?"

In answering that lingering question, the most original commentator accused the government. "The Israeli Government, and especially the finance minister," he wrote, "is pushing an entire social class to desperate acts with its general heartless conduct. The roots of the rage expressed by Ezra Buhbut in the atrocities he committed against Dalia Shushan can only be found in the growing frustration of the weaker classes, which have lost all faith in a social order not founded in violence and power."

These answers satisfied the public. The police were praised for their stellar detective work, and the case was quickly closed. Ezra Buhbut was sentenced to life in prison and was erased from Israeli memory as quickly as he had entered it.

The case, as it had been presented, was simple. Horrifying, but simple. An affair in which justice prevailed as speedily as it always should, if the universe only obeyed the proper rules. But looking at the police file, Elish was amazed by the number of holes. Was this on purpose? Superintendent Binyamini, the head of special investigations whose appointment Manny Lahav had pushed for, had signed off on the file that officially closed the case. Negligent police work? It was obvious to Elish that Buhbut had not received a proper defense. Any reasonably skilled attorney could have had him acquitted. The proof was weak and circumstantial. Buhbut had no history of violence. His criminal record, which was attached to the file, included burglaries and drug dealing, nothing more. Besides, many details were left unexplained. The odd position of Shushan's body, the strange gunpowder marks, and the simple fact that in spite of extensive searches by the police all over the area, the weapon—a Glock 17—was never found.

The case contained pictures of the murder scene: Dalia in a thin-fabric blood-stained dress, her arms sprawled by her sides.

A position that brought crucifixion to mind. Crucifixion? And what of the symmetry of how the gunpowder and tissue and soot were scattered? There was a pattern there. Someone had arranged the body. But to what end? It appeared that the murder had a personal significance–three gunshots, one in each temple and one in the heart. It was as if whoever shot Dalia Shushan intended on destroying her brain and her soul, or stealing them. But this was the only element attesting to any kind of ritual. There were no symbols or objects that were not directly connected to the murder to be found. And besides traces of gunpowder, tissue, and soot–which were microscopic and therefore not prominent–there was no other sign of any attempt to create a metamorphosis in Dalia's body, giving her new form. In addition–Elish looked at the pictures again, the many angles presenting the body's condition–there was nothing sexual or demonic, which was an exaggeration of a fear of sexuality, about the body's position. And yet, Elish couldn't help but think that the position and the traces had some kind of meaning–a metaphorical, and therefore ritualistic, meaning, or a literal meaning, such as a desire to damage that which aroused the killer's fury or desire. Elish was almost convinced that Ezra Buhbut was not the murderer, but he had to speak with him before he could make up his mind, and before he could do that, he had to find out what prison the man was in and what had happened to him.

"CAN I ACCESS THE *EVERYTHING TEL AVIV* ARCHIVES ONLINE?" he asked Lilian when he went into the office.

"Sure, honey. And we've got a membership. Don't you remember when I had you sign the credit card payment form?"

"No. Can you get me all the information in that archive about Ezra Buhbut?"

"The guy who killed Dalia Shushan? Sure, just give me a minute."

"I'm heading out to a meeting. Could you print out the results and leave them on my desk? And could you ask Eliya to wait for me?"

Lilian never asked him why he wanted her to pull certain information from the internet for him, or why his computer wasn't connected to the office web, why he never used email, or why he didn't have a cell phone. Perhaps she implicitly understood the answer, or deduced it, after he once said drily, "I don't use elevators. There's a mechanism in elevators that takes apart the user and then puts them back together. It's a government experiment that's been going on for close to a century and is meant to test the relationship between body and mind. Haven't you ever asked yourself why there's been a significant increase in schizophrenia in the Western world since the invention of the elevator?"

ELISH DIDN'T KNOW WHAT WAS TACKIER—THE TATTERED yellow sweatpants Levana Hacham was wearing, or the way she sprawled over the chair across from him. She answered his greeting with a reserved nod and lit a cigarette. Elish could have said something, but he preferred to observe her reactions. Not a second went by before an embittered female voice behind her said, "Could you please put that out? This is a no-smoking zone."

Levana didn't even bother to turn around. "Oh yeah? I didn't see a sign. Why is there an ashtray on the table?"

"Inside seating is always a no-smoking zone," the woman insisted.

"Get out of my face, leech," Levana said while waving the woman off with her hand, then concluded in a whisper that reached only Elish's ear: "*Ashkenazift*."

Elish watched the offended party, who was clearly skilled in this kind of battle. She raised her hand to signal to the server, who asked Elish and Levana to move to the glass-encased front porch. "*Yalla*," Levana muttered as they walked out, grabbing her black purse from the floor, "these days every bitch is a public health official."

Perhaps, thought Elish, it was unwise of me to say nothing. Within moments, Levana had turned into a knot of nerves. Or perhaps she was nervous about this interview.

"So?" Levana began, glancing briefly at the gas heaters overhead. "You don't look like a lawyer."

"Like I told you on the phone, I deal with the academic aspects of law."

"Yeah, yeah," she said impatiently. "So how can you help me?"

Elish smiled. "The work I'm doing will likely have some legal implications that will affect future suits and rulings."

"Does that mean I can sue the university now?"

"I didn't say that. I only said I personally can't prepare a lawsuit, but I know some people who can. But let's start with some background, the case at hand."

Levana examined him with suspicion. "You talk like some kind of professor, but you look too young, kid. It don't look right to me."

"My time is valuable," Elish said in a hard voice. "You aren't the only one who's been wronged. Do you wish to cooperate? If not, tell me now, and I'll move on."

"I told you I wanted to, but I also want to know what I'm getting out of this. How much money." She signaled to the server and ordered a club soda. "This is on you," she determined after the server left.

"On me," Elish agreed. "So I understand that last year, Dr. Yehuda Menuhin, may he rest in peace, placed a complaint about you."

"Don't say 'may he rest in peace' about that villain."

Elish gave her an encouraging look and she continued unwillingly. "Look, a year and a half ago, my husband was fired. We don't have children, so it was all right, because he collected severance and unemployment and I had a job. He couldn't find work for six months, and I started telling the girls at work about the situation. Every day. It didn't bother anyone. Then one day that piece of shit Menuhin came to the cafeteria and eavesdropped on me complaining for like ten minutes. All of a sudden he goes, 'How long do I have to wait just to get a cup of coffee?' I gave him a look, but he didn't care. The next day, he came back. I was standing there and telling my story, and he cut me off right away. I said, 'People have such cold hearts. What's the big deal? Just give me five minutes to finish my conversation." And that was it. The next day the manager said I was giving bad service to faculty members and that there was hair in the food I served and that he'd told me to use a hairnet about a million times. I cried and begged, but nothing. Stone cold. I've been cursing him every day since." She took a loud sip from her soda and sighed.

Elish said, "There's certainly grounds for prosecution here."

Levana leaned in eagerly. "A serious lawsuit?"

"There's still a few details we need to clear up. Is there any connection between the reason for dismissal and the fact that the deceased was your neighbor?"

Levana recoiled back into her seat. She opened her mouth, closed it, then demanded, "Who told you that? What do you want from me?"

Elish said gently, "Mrs. Hacham, if we intend to write up a suit, I need to be informed on every detail of the case. The last thing you and I want is for some seasoned lawyer to pull out a missing piece of information and strike us down at court."

"Yes," said Levana. "You're more of a snake than you seem. Maybe you are a good lawyer after all. Last year we sold the house in Rishon that my husband had inherited. After I was fired and my husband was still out of a job. We said, let's not overreact. We'll sell the house and live on the profit, and when we're in better shape we'll buy a new one. We found a cheap apartment to rent in Jaffa. About a week after we moved in, I saw that son of a bitch in the stairwell. I wanted to curse him. I blocked his path, but he looked right through me, like he couldn't even see me. He didn't recognize me. Son of a bitch, sent by the devil."

"And that was it? The extent of your relationship?"

"You're worse than the pigs with this interrogation." She fell silent, her eyes on the wooden table, then signaled to the server and ordered another soda. "No," she said softly. "After some time, I noticed he didn't have a wife. So I went to his apartment and told him, 'I need work. Maybe you need someone to clean up?' and he said, 'I was thinking about changing maids. Come by once a week. One hundred and fifty shekels.' That's very low for such a large apartment, but I didn't argue. I started working for him. There was one room he wouldn't let me into. Gave me hell. Kept yelling at me, 'This isn't clean,' 'You did a bad job.' And I said nothing. At night I heard yelling coming from his place and said nothing. The holidays came around. It's customary to give a little tip. Didn't give me a shekel. I went over there and told him, 'You aren't treating me right, respectable man like you.' He said, 'Don't come back anymore.' Whenever he saw me in the stairwell after that he looked at me with his mean eyes. I'd wait for him to pass and then I'd spit. He was sent by the devil. A bad man."

11

Elish's mind was racing, working hard to diagnose connections, when Eliya knocked on the open door to his office. First up, Levana Hacham. Why did that woman want to work for the man who had her fired? What kind of revenge was that? Did she hope to find something in his home, some secret she could use against him? Did she steal from him? Choosing the object that had collected the most dust since the previous cleaning? And did Menuhin truly not recognize her? Perhaps he did and wanted to continue humiliating her?

Elish tried to push away his thoughts about Levana and started to read. The printout that Lilian had left him contained news items that grew shorter as the public interest in Ezra Buhbut faded, and Elish could only imagine the items had also been pushed back to the end of the paper. The item that made him nod with sorrow was the shortest and probably the most marginal. He couldn't recall anyone ever mentioning it on the radio or on TV. "Dalia Shushan's Murderer Commits Suicide," the headline stated. The contents gave a bit more detail: "Two wardens at the Tel Mond Prison found Ezra Buhbut's body on Yom Kippur Eve. Buhbut, who had been convicted in the murder of singer Dalia Shushan in a court case that shocked the country, was found dead in his cell during a routine check. Buhbut had cut his veins with a razor found beside him. It is as of yet unknown how Buhbut had come into possession of the razor. Prison authorities have opened an investigation."

But that wasn't all. Another piece, taken from a local newspaper, mentioned that in his testimony Buhbut had admitted to breaking into Shushan's apartment with the intention of robbing the place, but instead had found her body on the bedroom floor. He panicked, ran outside, bumped into a bag on the living room floor, fell, got up, opened the bag, saw that it contained a mini-disk set, grabbed it, and fled the scene. This explained why he was limping when the two police officers had seen him, and why there was no trace of his fingerprints in the bedroom.

"It's open," said Elish, and thought about how, as a member of the generation raised during the 1980s on the toxic diet of Channel 1 broadcasts, he was always tempted to cry out "It's oooopeeeen," just like they did on that popular television show.

Eliya walked in and placed a stack of stapled pages on his desk. "This is the Gideon Menuhin report. Pretty boring, to be honest. There are two details I didn't include that are worth mentioning because I'd rather just tell you. I can also give you a briefing on the report if you prefer."

"Sure," said Elish.

"So, Gideon Menuhin is suspiciously clean. The typical past: he served in an elite military unit, fought in two wars, studied law, specialized in criminal law, forty-eight years old, married with three children, his wife is a department manager at a cell phone company, lives in Herzliya Pituach; he has almost no parliamentary experience, like many of the new members of parliament, so that the number of scandals or corruptions he's involved in is lower than average. If you want information about his children and wife—age, education, other occupations—you can find them in the report. And now, the cherry on top." Eliya removed her glasses and wiped them clean.

Without the glasses, her eyes lost their steel focus, thought Elish. Without the glasses, she looked on the verge of tears.

"There are no rumors about Gideon Menuhin in the Knesset hallways. Typically, every member of parliament is said to have an affair at one time or another. If you ask the right people, they can even point out their lovers and tell you how long it's been going on and what other party members have to say about it."

"Who are these right people?"

"Journalists, media people, security guards–anyone who spends enough time in the hallways or the cafeteria. Look, generally speaking, there's a code of silence between Israeli media and members of parliament. Everybody knows what's going on, who's cheating, who's sexually harassing. But nobody reports it. Even if you ask the lowliest, least inhibited gossip why they don't publish these stories, they would tell you something along the lines of 'lack of public interest.'"

"I really was always surprised by how few sexual scandals there were in the Knesset. Considering the fact that it's a power hub, I would have expected libidos to run rampant. But let's get back to Gideon Menuhin."

"That's just it–Gideon Menuhin has no rumors attached to him. He's so clean that his two secretaries are getting suspicious."

Elish swallowed a chuckle. "You mean to say that, in a place where infidelity is the norm, honest people become a persecuted minority?"

"Exactly. And nothing makes their antennas pop out like this kind of purity. So it's enough for something small to happen–for instance, for the secretary to answer a call from an unfamiliar female voice–to make everyone around start to whisper. You know as well as I do the way information accumulates from small details. Long story short, one of the secretaries told me about some suspicious activity on Menuhin's part up until three months ago–phone calls at odd hours, surprising absences, and unusual behavior."

"Is she a reliable source?"

"As reliable as any other gossip source. A mixture of hard facts and wishful thinking. The interesting thing about all this is that one day the mystery woman disappeared and life got back on track. But just before the holidays, wonder of wonders, Gideon was about to go into a meeting and left his cell phone with his secretary. It rang and she answered. On the other end was a woman on the verge of tears. By the way, I don't know if this girl's reports are accurate or if she borrows her descriptions from the TV shows she's addicted to. Either way, the mystery woman asked to speak to Gideon. The secretary went into the meeting to give Gideon the phone, and he stepped out of the office and out of earshot, but the big snoop did catch one thing he said: 'I told you never to call this number.' My remark about the accuracy level of these reports still stands."

"So what do you think?"

Eliya tilted her head to the right, narrowing her eyes. "My guess? I think the average Israeli tends to forgive indiscretion as long as it takes place between two consenting adults. That's why members of parliament aren't usually too careful about their love life. They know they're covered on all sides, both with the media and the public. But in this case, I think this is the kind of affair that can destroy a career. Otherwise, I don't get the secrecy. I'd guess it's an affair with a very young woman, maybe an Arab or an orthodox Jew. Those are the leads I'd investigate."

Elish nodded and turned this way and that in his chair. "Interesting," he said gravely.

Eliya gave him a few moments to digest this information before continuing. "Another thing, which might be none of my business, but I think you'd want to hear . . ." She paused, waiting for confirmation.

Elish waved away her hesitation. "You know I trust your judgment. Let's hear it."

"You know Shmuel Benita? From the Observation Investigation Agency?"

Elish shook his head, then changed his mind. "Hold on, isn't that the agency that Haim Sasaportas owns?"

"Bingo."

Haim Sasaportas was hard to forget, particularly because Elish had met him during the strangest investigation he'd ever conducted, which unfortunately was his third ever. A furious, jealous husband had hired their services to find out where his wife disappeared to every Thursday afternoon, coming home at night, and staying up until the following dawn.

For a full month, Elish followed the wife around every Thursday, learning her schedule. But each time he reached a dead end. Each week the wife checked in at a different hotel and stayed in till dark. The second week, Elish managed to spot her room number and roamed the hallways of her floor and the lobby, but nobody came to see her. No long-awaited man asked for the key at reception.

The fourth week, at the Dan Panorama Hotel, Elish noticed a man following her. A dark, robust, neckless man, panting, looking as if he were about to explode with anger. His right cheek was adorned with a scar that stretched up in a semicircle from the corner of his mouth. Elish panicked and summoned Eliya, who had offered her help as early as the second week that he'd come up empty. He covered the lobby while she went upstairs to check things out. Thirty minutes later, the same man crossed the lobby, smiling with satisfaction, which made his scar stand out even more.

"That's Haim Sasaportas," Eliya explained when she hurried downstairs. "He was bitten by a horse when he was seven. That son of a bitch stole our investigation. He's been following her too."

"What happened up there? What does she do in the room?"

"Nothing," said Eliya. "She just sleeps. The poor woman escapes for one afternoon a week to sleep by herself on a new bed with sheets she doesn't have to wash, without the kids shouting or her husband ordering her to fuck him."

The husband demanded his advance back from EE Investigations. A year later, Elish and Eliya heard that Haim Sasaportas had bought Observation Investigations. God only knew how he got the money.

ELISH SHOOK THE MEMORY AWAY. "SO WHAT ABOUT SHMUEL Benita?"

"It's bizarre. I don't know how he caught on that I was sniffing around Gideon Menuhin. I was sitting at a café and going over my notes, and he sat down beside me and said, 'I heard you've been asking around about Gideon Menuhin. Listen to me, baby doll, you don't know what kind of hornets' nest you're stirring up.' If he and I didn't go way back, I'd send him back to the 1940s movie he thinks he lives in. But he was really nervous. His eyelid kept twitching when he talked about Menuhin. I asked him why he was suddenly so interested in members of parliament, and he said he wasn't. Then he started singing like a canary. So, guess what? The man has a conscience. You get it? Shmuel Benita has a conscience. Three and a half months ago, Yehuda Menuhin hired his company to follow someone from the university." Eliya opened her notepad. "Professor Ora Anatot. He even ordered that her office phone be tapped. Benita was the one who set it up. Ever since he heard that Yehuda Menuhin had killed himself, he hasn't been feeling right. Truly, he told me so: 'I don't feel right. This whole thing is unpleasant.' That's it. I thought you'd want to know."

"You thought right. Excellent work, Eliya, as always. Did Benita tell you what they revealed in the tap that made him think the information would lead to Yehuda Menuhin's suicide? Anything like that?"

"He wouldn't tell me. He freaked himself out as soon as he spilled the beans about the wiretap. Then he said, 'Forget it, this has nothing to do with your investigation. Just forget it.' Then he practically ran away from the café."

"This only reinforces the intuition of the person who hired me, who doesn't believe Menuhin committed suicide."

"And what do you think?"

"I think it's entirely possible that our client is correct, but not necessarily entirely so. Something in the recordings might have led Menuhin to end his life. I want you to try to find out the content of the tap. Snoop around, but be gentle. Don't awake any demons and don't neglect your other cases. I want it to *look* casual, but I don't want you to treat it casually. I want you to devote every free minute you have. This is top priority."

"GOOD NIGHT, HONEY. DON'T FORGET TO TURN ON THE ALARM when you leave," Lilian laughed.

"Good night, Lilian. Hang on a second, I'll come downstairs with you and get something to eat. You never told me how that blind date went," he said as they descended the stairs. Sometimes, like right then, he was afraid he was taking Lilian for granted, as just another part of the office routine, essential for its function but invisible to the naked eye, like one of the body's involuntary actions–breathing, for instance–or something more prominent but still barely visible–the electricity in the walls, the phone line, the milk in the fridge.

"Oh, nothing new. The guy was an idiot, like all men," she laughed, then added, "except for you, of course, honey."

"So what happened?"

"The usual. We talked. 'What do you do?' 'What do you do?' He returned from India six months ago and is still caught up in that nonsense. The moment I realized it I said, 'What do you think about commitment? Marriage? Because I want children.' No better way to kill a blind date, take it from me. When you decide to get back into the dating world, let me know. I've got about a million tips for you. Okay, babe, I've got to run."

The remains of the day blew out of the sky. Winter retreated from Tel Aviv, emptying itself from it like a broadcast from a broken television. Soon thunder would start, God banging on Tel Aviv's back in an attempt to improve reception. Elish tried to organize his thoughts. Seek out the motivation, he told himself. Uncover the power structure. Gideon Menuhin must have had an extramarital affair, and if Eliya was right, and she most likely was, it was a forbidden affair. His brother, Yehuda, had Ora Anatot's office tapped and killed himself three months later. Gideon was convinced something was not kosher about it. And all these facts had something to do with Dalia Shushan's murder. She knew Yehuda and wrote the name 'Menuhin' on her demo. Did she mean Yehuda or Gideon? An affair between Gideon and Dalia, as ridiculous as it sounded, was possible. Yehuda could have easily introduced Dalia to his brother, and it would be just the kind of affair Eliya had referred to. The kind that could destroy a career. Especially now, after her murder, it would be doubly important to him that word never got out. So how did Elish reach Gideon Menuhin?

He bought a Diet Coke and a candy bar at the kiosk and walked back to the office. He was becoming more and more convinced that Ezra Buhbut was not the one who murdered Dalia. The more he looked into it, the more details came up that did not sit well with that assumption. Buhbut carried a gun in his pocket, but had to improvise with socks in place of gloves? What would a small time criminal be doing, carrying a gun? Buhbut had admitted to breaking into Dalia's apartment. That meant that whoever shot Dalia to death locked the door after themselves. Someone who had a key to the apartment. Someone she knew intimately. The affair option popped up again. But what was the connection to Ora Anatot? And Yehuda? Was there even one? Perhaps these were two separate cases. No. His gut instinct refused to accept this heretic thought. There was a connection. Someone made sure of it. It was too bad there was no one he could talk to and test his theories. Eliya and Manny Lahav were the most natural counterparts, but he didn't want to drag Eliya into a Dalia Shushan investigation, and didn't trust Manny Lahav, who he was convinced was hiding certain, possibly essential details regarding the investigation he himself had booked.

Elish climbed up the stairs. When he opened the office door and walked into the dark space, which remained entirely unilluminated by the scant light of Tel Aviv, three thoughts shot through his mind in succession: First, Ezra Buhbut killed himself in his prison cell on Yom Kippur Eve, two days before Yehuda Menuhin's suicide. Dalia's murder, if he remembered correctly, had also occurred around a certain commemorative date. He had to check the date on a Hebrew calendar. Second, according to Pinto and Elimelech's report, Dalia's neighbor who'd called the police did not report hearing gunshots or screaming, which would likely have been heard, since, according to the autopsy report, Dalia had been beaten before her death, and it wasn't likely she took it in silence. Besides, the neighbor's report did not mention that the suspect was carrying a gun. Third, Elish had locked the office door behind him when he left, but when he returned from the kiosk he didn't even have to pull out the key.

A punch to the back of his neck made the office shake around him, filling his head with thunder. He stumbled forward with the intensity, and the bottle of soda flew through the air, spilling everywhere. Elish rolled to his side on the floor with a surprise that was quickly replaced by anger. A dark figure was standing over him—his eyes had now adjusted to the dark—its face covered with a mask. Elish kicked the kneecap, rolled to the left, his head lightly grazing the leg of Lilian's desk, when he was hit by a kick aimed at his chest but blocked mostly by his left arm. He cried out in pain. Another figure now stood over him. A quick glance to the side revealed the first figure down on one knee. Elish's kick had hit the mark. The figure above him raised a narrow, elongated object, probably a club. But Elish had an advantage. He was familiar with his office. He reached his right hand over. Lilian was addicted to spare parts—spare pens, the emergency pack of cigarettes in the drawer, an extra pair of sunglasses on the desk, and a pair of high heels underneath it. He grabbed one of the shoes and slammed it against the glass of Eliya's office door. The figure recoiled from the noise and glanced at the door, a critical delay as far as Elish was concerned. He held onto the other shoe like a dagger and pierced the stiletto heel as hard as he could into the figure leaning over him with the club, taking advantage of momentum. Then he stood up quickly, ignoring the pain in his left arm. He kicked the person's crotch as hard as he could. "Son of a bitch," he said, snatching the club from the person's loosened grip and beating them as they doubled over.

He turned around to see what had happened to the other person, who, for some reason, he expected to find still kneeling, and then a powerful light filled his head. He felt his left cheek reverberating, deafening, and his eye swelling and trying to pop out of his face. He reached over to stop it from bursting, and fell backward to a seated position on Lilian's perfectly organized desk. A slap hit his face, then came a whack to the back of his neck. A leather glove-clad hand grasped his neck, and a crass voice whispered in his ear. "This is the first warning. Drop the Menuhin investigation, or else we'll have to come back here and drop you, get it?" This was followed by another encouraging pounding to the top of his head. The voice drew a bit farther away. "Leave it, what are you doing?" When Elish realized the question hadn't been directed at him, a volley of poundings shot him down onto the floor. "Enough," the voice ordered. "He got the message."

Then another, heavier voice, said, "I'll show him. That asshole hit me with a club and kicked me in the balls."

Another two blows to his back, and the men retreated. Elish tried to get up off the floor, aching all over, then giving up, spending a few more minutes recumbent, settling his breath. As he crawled over to the phone to call Eliya, he envisioned Manny Lahav laughing as he talked to the silhouette of Gideon Menuhin, speaking his name—Elish—voicelessly, then running a finger across his neck to mimic slaughtering. Elish thought: goddamn it, Manny Lahav, son of a thousand bitches.

PART TWO

THE OPEN, SHIMMERING ROAD

1

Elish had no memory of entering this room, which looked a lot like his mother's living room, but darker and more cramped. The pictures on the walls, the television, the VCR, the liquor and china cabinets gathering bits of tableware she'd received as gifts but never opened–the essential details–all fell away. He sat on the armchair. The living room table was naked of any tablecloth; the unified wooden surface was devoid of the scratches that would have attested to the lives of its users. Tahel was sitting across from him on the sofa, next to Yaffa, who was looking at him affectionately, just as she used to before that summer when he was ten. Tahel asked, "Elish, if God is all-powerful, can he make a rock so heavy even he can't lift it?"

Elish whistled and told Yaffa, "She really is getting smarter every day."

Yaffa nodded with sorrow. Horror climbed up the void in his stomach. Suddenly, Tahel buried her face in her hands, her body trembling with a whimper. She said, "Don't you get it? I have the disease. I heard Mommy talking to the doctor."

"I so wanted to spare her from this," Yaffa whispered.

"What disease?" asked Elish. "I haven't heard anyone talking about any disease."

"I'm growing up too quickly," Tahel sobbed. "I won't make it to age twenty. What difference does it make if I can already do fractions at age three?" A web of wrinkles flashed across the backs of her hands, then evaporated.

"Don't cry." Elish could barely speak. "We'll find a solution. I'll give you my bone marrow, my pancreas, whatever it takes."

"Everything's reversed, can't you see? You stopped growing when you were ten, and I'm getting old at age three." Tahel was bawling now.

He looked at his hands, then the rest of his body. He was small, young, a child. "But you aren't three yet, Tahel," he said. "You're barely two."

"Everything is reversed." Tahel raised her voice. "Look, you can't even see things because everything is reversed. Your eyes are wrong. Everything's upside down."

"Elish, Elish," Yaffa cried. "Elish, wake up."

The weight of his body and aches landed upon him at once. He sat up, panicked.

"Finally," said Yaffa. "Mom told me to wake you up. It's almost evening."

THEY ATE SILENTLY IN ELISH'S DINING ROOM. AN ESPECIALLY insistent buzz, accompanied with knocking, had woken him up just before noon. Elish dragged himself out of sleep and out of bed. His mother was in the doorway, Tahel in her arms, and behind them Bobby with a shopping basket in each hand, and Yaffa. Bobby said, "You know how hard it is to find parking on your street?"

Groggy, Elish said, "You should have called from downstairs, I would have let you into the parking lot. Make yourselves at home. I'm going back to sleep."

The remains of the dream were still glued to his eyes when Yaffa woke him up the second time that day. "Where's Tahel?" he asked.

"She's asleep in the other room. I took some linens out of your closet."

"I need coffee." He tossed off the blanket. His left arm hurt, and the left edge of his field of vision was blurry.

"Relax," Yaffa ordered drily. "I'll make you some. Go wash

your face. Mom said you have to eat something. I think she's cooked enough for a tribe."

Bobby was sitting in the living room, smoking in front of the television. Elish's mother was setting the table. "How are you feeling?"

"Like two intruders jumped me in the office and beat me up."

"Funny." Yaffa handed him a cup of coffee.

"So what are you doing here?" he asked.

"Lilian called Mom this morning, and then Mom called me and Zalman and he picked us up."

"You shouldn't have come. Isn't it a shame to miss a day of work?" he said, then regretted it. Yaffa fixed him with furious eyes that seemed to ask, Why do you always have to spoil everything?

They ate in uncomfortable silence. Bobby was the first to break it. For no apparent reason, he asked, "What do you need two bedrooms for?"

"Haven't you asked me that before? Precisely for situations like this," Elish snapped.

"Just tell me who did this to you and I'll finish them." It seemed to Elish that Bobby had been waiting to say that from the moment he walked in the door. Was Bobby truly angry? On his behalf? He hadn't always resented Bobby. Resented? He really did resent Bobby, it suddenly dawned on him. But Bobby hadn't always inspired automatic anger in him. When he was a soldier, Bobby got into a fight with his parents and they kicked him out of the house for a month. Yaffa never told Elish what the fight was about, but for a full month Bobby stayed with them, in Elish's room. Elish only came home from the military for a single weekend that month, and when he did he was forced to share his room with Bobby. On Saturday night he was trying to fall asleep, fighting against the gloominess that always took over him the night before he had to return to base. Bobby started talking to him, but Elish wasn't listening, feigning sleep. Bobby lit a cigarette, and Elish imagined the smoke blowing toward the ceiling, then hitting it and dispersing. He opened his eyes and glanced at Bobby's profile, illuminated by the light of the burning cigarette as he brought it to his lips, in the meek light of streetlamps filtering in through the shutters, sighing lightly as he exhaled. He must miss his parents, thought Elish. The loneliness he assumed Bobby was feeling hit him in waves, mixing with his own gloominess. Was this the meaning of masculinity—lying awake and tracking your own life in the dark?

"It's too big of a job," he told Bobby now. "Besides, I don't know who they were. At any rate, thank you."

"In Ashkelon you couldn't find a single bastard who'd dare lay a hand on you. In Ashkelon this wouldn't have happened," said Bobby.

"What are you talking about, Zalman?" asked Yaffa. "At least once a week you come home and tell me this guy was shot here, that guy was stabbed there. I'm getting frightened thinking what kind of city Tahel is going to grow up in."

"Every place is bad these days," said his mother. "Ashkelon included. So what did the doctor say?"

"I have a fracture in my left arm. There's not much I can do except wear this sling. The swelling around my eye will subside. But I've got plenty of bruises too, though no damage to inner organs. Every thirty minutes I find a new spot that hurts."

"Thank God nothing worse happened."

Bobby snorted. "Zehava, what's wrong with you? Do you have any idea how painful bruises are? What are you talking about, nothing worse happened?"

"They could have killed him."

THE PHONE RANG AND HE WENT INTO THE STUDY TO PICK IT UP.

Manny said, "Elish, I heard about what happened. Are you all right?"

"I'm fine," he said angrily. "How did you get my home number?"

"I'm a cop, did you forget?"

"What do you want?"

"Do you know who did it? Have you filed a complaint? Do you need any help?"

"Listen," said Elish, "I don't need anything from you, get it? Don't call me again." Then he slammed the phone down. He had no idea what kind of game Manny was playing, but what he knew for sure was that he was not going to play along. He was in this alone, just like he'd always been, and if anyone thought the threat of beating was going to stop him . . . seek out the motivation, uncover the power structure . . . The day after he requested Dalia Shushan's file and revealed Levana Hacham's odd behavior, the day he got closer to uncovering the dark secret concealed by Gideon Menuhin, who wanted to steer this investigation from his dark hiding, Gideon and Dalia . . .

He returned to the living room. Tahel started to cry in the other room, and his mother passed by him on her way to get her. Yaffa and Bobby were whispering in the living room. All Elish heard was Yaffa saying, "All the trouble he brings on himself, it's his fault alone, it's been this way ever since he was a kid," before they both fell silent at the sight of him.

"Everything okay?" Bobby asked in a garbled attempt to cover his embarrassment.

"Yes, but the office can't handle anything. I've been gone for one day and already they're calling me about every little thing." A film of anger colored his voice.

"Eyish!" Tahel cried with joy when she saw him.

"That's it, that's it, this girl is crazy about you," said Yaffa, perhaps having scruples about what she'd told Bobby earlier and thought Elish had heard.

Elish trembled as he looked at Tahel. Shards of his dream still dotted his consciousness. "Tahel, how's it going?" he said, smiling at her and offering the fingers of his right hand, which she gripped tightly. From the day she was born, Elish refused to speak to her like she was a baby. To him, she was a whole person.

Taking Tahel in her arms, Yaffa said, "We need to get back to Ashkelon. Do you want Mom to stay with you an extra day?"

"No," he answered, too quickly, thinking, What would I talk to her about for a full day? Her memories? Unlike Yaffa's, accusation never found its way into Zehava's body language, but a kind of remoteness did. She methodically refrained from touching him, even to wipe his forehead, since that day of his bar mitzvah, as he was burning with fever in bed, defeated by his dreams. This did not match her constant concern about his well-being. "There's really no need, I can manage. Besides, what would you do about Tahel? You both have jobs."

"We can leave her with Zalman's mother."

Elish's mother made a face. She'd learned to love Bobby with time. At first, Yaffa's love for him helped the process along. But she couldn't stand his mother. "Hicks," she'd remarked in front of Elish, on more than one occasion. "No matter how good you are to them, they never change. Their hearts are hard. It's disgusting how she carries herself around all day, with her makeup and her shopping, letting her kids run naked in the street."

"No, it's fine, it's really fine," Elish reassured her again.

"Call if you need anything," his mother said. Yaffa brought Tahel closer so she could kiss his cheek, and Bobby patted his back. "Take care of yourself, man."

"And fire your maid, she isn't doing a good job," his mother added at the door.

Elish turned around to glance at his apartment. It was spotless. His fridge, he just knew, now contained enough food for an entire week.

2

Professor Ora Anatot hopped like a drop of mercury around her office, which was too narrow to contain her frantic energy, as short and skinny as she was. She had a tendency to burst out laughing in all the wrong moments, at the sound of statements that contained no joke or even a hint of hidden humor. Her face twisted and wrinkled whenever she let out her laughter, which died out as suddenly as it had erupted. She sat down and got back up, fidgeted in her seat and lifted her body up to emphasize a certain sentence. Her movements reminded Elish, who'd spent a considerable chunk of his insomnia watching Looney Tunes on Cartoon Network, of the chaotic movements of Taz the Tasmanian Devil.

When he arrived she was lost in the papers heaped on her desk, perusing them, picking each one up in turn, getting a closer look, occasionally scribbling something on one of them and placing them face down. He watched her for a brief moment before gently knocking on the wide open door.

"I'm late," he apologized.

"Just five minutes," she said, then looked up and jumped to her feet. "What happened?"

"Oh, it's nothing, just a little accident." He walked over and shook her hand softly. "I got knocked down from my moped." His left arm was in a sling and his left eye was surrounded by raised skin. "My body landed on its natural side—the left."

She chortled. "Have a seat." Then closed the door and sat down. "You wanted to offer me something."

"Oh, yes." Instinctively, Elish retreated to a childish, embarrassed body language, his expressions apologizing for his very existence, his speech choppy. He knew this performance would emphasize every sophisticated statement out of his mouth, and that, coupled with his injury, this was the best way of buying Ora Anatot's affections. "I . . . well, last week I gave a lecture at the Department of Literature regarding the connection between poetry and serial murder, from an aesthetic point of view, and it got me feeling hungry. I thought I might be able to interest you in a lecture series about literature and aesthetics from a philosophical point of view."

"Who did you write your master's thesis with? Do you have any teaching experience?" She got up and paced the office, straightening the diplomas hanging on the walls with sharp, quick motions. Like mercury, Elish thought.

"I don't have a master's degree, and no real teaching experience. I attended the Department of Philosophy for two years, but I used to write about Israeli rock, and I had a book published, so, my background . . . I'm not sure how to define it. General cultural scholar, shall we say?"

"Did you write that book about television actors that made a lot of noise?"

"No, I wrote about Israeli rock. And yes, you could say it made quite a bit of noise."

"So why are you suddenly so eager to teach philosophy? And why did you quit the department?"

"Maybe I wasn't clear on the phone. I quit because I had an epiphany about philosophy. Perhaps because I was too young, I got caught in Wittgenstein's web. I read his writing about the foundations of math. There, in the heart of a complex discussion on the validity of mathematical proof, he said, seemingly apropos of nothing: 'The philosopher is a person who has to get rid of much sickness in order to achieve full insight. As in the mid of life we are in death, so in the mid of sanity we are surrounded by madness.' That quote stayed with me. Back then I thought: I don't know a thing about life and death, sanity and madness. How am I supposed to deal with meaning and the ways in which it is formed? I looked around me. None of the students in any department were concerned by this issue. They were all already addicted."

"Addicted to what?" Ora asked, riveted by the melancholic tone that had taken over his voice.

"The joy of destruction. A student enters the class Introduction to Contemporary Philosophy and leaves it enlightened, realizing that the function of time is to destroy knowledge and criticize it. This new jargon empowers them, and they don't yet understand that those who use the terms coined by others without fully investigating them are slaves to a passion which is not truly theirs. They destroy without fathoming the significance of destruction, criticize without understanding the repercussions of this criticism. That's why I want to teach. I want to instruct students in how to build. I want to raise the question of what happens after total destruction, what it means to be human in times like these."

"Times like these," said Ora. "These are hard times. Job openings are dwindling."

Elish knew where she was going and cut her off before she could commit to her conclusion and end the meeting. "I'm also friends with Eitan. Dr. Eitan Peretz, I mean. And he told me—I'm considering how to say this so it doesn't sound like a form of opportunism . . ." He shrugged apologetically.

Ora encouraged him. "Eitan Peretz from the Department of Literature? I hear he's a rising star. What did he say?"

"That you're in need of lecturers to fill in the time slot that was left after Dr. Yehuda Menuhin passed away."

"Yes, I've been thinking up ways of avoiding a drop in enrollment. His classes were very popular," she laughed, "and this week our offices were crowded with students who wanted to drop his introductory class. Even though it's a mandatory class for first-year students, considered foundational, it attracted students from other departments too, as well as from advanced degrees."

"Yes, I remember. I sat in on the first class of that course about seven years ago."

"And what happened?"

"I went up to him at the end of class."

"Completely understandable. You know, I'm not a big fan of this outlook, but there are moments when it can capture a certain truth. Sometimes," a brief, bitter laugh, "you can translate all worldviews, the entire intellectual universe of a certain thinker, into a simple line of mental complexes. I feel completely comfortable telling you that this was the case with Yehuda, may he rest in peace. There was a total disconnect between his intellect and his emotions. In practice, he wasn't able to admit his passions. As a result, he idealized passion as a concept, and wrote about it. In fact, he couldn't *stop* writing about it."

"I know what you mean. He preached uninhibited sexual behavior, while he himself avoided all sexual contact."

"That's not entirely accurate, but I'd be slipping into the realm of gossip . . ."

Elish could tell she yearned to talk about this with someone, someone with whom she wouldn't have to pretend, stand guard, watch her tongue. Someone who would not suspect she was being unethical or tarnishing the man's reputation out of personal motives. She wanted to talk to a stranger. He said nothing, only smiled and nodded empathetically.

"I think things were different. He behaved wildly, but would not admit to himself that he did so because he was giving in to animal urges, forces mightier than him that were burned into his basic makeup. So he made it all about the mind." She let out another laugh, which concerned Elish. It was her third burst of laughter, and he'd yet to detect a pattern. "Outwardly, he obliterated any recollection of his passions—in his body language, his appearance. But I'm sure that in private, how shall I put it? He made up for it, and then some." Her face twisted with sorrow. She seemed worried about the liberties she'd just taken.

Elish hurried to comfort her. "That's a very perceptive remark," he said, smiling, "and it reminds me of something he talked about in his book—how the greatest moralists are the most potentially heinous criminals, because their morality stems from the panic they experience when they look inside themselves and realize what horrors they are capable of."

"Yes. He certainly wasn't lacking in over-awareness. It's just a shame that over-awareness does not make one a better person. If you're a scumbag, all the awareness in the world won't change your scumbag condition."

She made her final statement almost angrily. What happened there exactly? Yehuda Menuhin had ordered her office to be tapped and found out something. But what? Whatever it was, he made it clear to her that he knew something. Did he extort her? Elish needed to keep her talking. If he didn't, he'd find himself promising to teach a class without getting any information of value. "When I was a student there were rumors about him harassing students," he offered.

"I wouldn't repeat those allegations out loud," said Ora, suddenly impatient, and stood up.

"A great loss to the humanities," Elish said without any specific emphasis, allowing her to interpret the statement as she wished.

"Indeed. *Lampoons* is certainly an intellectual achievement. Morally questionable and the product of a twisted mind, but an achievement nonetheless."

"Though it seems that he didn't quite match that achievement after that book."

"It doesn't just seem that way. He really didn't create anything worthy afterwards. In the past year he found his faith. He Jewified himself"–snorting giggle–"perhaps out of some desire to find new channels for his philosophy."

"Jewified himself? I don't think I'm familiar with that term."

"Oh, it's my term, but I'm sure you're familiar with the phenomenon. You know, all those culture and humanities figures who all of a sudden discover their Jewish roots, reading Gershom Scholem and quoting him without having any idea what they're actually saying, reading Levinas's commentary on the Talmud and cornering you at a dinner party or some other event so they can lecture you for an hour about why Kafka and Derrida are the strongest, most original embodiments of the Jewish spirit"–laughter–"and why their writing about its crumbling is more original and important than that of other writers and thinkers, who unfortunately for them were not born into the chosen people."

"Let's just say I've met more people with that kind of outlook than I would have liked."

"So that's the story. At first it seemed like Menuhin had just discovered one of his grandfathers had been a rabbi or something. He started to take an interest in Jewish mysticism, Kabbalah, the Zohar. That type always begins there. But he didn't make do with that shtick. At the seminar marking the end of the most recent school year, he gave a talk about how a researcher comes to a point where he can no longer be detached from his object of study and has to experiment with its practical applications. A few people thought it sounded like he was saying he was turning orthodox. I thought he was just saying it to irritate Gideon. His brother, I mean."

Elish looked at her imploringly and watched as the expression of sorrow and concern took over her face once more. Did Ora Anatot know Gideon Menuhin?

She walked to the far end of the office and watched student

traffic to and from the gate beyond her window, her hand resting against the curtain, as if prepared to flee if they were to look up and spot her. She returned to Elish with renewed impatience—"So how do we move forward?"—then gave a sudden smile, shifting her eyes. Elish turned his head. A boy of about sixteen was at the door. Curly hair, tan skin, grave eyes, quiet. Ora said affectionately, "Nathaniel."

ELISH TOOK THE STAIRS UP TO THE THIRD FLOOR TWO AT A time. What did it signify, the fact that Ora knew Gideon, knew him well enough to refer to him as "Gideon" rather than "Yehuda's brother," which would have left room for doubt, because Gideon was a member of a party that made its views on religion known? What did it mean? Luckily, Nathaniel had shown up just in time, forcing them to wrap things up. He left having made a vague promise to send a description of the course he was offering to teach, as well as a printout of the lecture he'd already given, and she would then give him an answer regarding next semester. It was already too late for this semester.

Eitan was on his way out, locking his office door when Elish called his name from behind. He turned around, patted Elish's shoulder, then recoiled. "What happened to you?"

Elish said, "I know you're rushing off, but do me a favor and answer two quick questions. Who's Nathaniel, the boy who just walked into Ora Anatot's office, and is there any connection between Ora and Yehuda Menuhin's brother?"

Eitan said, "Say, are you sure this detective madness isn't a kind of age-thirty crisis? I don't understand why you need to know all this crap. Nathaniel is Ora's son. He's been hanging around here a lot this past year. And as to your second question, you must mean that deputy minister from Shinui. I need to stop at the secretary's office to grab some worksheets."

While Elish waited, he watched, amused, as a student tried

in vain to shove a thick folder into the narrow opening of one of the professors' mailboxes. How is it, he thought, that in third-millennium Israel, ergonomics was still one of the least valued professions?

As he walked out of the office, Eitan almost bumped into the student, who had tired of her attempt to bend the rules of spatial distribution in her favor and was now storming in to see the secretary. "So," said Eitan, "it turns out our secretary knows Ora from college. Gideon Menuhin and Ora Anatot used to be a couple, briefly, when they were younger. You got time for coffee?"

3

Perhaps we never miss a person or a thing, but merely the moment when we wore a stronger, more beautiful body, which, in retrospect, had a better shot at redemption. Perhaps the entire memory and reminiscing endeavor is born from a selfish need to re-create a pleasure we had not taken full advantage of in its time. Elish listened halfheartedly to the excited tone with which Eitan unfurled the story of how he and his wife fell in love; how, in spite of the gloomy predictions of their friends, their relationship did not suffer after their child was born, and how hard she worked during their first two years together to prove to him that none of his fears would come true. Another moment, Elish thought, and the word "salvation" would be tossed into the air, hanging there, mocking gravity, like all the other empty words that had been spoken since *Homo sapiens* appeared on the superfluous muddy planes of planet Earth.

Fifteen minutes earlier, a ball of anger had been swelling in his chest. He descended the stairs two at a time. At the end of the first flight, he paused and turned back. Eitan was at the top of the stairs, his back turned to Elish, talking to someone whose face Elish could not see, only hands that sketched theatrical shapes through the air, accompanying, he deduced, a fiery tone. Elish spoke Eitan's name, and Eitan signaled to him—gathering the fingers of his right hand and moving it up and down—to wait, not even bothering to turn around. By the time they reached the cafeteria, Eitan had repeated the maneuver twice more. Then, at the cafeteria, he sat there, not apologizing, sipping his coffee carefully, as if the lukewarm temperatures of the cafeteria coffeemaker could truly singe his tongue, and looked at him, awaiting answers.

Elish said nothing, perhaps fearing that anything he said would offer his anger an opportunity to unfold into words. Finally, he asked with fake curiosity, “You know, it’s strange, after the lecture we talked and talked, but I never asked you what you wrote your dissertation about.”

Eitan answered with the same care he used while sipping, as if attempting to predict the direction Elish’s question was leading them in: “Mallarmé’s metaphysics.”

Elish snorted. “Mallarmé as a metaphysician, give me a break. The whole of Mallarmé’s poetry is a pile of spare parts that Baudelaire forgot in some storage space of the bourgeoisie.”

“Maybe he inherited some of those parts, but the machine he made from them is so perfect that any discussion of its operation can only be metaphysical, not poetic.” Eitan smiled. “I’m sure you don’t expect me to summarize a discussion that takes up a third of my dissertation. If you want to read it, I can lend you a copy.”

“Formal perfection,” said Elish, “has always been the refuge of those who lack artistic sense.”

“And abstract discourse has always been the refuge of those unable to operate in the world.” Eitan’s pleasant voice grated on Elish’s ears, even though it was the same pleasant voice that Elish had always interpreted as a direct fulfilment of Eitan’s affinity toward comfort. “I’m not going to let you off the hook so easily. A little over a week ago, you told me you own an investigation agency. I’m still not over that, and already you’re calling me to ask about dead people, then showing up clearly having been beaten up. It’s not hard to put two and two together. What’s the deal with that investigation agency? Was I right before? Is this an age-thirty crisis?”

"No, no crisis. I'm just accepting the full ramifications of my existence as a social creature."

"You?" Eitan cleared his throat. "You? A social creature? Don't take this the wrong way, Elish, but it's hard to come up with anyone who puts as much effort as you do in pushing away the people who want to be around him."

Elish weighed his possible responses, keeping his breathing and speech away from that ball of anger, lest they become infected, flexing his words. He said, "And let's say I accepted those people's intimacy? What difference would it make? Whatever you give others and whatever you receive from them in return, the basic reality stays the same. You never know the person standing before you. They are always an enigma refusing to be deciphered." Where did that phrasing come from, and why hadn't he thought about it before? And this preaching fervor, where did that come from? "We're all private investigators, all detectives against our will. The world around us is obtuse, but it won't stop signaling to us, drowning us in countless vague messages, as if we can speak all possible languages. I'm making my peace with the facts, aligning with axioms. Nothing more."

"Fine," said Eitan. "It's because you never stop formulating, understanding existence in a verbal sense. There are other ways, softer and less decisive."

"Do me a favor, don't tell me you're talking about love or faith. That argument got old in the nineteenth century." Elish knew how simple it was, this bait he'd placed in order to distract Eitan, but also how efficient.

"You might be right from an academic point of view, but that doesn't make the argument any less true," said Eitan. Then he began talking about love, and within moments deteriorated from general discussion to the detail-stifled space of his own experience, as if there were no gap between the two, and as if these fine-tuned meditations about love were nothing more than preparation for the precise flash in which Eitan could tell himself, Now I know what it means to be in, no, what it means to drown in love.

Elish did not interrupt him. He naturally retreated to the position of generous listener, in which he was so adept. Starting at thirteen, when he read Frank Herbert's *The Dosadi Experiment*—which described creatures able to mimic the brain activity of a specific person and predict their responses and choices—he'd practiced tracking the thoughts of the people around him, and even though he gave up eighteen months later, he unknowingly acquired the talent to interact with others as the perfect conversation partner, one who sees the entirety of his counterpart's soul, as if the counterpart were a sealed envelope that Elish could hold against the light and read through the paper boundary to the letter within.

Even as he was thinking all this, he continued—almost involuntarily—to follow Eitan's words. He nodded and smiled empathetically when Eitan described the expression of supreme pleasure on Daphna's face as she nursed their child, how the baby purred while he suckled, and how Eitan fell in love with her all over again whenever she looked up from the child to smile at him, her dimples revealed, and the wrinkles pregnancy had etched around her lips only deepening her beauty. Ten whole minutes, until finally he paused his flow of words, a little frazzled, and said, "Elish, you're such a trickster. Would you please tell me what's going on with you?"

"I'm sick of being a rock critic."

"That's not what I meant. You already told me that last week, and I don't mind repeating my response: it's a shame. A great loss."

"For who, exactly? All the nobodies I encouraged and promoted who ended up throwing me out of their concerts, cursing?"

"No. For me. For anyone who believes culture cannot sustain

itself on the collection of pale impressions of random critics, requiring instead a discussion of its wider arcs and its hidden messages."

"Isn't that what academia is for?"

Eitan smiled. "Don't be cynical, Elish. We're having a serious conversation."

"I'm not cynical. I don't believe in the establishment of cultural criticism anymore. It isn't appropriate for our time. Take your own example. People want to experience things, not think them. Academia is still able to maintain the illusion of its relevance. I can't."

Eitan shifted his eyes away from Elish and demonstrably examined the semibarren cafeteria deck around them. Elish's eyes followed his. The student to their left leaned over a book whose cover, a gray-green surface, disclosed the fact that it had been borrowed from the library. At the far edge, by the entrance, three students were chatting and laughing, the piercing in one of their eyebrows flashing whenever its owner tilted his head back to blow smoke mixed with a gasping cackle; a few hibiscus flowers peeked from the hedge behind them. In spite of the sparse traffic, the air was buzzing with activity. The enormous Gilman factory, with its concrete completeness, never stopped producing fabricated bustle.

"How can you bear to speak such heresy within the holy of holies?" Eitan asked, his eyes returning to Elish.

"Are we still having a serious conversation?"

"Always, Elish. You remind me of that Jewish scholar–what was his name?–the one who used to ride his horse in the synagogue yard on Saturdays."

Elish maintained his frozen expression.

Eitan insisted. "You know, that guy who lost his faith. I referred to him in a footnote in my dissertation, in the chapter on faith of the faithless. My memory isn't what it used to be. You, with your religious upbringing, must know this story. The guy sat in Ginosar Valley and saw a man sending his kid to steal baby birds from their nest, and when the boy climbed down from the tree, he was bitten by a snake and died. And the sage–what was his name? Avihu? Avey? Doesn't matter–after that Jewish sage watched it all unfold, he told himself: the child has performed two mitzvahs that should be repaid by a long life, but instead he died on the spot. What, therefore, is the point of the mitzvahs and their rewards?"

"I have no idea what you're talking about, Eitan."

"Whatever. So what about rock criticism?"

"What about it?"

"I looked at your book again after your lecture."

"And you changed your mind," Elish stated casually, as if he had known this moment would come as early as that day after the book came out, when Eitan called to tell him how impressive the writing was, though he wasn't convinced by Elish's theses.

"I still think the book is problematic, tending toward a certain simplicity in its social and historical analysis. But the chapter about Blasé et Sans Lumière is stunning. And you know I don't often use big words like that. But your claim, that Blasé's music is founded on aural deception, and that there is a gap between what the listener hears and what is actually played, astounded me. How could I not have noticed it sooner? Maybe because I never listened to their music side by side with your analysis. But this time I listened to the title song from their second album, *Like Under Water*, while reading your book. Suddenly I could hear all those little tricks you interpreted . . ."

Elish remembered his analysis. He recalled it every time he listened to the song itself, like that night after the lecture, sitting at Barbunia, the moment before Dalia Shushan's voice and image wounded him anew, dragging him into feeling once more. The high pitch of the guitar–a single note, clean for half a minute before drowning in distortion–and the flute–a fraction late–and the entrance of the acoustic guitar, and the violin that came in on the third quarter of the second chord, and the drums—a kind of complex programming that repeated itself only after a full chord progression, emerging in the second quarter of the last chord in the round, which was the only chord that changes on each round, a non-loop loop, a broken universe of sound. Dalia Shushan's voice cracked at the edges of the high range, scattering in the low range, but always clear. When the singing was over, an instrumental segment erupted—wind instruments spinning into each other, swallowing up the flute and violin, a hypnotizing section that he thought bordered on genius. Elish had no formal training, but he assumed the musical ruse had a name, such as sleight of ear. The wind instruments changed the harmony, developing it, dragging it another way, attracting the listener's attention. That way, the chorus, on its second iteration, seemed to appear out of nowhere, from within an acoustic abyss. But for those who'd been following the flute and the violin, which insisted on repeating the same melody over and over again, its recurrence made sense. The instrumental segment pretended to present a melody, a musical progression, that were not really there.

Eitan kept talking, offering his own detailed version of the song's analysis, which afforded Elish a fresh view of it. This analysis contained, he felt without being able to point to any practical reason, something to do with Dalia's murder investigation. Not the content itself, but the principle it revealed. What was it? What? Elish refocused his attention on Eitan's words. His lecturing skills must really be taking off, he thought, if he's able to lecture to me at such length about ideas that I myself came up with. Had Elish believed people could or might change with ease, he would have started to hope that Eitan's level of intensity would also lower accordingly. Which, of course, did not happen. Eitan finished by saying, "You should write a rock music listeners' guide. I don't understand how you let yourself waste time following people around when you have the ability to make them follow you. How can you replace all of that with this?" He gestured toward Elish's injured shoulder. "Which brings me back to the question you've been evading. What happened to you?"

"Nothing important," Elish lowered his voice, "but if you must know, two thugs broke into my office the other day and beat the shit out of me."

"Why? What did you do?"

"You know how it goes, that ancient philosophical question. You're so skilled at asking questions that you don't even notice the one you were not allowed to ask."

"And I'm so used to your answers that I can see when you get tired of answering directly."

"Meaning?"

"Meaning that you're clinging to vague, semiparodic statements, letting the person you're speaking with understand what they choose to understand. That doesn't work on me, you know."

"Okay, if you say so."

"You can signal to me to back off as much as you want. Maybe, under different circumstances, I would do that without taking offense, but I learned years ago that even you don't buy your own act."

"You think I buy yours? You think I believe your collection of shallow insights about love? About being in love? About being able to be happy? You think I could have even talked to you if I hadn't recognized in you that same profound understanding I have?"

"No, Elish, I've never agreed with you on that, but you've bothered to interpret everything I say as if it confirms your desired subtext. I'm not like you. I don't even know what it means to be you."

The fury Elish had felt earlier burst inside his chest, acidic, setting his vocal cords and airways on fire. "That's bull, Eitan, and you know that very well. Just like you know that academia, the military, senior management positions that seem to require that you become a workaholic—that all those are established places of refuge for people who cannot truly share their lives with others. People who are socially disabled. So you hide here, believing you've figured out the trick for living a normal life, being happy, kids, a family, being normal. Normal, Eitan? You? How can you be normal? You weren't born with the glassy eyes that ninety-five percent of the world's population have. What are you going to do, look directly at the sun through a piece of glass? That won't make you any less blind."

Eitan didn't flinch. He continued with the same pleasantness that had slipped into his voice at the beginning of the conversation, "Elish, you're using broken metaphors. Maybe it's your way of preserving the sorrow you think is a condition of existence. And I've got to admit, I understand your insistence on it. After all, we both came of age in the decade when the most beautiful song was called 'Cemetery Gates.' That's why we imagine that suffering is deeper, more real. But it's nonsense, Elish, complete nonsense. What I'm concerned about is: why are you turning this insistence into your instrument of criticism? You're too intelligent for that. And, if memory serves, more fair. Why are you attacking my life choices while expecting me to empathize with yours?"

Elish thought, with sadness, People betray you by never being who you want them to be, and then, But what exactly do I want from Eitan? He's simply moved on to the promised happiness that too many generations of humans fought to formulate. Who am I to convince him otherwise? Misery is a boring way of making the world a bearable place, but also ordinary, so ordinary, no less ordinary than happiness.

4

Elish crossed the university quad, taking the stairs down toward the main entrance. The grass glistened to his right, and to his left rose the Economics and Business School, with students swarming in and out. And to think this used to be life in all its glory—being able to walk someplace without looking up at the sky, waiting for war. Once more, the morning papers discussed the American attack of Iraq that was expected to take place at any moment and its repercussions on the entire area. Bits of conversation blew toward him from every direction, the topics ranging from the obtaining of gas masks to apocalyptic predictions.

He bought a new copy of *Lampoons* at the university store. He'd thrown the old, marked-up, weather-worn copy out his apartment window that day Menuhin had refused to speak to him. He'd walked out the university gates and hailed a taxi with the hand holding the black bound book. He had thirty minutes before his meeting with Malkieli, and his left arm still hurt. The day before, rage flowed through him whenever he moved and his arm bothered him or whenever a mirror showed him a reflection of his wounded face. He cursed and shattered some glasses. Perhaps he should have asked his mother to stay with him another day. It wasn't a good time to be alone. That son of a bitch Manny, how did he have the nerve to call? Elish still had to find out how Dalia was connected to the whole thing. The day after he requested Dalia's case, those two guys jumped him. Was there a connection between Dalia and Gideon Menuhin? She was his brother's teaching assistant. Something was rotten. Rotten. The neighbor knocked on the door to make sure everything was all right because she thought she heard yelling and things breaking, and he told that old snoop to get bent. I'm getting as bad as Lior Levitan, he thought. Oh, of course. Lior Levitan was the place to start. He had to find out something about Dalia's life, some information that might be negligible to Lior but would give Elish a foundational point from which to raise this entire mess to hell, and the easiest way to reach Lior Levitan was through Malkieli. Malkieli was delighted to hear Elish's voice on the phone. It was like an old friend she hadn't seen in years had reached out to her. Yes, she'd heard he'd gone to the concert, Nicole told her, that was great. And yes, she'd been waiting for his call because she heard he was working on an article about Dalia's legacy, and of course she'd be glad to assist in any way she could, and why not, he could come by today. Today wasn't convenient? Tomorrow afternoon was great too.

He got out of the taxi on Balfour Street. Malkieli hadn't changed much since he'd last seen her, when she apologized unconvincingly to him outside of the Barbie, repeating over and over again that she couldn't control her artists' decisions, and that if Dildo wouldn't allow him into their concert, she was helpless to do anything. She'd dyed her hair platinum blond and cut it short, so now golden-white spikes popped out of her head. She walked over to greet him with open arms, smiling wide, kissed his cheek, examining his arm and face with concern, laughing at his "the left" joke. "Welcome back," she said cheerfully. "Coffee?"

"Why not?"

She called out a coffee order from her office door, lit a cigarette, and pushed the pack toward him. He pushed it back with a smile.

"So what's this I hear about you becoming a private investigator?"

"Got to make a living, and it doesn't look like music reviews are still an option." Elish waved the question away, concealing his surprise. He gave a wide, open smile, as if taking pleasure in the concept of a renewed acquaintance, the fact that it was possible to sit with her after two years of hostility that evaporated as soon as he walked into her office.

Malkieli looked him over carefully, but if there was any doubt in her gaze, it was completely absent from her voice. "So what do you think about Neriah Tzahor?"

"Who?"

"Neriah Tzahor, the singer that sang the first song at Dalia's memorial."

"Oh, her. She's got potential, but she needs some guidance."

"We're recording her album now. She's going to do a version of 'A Superfluous Eternity,' Dalia's song that she sang at the Barbie."

"Okay," Elish muttered.

"I know what you're thinking," Malkieli bared her teeth in a tense smile, "and I'm with you on that. No one can replace Dalia. But Neriah is a huge fan of hers. I played her Dalia's demo so she could pick the song to sing that night, and she got so excited. She said, 'Let's record an album of my versions of all of Dalia's new songs.' Of course I talked her out of it. I told her, 'That wouldn't serve you well as a debut album. Maybe for your third or fourth album, once you're a little more well-known.'"

"You're right," said Elish. "So what's the deal with the demo? Nicole told me you received it the day after Dalia was murdered." He placed a small recorder on the desk. "This is okay, right?"

"Sure. To this day I get chills whenever I think about it. Nicole walked in with a package, all shocked. 'Look what I found in the mailbox.' I opened it and my heart broke. Did Nicole tell you what was written on the CD?"

"Yeah, 'Menuhin.'"

"At first I thought it was some kind of code or wish. It took me a whole week to figure out that Menuhin was someone's name. I was watching TV, and on some news show someone was talking about new members of parliament, and they mentioned that guy, Gideon Menuhin."

The coffee arrived. Malkieli blew smoke at the ceiling.

"So what are the plans for Dalia's estate?"

"That's exactly what I wanted to talk to you about. The timing. I'm planning on putting out a double album next February. The first CD would be Dalia's demos, and the second one would be different artists' versions of some of the new songs. Maybe we should postpone the article till the album comes out?"

"No problem, I'll talk to my editor. I'm actually gathering background material right now. This might be used for a broader piece."

"You should write her biography." Malkieli's eyes sparkled. She had recognized a business opportunity and pounced on it, running her tongue over her nicotine-stained teeth. "It's genius. You'll write her biography, and we'll publish it together with a special best-of album. It'll be a huge hit."

"That's not a decision I can make on the spur of the moment."

"But think about it. Think about it, it'd be the bomb."

"I'll think about it. Do you plan to include Rami Amzaleg in this album?"

She looked at him beyond the smoke. Had her eyes always been so watery? "That depends on whether he wants to collaborate and agrees to my terms. But that's got nothing to do with your article." She gestured with her chin toward the recorder. Elish turned it off and crossed his arms against his chest.

"Look, I talked to Rami about Dalia's memorial. He refused to perform and called me a vulture. So I don't see a bright future for any collaborations between us. I think he was angry about the fact that Dalia sent the demo to me and not him."

"He told me that no one ever approached him about the Barbie concert, and that you have a vested interest in keeping him out of anything to do with Dalia's estate."

"Nonsense. Blasé weren't only admired because of Dalia. I know how talented he is. Why wouldn't I want to include him? He was half of the band."

"He says there was tension between you regarding some financial issues related to royalties and rights."

"Is this going to be a mutual slander piece?" Malkieli asked, irritated. "That's not your style, Elish. Did you become a tabloid writer?"

"Of course not! I'm trying to paint a portrait of Dalia and the importance of the songs she left behind. I have no desire to report inheritance battles. I'm just clearing the desk so I can do a better job and verify my sources, nothing more."

This seemed to satisfy her. "If we're talking about reliable sources, I have information from a fairly reliable source that Rami and Dalia were not on very good terms before she died. In fact, they had a fight the day she was murdered."

"Can you elaborate?"

She glanced at the recorder to make sure it was still off, then pulled on the end of her cigarette. "My niece works at the Espresso Bar on Herzl Street. She told me Dalia and Rami met there that afternoon. Dalia had spent all morning there, and then Rami came in around noon. She recognized both of them and wanted to talk to them, but Dalia looked depressed, and that horndog Rami wouldn't take his eyes off my niece's ass. So instead she watched them from a distance and saw them getting into a fight. Rami pushed a table over and left."

"Really? That bad?"

"That's what I'm telling you."

"And what about the royalties and rights?"

"We had a small misunderstanding about the first album. After all, I took a gamble on them and paid for all their studio time out of my own pocket. I thought we'd reached an agreement about how my investment would be paid back. They claimed they hadn't been informed. Things got a little heated, but we worked it out. The fact is, we made a second album together, and Dalia sent me her new demo."

Elish turned on the recorder. "Okay," he said into the mouthpiece, "Debbie Malkieli, interview regarding Dalia Shushan, part two." Then, to Malkieli, "Tell me a little bit about Dalia from your point of view."

Malkieli broke into cheerful chatter about how close she and Dalia had been from the first time they met, and how wonderful Dalia was, so sensitive and compassionate, and how happy she was for the privilege to have known her, and how she cried, cried for days, after Dalia was buried, and how, ever since, whenever she hears a song Dalia loved on the radio, she tears up.

Elish half-listened, occasionally interrupting the emotional confession with a guiding question. He smiled as he turned off the recorder. "That was excellent. Very moving too. I need two favors from you."

"Name them."

"A copy of Dalia's demo, and for you to ask Lior Levitan to talk to me. It's very important to me to get an interview with him, you know, because of the close relationship he had with Dalia. Right now our relationship is pretty much restricted to him hanging up on me."

"I'll talk to him right away. Give me your number. I'll make sure he calls you. I'll have to think about the demo."

He wrote down his home number on a piece of paper. "Thanks for all your help, and thanks for the invitation to the memorial concert. I haven't had a chance to thank you yet."

"Don't mention it. The truth is, I wasn't sure whether or not to invite you. I hadn't seen you at a concert in years."

I wonder why, thought Elish. Then he asked, "So what made you decide to invite me?"

"Don't be like that. I truly am happy you called to ask for the invitation. Now that I know you're back, I'll be sending you invites on a regular basis."

He furrowed his brow, placing two fingers on the bridge of his nose. "Do you remember who I talked to when I called?"

"I don't know. Nicole left me a message from you on my desk."

THAT EVENING, HE PLOPPED DOWN ON THE SOFA AND OPENED *Lampoons*. How could he have forgotten? The words, familiar and glittering, surged at him, those same sentences he'd highlighted in the introductory class, once again fulfilling the central idea of the book: "Philosophy is universally valid and capable of revealing eternal truths only in times that require it to function thusly. This is not the case for our time. There is no longer any justification for the detachment between contemporary life and the contemplation that stems from it. Our times dictate that its philosophy emerge from its strongest emotional foundations: bitterness, rage, depression, and frustration. Only when philosophy harnesses those as its sources of energy, will it have the authority to say something important to our generation. The lampoon, the slander, the scorn, and the wallowing are therefore the sole means of philosophizing in our time."

That personal, exposed tone that was such an important component of the book's innovation returned to Elish: "At times I awaken and listen. Breathing. The nighttime bosom rising and falling heavily. Warm breathing near my ears. Darkness leans against me. Breathing. I'm one of the only people who acknowledge the fact that they are sentenced to die. Therefore, I watch others with amusement—their ridiculous little races, the ridiculous gravity with which they carry on, the frivolity with which they risk their passions for the sake of comfort. But like an adult smiling condescendingly at children fervently engaged in a game I find baseless, I am the fool. And all those damn existential thoughts now storming are a winged herd of hyenas. As it turns out, the weaklings have won. All those rejected lepers whose mental development was stunted at puberty, who spent the remains of their lives planning their awful revenge, who in their dark cellars created the lethal virus called existentialism, worshipping the detestable aggression either in hiding or out in the open. Ubermensch my ass. How I loathe them. I am them. At times we awaken and listen. Breathing."

And there's Qalqilya. The sound of the muezzin's voice rises, and Menuhin's sweeping statements interweave with it well in their fervor and naivety. "Every great artwork is at its foundation romanticist, even if it is written in a cognitive environment that resents the Romantics."

And then came the crude language that dotted his eloquence, inspiring Elish to consider the cleanliness of philosophy. "Kant was wrong. I would give up the right to write *The Critique of Pure Reason* for a good fuck any day." Then the lines for which he had been condemned, which were not necessarily the strongest in the book, but still stood out: "These days, every average dump contains the raw materials necessary for producing a lethal bomb. The only two things preventing it from being produced are knowledge and morals. We've got too little of the former and too much of the latter."

And the next paragraph, which had become revived in his memory when he spoke to Ora Anatot: "Every human being is a potential criminal, and the biggest criminals are the inventors of morality theories. The more expansive and detailed the theory, the bigger potential criminal the person behind it. Moral theories are always born from the horror that rises in a person when they realize how boundless they can be in their imagination. And all it takes to make a potential criminal a practical criminal is the right kind of temptation or the right kind of desperation."

Elish got up to boil some milk. No. Such a life force does not destroy itself. Does not break so easily. Yehuda's brother was right, something didn't fit. He picked up the book from the coffee table, shifting his eyes from the written lines and the pot on the stove, lest the milk overflow. A person who writes like that does not kill himself. No existential doubt is horrible enough to cause him to lose his mind, unless the tapped phone uncovered a piece of information that could completely ruin his life, right? Elish recalled the sedatives and wine Yehuda had consumed. Maybe Eliya was right. If so, what was the source of his distress? No, no, it was more likely that Gideon's suspicions were justified and he knew something he wasn't telling. The possibility that someone had forced Yehuda to kill himself made complete sense. Or he could have even been murdered. But either way, who was behind it?

Good question, he thought, but perhaps I should focus on a different, no less urgent question. What drew him to this book when he was a soldier? Was it the loneliness and the desolation of the guard posts? And why did it now rile him up again? He rolled the questions on the margins of his mind. Perhaps he was in love with the mythology of darkness, like some depressed poet, in spaces within the human existence that annihilate faith. He had not had a proper bar mitzvah. He'd been too sick. And the memory of the synagogue dwarfed in his mind until it became a weak flicker. But there was more than that in Menuhin's writing–a desperate desire to create an alternative world that would be perfectly clean of the wait for redemption, to establish the satanic mirrors of nature. Who phrased it like that? And was it within this context? He couldn't remember and it didn't matter, the expression was appropriate. The urge to see a fully human kingdom on earth, to forget the nights and days in which he'd tried to hide, terrified, from the ever-open eye of the Lord. Someone told him about breaking the rules, and he sought the sparks in the vulnerable blossoming of dandelions, watching as the light faded since creation, as growth went blind. Forgetting the glimmer emptying out of the creator's skull, erasing the longing for paradise, being alone, a human. This was the frequency in which Yehuda Menuhin spoke to him, not like some fucking antichrist, as Rami Amzaleg would put it. Not through the aimless chatter of existentialism, embracing the absurdity of existence, yeah right, they could get bent. He was starting to like that expression. No, Menuhin was talking about something deeper, truer–about the recognition that the world was full, happy, but operated only by human hands. Not replacing one faith with another, not standing brave before the metaphysical void, that was truly an expression for tuberculosis patients who wanted to feel better about themselves. To be human, but what did that mean?

Elish read on, taking small, indulgent sips of his milk, arriving at another accumulation of sentences, the smell rising in his nose of the sweaty undershirt he'd worn as a soldier and hadn't changed in three days in the awful heat of the Jordan Valley. "At first, reason denied the living nature of the world. Next, it called it animism. In suggesting that its roots were in the structure of the mind rather than the order of the things exterior to it, in institutionalizing this false explanation for the belief in its existence, it wished to ruin it once and for all."

He trembled and paused, looking up from the heavy waters of memory. Ora Anatot said she knew Gideon Menuhin, but in the same breath she may have told him something more important, that his excitement over their acquaintance had concealed. She said that Yehuda had declared he no longer wanted to be detached from his object of study, but his object of study was Jewish mysticism, not the Talmud or Jewish Law. So, in fact, he wasn't announcing that he was becoming religious, or trying to anger his brother. If he seriously meant what he'd said, then he was referring to the applicable aspects of mystical thinking: ceremonies, magic. Elish lunged from the doorway and into his study, where he kept a Jewish calendar. Yes, he'd remembered correctly. Dalia Shushan had been murdered on the Ninth of Av. Menuhin had killed himself the day after Yom Kippur. A ritual? The image of Dalia Shushan's murder scene, which he'd constructed in his mind during that Monday dawn, floated before his eyes again: Dalia sprawled on the floor of her bedroom, one bullet in each temple and a third in her heart, arms spread beside her, traces of gunpowder on her palms, on the sides of her wrists, around her ankles, someone standing over her, slipping the gun into his pants pocket, and mumbling an incantation in a hard voice, in a language laden with throaty consonants.

5

How do you live without me, in the morning?
Evil birds sing in the late rain.
How do you wake up?
How are you not there,
Beside me?

Elish had no idea what made Malkieli make up her mind so quickly, but the fact was that on Friday morning a messenger delivered to him a copy of Dalia Shushan's demo, and her voice emerged from his car speakers. The weekend rest had improved the state of his arm, and if he was willing to pay the price of bearable pain, he could remove the sling and drive. He was on his way to Sderot to meet Dalia's parents. He had no idea what he was hoping to get from them. They must have known less than the average Tel Aviv resident about the last seven years of their daughter's life. But he had to go see them if he was going solve their daughter's murder. Was that his intention, to find Dalia Shushan's murderer? Esther Shushan's broken voice pierced through her daughter's singing. Was he not about to do a terrible thing—reopening a horror that they'd already sealed? Perhaps that was what he was after—permission.

And what silences me,
Until I can no longer talk,
Cannot command the mouth,
Trying love, but time

Is killing me,
Killing me so much.

The chorus rattled him. Had he believed that Menuhin's name on the CD truly had given Malkieli chills, he would have feared that the song would cause her to pass out, but he had trouble imagining that anything had the power to shock Malkieli or affect her with extraordinary intensity. Her niece, on the other hand, was a fragile creature.

On Friday afternoon, the dead hours of southern Tel Aviv, he'd walked into the Espresso Bar on Herzl Street, armed with a CD player and Blasé's album *One Mile and Two Days Before Sunset*. He sat down, put on the headphones, and lost himself in the liner notes. The server waved at him. "Do you want to order anything?" she asked when he removed the headphones.

He smiled awkwardly and looked at the CD player. "I always lose contact with the world when I listen to this album."

The server looked at the CD, read the name on the box, and said, "I think the guy from that band comes here a lot."

"Who, Rami Amzaleg?"

"That's the band where the singer got murdered, isn't it?"

"Yes, Dalia Shushan."

"So her partner in the duo comes here often. I heard he's a super irritable guy."

"What does that mean?"

"He kicked over a table a little while ago. Something like that."

"Really? That's an incredible coincidence. I'm actually working on a piece about Dalia Shushan for the newspaper. Can you give me more information?"

"Oh, I don't know the details. I wasn't here. It was Chava's shift."

"You think I could talk to Chava?"

"Her shift starts in thirty minutes, but she might get here earlier."

"Awesome. Can I get a latte?"

He put on his headphones again and kept reading the liner notes. After four songs, a hand touched his shoulder. "Hi, I heard you're looking for me," said the girl standing over him. "I'm Chava."

"Do you have a few minutes to talk?" he asked, closing the liner notes. "Can you sit down, or does policy forbid you from sitting with customers?"

She laughed. "My shift starts in ten minutes, so for now I'm just a civilian. I heard you wanted to ask me about Rami Amzaleg." Her eyes focused on the Blasé CD cover.

"Uh-huh. It's just such a surprising coincidence. I'm working on a piece about Dalia Shushan's estate, and then I hear she came here the day she died."

"Yeah, she was sitting with Rami Amzaleg, that creep." Chava made a face.

"Can you tell me a little about it?"

"I don't know. These are people who have a relationship with my aunt."

"Oh, yeah? Who's your aunt?"

"Debbie Malkieli."

"I can't believe it. I recently met her about the same piece. I'm sure she wouldn't mind. Besides, I won't quote you or anything. This is more like background."

"Okay. Dalia was sitting here all morning. It took me a while to realize that something was wrong with her. She didn't take off her sunglasses the whole time. Then he came by around noon, and within a few minutes they started fighting."

"A real fight? With yelling?"

"Not really, more like an argument. I heard them because they mentioned my aunt's name and I wanted to know what they were talking about, but I could have easily ignored it. After all, this is a café. Lots of times people raise their voices because of the noise from the espresso maker."

"So what were they talking about?"

"I think she told him she was going to make a solo album, and that's when she mentioned my aunt's name. She said she wrote twenty new songs, and he was very surprised, and angry too, because he thought she wasn't writing at all."

"Are you sure?"

"Pretty sure. He told her like three times, 'You're going to make a solo album? I thought you weren't writing.' And that was it. Then he got up, slammed his fist on the table, and it fell over. When I came over to help him he cursed me."

"He had to be a real brute to curse a girl like you," Elish said, watching her smiling and blushing, the dimple in her cheek deepening. "You were a great help, Chava. Thanks for the information."

"No problem. My shift just started. Can I get you anything? Another latte?"

ELISH TOOK A LEFT ON HODAYA JUNCTION, TRYING TO AVOID driving through Ashkelon. The road twisted, tangling in the greenery. Eucalyptuses and orchards, a weighty shadow. He couldn't remember ever driving down it. At Givati Junction, he bent down to turn off the music. Driving into the heart of Sderot along with the ghost of Dalia Shushan was too monstrous. When he steered left and looked up again, the light hit his eyes, and he felt around for his sunglasses. He couldn't blink, he remembered. He had to look ahead. He turned right and the pressure on his eyes ceased.

WELCOME TO SDEROT—MUSIC CITY. Elish chuckled at the sight of the sign covered with the names of famous bands alongside entirely anonymous ones. Dalia Shushan's name was in the center, in bold letters. Elish wondered if the sign had been put up after she died, and who had taken it upon themselves to keep her alive, stripped of the person she used to be. The name of her band, Blasé, did not appear, as if someone had known of her plans to record a solo album. He ran through his conversation with Chava in his mind. He had no doubt she'd twisted the truth a little, and that she'd in fact eavesdropped on Rami and Dalia carefully, but that didn't change the content of the information she'd given him. Rami hadn't known of Dalia's intentions. He hadn't known she'd been writing songs for a new album. This piece of information didn't sit well with something else. But what?

Sderot spread on both his sides. He followed the directions Esther Shushan had given him on the phone. She'd mentioned the sign. He took the correct turn. To his left rose gray block projects, very similar to the ones in his old Ashkelon neighborhood. Clotheslines, clothes that looked like they'd never be clean again. A few children crossed the street, ignoring traffic, causing him to slow down. He decided to adhere to the pace dictated by the children and the landscape. Ugly brick buildings licked the sky to his right—the sky was lower in Sderot—a crude mosaic reproduction of a Renoir adorned one of the buildings. Another short and stout building of concrete, glass, and decorative ceramic was surrounded with a lawn on which Bukharan and Caucasian immigrants spread their wares. Women sprawled beside blankets, adjusting their headscarves, while the men improvised a neighborhood café, sitting under the bare jacarandas, tossing cards onto tables. Esther had warned him not to be deceived by appearances—"It's the public library. Dalia used to go there almost every day." To his left was the colorful playground she'd mentioned, turn right at the gym, turn left at the soccer field—a grassy field dotted with brown bald spots, the goalposts' nets waving in the light breeze. The Sderot cloudiness stifled October, Elish thought as he parked under a pomegranate tree beside the field.

Esther, a middle-aged woman in a headscarf, was waiting for him. Her eyes were the first part of her he met, two velvet wells.

That's how he wanted to describe the sorrow, a profundity of quiet burning, demanding nothing from the world, resting a merciful look without a hint of condescension upon him, only a piercing knowledge of what was to come for all things. This woman, he told himself, had been six and six hundred, eight and eight hundred, and now she was just tired. Something of the wisdom in her eyes was inherited by Dalia, whose gaze had been more sober and less faithful. Esther said nothing, waiting. How long had she been waiting there for him? He was fifteen minutes late–an unexpected traffic jam just as he was leaving Tel Aviv–and yet she looked like she'd been waiting for generations. The light breeze loosened a lock of hair from her scarf. Her hair was white. She was too young for white hair.

"Welcome," she said when he opened the small green gate and walked into the yard. Rose bushes were sprouting. This wasn't their season to bloom, but he knew that with time they would grow as large as fists, their smell furious and flooding. His heart pinched. He noticed the web of wrinkles on her face, delicate, pulling on the corners of her mouth, or perhaps it was that makeshift garden that erupted in his memory again, what lay between a child and his mother. Esther's voice came from somewhere in the distance, "Come in, it's getting chilly outside."

He followed her. At the end of the hallway that forked to the right of the foyer, he noticed a door hung with an enormous poster of Robert Smith, tattered with years of wear. Next to the man's wild, gel-hardened hair, a thought bubble read, "I want the person farthest from stage to see my lips moving." That statement summarized the entire philosophy of eighties pop, he thought–the mask of makeup and color that concealed a pain and a desperate desire to be heard–a false desire, because all that was left of it was the movement of lips. Even though young boys experienced their first sexual release to the voice of Samantha Fox, and girls felt their loins burning before centerfolds of Simon Le Bon, and even though pop music attempted to speak the language of clubs and dance floors, the language of the melted masses, ultimately adolescents listened to it with low spirits, at dark hours, in the fortress of their bedrooms, pouring the bitterness of their hearts over it. From behind him, Esther said, "Dalia never let us take down that poster, even after she moved out, so I'm keeping it up until it falls by itself."

He followed her into the living room. She pointed to the sofa. There were already plates of nuts and fruit on the table. "Turkish coffee?" she asked.

When she left the living room, a short bespectacled man showed up in the doorway to the living room. "Hello. Are you the journalist?" He had a heavy accent, his voice almost a growl. Elish could only deduce what he'd said.

He stood up and walked over to the man. "Elish Ben Zaken," he said, offering his hand.

The man offered his blistered hand in return. "Yossef Shushan." An extinguished man, speaking with the smallest effort, flattening his syllables.

"Nice to meet you."

"Ben Zaken?" he added in his broken speech. "Are you Moroccan? Where's your family from?"

"My parents were born in Marrakesh, but they met in a transit camp near Ofakim."

"Ah, Marrakesh," Yossef said longingly, then walked away.

Elish returned to his seat and looked at the pictures of Dalia that hung on the wall across from him in chronological order: Dalia in her crib; Dalia at age three, sitting in the yard, hands on her lap; Dalia at age five, bottle feeding a doll; Dalia at age six, holding a Bible; Dalia at age seven, dressed up as the queen of the night for Purim; Dalia at age nine, waving hello; Dalia at age ten, hanging upside down from the monkey bars at a playground, laughing; Dalia at age twelve, surrounded by birthday gifts, her cheek against her mother's. He forced himself to look away, to stop his eyes from wandering toward the moment when the chain of images was cut within Dalia's time, afraid he might see her body, arms spread, lying in a puddle of blood.

"Was Yossef here?" Esther interrupted his thoughts. She placed his coffee cup before him.

"He came and left."

"I don't know what's going on with him. Where he's going, when he's back. Ever since Dalia . . ." She sighed.

"That's all right, Mrs. Shushan. I think a conversation between you and me would be fine."

She took a seat across from him. He sipped his coffee. "Excellent coffee," he said appreciatively. "So, like I said on the phone, I'm working on a very big article about Dalia. I really hope it doesn't hurt your feelings, or your husband's. It'll be very dignified, I promise you." He placed the tiny recorder on the table.

She smiled. "It's a shame that the most important person can't talk anymore."

"Do you mean Dalia herself?" His throat soured.

"No. I'm talking about Ezra Buhbut, may God forgive him."

"And why should God forgive him?"

"He was a thief and a junkie, but his punishment was worse than he deserved."

"Mrs. Shushan . . ." Elish began carefully after a brief pause. Her voice was so decisive.

"Esther, you can call me Esther."

"Esther, Ezra Buhbut was found guilty of your daughter's murder."

"I don't care what the judge said. He's just a person, and people make mistakes. Buhbut didn't murder my daughter."

"Look, Esther, this isn't exactly connected to my article. I'm writing a profile piece, but I'd still like to hear why you think that."

Again those eyes landed on him, knowing and restrained. "I know his type. He'd steal, that he'd do. He'd steal a blind beggar's last piece of bread, but he'd do it when no one was looking. He wouldn't kill for it. From the moment I saw his face on TV, I knew it wasn't him."

"Who is it, then?"

"That's for the police to figure out, not me. I've done my part." She looked around. "I don't want Yossef to know, but I went to see him in prison after his trial."

"And they let you meet him?"

"Of course they did. He had no family, so his visiting hours were open. The cops gave me dirty looks, but what do I care? They're just humans. I wanted to be sure. I wanted to ask him if he knew who could have done such a thing to my daughter." Her voice choked. "He said he didn't. He kept swearing to me that all he did was steal that bag from her apartment. I believed him. I told him I did. But now he's dead, and the dead don't talk."

"Did you tell anyone?"

"A reporter called, so I told him. The day after Dalia was murdered, everyone wanted to know what Yossef and I had to say. But as soon as I told him what I thought he politely ended the conversation. So I called that officer who's in charge of the police."

"Manny Lahav?"

"Yes. And he was polite too. As friendly as it gets. But he didn't lift a finger, either."

"I'd like, with your permission, to ask you something crass, Esther."

"Go ahead."

She looked at him. He finished his coffee, didn't touch the food. This guy doesn't eat. He could read the thought as it bounced across her eyes, and smiled. "What kind of justice can be done with the dead? What would you want to have happen?"

"I know what I should want. I should want the truth to come out. People are so afraid of their own truth, that they believe the truth is the worst punishment anyone could get. But what I want is simpler. Something my heart, not my brain, can understand." For a moment, her eyes lost that peaceful knowledge in their depths and a wave of anger flowed through them. "I want whoever did it to suffer, to suffer like I do, to wake up in the morning, knowing Dalia would never call again, won't come on Saturday. I want them to go out in the afternoon to look for Yossef and find him crying in the synagogue yard. That's what I want."

"That's more than one person can sentence another to."

"I'm waiting for God to do it," she said, her voice hard. "Not people."

Elish said nothing. What could he say? Yossef wandered inside, leaves stuck to his thin hair and his yarmulke.

Esther walked over to brush them off. "Where were you, Yossef?"

"Under the tree," he said. "I went to make sure the neighborhood kids didn't touch his car," he said, pointing at Elish.

"Thanks," said Elish. "Tell me a little bit about Dalia."

"What's there to tell that I haven't already?" Esther asked, her voice shaking. "Dalia wasn't an easy child. Nothing about her was easy. Yossef and I waited for her for ten years. After she was born, the doctor told me I'd never be able to give birth again, and that she was a medical marvel. We gave her anything she wanted, and she never wanted too much, not like those kids that are always saying buy me this and buy me that, then a week later push aside the toys they got and never play with them again. She always knew exactly what she wanted, even when she didn't talk. That's another story. She didn't talk until she was three years old. People thought she was retarded. The neighbors told me, 'What's wrong with you, Esther? Take her to see a doctor. She may have a hearing problem.' But I knew. I told Yossef, 'Once this girl opens her mouth she won't close it. People will be sorry she started talking.' Until she was three she spoke with her eyes. It was no problem figuring out what she was thinking. Then, when she was three, she started speaking in full sentences, as if she'd been talking for a million years. People said, 'This girl is a miracle! Take her to the Baba Sali to get his blessing.' But Yossef and I didn't want to. We didn't believe in those primitive superstitions. At age five she taught herself how to read, I have no idea how. She would sit with Yossef when he read the Bible and ask him, 'What's this word? What's that word?' until he lost his temper and shouted at her. Her teacher came up to me at the market one day and said, 'You're raising your daughter so well, it's so wonderful she can already read.' When I got home I found her reading a book the teacher gave her as a gift."

She stood up and left the living room. Yossef watched her go. She returned with a tattered book whose remains of glisten reflected from the living room light. *The Blue Bird.* On her way out of the living room, or perhaps while she was telling her story, he hadn't noticed, the tears had shattered her walls, streaming down her cheeks, making her voice tremble further. "She learned it by heart and told it to us every night. She even made up a dance for the bird."

Yossef reached out to take her hand.

"But she wasn't easy. She had an opinion about everything. She would argue with her teachers. At fifth grade her homeroom teacher slapped her for arguing. Dalia sent a letter to the radio about it. They read it on the radio and the teacher was fired. She would argue with Yossef about God, and there's nothing Yossef hates more than arguments about religion. When she was a teenager she stopped going out. She had no friends, was sad all the time. One time, I remember, she came home late at night and cried for three days afterward. She didn't go to the military. Told them she didn't want to join a military that controls another people. When she was twenty I convinced her to move to Tel Aviv with her cousin Ronnit, who used to be her best friend when they were little. She was difficult there too, and they got into a fight two weeks in. Same thing when she was here: she came to Sderot to perform once, and the local council gave her some grief, so instead of singing she cursed them out up onstage and then didn't come to visit again for two months. But it looked like Tel Aviv was good for her. She was successful, and a little happier. And now she's dead and I blame myself." Esther began to sob. "Excuse me," she said, then left the living room.

Choked up, Elish turned off his recorder. This whole dead people and brokenhearted people business was not for him. This was the world that God created; let God handle it. What was he thinking? This wasn't his anger, it was Esther's. It was an anger that concealed a different anger, a different shame.

WHEN HE PULLED OUT FROM HIS PARKING SPACE, WAVING goodbye to Esther and Yossef Shushan, he felt as if he were fleeing. Sderot was a crater of pain, and he wished to leave it behind as quickly as possible.

Esther had locked herself in the kitchen. From behind the door he told her he was leaving and asked for Ronnit's phone number, which Esther dictated. Then he added, "Esther, I have Dalia's last songs on a CD. I can leave it for you."

In a stifled, effortful voice, muffled by the thick door, Esther said, "I never liked the way she sang, like she had broken glass in her throat. Music is supposed to make people happy. I don't want to hear her songs. I want to see her one more time right now, my little girl."

What the hell was he doing? Elish wondered on his way to the car. He had gotten the permission he'd been seeking, but you had to be mad, seriously mentally disturbed, to investigate people's deaths. How many wires of sorrow did he have to cut to appease the ticking bomb in his chest? What were all those Sherlock Holmeses, those Hercule Poirots, those Jane Marples, those Father Browns, those Peter Wimseys, what were all those nutjobs doing, untangling the thicket, one thread at a time? You had to be at least as cold and calculated as a murderer to stay sane when you faced the paralyzing lonesomeness of those the dead left behind.

Yossef stood by the gate. “Is the car okay?” he asked. “Ben Zaken? From Marrakesh? I don’t know them.” He looked toward the house, and his voice brightened. “Esther was pretty when she was young. Hair down to here,” he placed his hand at his waist. “Black, straight. And eyes. Everyone wanted her. But her brother gave their mother hell. He was no good. He stole. He bought drugs. The police would come by every other day, banging on the door. They’d go into her shack and turn it upside-down, looking. Esther would sit in the corner and cry. When I came to ask her to marry me, her mother said, ‘It’s good that someone is taking her away from here.’ They lived in the transit camp, poor souls. Even after we got married, Esther would wake up in the middle of the night, screaming. She’d say, ‘Hold me, Yossef, I’m afraid.’ For two years. Isn’t that a crying shame? She was pretty when she was young. She was so happy when Dalia was born. Dalia was her light. She knew how to respect her parents.” His voice thickened and trailed off. Then, without saying goodbye, he turned to leave.

Dalia knew how to respect her parents. And Elish? He was already in the middle of his drive home, and a desire he hadn’t tamped down in time took advantage of his distraction and took over his body. When he tried to concentrate on the road ahead, he noticed he’d been driving toward Ashkelon. Why not? He could go see his mother. Their time was limited too.

6

I'm getting soft, thought Elish. He was dancing with Tahel in his mother's living room. On television, a screechy pair of actors were butchering classic children's songs. Tahel was not familiar with the originals, so she beamed with joy. "Dance," said Elish, taking her by the hands and shaking her arms.

"Das," she repeated, trying to skip.

His mother had popped down to the grocery store, leaving him in charge of Tahel. He was surprised by her boldness. Yaffa could never find out.

"That's it, I'm tired," he told Tahel.

"No, Eyish," she protested.

He sat her down on the couch and changed the channel to a kids' TV show. Tahel stared at the screen, charmed. "Bob," she said, pointing.

"Uh-huh," Elish responded, as if he knew what she meant. I'm getting soft, he repeated to himself. Whenever anyone claimed that any aspect of Tahel reminded them of Bobby's family, he denied the allegation. Tahel belonged only to Yaffa, a Ben Zaken offspring. But how simple it is to hold a grudge, and how much simpler to melt it away, he thought, as soon as you figure out its source. Zalman Danino was his best friend until he turned ten. Looking back, he wasn't sure why. They were utterly different children. But maybe children didn't make those sorts of calculations.

One Purim, Bobby had dragged him into the neighborhood bomb shelter. They were almost ten years old, and Zalman's new nickname rested on Elish's tongue, squeaky clean. A few months earlier, Bobby had figured out a way to pick the lock to the bomb shelter in the yard of the HMO clinic, a shelter that, if Elish's memory served, was used and maintained by no one. When Bobby opened the heavy door, Elish knew he'd been right. Many winters had left their moldy marks on the walls, and the smell was almost unbearable. There was no electricity, only a bit of sunlight filtering in. They cleaned up one of the rooms, and though they could not get rid of the powerful aroma of mildew or install any light bulbs, the room became the preferred neighborhood kids' hangout, formally named "the shelter." They gathered there, equipped with candles. They learned they could leave sooty graffiti on the moist whitewash if they brought the flames close enough. Many sketched out their names with the unavoidable superlatives "the king," "the biggest man in the hood," "forever," or simply "was here," accompanied by arrow-pierced hearts. Elish didn't bother.

That day, Bobby opened his hand. "Look what I lifted from my dad." In his hand was a green, shiny, rectangular box. "A pack of Nobles," Bobby explained, not leaving any room for guesses. "I'm going to the shelter to smoke. You coming?"

"Forget it. If my dad catches me he'll kill me."

"Come on, you chicken, don't you know smoking is allowed on Purim?"

"Who told you that nonsense?"

"Everything is supposed to be opposite," Bobby chuckled, "am I right?"

Elish wasn't easily swayed, but he was tempted by the notion of smoking. At the end of the day when Yaffa and his father had shooed away the pigeon, he'd heard his father humming in the kitchen. He drew nearer to listen. It wasn't exactly a hum, more like a tune reminiscent of the way cantors sang Bible passages, a kind of low, bewitching recitation. That evening, he began to spy on his father, watching beyond the thin crack left between the kitchen door and the doorframe. He watched the way his father smoked, ponderous, painting rings of smoke through the air, staring, sighing, and finally tossing the butt into his coffee cup.

At the shelter, the smoke glided down his throat. After two coughing fits, the roughness was painfully sweet. He pulled on the cigarette with pleasure.

"Relax," said Bobby. "There's an entire pack here."

He'd never heard of this phenomenon, but a light feeling of floating took over. "Say, what's in these cigarettes?" he asked Bobby.

Bobby leaned against the wall, looking up. In the light of the candle, his face looked mature. He held the cigarette between his thumb and middle finger, smoking knowledgeably. "This is a good way to be," he said. "This is how it should be."

Elish only later considered this remark, which meant nothing to him at the time. Just then, his attention was grabbed by the sound of the shelter door creaking. He looked at Bobby, who had his eyes fixed on his fingertips. "Is anyone else coming?"

"No, nobody."

"Did you lock the door behind us?"

"Are you crazy? Locking us inside? Didn't you hear about the girl who got stuck in this shelter fifteen years ago? She couldn't get out and was drowned by rainwater."

"That's just a story they told you to keep you from breaking into the shelter. Not that it worked. Listen! Somebody's coming."

Elish and Bobby fell silent, listening to the rustle on the steps, the rubbing of jeans and heavy footfalls. "Put out the cigarette, toss it, and hide the pack," Elish said urgently.

"Where's the fire?" said Bobby, "we're just—"

"Elish!" Prosper's rumbling voice cut off Bobby from the doorway. "Elish, you idiot, if I catch you down there you're a goner." Prosper walked into the circle of candlelight, the angry energy accumulated in his body making him look threateningly large. He was about to explode. Elish froze with fear, lines from a book he once read running through his mind, about predators that hypnotize their prey or paralyze their bodies with toxins. But Prosper's rage was entirely directed at Bobby. "Danino, you stinking hick," he said, grabbing Bobby by the collar and pulling him up to stand, "I knew you were involved in this. Fuck off." Elish heard the flesh of Bobby's face screeching as the palm landed on it. He raised his arms to protect himself. Two of Prosper's fingers grabbed his ears, forcefully levitating him, then pushing him forward with the force of the momentum. Prosper kicked him toward the stairs. His left palm rubbed down the wall and he kneeled on the steps. Bobby was ahead of him, fleeing up the stairs while cursing, "You motherfucker, Ben Zaken."

Outside of the shelter, Elish was blinded by the light waves of March and placed a hand over his eyes. Bobby was six feet away, holding a small rock in his fist. "Ben Zaken," he yelled when he saw Prosper coming out the door, his voice breaking into a whine, "Ben Zaken, if you lay a finger on me one more time, I'll mess you up, you hear me? I swear to God, if you—"

"We know all about you, Danino," Prosper said with contempt. "You and your hick family. If I see you hanging around my son again, I'll break both your legs, you got it? Now get out of my face." Then he turned to Elish: "I'm not through with you yet," he said, slapping the back of his son's neck. "Go up to your room, and you'll stay in there until school starts up again after the holiday. We'll talk about this tonight."

Elish walked toward the clinic gate, fighting against the urges of his rebellious eyes. Yaffa was sitting on the sidewalk by the gate, sketching an imaginary picture with her finger over the rocks. She stood up when his shadow fell on her. "Elish," she said, adding nothing more.

His red face must have revealed his insult. "You snitch, revenge will come," he said, pushing her aside and crossing the street.

That afternoon, lying in bed with his face to the wall, he heard the door opening. A moment later, he felt Yaffa's hand tugging on his shirt. "Elish," she whispered, "look at what I got you."

He didn't turn to face her. His eyes were still moist and he didn't want Yaffa to see. His voice thick with tears, he said, "You snitch. Don't think you can get away with this."

"Elish," Yaffa whispered. "It wasn't me. Bobby's dad came by this morning, saying he was looking for Bobby because Bobby stole money from his wallet and another kid's mother had seen the two of you together. I saw Dad losing it, so I ran after him to warn you, but he knew you were in the shelter."

"Where are Mom and Dad?"

"Mom's sleeping and Dad's out. Look, I got you the Mishloach Manot I was saving for after the holiday."

He didn't touch another cigarette until military service. There, on one of the freezing night-guard duties, he bummed a cigarette from another soldier in his company, and that burning-sweet sensation filled his limbs again. He smoked nonstop for a year, until his company was sent on an educational program at Givat Olga. The moment Elish set foot in that resort, he smelled the sea, and spent the rest of the day coughing out all the nicotine that had been piling up in his lungs for the past twelve months, which had been truncated into the recurring pattern of inhale, exhale, wanting to die.

"EYISH!" TAHEL SCREECHED. "HORSEY!" SHE RAISED HER HANDS.

"Yes," he said, watching the show's credits on the screen. "Who's a smart girl? You're right, Bob the Builder is super boring." He linked his fingers and lowered his arms so that Tahel could sit on his palms. "Horsey, horsey," Tahel hummed without any kind of rhythm, curling up in her hand hammock. "Horsey." Yes, Tahel had inherited something from Bobby's side–a talent for joy that was uncommon among the Ben Zaken family. At

Yaffa's wedding, the Ben Zakens sat sulking at their tables while the Daninos, whose relationship with Bobby had already started to unravel, rejoiced, filling the dance floor with their high spirits. Elish looked at his sister, twenty years old, so young, mummified in her white dress. "You're going to throw away your future like that?" their mother said when Yaffa announced that she and Bobby had decided to get married. Yaffa got angry. Elish would have been angry too, had he not thought their mother was right. "Come on, Zehava," Bobby's mother cried, dragging his mother onto the dance floor. "Your daughter's getting married! What could be happier? Dance!"

Elish decided to implement the advice his mother had received in an original way. He'd never had alcohol before that day. Prosper abhorred booze and had passed his distaste on. Elish gave Yaffa one last look–dancing with a measured step, afraid of shattering the evening–and went to the bar to get a cocktail.

"That," he said, pointing at a red drink.

"Kir Royale?" the bartender asked.

"Uh-huh," confirmed Elish, then drank.

In the tumult of guests approaching the bar and calling out their orders, the bartender didn't notice Elish mixing drinks with the foolishness of the novice. "Tequila," Elish heard someone saying, and did the same, as he did with vodka and orange juice, arak, piña colada, beer, then stepped outside, the thought flashing through his mind that he threw up much more than the average guy before he spilled out the contents of his stomach on the sidewalk outside the event hall and dragged himself home by foot.

"HORSEY," TAHEL INSISTED WHEN HE SAT HER BACK DOWN ON the couch. "Horsey."

"Enough," he told her. "You need to learn how to be bored at a young age. Believe me, it's life's secret sauce. Let's read a book."

He randomly picked up one of the colorful books that were strewn over the coffee table, and without looking at the words, began to recite: "There once was a king who'd grown despondent with his garden. No, not grown despondent, he just grew tired of wandering. And his wife, the queen, a serious pest, also complained about resting her eyes on the same views for three years straight. So the king summoned the royal architect, who everyone claimed was the most gifted architect in the land, and gave him a year to design a garden that would move even the most jaded heart. For a full year, the architect locked himself in an enormous, fenced-in area in the southern tip of the kingdom. And when the time was nigh, no, not when the time was nigh, when the twelve months allotted to him had elapsed, the king stood at the gate of the fenced garden and looked at a large arrow bearing the words 'To the Exciting Gardens.'

"The king smiled to himself, struck his hands together with joy, no, not struck his hands together with joy, rubbed his hands with satisfaction, and walked inside. The arrow pointed toward a path twisting within a barren landscape, and a few hundred feet away was another arrow. The king almost ran toward it. At a bend, a lucid ray of light hit him, but the king tented his eyes with his hands, no, not tented, covered his eyes with his hand, to protect them from the sun. When he reached the arrow pointing toward 'The Fragile Flowers,' he looked ahead. Another arrow waited in the distance, and the king hurried over. A lone rose leaned against the side of the path, but the king hurried past it, gritting his teeth.

"Thus, for a full hour, the king dragged his legs from one sign to the next, ignoring a jasmine bush to the right of the path, a colorful rock to the left, a weak tune carried by the wind. When he arrived at a sign reading 'Exit,' where the architect waited, he was beside himself, no, not beside himself, he was about to explode with anger.

"'So, what do you think?' the architect asked quietly.

"'Where's my garden?' yelled the king." Here Elish raised his voice and made a threatening face. Tahel, riveted, giggled.

"The architect answered calmly, 'You've been walking through it this entire time.'"

"Don't overstimulate the kid," his mother said, swinging the front door open, soaking wet. "This rain, God help us. She didn't cry or whine," she added, half-imploring, half-wondering.

"No, of course not, she's a very good girl."

"Stay for lunch? It's no good, driving in this rain. Wait for it to end."

"Let me just check my messages first."

"*Medura yana*," his mother said, making a kissy face at Tahel and putting her down on the rug, away from the danger of heights to which Elish had exposed her.

Lilian told him that everything was fine at the office, and that other than Manny Lahav, who called and whom she told, as Elish had instructed, not to call again, there was nothing urgent. Oh, and Eliya said to tell him she hadn't been able to track down Shmuel Benita yet, and that he'd know what she meant. On his home answering machine, Lior Levitan had left a stuttered message, saying he was willing to meet. Elish called him back and set an appointment for that afternoon. Then, in an impulsive decision, he called Rami Amzaleg and told him he'd love to go out with him that night and have a drink in Dalia's memory at Abraxas.

"No, Mom," he said as he put down the phone. "I can't stay, I have things to do in Tel Aviv, and I'm afraid I may have left my windows open."

"How's your arm?"

"I'm okay without the sling."

"Have they caught the person who did it?" his mother asked, heading out of the living room.

"No, I didn't file a complaint." He walked over to Tahel, who had her eyes fixed on him.

"Why don't you take something for the road? Wait fifteen minutes, I'll throw some schnitzels on the stove. The meat is already defrosted. And I'll chop some salad. You know, how about I make some fries while I'm at it? Twenty minutes, tops."

"Long story short, Mom, you're keeping me here for lunch," Elish said thirty seconds later, thinking she'd walked away. Then he leaned down toward Tahel and added, "Don't end up like Grandma."

But his mother was at the doorway, and heard.

7

So much for respecting one's parents. Why did he have to insult his mother? The wipers worked overtime on his windshield, shoving away the torrents of rain. Elish's eyes grew blurry. What was happening to him? He wasn't even certain he'd hurt her feelings. How could he? She hadn't shown any emotion but hollow, mechanical concern for him since the day of his bar mitzvah. He wasn't sure she even understood the motive behind the gifts he was always showering on her, or if she'd noticed the fact that she hadn't given him a single gift since his tenth birthday.

In the spring when he was nine and nine months, three months before his tenth birthday, he read in a book—The Famous Five, or Nancy Drew—that ancient buildings sometimes play auditory tricks, so that in a main sitting room of a castle, one might be able to hear something taking place in a remote wing.

Their home was barely fifty years old. For some reason, that day he and Yaffa had decided to stay in and play spot tag. Each one of them was able in turn to take one step toward the other or away from the other. The winner was whoever was able to step on the other's foot first through this series of movements. It was obvious that Yaffa was cheating, moving forward when she thought he wasn't watching. She'd always been a sore loser, and he let her win time after time, witnessing the expression of joy washing over her face.

That spring he did a cartwheel, moving away from Yaffa, then stood still. He was filled with excitement: the book had been right. His feet were planted in the living room, but he heard his mother singing in the kitchen as if she were standing right beside him. A trick of sound. Magic existed. Yaffa stomped on his foot when she realized he wasn't paying attention to the game, breaking the spell. He chased her through the apartment, listening to her squealing with delight, pretending that his foot was injured, limping slowly to prolong her pleasure.

That evening, he returned to the same spot in the living room and stood still. The kitchen door was closed, but he could hear his mother and father arguing at a whisper.

"But Prosper," his mother said decisively, "you know how much Elish has been looking forward to that video game. All the kids in the neighborhood already have one. Last year you bought him that skateboard even though I told you he didn't want it and that it was going to lie in his room, collecting dust."

"I know." Prosper's voice was made for yelling. Whispers broke it apart. "I know, Zehava, but none of my brothers will give her any money and she's broke. I won't let my mother die like a dog."

"Well, it's her fault for treating your brothers and sisters like trash, and you, too, don't you forget. She didn't even come to see me at the hospital when Elish and Yaffa were born. So now you want to give her the money we've been saving up for his present?"

"Zehava," Elish heard Prosper's voice cracking–it was more than a whisper; for the first time in his life, Elish heard his father in distress–"Zehava, just this once. My heart won't let me turn her down. Respect for parents is a big thing for me. I–"

"Prosper, can't you see that's why she comes crying to you and not your brothers and sisters?" Zehava said, tired. "I could spend a thousand years with you and never fully understand you. Do whatever you want. But you're the one who's going to explain to Elish why he didn't get that video game, not me."

"Well, I haven't really punished him yet for what he did last Purim."

Elish trembled away from his secret spot in the living room. His parents' voices faded. He went to his room, mad, refusing to accept the fact that the Donkey Kong game he'd been feverishly dreaming about for nearly six months had slipped between his fingers with such casual cruelty. He spent all night hating his grandmother, with her dry cakes and her hard kisses and her gross hands and her mouth that smelled like spoiled milk. He'd never forgive his father, he promised himself, fuck respecting one's parents, and fuck his father.

Three months later, on his birthday, he didn't even bother to feign surprise when his father told him in a hard voice that he and his mother had decided that this year he didn't deserve a birthday gift because of his unruly behavior, and that he hoped Elish had learned his lesson. But in the following days, he roamed the apartment frowning and mean-spirited, even though it was summer vacation and the beach was calling, evading his mother's attempts at appeasement, standing chastised before his father, but refusing to say a single word, carrying out his chores passively, with heavy movements, until his parents finally broke and his father announced, "Next week we'll compensate you. We can go to the amusement park in Tel Aviv and you can play all the video games you want."

"SO YOU'RE WRITING A PIECE ABOUT DALIA SHUSHAN?" LIOR Levitan asked, standing in the doorway to his apartment. In spite of the chill and the rain that had polished Tel Aviv in the late morning, Levitan leaned against the doorframe in nothing but long johns with holes in them, his torso bare, a thin tuft of hair adorning his flat, pale chest. His long, ponytailed hair was mussed up and hard. It must not have been washed in months. Then Levitan added, "Before you come in, I have one condition: you need to give me your word that you won't make Dildo look bad in your article. That was my deal with Malkieli too."

"No problem," said Elish, pushing him aside. "Like I told you on the phone, the article is about Dalia Shushan, not you guys."

Elish was a little worked up from his drive over. The thoughts he'd lost himself in on the way to Tel Aviv almost caused him to crash into another car when he switched lanes, entering the Ashdod freeway, and for the rest of the way he'd forced himself to be consciously concentrated. Levitan didn't offer him anything to drink. Instead, he said, "All right, let's get down to business. I'm not about to reminisce with you here."

Elish looked around. It was better not to have been offered a beverage. Levitan's cramped one-bedroom apartment was in disarray: a guitar tossed on the bed, cups with hardened and cracked coffee sediment topped with cigarette butts, a bent-up rattan bookcase, clothes over every chair, on the floor, on the beanbags, a humming computer with a Da Vinci screen saver darkening its screen. Elish walked over to the computer, ran a hand on the screen as if to wipe away dust, and shifted the mouse. The colorful surfaces representing recording channels on the Acid software appeared. He noticed that Cubase and Sound Forge were also open. All this software must be pirated, Elish thought, but how did that help him? In a bored voice, he told Lior Levitan, who stood behind him, "Don't you know it's bad to use the screen savers that come with Windows? They flicker at a frequency that makes you become addicted to Microsoft products."

"You always were an idiot and a snoop," Levitan muttered with disgust, turning off the screen.

Elish decided to broach the subject with all the callousness he could muster. No other ruse would motivate Levitan to talk. He placed his recorder bluntly on the coffee table, sat down, and spoke into it: "Lior Levitan, conversation number one.

"So, in fact," he said to Levitan, who'd lit a cigarette without offering Elish one, "you were Dalia Shushan's partner in the last year of her life."

"Yes," Levitan said importantly. "We broke up a month before what happened."

"I have to admit this seems odd to me," Elish smiled mockingly, "because five years ago she said in an interview, and I quote: 'Unfortunately, rockers are the worst chauvinists, no matter what part of the country they come from.'"

"So what do you want? You want me to tell you why she changed her mind? Five years is a long time. At any rate, I never got any complaints from her about that."

Elish embarked on his crude attack. "Maybe that's because she was using you. Maybe it was more about needing you than loving you?"

Levitan narrowed his eyes suspiciously. "Did you talk to Rami Amzaleg?"

Elish nodded coolly, maintaining his ridiculing smirk. Who am I fooling here? he thought. This is more than an information-gleaning technique. This is revenge. Petty, disgusting revenge, stinking of humanity. And nevertheless. He had no intent of concealing his loathing for Levitan, who, like so many other performing artists, he suspected, had no idea how to cope with direct contempt, with such a blatant rejection of who he was. Scornfully, he said, "Rami said you couldn't last a year with a girl without being cheated on."

The blood rushed into Levitan's face. His right hand closed into a fist around the cigarette that was vibrating between his lips. He crushed it in the ashtray. "That son of a bitch. What's he butting in for? He was all over Dalia from the start. Everything he achieved was thanks to her. Ever since Dalia decided to break up Blasé, all he's done was write those stupid dance tracks and work the graveyard shift at the *Everything Tel Aviv* archives. And believe me, that's exactly what he's worth—a shitty gig."

Elish said nothing.

Levitan shot up to his feet, angry. "That loser. Blasé's success wasn't enough for him. He wanted to be involved with everything to do with Dalia. He drove her crazy. Every other day he called to tell her about his problems with Nicole or some other girl he picked up at a bar. Why was it Dalia's business who he fucked? They were just making music together."

"Did Dalia say it was none of her business?" Elish asked. He was on a roll. Levitan had dropped all his defenses.

"No, of course she didn't. If Dalia thought so, she would have told him to his face. She thought Rami was like a child. She felt sorry for him. 'He's not prepared for adult life.'" Levitan went up an octave, squeaking in what was supposed to be an imitation of Dalia. "Not prepared, my ass. But Dalia was no phony. I could say a lot of bad stuff about her, but not that."

"What could you say?"

"That she was a cheating bitch." Rami's comment had really unhinged Levitan, and he was losing control. "Everyone always says—even me—what a wonderful girl Dalia was, but between you and me, she was a cheating bitch."

"You say she wasn't a phony, so I'm assuming she was up-front with you about it."

"I wish she'd hidden more from me." He paused, considering his words, but the fury Elish had ignited inside of him was too great for him to keep quiet. "She had another guy." He paused again, his tone changing. "She didn't want to tell me who he was. She was always saying that people can't just make do with one relationship, that it's a cultural lie, something like that, but there's always only one relationship where you feel at home, and that's what she had with me. She said that was the closest I could be to her."

"Were you in love with her?"

"What do you think? You think I'd have compromised like that otherwise? There's a ton of hotties waiting in line for me to just shoot them a smile."

Elish was amused. Even when he was mad, Levitan maintained his clichés. "So how did you two meet?"

"I saw her at the Logos after our show. I jokingly asked her what she thought about our set, and she said we needed some work, and that if I invited her to rehearsal, she'd explain how, exactly. So I did, and by the time rehearsal was over it was clear to me she was something else, not like all those girls who hang around you so they can see their names in gossip columns."

"I understand. Why don't we take a little break? Have some water, roll yourself a joint," said Elish. Self-pity did not become Levitan, washing over his image, making it glare. Why? He walked over to the bookcase and quickly scanned the row of books. It was the usual teenage crap: *The Alchemist*, the second Harry Potter, *The Catcher in the Rye*, *Zen and the Art of Motorcycle Maintenance*, *The Monk Who Sold His Ferrari*, *Jonathan Livingston Seagull*, *The Little Prince*, *Steppenwolf*. Two thick volumes at the end of the row caught his eye: the Zohar books, both parts. Kabbalah. He pulled them out and turned toward Levitan. "Interesting," he said, waving the books.

"Uh-huh," said Levitan. "Whoever wrote the Zohar must have had a close acquaintance with Dr. Hofmann." He laughed, probably repeating a joke someone once told him that he thought was witty. "I've been recording passages from it and composing electronic music over them."

"Awesome," Elish said drily.

"Amazing," Levitan confirmed. "Malkieli thinks it's going to be the next big thing."

"Experience has taught me to trust Malkieli's instincts. How did you come up with the idea?"

"Dalia gave me those books as a gift and they seemed too heavy, but after what happened I started reading them. She was into Kabbalah, big time. I got this tattoo because of her." He turned his back toward Elish. On his right shoulder blade was a broken, twisting line creating a circle full of cogs and bends. "Dalia called it a rune. Had a book full of those signs."

"She was interested in the occult?"

"In what?"

"The knowledge of the hidden."

"Didn't I just say she was into that stuff, big time?"

"That's surprising," said Elish, though he wasn't surprised at all. A cloud of guesswork shaded his brain. "When did it start?"

"I don't know. Before I met her."

"Did her parents know?"

"No." Levitan plopped down on a beanbag. "They were afraid she'd become a junkie, not just a weirdo. Because of her mother's brother. Her mother once searched Dalia's bag and found some pot. Don't ask. She was yelling like crazy. Such a mess."

"I won't ask." Elish also sank his body into a beanbag. "Did you know the songs on the demo Malkieli got?"

"No. When we were living together at her place she wasn't making any music. She must have written those songs the month we broke up. It came as a surprise to me too."

"Did anyone know about them beforehand?"

"How should I know? All I know is that Malkieli called me two days before what happened and told me that Dalia told her she'd written twenty new songs. You have no idea how badly Malkieli wanted those songs from the moment she heard about them. She knew, without even hearing them, that they were worth a fortune."

"And what did you think when you heard that?"

"Only that if anyone else said they'd written twenty songs in a month I would have thought they were lying. But Dalia didn't lie, it wasn't her style."

"And yet, she went out with you and was seeing someone else at the same time. Doesn't that count as lying?"

Elish realized too late that he'd taken it too far. Levitan had time to pull himself together. He stood up threateningly, turned off the recorder, and before Elish could protest he opened it and pulled out the tape. "What do you think you're doing, huh?" he yelled. "Did you come here to talk about Dalia or to dig up dirt?" He slammed the tape against the floor, then stepped on it. "Get out of here, you asshole."

Elish got up with a smile. He brushed off his pants slowly, taking a long look at the shattered tape. It was brand-new, and he remembered their conversation perfectly. "So I take it this interview is over," he said.

"Go on, get out of here." Levitan pointed at the door, and when Elish walked out he shouted after him into the stairwell. "Ben Zaken, go fuck yourself. You were always a dipshit and you'll always be a dipshit."

8

All cities are sinking, but Tel Aviv will last forever. What a crime against humanity it would be if Tel Aviv ceased to exist, thought Elish, possessed, as he walked up Allenby Street. You could already taste the American attack on Iraq in the air. The minister of defense kept repeating that he was sleeping soundly at night, free from concerns—empty remarks that helped no one, only encouraging those long conversations about everybody's plans to escape the city as soon as the first missiles hit. This time, unlike the last Gulf War, there was no question of civil loyalty. Fleeing Tel Aviv was the preferred solution. Good, more of this city for me, he thought. In those moments, his body was an echo of the urban drama, and the crack in his arm its prophecy of ruin, the fear running through it.

It was almost the middle of the month, and he looked up at the clean, gestating moon. It was like looking into the sun but without burning his eyes, without the desire to go blind, which had awoken in him at age ten, when he started fifth grade, expressionless and staring, and took a seat, half-listening to the cheerful voice of the substitute teacher. Their regular teacher was on maternity leave, and the new teacher, young and excited, knew nothing about Elish's story, which must have been whispered from one student to the next behind his back. They were stuck in the middle of Deuteronomy, detailing decrees and prohibitions ad nauseam. The teacher said, "About the decree of respecting one's parents, the Bible says 'so that you may live long in the land.' Who knows what other decree that appears in Deuteronomy promises a similar reward?"

One of the smartass kids, the son of the rabbi of the local synagogue, who dreamed of becoming a cantor, called out, without raising his hand, "Sending the nest. If you see a bird sitting on eggs, you can take the baby birds, but you have to chase the mother bird away first."

"The sending of the nest," the teacher corrected, but Elish didn't hear her, because the cry hiding in the bottom of his throat stood him on his feet and shattered into the air of the classroom. The teacher stared, stunned, for a moment, then got ahold of herself and sent him to the principal's office. Rather than go, Elish went out into the schoolyard and looked up into the sun. The holidays were behind him and the end of Tishrei still scorched. He looked directly into the ball of fire without blinking. That evening, when he got home, he had his first fever attack.

He lowered his eyes back onto Allenby Street, where he'd been standing, frozen, for several minutes. The city had quickly cleaned off the rain, but not the smell of ozone and asphalt. The night was cold. Shards of the ancient grace of Allenby Street peeked from the ficus trees and their mush of fruit, turning the sidewalk slippery, from the synagogue that overpowered the fluorescent windows of sex shops and bookstores, from the flickering of traffic lights approaching Rothschild Boulevard. He would have spread his arms, letting the breeze comb through his fingers, but the pain in his left arm, dull but present, reawakened with every effort. Rami had accepted his invitation with suspicious speed, and had chosen an odd hour, 9:30 at night, when the Abraxas was still deserted, save for three servers, two idle bartenders, and one bored security guard, as if he predicted that Elish was more interested in a conversation than a drinking companion.

He sat down at the table near the door, scanning Lilienblum

Street, its banks cleared of their dwellers and its glowing darkness swiftly growing, a shortage of parking spaces already commenced. Rami arrived late, after Elish had already downed one glass of arak. "I see we're starting with anise," he remarked, shaking Elish's hand, and told the server who'd hurried over, "Pernod, please." Then he turned back to Elish: "Say, is it just me, or is this city fucking emptying out in honor of the attack in Iraq?"

"Somehow, you seem pleased."

"Because I'm convinced we're going to get something out of it."

"Huh?"

"You know, we'll be able to really slam into the Palestinians without a peep from all those European hypocrites."

"Again, I have to ask: huh? You've gone political now? What's up with you?"

"Nothing. I was just thinking about it the whole way over. The previous Gulf War, with all that Scud missile fun and the bad jokes on TV—there was still something good about it, right? It ended the First Intifada."

"And you think history is going to repeat itself?"

"Why not? With some changes, because I don't think I'll be able to tolerate that Channel 1 humor this time. I've had enough of these suicide bombings, and this is a fucking great opportunity for the IDF to act without international pressure."

"Don't be naïve. Do you really believe military action can annihilate terrorist infrastructure? The source of Palestinian terrorism isn't the availability of ammunition and explosives. It's first and foremost a social and psychological matter." Elish couldn't believe he was getting dragged into this pointless argument.

"Fuck that. A few assassinations and the leaders of Hamas and the Islamic Jihad and the Izz ad-Din al-cocksuckers will start shaking in their boots. Just wait and see how quiet things are going to get."

"What are you talking about, Rami? It won't be quiet here, no matter how many leaders you take out from their side or ours, which, by the way, is the only good thing that could come from an all-out war between our top government and theirs. For the time being, neither side has a real interest in ending this conflict."

"That's fucking nonsense."

"Think about it. This struggle is what allows both sides to define themselves. How can you even talk about Israeli identity without bringing up the feeling of persecution experienced by the Jewish majority in Israel, without bullshitting about our right to be here or the existential threat from the Arab countries and the residents of the territories? Huh? And what even is the Palestinian nation? Could there be one without IDF occupation and oppression? What kind of national tradition do the Palestinians have outside of Israeli occupation?"

"You leftists always have to make everything complicated."

"So besides this political philosophizing, how are you doing?" Elish asked. This tiring argument was identical to the one he'd had with Bobby dozens of times before.

"Hanging in there," Rami grumbled. "So you're doing this article after all. I'm glad someone on the inside is working on it, because that *Yediot* supplement they dedicated to Dalia after the murder was moronic."

Elish nodded. The warmth from his final sip of arak quickly dissipated in his throat. "I'm not writing it yet. I'm gathering materials. Normally I record my meetings. I hope you don't mind, even though this is more of a social call."

"No problem," said Rami. "Who have you spoken to so far?"

"I met with her parents, Malkieli, and Lior Levitan." Elish had trouble reading Rami's expression in the low lights and couldn't tell which name had left the biggest impression on him. But there was no need for that. A few seconds later, Rami said, "Malkieli is cooperating? After Dalia was murdered she wouldn't let any of her artists comment on it."

"Maybe after throwing that memorial concert she feels like she's ensured her ownership of Dalia's legacy. Anyway, the reasons aren't important. Not as much as the fact that she's willingly cooperating."

"Bitch," muttered Rami.

"Look, I know from what you told me at the concert that Malkieli tried to swindle you, and I'd like to clarify a few points I thought about later. By the way, she's denying it. She claims it was a temporary misunderstanding and that you've already squared everything away."

Rami chuckled and sipped his Pernod. "What did you expect, for her to tell you on record that she cheated her artists?"

"It was off the record. I'm guessing it's a question of perspective."

"Perspective my ass," Rami said decisively. "She cheated us, and I don't mind if you record me saying that. I already told you: we got a tenth of the revenue from our first album. You dig? A fucking tenth. And it wasn't innocent. In the publishing clause of her contract, she made sure to take care of her percentage."

"I don't understand. You could have hired a lawyer to check that the contract was legit."

"After we realized she was stealing from us we went to see a real shark, and he said there was nothing we could do about the first album. But he found a loophole: we were obligated to give Malkieli the demos for our next albums, but if she turned them down, we would be released from the contract. He suggested we give her a demo that was just white noise, get it? The contract didn't specify that the demo had to include songs. Malkieli lost her shit. She yelled at us that she was going to lawyer up, but Dalia was so cool. She told Malkieli that if she took us to court, Dalia would give a newspaper interview and tell all. We might lose the suit, but Malkieli would be screwed, big time. No artist would even talk to her again." Rami fell silent.

"And?"

"And Malkieli called us two days later and offered us a new contract. She gave up her royalties, but we had to commit to give her demos for the next two albums that had songs with at least one verse in them, and then they would stand the test of a lawyer who specializes in this stuff—what did our lawyer call it? Let me think. Oh yeah, the new songs would have to be clear of any concern for not fulfilling our obligation—and then she would have the right of refusal. It was a good compromise for both sides, so we continued working with her. Our second album made a lot more noise, and then Dalia announced that she was quitting."

Elish remembered the debut concert of their second album very well. The excitement in the audience, the silhouettes of ticket scalpers, whose numbers were doubled or tripled by the limited seating in the large concert hall in southern Tel Aviv. The stage was empty. For fifteen minutes the sound system emanated a captivating, monotonous instrumental segment. Dalia and Rami walked out onstage, and Dalia said, "Good evening. Before we start, I want to let you all know that this is going to be Blasé's final show."

The audience, which had been rustling from the moment the musicians had set foot onstage, fell silent. Elish thought that even Rami looked stunned.

"I didn't get a chance to ask you before—were you surprised by Dalia's decision to quit?"

"Surprised? I wanted to kill her. When Dalia wanted to be secretive she'd turn as quiet as a mouse. Then she'd tell me about something she did, which sounded made-up, a lie. But Dalia didn't lie. She would disappear for like three days, and when she came back and I'd ask her where she'd run off to, she'd say something like, 'I read all of Shakespeare.' When she was in a good mood, which wasn't often, we could joke about that kind of thing for hours. We would say that one day I'd ask her where she'd been and she'd say, 'Oh, I just got back from a trip to Mars,' or, 'Nothing much, I was just mapping the human genome.'"

So close, thought Elish, so far. His voice filled with a yearning he hadn't noticed in time, hadn't bridled in advance, he said, "Dalia was the original artist par excellence. Everything she touched was only hers."

"You sound like you were in love with her or something," Rami said sharply.

Elish made a face. "I can't stop thinking about her death and how unfair it was. Myths lie to us just when we need them the most. It isn't right. Music is supposed to lead us toward life, not death. Not this kind of death. Not like this."

"When you find the number for God's complaint line, let me know," said Rami. "Dalia changed my life. Ezra Buhbut got what he deserved, but I still want to scream. So when you find that number, let me make the first call."

"Ezra Buhbut got more than he deserved. I don't believe he murdered Dalia." Elish's tone was angry. What had angered him about Rami's words? His appropriation of Dalia's death? The injustice Elish believed Buhbut had suffered?

"And why don't you believe it, if I may ask?"

"Because I met with Dalia's mother yesterday and she convinced me, that's why."

"I know she doesn't believe it. In any other case, her argument would have been published in newspapers and the TV would show her image, crying with pain. Don't think I don't know how these things work. But in this case, everyone wanted to see Ezra Buhbut punished, so nobody listened. She told me what she felt when I called to check on her. Esther's a good soul. She isn't built for this world. I saw her breaking. You know how much she loved Dalia? I would have done anything to spare her this pain. More than I want Dalia back for my sake, I want her back for Esther's sake. So don't get me wrong when I say Esther isn't ready yet to accept the fact that Buhbut murdered her daughter. If they continued searching for the murderer, it would have kept Dalia alive for a little longer."

"Isn't it usually the other way around?"

"No one talks about Dalia as flesh and blood anymore. They've turned her into a goddess, which is less than human. Dalia wasn't perfect. She had her bad qualities. I, and her mother, want to remember her the way she was. We want to remember the . . ." Rami lingered, searching for the right word. Elish knew what he was trying to say, but went against his habit and let Rami find his own phrasing. ". . . Flaws. That memory of the flaws is what keeps other people alive."

Elish took a close look at him. A momentary anxiety climbed up his throat. I have to watch what I say to who. His left arm was a reminder. Somehow, he got the sense that Rami was smarter than he'd remembered. He knew where this thought was leading. The holes in Dalia's temples, the rune on Levitan's shoulder blade, that passage from Menuhin's book, all floated before his eyes. No, that's preposterous. That kind of thing doesn't happen in real life. Involuntarily, he waved his hand in derision.

"What? You think I'm wrong?" said Rami.

"No, I think you're absolutely right. It's just that one of the obvious conclusions from what you just said seems baseless. But forget about that. I have other reasons to believe that Buhbut didn't murder Dalia."

"Don't tell me your article is going to be a case for reopening her murder investigation."

"Nothing of the sort. At any rate, this article will only come out a few months from now, so I have some time to ponder the ramifications of all the things I'm hearing."

"Okay," said Rami, sounding utterly unconvinced. His glass was empty, and he ordered an arak. "Abraxas is the best spot I know in Tel Aviv, but still, the bars in this city are so overpriced. I could get a bottle of this arak for ten shekels at any kiosk."

Elish didn't like this new turn in the conversation. Flatly, he said, "You should get your arak with mineral water. They've started adding captive trout urine to the tap water in Israel. It makes you racist."

Rami's eyes were following the server. A few seconds later, Elish added, "You said that Dalia was secretive about certain aspects of her life. Is that why she didn't want to be interviewed?"

"No. When our first single came out she gave an interview to a local paper, and that convinced her she should avoid the media. She told me she got really bummed out by the piece. 'We need to adopt an attitude of mystery.' It matched her personality—never giving interviews, never explaining our name. There were lots of theories about our name, by the way. I don't know if you were following that. Someone once wrote that the name of our band, just like our music and lyrics, was an 'uncompromising metaphor for inner exile.' Dalia said she imagined he meant it as a compliment, but that there was nothing she respected less than the sense of inner exile. 'People have put so much emphasis on their sense of inner exile as the most crucial component of their identities,' she said, 'that they've forgotten that humans have to fight to feel like they belong.' You know, it's strange. I seem to remember all of Dalia's observations by heart, though I had no idea what she was talking about at the time. Only now that she's gone am I beginning to understand."

"So the secrecy issue was deeper? From what I recall, at the concert you insinuated that Dalia had cheated on Lior Levitan. I talked to him and he confirmed it. But he didn't know who she was having the affair with."

"Oh." Rami drained his glass and ordered another arak. "She had someone before Lior. She wouldn't tell me who. I had my reasons for suspecting that they were still seeing each other even after she and Lior started dating. But after I tried questioning her about who it was once and she responded aggressively, I let it go. I assume if I'd asked she would have told me she was still seeing him, but I always felt that our relationship wasn't symmetrical, that it was more important to me to share with her than it was important to her to share with me, and I had no problem with that."

Why was Rami playing along so easily? Was he that eager to talk about Dalia? Was he missing her so badly? Or was the anise doing its silent, soporific work? "What were your reasons?"

"First, Lior Levitan wasn't her type, to say the least. I think the only reason she was able to stand him at all was because he loved her so much, and his love was like an anchor. Second, the sharpest turns in her mood, her self-esteem, continued even after she supposedly broke up with this Mr. X. Look, she didn't have a lot of romance in her life. I think this anonymous guy was her first meaningful relationship. Also, I think he was married, and a good deal older than her."

"Why's that?"

"I don't have real proof, just a hunch, based on things she said or looks she gave me. I think she was attracted to older men. I'm not the only one who thinks so. Nicole once told her–you've met Nicole, right? The woman has no shame or inhibitions–she told Dalia one time, when they were talking about Hollywood actors, 'I think you have daddy issues.'"

Elish, who had the phrasing on the tip of his tongue, chose instead to ask, "And what did Dalia say?"

"She said, 'You're just buying into the false superstructure of the secular West, which has abandoned belief in God, faith, and the stars, replacing it with obedience to smaller and weaker forces, such as complexes and personality types. The result in both cases is the same: humans become numb slaves. But the way there? Who would want to give up the open, shimmering road in favor of airless paths through a dark forest?' I think Dalia was the only person in the world who could get Nicole to shut her trap."

HAVE I BEEN WRONG ALL THESE YEARS? ELISH ASKED HIMSELF up on the roof of his home, in the clean air. It wasn't long before time would make its refined plummet into November. His head was clear, refusing sleep. How could there not be a single person in the world with whom I can discuss the Dalia Shushan case? Eliya can be a wonderful conversationalist, but she wouldn't understand the emotional layers involved in the facts. She would treat the facts like pieces in a complicated yet solvable puzzle–an intellectual challenge, nothing more. But my heart is telling me a different story. The key to this mystery is different, more than an appropriate arrangement of facts. The stain of Dalia's death seems to be spreading, infecting more and more people that have passed through her life. How did Nicole get in there? When he challenged Rami with Malkieli's claim that Rami had, in fact, been asked to perform at the Barbie memorial concert and had turned it down, as opposed to what he'd reported on the night of the show, Rami simply said, "Somebody's lying. All I got was a call from Nicole, who told me, with a kind of obnoxious joy, that she was planning a memorial for Dalia that I wasn't supposed to take part in, but that her contract obligated her to inform me of every use of Blasé songs."

He had to talk to Nicole. He had to start getting things in order. But did he have to do it on his own?

The dwindling moon, the heart of October, was a weak note in the tune that sang and swept across his face from the night sky, and the heavenly bodies took advantage of the low light and grew like students chasing the teacher out of the classroom with their ruckus. After that age-ten summer in Ashkelon, he'd thought he heard something else in that growl on moonless nights–the roaring of engines. In the mornings that followed he prepared for invasion, recognizing in the scarves of insects carried by scorching late August the hidden tapping devices, the satanic mechanisms of cognitive control, the early stages of the conspiracy. What had he just been thinking about? His eyes never left the perforated spaces of darkness above him. Oh, yes, the open, shimmering road as opposed to airless paths through a dark forest. What did he prefer, if the results were the same? If, ultimately, he was alone? Yes, fate would have made his life much simpler, as would a merciless diagnosis of his personality, but what about those who turn down both options of walking through the world and choose a third way? Is there a road in which humans do not become numb slaves? Had he found this road? Yehuda Menuhin had found that road, as well as his death. It was obvious to Elish, though he had no concrete evidence that it had not been a straightforward suicide, but Menuhin's path was miserable, the way of elimination. There was passion there, but no actuality. What was Dalia's road?

I remember her. My grief is meant to exacerbate, but instead it's weakening. As long as the memory was merely a meek, trembling flame flickering against the walls of consciousness, the sorrow was greater, but now it's exposed, lying before me, nothing but a rip that will not be mended by the tapestry of years. A rip among the thousands of flaws and cuts, numbered as many as the stars in the sky. He almost smiled–he hadn't prayed in nearly twenty years, but his tongue was still evoking the words. No, he pushed away the thought that attempted to divert him. I can't ignore it any longer: I become indifferent as soon as I learn the magnitude of the pain. Does this mean I'm incapable of love?

He had never minded being alone before. He told anyone who asked, straight up: I choose to be alone, I don't need company. But if this meant an inability to love, what then? No, he insisted, I won't accept that. I do love. Yaffa's face, Tahel's, Zehava's, all floated before him. But it's so easy to love the ones you'd been trained to love, those you can't help but love. Esther said Dalia had cried for three days. Over him? There was a small chance that was true, while all he'd done was run a wet wipe over his memory, burning with fever and recalling the sea. "The sea. There's another sore travail for you to be exercised therewith, Elish Ben Zaken," he said out loud. "Go to sleep, Elish, the night is leading you down its evil paths."

9

Time charged at Elish like a flamethrower, and Elish didn't notice. When his flesh was singed and roasted, he decided to fight back. He sat on the stoop of the HMO clinic that had been abandoned for a year, golden with summer and sweat, eleven years old, or just one. The clinic yard was strewn with weeds, wild growths, one acacia yellowing with force, hibiscus flowers as red as lipstick, as white as a bleached shirt, attracting bees. Elish was surrounded by their buzzing when he climbed over the locked gate and crossed the yard gently, careful not to interrupt ruin in its labor.

"So what's up, Elish?" he said into the air, straining to hear the answer. "Did something specific happen, some disaster or cause for festivity?" He listened in again. He thought he heard a whisper, a rustle, perhaps just the assimilation of light into foliage. At any rate, he could not hear the answer, if one had been given. "So I'll speak to you the day after tomorrow," he said, "when I'm here and you're on the other side."

The next day, he returned to the abandoned yard. Little had changed: thorns and brambles, little purple flowers he hadn't noticed the previous day. His exposed leg was scratched in the climb. He stood before the stairs and tried to see. Nothing appeared. He said, "Everything's fine, except for the scratch on my leg."

Perhaps a stray cloud. He thought he spotted a fraction of movement on the steps, a hint of action. He paused for a moment, then said, "No, nothing happened, no disaster or cause for festivity, unless you count the scratch." Then he fell silent again, straining his eyes. "Yes, I'll talk to you the day after tomorrow, when I'm on the same side again."

For two weeks he had these conversations with himself, switching sides each day. He assumed that was the right way, that if he continued to ask himself and then answer on the other side of the day, the boundaries of time would thin out, and he'd be able to see and hear the Elish of yesterday, the Elish of tomorrow, until he returned whole, able to move freely between past and future, all over the present, master of his own destiny.

WHAT A SHAME, ELISH THOUGHT WITH FRUSTRATION, THAT HE hadn't improved his technique to challenge the boundaries of time. What a shame he'd deserted the effort when it was newly born. At the very least, he could have asked last week's Elish not to waste hours on fruitless conversations, and instead corner Nicole for a longer conversation on the night of the concert, since the next day–as Malkieli Productions had informed him that morning–she'd left for a three-month-long tour of India. Nicole was the one who'd given Malkieli the made-up message from Elish, his request for an invitation to Dalia's memorial concert. Why would Nicole need to get him there? She was also the main channel of communication between Malkieli and Rami, and–unless one of them had lied–had been the one in charge of torpedoing Rami's participation in the concert. Who was Nicole, anyway?

Seek out the motivation, uncover the power structure. Dalia Shushan had a secret, older lover, possibly married. Gideon Menuhin was having a forbidden affair he wished to keep under wraps. Yehuda Menuhin was most likely extorting Ora Anatot, and then was either murdered or forced to commit suicide. Levana Hacham wanted to take revenge against the man who got her fired and forced her and her husband to sell their home. Manny Lahav lied and tried to deceive him. Malkieli wanted

Dalia's songs, which were written in the last month of her life, and which no one had heard before she died. Dalia was on the outs with Malkieli, and must have fought with Rami Amzaleg, her band partner, the night before she died, and sent her demo, with the word "Menuhin" on it, to Malkieli the same day. Dalia cheated on Lior Levitan, her partner. Someone murdered Dalia and placed her dead body in a position crying out to be deeply investigated and interpreted, but the case was quickly closed. Dalia was murdered on the Ninth of Av, Yehuda Menuhin died the day after Yom Kippur, one man of shadows tried to drag Elish into the heart of the labyrinth, another used violence to prevent him from entering the labyrinth, and Elish Ben Zaken was incapable of love. That was all he knew so far.

On the third floor of the Azrieli Mall, leaning over the railing, Elish tried to leave this storm of facts outside the clear expanses of his thinking. He had a few conjectures, but he was still missing the key fact, whose pins would force all the others to lock into place and stop moving so fast, so many revolutions per minute, like the flow of people riding the escalators between the bottom two floors, rustling between glass and metal, flowing between stores, even though it was the middle of a workday, no excitement on the horizon—unless you counted the clouds of war and a rain as light as a guess.

He was waiting for Ronnit, Dalia's cousin, who was coming on the train from Beersheba especially to meet him. The previous night, when they spoke on the phone, she sounded eager to meet, and cleared her morning. Elish wondered what she was hoping to accomplish. She hadn't spoken with Dalia, she told him, since they'd gotten into a fight and she'd moved out. And yes, her mother had told her that Dalia had rented the apartment they'd shared a few days after Ronnit moved out. "I can't quite explain it," she said over the phone, almost straining to prove she'd known Dalia, "but that's so like her."

Ronnit had given him an accurate description of herself, and he recognized her right away as she rose toward him on the escalator: tall, skinny, hair gathered into a tight braid, large brown eyes, black dress, a pretty woman—not just pretty, but strikingly pretty—smiling at him, perhaps out of a habit she'd acquired after a decade of male ogling, or perhaps she'd noticed his widening expression as recognition and deduced that he was waiting for her. Elish offered his hand awkwardly, she offered her hand in return, and he held it for a moment longer than necessary. "Shall we sit?"

Ronnit smiled her agreement. "Do you smoke?" she asked. "I know it's rude, but I'd love it if we can sit in a nonsmoking zone. One person smoking is not a problem, but ever since that law was passed against smoking in public spaces, the designated smoking areas have sort of become, how should I put it . . ." She paused and looked at him, trying to discern whether she was crossing a line, and Elish guessed the rest of her sentence and said it for her: "A depleted version of a gas chamber."

Ronnit nodded. "With all this smoke, I don't understand how people are still panicking about chemical warfare. There was a piece in the paper today about how 1.5 million of the renewed gas masks aren't even properly functional. Besides, I don't know if you've noticed, but smokers have a tendency of focusing their entire body language on the tip of the cigarette. It's disturbing."

"What's disturbing? The exposed way in which they signal to the world with their cigarette? Quick, short inhalations when they're nervous, slower ones when they're desperate, or the flattening of body language into a general series of signals devoid of nuances?"

"Hell of a phrasing," said Ronnit, placing her bag on the chair to her left, making Elish sit across from her. "Both."

"You sound like an ex-smoker."

"We recognize each other anywhere." Again that smile. What was so charming about it? Elish wondered. She was left-handed. The muscles on the left half of her face were more adept at facial expressions. That half was charged with a greater sense of liveliness with that smile, but it was subtle. The difference wasn't apparent to the naked eye, not snooping or investigating, but Elish wanted an explanation. This is the essence of beauty, he thought—the temporary injustice, light and shadow unable to share the world equally. One of them must tip the scales for a moment for beauty to appear.

"In America, this is the moment when someone would say, 'a penny for your thoughts.' That's probably the most useful phrase I learned there."

"My thoughts have been getting the better of me lately. You've been to America?"

"Sounds like you haven't traveled much. Lots of Israelis have been to America."

"I don't like going abroad," said Elish, his voice indifferent, toneless. "I left the country once, for France, and it felt as if the entire flight was a scam. Like I hadn't actually traveled to another country, the plane was just standing in midair while a team of professionals disassembled the Israeli landscape and replaced it with a French scene. I can even expand my experience into theory. That's always the case. It's easy to install Europe, so the flight is only four, five hours long. The United States and Southeast Asia are more complicated. Turkey's so close because there's really no work to be done there. You just throw all the spare parts that are piled up in storage into the Israeli landscape."

Ronnit laughed, and Elish wrinkled his forehead quizzically. She was prettier. Beaming. "What a strange sense of humor. I have to remember that joke, my boyfriend is crazy about nonsense."

"So what did you do in the U.S.?"

"I was studying. After military service I went there to get a biology degree. But I quit. Then I came back to Israel and enrolled in med school in Beersheba."

"Why biology?"

"No real reason. Some childhood belief that there's something out there you could truly call 'the secret of life.'"

"Did it not reveal itself to you, or did you conclude it didn't exist?"

"What difference does that make to me? Either way, I still have to live in this world without it, don't I?" Her eyes were filled with a distance; the smile was gone. To maintain beauty, Elish thought, balance has to be restored. What a dull dynamic. But the earth hath he given to the children of men, that is . . .

"You're hovering again," said Ronnit. "I miss Dalia."

Elish pulled out his tape recorder with a gesture and a statement that had nearly become ritualistic. "I record all my conversations. I hope you don't mind." When she nodded he spoke into the recorder: "Ronnit Abraham, conversation number one." Then, to Ronnit, a line that by this point had begun to amuse him: "Tell me about Dalia."

"Dalia was my best friend when we were kids. We're cousins. Our mothers are sisters. But I don't think that makes anything obligatory for children. We're the same age. Were. Dalia was born two months after me. Up until we turned eight we spent every free moment together. Her mother didn't work. My mother was an elementary school teacher. So when we were little we would hang out at her place, and when we got a little older and were allowed to spend time alone, unattended, we would go to my house, which was empty. My little brother was born in Beersheba when I was nine years old. Dalia had no brothers or sisters. So back then we were both only children. We often imagined we were alone in the world. When we were seven we watched—you remember that *Alice in Wonderland* cartoon? The Japanese one?"

Elish shook his head.

Ronnit carried on. "Anyway, there was one episode where Alice stepped through the looking glass in one place and stepped out in a different place. It was exciting, all the mirrors had become doors and secret portals. We would dream we stepped through the looking glass in one of our homes and into a Sderot that looked exactly like ours but was completely empty. Dalia would say, 'Now let's step into the bathroom mirror and come out through the mirror in the grocery store and eat all the chocolates.' And I would say, 'And they're magic chocolates, the kind that don't give you a stomachache no matter how many you eat.'" Ronnit smiled, wrapping her hands around her herbal tea. "See? I was concerned about my health even then. Dalia was a tough kid. She never let go of anything, never held back. One time she told me, 'I wish we could actually step into the mirror in your house and come out through the mirror at the Romanian's son's place at night, then pull his hair till he cries, and run away.' The Romanian's son was the kid on my block who used to call us two fat-asses. I may have been concerned about my health, but I didn't pay much mind to my figure." She smiled again.

She's aware of her power, Elish thought.

"As a child, she was full of joy and her imagination was incredibly vivid. For example, she made up a way of tying chrysanthemums by the stems to make a necklace or a ball. And all the games she improvised–I remember them all. I also remember I was always jealous of her." Then she added, "And I did an awful thing."

Elish said nothing. This was Ronnit's moment. The moment for which she'd boarded a train to Tel Aviv. She'd come to beg forgiveness, he thought, just like me, just like everyone I know.

"When I was eight my father was appointed principal of a high school in Beersheba. We moved there and I lost touch with Dalia. Our moms were the only ones who still spoke. Occasionally my mother let me know what was going on in Dalia's life, so I followed her issues from afar. She stopped speaking for whole days, would break into tears for no apparent reason. She cut off contact with all her childhood friends. Her mother had no idea what was happening to her. She would talk to my mother, who would reassure her, telling her it's just an age thing, the body changing, the hormones raging, and that some girls get it worse than others, you know, that some girls have searing pain when they get their periods, that the first period is a nightmare, that some girls bleed a ton. You must have heard this a million times, but you guys have such an easier time with your bodies.

"I would listen to Dalia's problems from a distance and ignore them. But that wasn't the awful thing. When we were fourteen, I ran into her on a field trip to the Museum of the Jewish People. Actually, she ran into me. I was with friends from my class out front, and there was a guide walking through the quad, mumbling to himself, and it made us laugh—but you know how every little thing makes fourteen-year-olds laugh—and suddenly, while we were laughing, Dalia appeared in front of me, and at that moment I thought, What a cow she'd become, I hope she doesn't start talking to me. But she just stood there, staring at me, so I said, 'Dalia, you haven't changed a bit.' And I expected her to leave. In elementary school in Beersheba I was always an outcast, but suddenly, in the course of a single summer before I started junior high, I became popular, really popular, and I felt I'd earned the right to tyrannize anyone who was below my new status. But Dalia joined our group without asking permission. She felt clingy to me, and my friends thought so too, and all day long we made nasty comments, not even witty ones, as if by chance, about fat girls, and people from Sderot, and leechy girls from our class, and about things Dalia said. I don't know what got into her that day. Maybe she'd just changed. The Dalia I knew would have attacked us with her toxic tongue or humiliated us with her knowledge, or found some other quiet way of getting back at us—something so sophisticated that it would have taken us a year to figure out it was her all along. But the new Dalia that joined us that day quietly took all the insults we shot at her, and because she spent the rest of the day with us and hadn't noticed the time, she missed her ride back to Sderot and I had to lend her bus fare."

She looked at him apologetically. He wanted to say, First World Problems, people carry heavier burdens than that, but instead he said nothing, because her confession was not yet over.

"I think only when I turned eighteen did I realize what a horrible, condescending girl I'd been. That day at the museum never left me. I was so glad when I overheard Esther asking my mother to get me to let Dalia stay with me. I was an officer in the Intelligence Corps, serving at the Kiryah. My parents had rented a place in Tel Aviv for me. It was my chance to make amends. It took Dalia a long time to call me, and in the meantime I made elaborate plans about how I was going to introduce her to the city, how we would go out on the town, how she would forgive me. Yeah, right, what an illusion. As if I was rescuing the country girl from her naivete.

"When Dalia finally came she was depressed. I was all over her, inviting her out to movies or pubs or shows, but she always turned me down politely. I tried to find out without asking her outright if she was mad. It seemed like everything I said infuriated her. She asked, for example, how we should split the water and electric bills, and I told her fifty-fifty. That answer angered her. She asked if we should get someone to fix the buzzer and the front door, and I told her the building committee had received a price that was very high and that the other tenants wouldn't pay. She lost her mind. I assumed that growing tension had to find a way out somehow, so when things exploded between us after two weeks of living together, it was inevitable, but I regret that too. The reason was silly, but you know how long-term hatred and big anger are channeled into forgettable and mundane events like dishes left in the sink or someone forgetting to buy milk or an open tampon wrapper that someone accidentally leaves on the toilet tank. You know, a world war over nonsense. Have you spoken to Eran Shitrit as part of your research?"

"Eran Shitrit?" Elish marveled. "The neighbor who reported Ezra Buhbut? He lived there back then?"

"Yeah, he owns an apartment in the building, that pervert."

"Pervert?"

"He tried to watch me. Or at least I'm convinced he did. There was a French window in the apartment, facing the balcony and the yard. Even though the apartment was fairly high up, if you stood at the far corner of the yard, you could see inside it. Eran had a small dog, a cocker spaniel, and somehow, during my early days living there, whenever I looked out the window I saw him walking his dog through the yard and glancing toward my window. So I bought a thick curtain, and when Dalia moved in I warned her not to walk around undressed if the curtain wasn't closed. One day I was in my bedroom and I heard screaming. Dalia was at the window in a bra and underwear, and the curtain was open. Eran was watching her from the yard while his dog was peeing or pooping, I don't know. I slammed my hand against the glass and Eran walked away, indifferent, as if nothing had happened. I closed the curtain and Dalia yelled at me. It turned out she'd called out to me from the bathroom, asking if the curtain was closed, and she thought I'd said yes. I hadn't even heard her, but she wouldn't let me explain myself. All the resentment she'd gathered in the two weeks we lived together and in who knows how many years before that came out. The poison I knew was inside of her came out. She still knew how to be cruel when she wanted to, believe me. She interpreted all my efforts as proof of my condescension and my supposed ridicule. She said, 'You loser, I feel sorry for you. Do you really think your education and your officer training can save you from who you are? You're going to spend your entire life chasing after who you want to be, and only realize how pathetic you'd been thirty years too late.' Sometimes I think she was right, but that's none of your business and irrelevant to your article. I didn't stay quiet either, I told her everything I thought about her, that she was ungrateful and vindictive. Now I wish I'd just said, 'Dalia, what are you talking about? I've been missing you this entire time.'"

Ronnit looked at him, awaiting understanding or approval. Elish said nothing. She rummaged through her purse and pulled out her wallet. Elish signaled to her not to worry about it. She stood up and said, "I'm glad I told you. I tried to tell my boyfriend and he didn't understand what all the fuss was about. My mom won't listen."

She lingered at his side a few moments longer, and Elish knew he should say something, that she deserved some kind of reward for her confession, but he had nothing to give her. The tension had made her stand taller, and had it not been for the sorrow of the conversation that had appeared and retreated alternately on her face, he would have let her stand like that beside him, breathtaking in the brightness of winter that descended from the Azrieli Mall dome, in her tight, black cotton dress, which emphasized how natural the wholeness of her body, its height, its simplicity, was to her. If she lingered long enough, waiting for him to speak, he thought, one could mistakenly believe she'd been here before the bricks and the lead foundation, the glass and the pale neon lights, and that the architect of the structure had designed them around her. He was afraid to speak the necessary words, to tell her, You're wrong if you think you could have changed anything. If you acted differently, if you said the right thing, maybe Dalia wouldn't have gone back to live in the apartment, wouldn't have stayed there, wouldn't have been murdered. Those are pointless thoughts. You could not have prevented it. I don't know if this is any consolation, but I've been gathering evidence, and I don't believe Dalia's murder was random. I don't believe Ezra Buhbut killed her. It was premeditated and would have happened no matter where she lived.

But what could he tell her instead? What? His thoughts didn't go far. Ronnit interrupted them. She shifted, releasing herself from the gaze that had held her in place. "I've really got to run," she said. "Thanks for listening." She shrugged, and in a sudden burst of emotion leaned in and kissed his cheek, a dry kiss. She looked back as she descended down the escalator, her eyes fixed on him.

ELISH WENT TO A PAY PHONE AND CALLED LILIAN, WHO TOLD him Manny Lahav had been looking for him again and asked her to give him the message that he wanted very badly to speak to him.

"Let him take a number and wait in line like everybody else," Elish said, then gave her the phone number of the pay phone and asked that she connect him with Eliya. Thirty seconds later, Eliya's voice emerged, dull and distant, swallowed in background noise. "Elish? Can you hear me?"

"Where are you, Eliya?"

"I'm driving to Netivot. I have news for you, but it'll have to wait till tonight. I can't talk right now."

"Can you come over to my place around six? I don't want to stay late at the office."

Eliya blurted a laugh that reached his ears in segments. "I have news about that too. See you later."

He replaced the phone and thought about Ronnit, the amount of fake forgiveness and comfort he would have to give until he untangled this mystery. The beating and shock of the break-in had made him forget one of the insights that had passed through his mind that night, and now the conversation with Ronnit had made it reemerge: the police file hadn't included any report from Eran Shitrit about hearing any shouting or gunshots.

ELISH CLIMBED THE STAIRS AT 17 ISRAËLS STREET AND STOPPED after the first flight. The door to Dalia Shushan's apartment was locked. What had he expected, a stream of visitors? A small wooden name on the door bore the name "Shushan," under which someone who may have meant it as a joke had added the letters "RIP." He kept going up, ringing the bell of the apartment on the second floor, on the front door of which a bright sign read "Eran Shitrit." On the floor was a hairy doormat.

A thin-faced man of about thirty-five, possibly older, appearing younger only because of his narrow frame, cracked the door open and looked at him, the chain kissing his forehead. "Can I help you?" he said impatiently.

"Good afternoon, Mr. Shitrit," Elish said, emboldened. "Could you spare a bit of your time?"

"What's this about?" Eran asked suspiciously. "Who are you? What are you looking for?"

"My name is Elish Ben Zaken and I'm a private investigator reopening the Dalia Shushan murder case. I'd love to—"

The thin man closed the door, calling out, "Sorry, but I've got nothing to say."

Elish had prepared for this. He pulled out a notepad from his bag, opened it to a new page, and wrote, "I've just come back from a meeting with Ronnit Abraham, the woman who lived in the apartment below you before Dalia Shushan. She's crazy, looking for revenge. She's considering suing you for sexual harassment retroactively in her and Shushan's name. I can convince her to drop the lawsuit. I'll be waiting for you at Segafredo Espresso Bar on Dizengoff Street in five minutes. Elish." He tore out the page, folded it, and slipped it under Eran Shitrit's door.

ELISH DIDN'T HAVE TO WAIT LONG. THE THIN-LIMBED ERAN walked into the café, strutting oddly, his limbs limp and swinging, eyes darting here and there. Elish signaled to him and he hurried over. His face was pale, his bottom lip trembling.

"This is extortion." He placed Elish's note softly on the table. "Extortion."

"Let's think of it as one hand washing the other. I suppose you're familiar with this manner of symbiosis from your military work."

"I'm no longer an officer. I quit. What do you want? What did Ronnit Abraham sell you? I'm not looking for trouble."

"Neither am I. I'd love some answers to a few questions, though."

"Is she serious, that Ronnit?"

"Relax. Everything's under control. Play along with me and I'll get her to drop the idea. She's just mad with grief and searching for someone to blame. Dalia Shushan was her cousin."

"Yes, I know. What is she grieving about? They didn't get along well when they lived together."

"How do you know that? You seem to know more than a neighbor ought to."

"What are you insinuating?" Eran asked, startled, growing even paler.

"I'm not insinuating. You had that dog you used as an excuse to spy on them. I'm assuming that habit didn't end even after the excuse dropped dead and after Ronnit left. I think you were spying on Dalia Shushan. It excited you, peeping on a famous singer, didn't it?"

"Shh, keep your voice down," Eran whispered. "People can hear you."

"I think it was no coincidence that you spotted Ezra Buhbut the night Dalia Shushan was murdered. I think you were standing outside in the dark, looking into her apartment. I think it was routine. But that time, to your surprise, you saw Ezra Buhbut in there and you panicked."

"Yes," said Eran, "I was so scared. But who did it hurt, my taking a look? I wasn't hurting anyone. Then, all of a sudden, that night I saw a strange man in her living room, fleeing from the bedroom and falling over. I freaked out. I called the police."

"It's odd that when you called them you never mentioned yelling or gunshots. In fact, you didn't mention anything out of the ordinary. Not even that you saw that whoever was inside the apartment was carrying a gun."

"I didn't see a gun. They asked me about it in the trial when I testified. You can't see a gun from so far away. Anyway, I identified Buhbut beyond any doubt as the suspect whom I'd reported to the police that night."

"And yelling?"

"I didn't hear yelling. Why? Was I supposed to?"

"Yes. If someone beat Dalia Shushan before murdering her, she would have yelled, no? What about gunshots?"

"I didn't hear gunshots. I didn't make anything up, if that's what you're saying. I simply described what I saw. At any rate, they didn't need me. They found a bloody shoeprint that matched Buhbut's shoe, an old Puma."

"Still, Ezra Buhbut got life in prison based on your negligent reporting."

"What do you mean? I was watching the living room. How could I have known that Dalia Shushan was dead in the bedroom and that the intruder was just running away from the body? When the police came they dragged him out while he fought and cursed them out. I think he even bit one of the officers, who then whooped his ass. One cop walked out of the apartment white as a wall. He told another one, 'I understand why he didn't want to go back inside, there's a dead girl in there.' Then a commotion started and nobody needed me or asked if I'd heard gunshots or yelling, not even when they took my deposition. But as the trial was going on I kept thinking, But I didn't hear gunshots. Maybe he used a silencer? And how did he get rid of the gun? Someone will ask me at some point. But nobody did. Still, I knew the day would come." His bottom lip continued to tremble as he spoke.

Elish said, "Are you aware of the fact that Buhbut committed suicide in prison?"

Eran looked shocked. Elish took advantage of this opportunity: "I don't think that's your only sin. I know you were sitting and waiting for the right time to spy on Dalia Shushan, and I imagine other people walked into the building that night, and that you're worried the day will come when someone asks you about everything else you saw, not only what you chose to report."

"Did he kill himself? Are you sure? I didn't read that anywhere, and I've been following–"

"Trust me. Google his name and you'll find it. So what do you say?"

"I saw two people that night. A guy and a girl."

"Describe them."

"The girl had short blond spiky hair. She walked into the building at six thirty. She and Dalia argued for like ten, fifteen minutes. Then it was quiet."

"Did you hear what they were saying?"

"The walls in that building are thin, but not *that* thin. I took the dog upstairs, then I saw the man leaving Shushan's apartment when I went downstairs for my evening walk. Now that you mention it, I heard yelling coming from her apartment before he left. Every night at seven thirty I take an exactly forty-five-minute walk. I looked over the railing in the stairwell and saw him closing the door behind him. I'd seen him in her apartment a few times before, once in his underwear. He was skinny, kind of shriveled, with graying hair. He had evil eyes."

Finally, something in this mystery was beginning to clear up. Debbie Malkieli and Yehuda Menuhin had come to see Dalia before she died. Interesting. "What time did you start watching?"

"Five o'clock."

"Do you think either of them saw you?"

"No." Eran chewed on his lower lip. "So what are you going to do with this information?"

"Nothing. I'm interested in truth, not punishment. Now that you know you weren't truthful, you know that one day you'll pay the price for this awareness. Don't you think that's sufficient?"

10

These past few days, Elish thought, shards of time stick to my skin like a pack of fleas. No matter how much I scratch or sterilize, they continue to suck my blood like a torrent of shattering glass, and memory opens, denying the principles it has followed for the past twenty years. How much simpler it was before, when all the memories were dark and dormant, and only occasionally, upon an uncautious movement, did one of them turn in its sleep, hurting the sentries of consciousness with their soporific spells, arousing a general distress that hinted, You'll find something that way, but nothing more than that, and there was a power in them that evaporated as soon as they rose to the light, having been flattened into an image and a word. All memories are monsters that ought to be left to sleep uninterrupted. I want that blindness back. Remembering means emptying of all inner force.

He paced nervously through his apartment, thinking, Why these memories, flowing the summer of age ten toward me? He wouldn't give in, he was skilled at erasing, he would say no. He continued wandering, up to the roof, back downstairs, touching the rows of books in his bookcase, pulling one out, reading a few lines, losing concentration, plopping onto the armchair, turning on the television, watching episodes of *The Powerpuff Girls* he'd already seen before, *Eerie, Indiana* on the children's channel, so boring, flipping through his CD collection. Not this one, not that one. Where was Eliya?

Yehuda Menuhin was Dalia's secret lover. He should have guessed it. Eran Shitrit's account was not the only last nail in the coffin of this hypothesis's certainty. He rushed home from Dizengoff, found his copies of Dalia's and Menuhin's police files, and pulled out their pictures. Then he drove fast to Jaffa.

Elish could appreciate irony, but this seemed excessive. Yehuda Menuhin had lived in Ajami, a few hundred yards away from Ezra Buhbut, according to the address in Dalia's file. He went up to the third floor, then descended back down to the ground floor. He didn't find a thing he hadn't expected. The dirty, derelict appearance of the first two floors was replaced between the second and third floor by a perfectly renovated and painted stairwell. The entrance to Menuhin's apartment was too well-done and polished, a sin against the neighborhood aesthetic. It suited him to live here in luxury, in the heart of the wounded distress, in the maximal conditions for creating friction with his surroundings.

Elish walked around the building for a few minutes after having knocked on Levana Hacham's door to no response, looking around for neighbors willing to talk, but the building seemed deserted, blanketed by an atypical afternoon slumber. Where was the chatter of neighbors, the shouting as they hung their laundry? Where was the low, tyrannizing voice of men? He walked over to the shopping center, which did not disappoint–full of customers, coffee shop loiterers, and random diners. He walked through the coffee shops, showing owners the images of Menuhin and Dalia and receiving head shakes and shrugs in return. He got similar responses at candy stores and bakeries. Only at the corner store, whose Arabic name he could not pronounce, did the clerk say, "*Hada, l'brofessor al-yahudi, mat, maskin.*" Elish handed over Dalia's picture and the clerk examined it. A small group of customers gathered round. Perhaps his persistence as he moved from one store to the next had aroused their curiosity, and the regulars wanted to know what the commotion was all about. He handed one of them Menuhin's picture, and they passed it around.

"No, not a poor guy, not a poor guy at all," someone cried from the doorway. "A bad man."

Elish turned toward the voice. Levana Hacham was standing behind him, waving Menuhin's picture. She was wearing the same yellow sweatpants, her face flushed with anger. She pulled Elish outside by force. "What are you doing, embarrassing me in front of my neighbors, huh? What are you asking them about me?"

"What are you talking about?" asked Elish. "I wasn't asking about you."

They were standing in the corner of the store, their words swallowed in the chaos all around.

"What do you mean you weren't asking about me?" Her furious body language relaxed a touch. "Then what are you asking about him?" She held the picture in her left hand. "If it isn't about me . . ."

"I found out some interesting facts about him in my research and I'm testing the possibility of a class action."

"Stop bullshitting. I may not understand your pretty words, but I know when someone's taking me for a ride."

"Look, I can't explain right now, but anyway, this won't hurt you, even though your behavior with regard to him was suspicious, and understand, his suicide isn't as straightforward as it looks, but I believe you have nothing to do with it. I'll defend you when people start asking questions, and you're going to need that defense, take my word for it."

Levana lowered her eyes, sunlight flickering off the black roots of her hair. "I knew it, I knew you were a *manayek*, I knew it from your questions. I knew there would be no lawsuit, no money. The night I came back from meeting you I told my husband, 'I met this lawyer today, looks weird, asked questions, promised to get money out of the university, looks like a bullshitter, they're all the same shit.'"

"What's the deal with Menuhin?"

"What do you want from me?" she whispered. "Why are you hunting me down? Are you a relative of his? You think I did something to him? Tell me."

"Relax. I don't think you have anything to do with his death. But I still need to know why you chose to live here, in the same building as a man who hurt you and humiliated you."

"It wasn't on purpose. I wasn't looking for him, and my husband didn't even know about it. When we came to see the apartment, we were waiting downstairs for the realtor, and I looked at the names on the mailboxes. I saw his name and all this shit resurfaced, all the hatred. I told my husband I liked the apartment, even though we'd seen ones that were much nicer, and that I wanted to take a walk and check out the neighbors. My husband was nervous. He said, 'Levana, what are you talking about, check out the neighbors? This is Ajami. You leave the apartment for ten minutes and when you get back there's no TV.' But I calmed him down. I told him I had a good feeling about it. He waited outside while I went upstairs, and that's where I ran into him. He was just leaving his apartment. Damn his name and his memory. He looked at me like I was air and barked, 'Who are you? What are you looking for?' And that's when it clicked. All the hours I spent cursing him in my heart and fantasizing about torturing him–nothing. This was the worst. He didn't even remember who I was. So I just said, 'Nice to meet you, I'm Levana, your new neighbor.' He went back into his apartment without answering me."

"So you came back and offered your services as house cleaner. What were you hoping to achieve?"

"What were you hoping to achieve?" Levana repeated mockingly. "You tell me, because you seem to have some head on you. What do you think I wanted? I'll give you three guesses."

Elish didn't answer.

Levana sighed deeply. "I wanted to study him and find out what would hurt him the most. I wanted what everyone in this country wants, what they taught me when I was a little girl and they made me stand and cry at all those stupid Holocaust Remembrance and Memorial and Independence Days." Her voice grew louder, filling with fury. She looked up, her face the expressionless antithesis of her voice. "I wanted the thing people say is best for a Jewish person's soul. I wanted revenge."

Elish tapped Dalia's picture, which he'd managed to retrieve from the clerk's hands before being pulled outside. "Revenge," he mumbled, appalled, then handed the picture to Levana. "Do you recognize the girl in this photo? Did you know her?"

She glanced briefly at the image. "Yeah. I know her. She came over a lot. Came at night, left in the morning. One night I heard crying outside. I asked my husband, 'Who's crying in the stairwell at this hour?' I looked through the peephole but I didn't see anyone. I opened the door and saw her standing outside of his apartment. The automatic light in the stairwell was on; she must have put a match in the button. I said, 'Why are you crying?' She said, 'He won't open the door.' Then she yelled, 'Yehuda, I'm not going anywhere, you hear me? I'll sit here all night. I know you're home.' Then she said, 'Sorry, I won't make any more noise.' I said, 'You want some water? Come inside, have something to drink. That's a bad man.' She said, 'Thanks, but I'm staying here.'

"She stayed till morning. At six o'clock I went out to the market and saw her sitting on the stairs, her eyes puffy, like this"—she placed her two fists over her eyes—"I said, '*Ya binti*, you don't need him. That's a bad man.' He was also too old for her, but I didn't say that. She started to cry again. I told her, 'Go on, go home.' Then I took her by the hand and took her to the bus stop."

"Do you remember when this was?"

"The day of the suicide bombing at the central bus terminal."

And Elish thought, eve of the Ninth of Av.

• • •

SO YEHUDA MENUHIN WAS DALIA'S LOVER. ON SECOND thought, Elish should have suspected that when he read in that article that Menuhin had asked her to be his teaching assistant. Dalia was brilliant, but Menuhin seemed to him like a man in love with his own bright light, unable to appreciate it in anyone else. Perhaps he'd refused to reach the necessary conclusion because he believed Menuhin had tried to seduce Dalia, but had trouble believing that he'd succeeded. So Yehuda Menuhin was Dalia's lover. Why was he repeating this conclusion to himself? To torture himself? It was deplorable, but it didn't justify murdering either of them. Why did someone decide to kill them? He'd been lingering too long on the how and the who, and had neglected the question of motives. Why?

Information, information. Why did Dalia send Malkieli a demo on which she'd written the word "Menuhin"? Why didn't she give it to her that night? Clearly, Malkieli had made a pilgrimage to see her and receive, or at least listen to, the demo. Dalia was her goldmine. Did Dalia intend to send a message from beyond the grave? For instance, that Malkieli had murdered Dalia for the demo? A pathetic reason, and yet, for the sake of argument: Let's say Malkieli took the demo, put it in her office mailbox, and feigned surprise the next morning when it turned up there. At first she hadn't realized that Menuhin was the name of a man. Then, once she'd tracked down Yehuda Menuhin and learned he'd been Dalia's lover—how? Through Lior Levitan?—she contacted him. He knew that Dalia hadn't intended to give her the demo, and so she murdered him and made it look like a suicide. Sounds like an episode from the third season of *Profiler*. What are the odds of something like this happening in real life? And even assuming that people in this world would murder for twenty songs' worth of fame and fortune: the time of death didn't work. Malkieli arrived at six o'clock. Unless she stayed at Dalia's till eight, then murdered her, which would mean that was how she met Yehuda Menuhin.

Then why did she wait two months to murder Yehuda? Because of the demo? At some point she realized that the demo bore Menuhin's name. Maybe Yehuda started extorting her because he knew Dalia hadn't meant to send Malkieli the demo, and this extortion and the abuse that came with it made her life so bitter that she decided to act? No. No. Eran Shitrit's report was missing an hour in which he was out of the house. She could have come and gone during that time. And what was the explanation for the odd position of the body? The seeming ritual? What was the point of that? Did Malkieli hate Dalia so much that she decided to give her body the shape of her hatred in death? I hate your talent for emotion, she said and shot her through the heart. And your intellectual prowess, added Malkieli, shooting Dalia through both temples. She knew Dalia was interested in esoteric dogmas, so she touched the smoking barrel of the gun to her palms and feet, beaming with satisfaction.

No, this was all ludicrous. How did she get the gun? Yes, he checked. The gun that killed Menuhin had a silencer, and the bullets–nine millimeter–matched the ones found in Dalia's body. Was it the same gun? If so, why didn't the police look into that? How did Manny Lahav fit into this general tangle, and why was he trying to pull Elish into the heart of darkness? Who was he protecting? Were Malkieli and Gideon Menuhin having an affair? Malkieli persuaded Gideon to plant a bait in his brother's police file, luring Elish into his trap, and when she was afraid he might have uncovered something meaningful, she hired thugs to beat him up. No. That was too complicated. Why would Malkieli want to hurt him, besides the general malice that all people distractedly harbor for their counterparts? And since when was Malkieli interested in men? Perhaps she was having an affair with Ora Anatot, who had a certain influence on Gideon Menuhin, and that was what Yehuda had found out, leading him to extort her and his brother and finally be killed? Such insipid horror.

Maybe he should start from a different direction. The thugs. They beat him up when he discovered the connection between Yehuda's suicide and Dalia's murder, received hints of Ora and Gideon's intimacy, when Eliya told him about the wiretap and he discovered Levana Hacham's obsession with Yehuda. That was a good point, which could help him erase some of the facts that seemed connected but were not. Because, he'd decided, there was more than one story here, just as there had been when he'd started looking into this case, but the organization of facts was different. Now there was a clear connection between Dalia's and Yehuda's deaths and Ora and Gideon. What wasn't fully clear was which reasons and motivations had to do with one story and which with the other. There were so many facts that he couldn't identify the pattern. And how did Levana Hacham, the pathological neighbor, who wished, by her own testimony, to take revenge against Yehuda, and had met Dalia, fit into this? Could she have some connection to the thugs? In a few minutes he would have Eliya's information, something to do with the wiretap and the thug attack. Then he would be, if not wiser, at least less confused. Oh, the wonderful doorbell. He flung the door open. What perfect timing.

"Welcome back from the far south," Elish greeted her cheerfully.

"Such uncharacteristic high spirits." Eliya was also in a good mood, which was not a bad sign. "I'm already wondering what you aren't telling me. Maybe I should ask Lilian. She'll definitely know."

"Lilian should start a gossip column. Let's get right to business. I can't wait any longer. Drink?"

"No, thanks. I haven't had a chance to print my report, so you'll have to listen to me telling it. So, remember Shmuel Benita? The one who told me about the wiretap? Turns out, the next day it was like the ground had swallowed him. After the attack in your office I became suspicious, though I didn't know about the other demons you'd awakened. In fact, I know nothing about your investigation."

"Forget it, it's too complicated. Believe me, I would love to share with you, and you would love to try and put together the puzzle pieces I've found, I have no doubt about that. I would enjoy it too if the whole thing didn't feel a little too personal."

"Okaaaay," Eliya pulled on the final syllable and pressed on the right arm of her glasses. "The next day I started searching for him. There was no answer in any of the numbers I had for him. At his firm, Observation, nobody knew anything. After two days of failed attempts at tracking him down, I realized that Benita had gone underground. I won't waste your time with superfluous details. I knew he wasn't originally from Tel Aviv, and it took me a week to find his family. Pretty dull busywork. But I finally tracked them down. They live in Netivot. I went down there yesterday to stake the place out and get to know the people. I bribed a little girl to tell me where Shmuel Benita lived, and she pointed out the house, no hesitation. But there was no sign of the man. This morning I called the number I got from information and the idiot picked up. I started speaking Arabic and he hung up on me. He hadn't recognized me. I drove right down, waited outside for about thirty minutes until he came outside, then cuffed his arm to mine and told him he would stay attached to me until he told me everything that was going on, and if I needed to I would drag him back to Tel Aviv with me, right to the doorway of his office. The loser started singing, as if he'd just been waiting for the opportunity. Or maybe he was that scared of going back to Tel Aviv. He got so scared after he warned me at the café that one time and told me about the wiretap that he ran to see his boss, Haim Sasaportas, and told him we were sniffing around Gideon Menuhin. It freaked Sasaportas out, and I'll tell you why in a minute, but first give me some water."

Eliya gulped it down, paused to arrange her thoughts, and then continued in her flow. "This will surprise you. Ora Anatot has a child, but the biological father isn't her husband. It's Gideon Menuhin."

"I had a feeling. I knew the two of them had known each other when they were younger, and I saw the kid in her office. Still, I am surprised. How did you find out?"

"You wanted to know the content of the tap, right?"

"Yes, but how do *you* know?"

"Simple. Yehuda Menuhin ordered the wiretap. Ora Anatot called Gideon Menuhin three weeks ago, terrified, and told him she thought Yehuda knew about Nathaniel—that's the kid. How did they come up with that name? Nathaniel Anatot. Kind of a heavy name for a child, isn't it?" She smiled, tilting her neck. "With a name like that you've got to end up a prime minister. Anyway, Benita saved a transcript of the conversation. The man can smell the potential for money. He gave the tapes to Sasaportas, who was furious when he discovered they'd been eavesdropping on a deputy minister. He called Yehuda and told him they were dropping the case. Must have given him the regular excuse—ethical reasons. I'm summarizing, okay? I'm also filling in with my own guesses, but the main facts have been verified. Yehuda Menuhin secretly approached Benita, who sold him the transcript, and Yehuda used the information, I'm guessing, to extort his brother, though I'm not sure how."

"No, he extorted Ora Anatot. He wanted to become a full professor and she objected. Because she's the head of the department and a member of the appointments committee, she had the power to block his promotion."

"Okay. Sasaportas threatened Benita that if any part of the contents of the wiretap leaked it would be his head. Benita told me he panicked because he knows what Sasaportas is capable of."

"For instance, sending two thugs to beat up a guy and make him lose the urge to carry on an investigation." In his mind's eye, Elish saw Sasaportas—tan, firm, his entire body spouting fury, the scar from the horse's bite pulsing terrifyingly on his face.

"Exactly. That's why he ran away from Tel Aviv. Yehuda Menuhin was murdered and we started sniffing around his brother. Benita got worried we might find out about his secret deal with Yehuda. To cover his ass, that snake ran crying to Sasaportas, telling him that he just happened to run into me by the Knesset and got some information out of me—that I was investigating Gideon Menuhin. Sasaportas is terrified that if you keep investigating you'll discover the content of the wiretap. What I don't understand is why Benita is playing double agent."

"He's convinced that Yehuda Menuhin was murdered because he found out that Gideon and Ora had a child, and he's scared to death. Then, all of a sudden, we show up, and he sees his chance to get Sasaportas off his back. Our investigation can ruin Sasaportas, which would mean freedom for Benita. If nothing changes he won't get hurt, because it would mean that throughout the investigation he remained loyal to Sasaportas and updated him on its progress." When Elish realized the meaning of this, he fell silent. He recalled the phone conversation when his mother told him someone had called to ask for his office address. Until now, he'd assumed that call truly had been intended to find out the address to which the caller was going to send their thugs, but what if it was actually meant to confirm that the Ben Zaken family in Ashkelon was actually *his* Ben Zaken family?

"Eliya," he said, startled. "What time today was it that you spoke to Benita?"

The ringing of the phone startled them both. Elish snatched up the living room phone, his heart contracting.

11

Elish slammed both his hands on the steering wheel and the horn. "Move!" he cried. "Come on, move already! What's wrong with you?" In the closed interior of his car, his voice mixed with that of Frank Black, who sang "Wave of Mutilation" over the speakers. The best way to move right now–on a wave of mutilation. A wave of destruction. A traffic jam at the entrance to the Ayalon Highway at eight o'clock in the evening. What happened? It began to rain, slowing traffic even more. Elish hoped the rain was the only reason, and not some inexplicable upsurge toward the south. His mother had been on the verge of tears over the phone. She said–while Tahel whimpered in the background–"Elish, you've got to come. Someone broke in. The police are here and I can't get ahold of Yaffa and Zalman. They're at the movies."

Eliya had already guessed what was going on, and muttered under her breath. "I'm coming with you," she said as they walked into his building's parking lot.

"No need," he said. "The police already caught the intruders. I don't understand how they got there so quickly. If my mom's description is accurate, the people who broke in are the two guys who jumped me. She was pretty confused though. She was in shock."

"I can understand that. Are you sure you don't need me?" she asked. When he nodded furiously, she added, "I never told you this, but I've been thinking about it a lot lately–you're very bad at asking for help."

Of course she was right. But he said, "Eliya, this isn't the time for this conversation."

"Drive safe and be smart. The problem with these conversations is that there's never a good time to have them."

The rain grew stronger, but the road opened up a little. Elish was just about to turn off the radio, because the music bothered him when he stood in traffic or waited at lights, but then the cars ahead of him were starting to gain speed. Sons of bitches, he thought, sons of bitches. What were those two gorillas going to do? Threaten an old woman and a baby? What? Beat them up? Break one of their bones just to scare him? The thought of his mother and Tahel, holding each other, terrified, facing two figures in black, gave him chills. The image froze before him, bathed in harsh light: His mother protecting Tahel, holding her against her chest as she cowered, and two silhouettes with bats in their hands towering over them. He didn't dare take the thought further, picturing any real damage. The road spread ahead of him, a wet nocturnal freedom. Elish cut through the dark, speeding up, worrying. The rain didn't help, it only brought the sea closer. The problem with these things is that there's never a good time for them. He was thirteen and woke up on the day of his bar mitzvah with seawater flooding his lungs and salt running through his veins, clogging his sinuses. It wasn't a dream, it was a lot more than that. He didn't know what had led him to leave the beach from which, every night as he was falling asleep, he safely watched the enormous, rustling blue tranquility, and walk toward the waves, leaving the light of day behind him and answering for once the call of the depths. He put one foot in the water, then the other, and could no longer go back. His thoughts calmed. He could feel the seaweed wrapping around his ankles, the jellyfish sucking on his flesh, taking away what he didn't appreciate as much as they did. He kept walking, the surface of the water breaking under his weight, one step and another, until the bottom fell and the blessed heaviness of the body, of which only clean bones remained, and face and lungs—after the piranhas and the sharks ate the rest—dropped down, and the water roiled, through the mouth that opened, yearning, and through the nose that was stuffed with many winters of cold, free to breathe in the new, bewitching air, and awoke to this body he'd thought he had lost and was thankful for losing, coughing to the point of losing oxygen, dizzy, dizzy, dizzy and nauseous, and his mother, who from the time he was ten followed with concern the trails of noise that he and Yaffa left in their wake, swung into the room and grabbed him. "What's wrong, Elish, baby? What's wrong?" She placed her palm on his forehead, and he said, "Mom, I think I'm going to die." She wrapped her arms around him, bringing his body close to hers, and said, "You're not going to die, you're just having another fever attack, you can't die, we named you Elisha."

THE STORM DISAPPEARED JUST AS EASILY AS IT HAD COME, with a cry of defeat. Elish forced his eyes open. He couldn't blink, the memory fell silent. He felt that another bit of it had torn off, another relief arriving, which he did not welcome either. The rest of the drive went calmly. He slipped Dalia Shushan's demo into the CD player. From across death, she sang to him:

I am left with only the body
To rely on.
And what is the body?
An anatomy lesson, muscles and tendons.

From one moment to the next, my life is
becoming a museum
The clothes I place in the closet,
A shelf for every shirt,
The books in their plastic sleeves,
The silverware in its glass cages.

And this flesh is a delaying in-between
Like aether driving the sun
Eight minutes and one second
After it took place.

In perfect coordination with her voice, the rain hid behind him, in the north. By the time he arrived, the police car was already parked by his mother's building, and so was Yaffa and Bobby's car. He ran up the stairs and into the apartment. His mother looked at him, her eyes red, cradling Tahel, who had fallen asleep in her arms. He heard Bobby and Yaffa arguing in the kitchen with a third voice, which he recognized but could not place. A male and a female officer in uniform were sipping coffee in the living room. The female officer spoke softly into a cellular phone. A few neighbors, who were filled with a sense of camaraderie over the action, fussed around his mother, spouting curses aimed at the intruders, who were no longer there.

"Mom, are you all right? How's Tahel?"

"We're fine, we just had a bit of a scare."

"*Wuld l'hram*," one neighbor cried with anger. His mother shushed her.

"Can you tell me what happened?" Elish asked.

"I left Tahel in the living room to play and went into the kitchen to make her hot cocoa. Suddenly, I heard the door open. I came out of the kitchen to see what was going on, and these two tall guys with masks on their faces were standing in the doorway. Without thinking, I ran into the living room and picked up Tahel, who started to cry. One of them said, 'She has a little girl,' and the other one said, 'What difference does it make? An old woman is okay but a little girl isn't?' Then the first one said, 'I don't know about any of this.' Then all of a sudden two cops ran inside, the ones who are in the living room, with guns, and yelled at them, just like on *Walker, Texas Ranger*, 'Hands up!' And that's it. They cuffed them and held them against the floor. Five minutes later a whole mess of cops showed up and took them away. Another man came with them, without uniform. He asked the guy and the girl to stay here and take care of us until Yaffa and Zalman came back. So I made them coffee. Yaffa and Zalman are talking to the man in the kitchen."

"Sit down, Mom," said Elish, then turned to tell off the neighbors—"What are you standing around here for? Can't you see she needs to rest? Go on, go home. You can talk tomorrow." He pushed Tahel's hair out of her face and watched her slumber, thumb in mouth. "I'll be right back," he said.

YAFFA, BOBBY, AND MANNY LAHAV FELL SILENT AS HE WALKED into the kitchen. "Elish," said Yaffa, accompanying her words with tired eyes, a hint of anger peeking out of her calculated, businesslike tone, "this officer is trying to explain to us what's going on, but he can't promise us that no more intruders are going to show up. He says it's got something to do with your work."

"What are you doing here?" Elish asked Manny.

Bobby turned to Elish, "Are these the same guys that beat you up? They're lucky I wasn't here."

"Yaffa, Bobby, can you give us a minute? I promise I'll come right out afterwards and explain everything."

Once they were alone, Elish said, "You didn't answer me. What are you doing here?"

"What have I done to deserve this cold shoulder?" Manny asked. "I tried to warn you but you hung up on me. I left you several messages and you never even bothered to call me back. Can you explain what's going on?"

"I asked you first," said Elish, crossing his arms and taking a seat at the kitchen table. "Did anyone offer you anything to drink?"

"Yes, I've had enough. Your mother's an amazing woman.

Look, I expected something like this to happen after you were attacked."

"I thought you were involved."

"Why?"

"Because my investigation revealed something you and Gideon didn't want me to know."

"Gideon and I are not the same person."

"Okay, go on."

"You found out something that someone wanted to hide so badly that it made them pull out the big guns. That's what I wanted to talk to you about–to find out what you uncovered. Maybe my knowledge and experience could have helped you make connections you couldn't make by yourself."

"I doubt it."

"You trust yourself so much that you forget others have something to offer you too."

"Hey," Elish said, getting angry, "am I wearing a sign saying 'Analyze my personality' or something? You're the second one to say that to me today."

"At any rate, our two pals who broke in here are refusing to talk for now. But don't worry, I'm putting pressure on the chief of police to make every effort to get information out of them."

"No need for that. They work for Haim Sasaportas, owner of the Observation Investigation Firm."

"A professional competition?" Manny joked, laughing his free, captivating laugh. "I'll take care of it first thing tomorrow morning."

"I already know how to take care of it," said Elish. "As far as I'm concerned, Sasaportas is an acquaintance of Gideon Menuhin."

"Come on, Elish," Manny replied to the hidden accusation, running a hand through his hair, "give me a little credit. The first thing I did after I heard about the attack–which, by the way, if you were wondering, I heard about from your secretary–was call

Gideon. And don't worry, I didn't mention your name. He doesn't even know who you are. I asked him gently if he'd reached the conclusion that it was time to stop the investigation of the circumstances of his brother's death. He had no idea what I was talking about."

"Yes, there's a good chance that Sasaportas was acting independently."

"Besides, unless Gideon's changed a great deal, he would never send thugs. That's too crude for his style. He's a master of manipulation and getting people to come to their own conclusion that it would be in their best interest to do what he wants. He's not a bone breaker."

"Look–" His anger at Manny was dwindling, and once again Elish couldn't say why. "I'm sorry if you feel that I'm not giving you enough credit, but you still haven't answered any of the most basic questions I've asked you. Why are you so eager to help? What are you even doing here?"

"Like I started saying earlier, after I couldn't get ahold of you, I called the Ashkelon police commander and asked him, as a personal favor, to send a squad car to patrol your mother's block in the evening. I know how those threats work. If they can't deter you personally, they'll always turn to your loved ones. I didn't know if the first attack would make you stop the investigation, and as long as I had no way of finding out if the danger was still imminent, I decided to play it safe."

"If your cops hadn't been around tonight, if something had happened to my mother or Tahel . . ." Elish was choking with gratitude.

"I know, Elish, I know," Manny said softly, "but we have to talk."

"Yes," Elish agreed, "we have to talk. Tomorrow, early afternoon? Let's say noon, at the café across the street from the Dizengoff Police Station? There's something I've got to do in the morning, and then I can answer all of your questions."

12

Elish ignored the secretary's physical protest. He passed her by, though she stood up to block his path and waved her arms after he asked if Ora Anatot was there and didn't bother listening to the response, instead confidently crossing the threshold connecting the two offices, calling, "Hold her calls for the next twenty minutes," then slamming the door in the secretary's face, which wore an expression of disbelief, her lips rounding to speak, but since she was not accustomed to anyone treating her with the same disdain she reserved for students, she found no ready-made rebuke.

After the previous night, he felt that the remains of his passion for games, pretense, and ruses had evaporated. He'd sat in the living room with Yaffa and Bobby—his mother having retired to bed, exhausted from the panic and the excitement, taking Tahel with her—and talked to them till the small hours of the night. It was hard for him to maneuver between the different stories he could tell based on the mess of facts at his disposal, and it was impossible to escape Yaffa's small accusations, which grew more and more frequent. Every question she asked was another manifestation of grievance toward him for not having sufficiently reined in his death curse. Bobby was devoid of defenses, baffled. In an unexpected turn of events, he was now meant to be grateful toward those who represented to him the evil, rot, and arbitrariness of the country—the Israel Police, the *manayek*, the blue eye.

Elish told them about the investigation of Yehuda Menuhin's odd suicide, offhandedly mentioning Manny Lahav, who had hired him, explaining his connection to the case—"a friend of Gideon Menuhin's."

"The guy from the Shinui party?" Yaffa asked.

And Bobby said, "All of them shits."

Then Elish continued to tell them about his personal connection to the case, about the professor that Menuhin had been, and about his book *Lampoons* and how much he'd loved it, and how he came up to Menuhin after class only to have the man condescend to him. Bobby cursed quietly, and Yaffa said pointlessly, "Would you look at that, university professors." Elish didn't share the suspicions he had about the motivations behind his hiring. They were satisfied by his explanation about his personal acquaintance with the deceased and the deceased's workplace. He told them, as if weaving a legend, remote from all events, about Eliya, how she met Benita, about Benita's warning and the break-in at the office, and about how—giving too much detail, distracting them—Eliya staked out Benita in Netivot, and how she handcuffed him—"Like something from a movie," Yaffa said indifferently, obligated to offer some kind of response, and Bobby added, "Hell of a girl." Then Elish told them about the wiretap and Sasaportas's threats, making due with muttering, "We already know the contents of the wiretap but I can't tell you that right now, maybe after this is all over," and how Sasaportas sent his thugs after an old woman and a baby.

"You were busy," said Bobby, "and quiet. You didn't mention any of this."

"It all happened so fast," said Elish.

"You wouldn't have told us even if it had happened slowly. You've been keeping secrets ever since you were a boy," said Yaffa, who could no longer keep her grievance, that Elish had been evasive, at bay. This grievance now hit him in its most innocent form: a clear, righteous accusation of a breach of trust. "How dare you?" Yaffa raised her voice: "Isn't everything you did as a child enough? Isn't it enough for you? Now you're putting

Tahel in danger, and Mom? I always knew you were cursed, and I tried to restrain myself. I told myself, Maybe it isn't his fault, though deep inside I knew it *was* your fault. It was always your fault. Look at what's become of Mom, look at what's become of you, I'm sick of it."

Bobby, who'd never heard her speak that way before, not even to her brother, took her arm. "Yaffa, all this excitement isn't good for you."

"Leave me alone, Zalman." Yaffa stood up, sobbing, inhaling through a runny nose. "I'm sick of talking to him all the time," she said as if Elish wasn't in the room. "I'm sick of talking as if nothing's happened, I'm sick of keeping quiet, sick of being a good sister, letting him hold Tahel as if my entire body isn't screaming against it, as if my stomach isn't twisting. You know very well what he caused, and you've known, like I do, this whole time, that this curse of his would come back again. So here, it's back now, and it's his responsibility. He brought these people here with his games, becoming a detective, investigating murder mysteries, as if he doesn't already have enough death to pay for." She turned to Elish, her voice trembling. "Do me a favor, when you come visit Mom, let me know in advance, so we can make sure not to be here." Then she left the kitchen, Bobby following, shooting him an apologetic look and signaling with his hand that he would call him.

When he tried to fall asleep on the living room sofa, after having watched in silence as Yaffa and Bobby carried the sleeping Tahel out gently, to keep from waking her, he pondered with bitter righteousness the way he'd told them the story. Had he not tried to protect them enough? Had he not obeyed the inner resistance that had roused in him whenever he meant to disclose the dark aspect of his investigation? He hadn't reported his certainty that Menuhin had been murdered or forced to commit suicide, or the explicit connection he'd discovered to Dalia Shushan's murder. And perhaps Yaffa, with her difficult words, which he refused to repeat to himself, had been right. Did he want to escape the final proof that he was destined to harm the ones he loved?

ORA ANATOT RAISED QUESTIONING EYES AT HIM. SHE WAS fairly calm, her franticness concentrated in the tips of her fingers. She leaned on the wall near the bookcase in her office, leafing wildly through a book, reading a paragraph and then flipping the page with a sharp, impatient motion. "Elish," she said, "what is it? I haven't yet received the materials you promised to send me."

"We have more important matters to discuss," said Elish. He pulled an envelope from his pocket and placed it on her desk. "Please, take a seat."

When she sat down obediently before him, he said, "I've lost my patience, so I apologize in advance for the vulgarity I'm about to express, especially since you've been so generous toward me." The things he said were empty and too few. None of the recent events had been Ora's fault. She'd been unwillingly caught in the line of fire. He could show her of all people some empathy, at least, but though the previous night rested, locked behind him, anxiety shook him here and there, Tahel's face floating before him, almost trying to tell him something. He carried on, stifling the sense of urgency that beat through him. "I apologize again. I know Yehuda Menuhin had your phone tapped. I know he found out that his brother, Gideon, is the father of your child, and I know Yehuda extorted you in an attempt to force you to approve his full professorship."

She looked at him, suddenly relaxed, and asked, "Who are you?"

"I'm everything I told you when we first met, plus a private investigator. Gideon Menuhin hired me, without his knowledge, through a mutual acquaintance, to investigate the circumstances of Yehuda's death."

She nodded, her mouth tightly shut. For some reason, it seemed to Elish that she'd already deduced who he was and what he wanted from her before she even raised the question of his identity out loud. Years of teaching logic must train a person for something besides memorizing the decisive basic assumption that all people are mortals. "Yes," she said, without bitterness in her voice, or even the shadow of anger that should have been present in the voice of someone who had just learned they'd been deceived. "He told me he was planning on doing something like this, but said that as far as he understood, the investigation had reached a dead end. By the way, I share his opinion that something about his brother's death isn't right. Though it makes no difference to me, and I don't mind admitting that a great weight was lifted from me when I heard about his suicide. How do you know about Nathaniel? Gideon promised me it was being kept secret."

"I found out by chance, and don't worry, your secret's safe with me. That's why I came here today." He tapped on the envelope he'd placed on her desk. "I need you to get this letter to Gideon."

"I don't understand."

"Let me tell you a story. The person who was in charge of tapping your phone is a guy named Haim Sasaportas, owner of the Observation Investigation Agency. A week ago, he sent two thugs to beat me up in order to stop me from continuing to investigate Yehuda Menuhin's death, and when I didn't, he sent them over to my mother's house, to hurt her—physically or emotionally, I'm not sure. Luckily, the police arrived in time."

"I'm sorry."

"Me too. In this letter, I offer Gideon a barter deal. He'll remove Sasaportas's threat from my family and myself, I don't care how. I know Sasaportas is panicked about having tapped Gideon's calls, and I'm sure Gideon can work it out. In exchange, I'll keep the information I have confidential. As a gesture of good will, the letter also includes information on Shmuel Benita, who's behind the wiretap content leak. As far as I'm concerned, Gideon can deal with him as he sees fit."

"I feel sorry for Gideon, though looking back I could see the seeds of calamity. When I met him, twenty-three years ago, he was still innocent. We met in college. He was a law student then. We lived together for a year, and then he started his internship at a large law firm."

"And the engines of ambition began to turn."

"The engines of ambition began to burn." One of her surprising bursts of laughter, which had been missing from the conversation, sounded now, meek and hollow. "The usual, ever-boring story. The boss's daughter. I met Amos, my husband, and we got married, but I couldn't get pregnant. Five years of failed attempts. We put our hopes in modern medicine. It was the early eighties and fertility treatments were just emerging. Test tube babies were the next generation, destined to replace good old man-and-woman-made humanity. I'd lost hope and was getting used to the thought of life without children, but Amos wasn't prepared to give up. We went through a series of treatments, and in the meantime I just happened to run into Gideon, who was married and climbing the career ladder. I don't know what drew me to him a second time, after he'd abandoned me once. Actually, I do know. You're not married?"

Elish shook his head.

Ora spread the fingers of her right hand, lowering her eyes to her ring. "Even if you were, you wouldn't necessarily experience it—the periods when your attitude toward the body becomes mechanical, when you have to want. Do you understand what I'm saying? It's a little embarrassing to talk about." She shifted uncomfortably in her seat, and her extinguished franticness began to bubble again. He could hear it sneaking into her voice.

"I understand. Because of the fertility treatments you had to try every night."

"Yes, and it was difficult. So difficult. Without a hint of humanity. Amos stopped talking to me. The only words he said to me were at night: 'Ready to try?' I started seeing Gideon on the sly. It only lasted two weeks. We only slept together once, but that was enough. After five weeks, the fertility treatments had succeeded. Amos's joy knew no end." A small, bitter laugh. "I couldn't get an abortion, though I wanted to. And Nathaniel was born. Amos suggested the name, feeling the need to show his gratitude for this miracle. Nathaniel–Hebrew for 'given by God.' Amos wouldn't stop saying how much the boy looked like my father, and whenever I heard that I didn't know whether I should feel grateful for it. With the years, my defenses weakened, and I started to believe that Nathaniel was Amos's. Out of a principle of cosmic justice, if not biology, I never told the truth to Gideon or Amos. I didn't notice how Nathaniel was growing to look so much like Gideon's father, whose face I'd forgotten." She got up, laughing briefly, and started pacing the room. "Six months ago I ran into Gideon again, at a conference where his brother was the keynote speaker. Yehuda gave that talk I told you about, about theory and practice in Jewish studies."

Elish nodded.

She continued, her voice bubbling with bitter laughter. "I can't explain it, but Gideon has this knack for showing up at crucial points in my life. A year ago, after Nathaniel's sixteenth birthday, my relationship with my husband started growing distant. How should I put it? We'd reached a point after which we returned to being strangers. Emotion died out, as if we'd awoken from some deep slumber and didn't know what we were even doing there. And then Gideon showed up, and all those years were erased. We met in hiding over and over again. Gideon is a secretive type, so it's possible that the discreetness is what excited him. I thought we'd finally found our place, and what had been meant to be years earlier was finally happening. I toyed with the illusion that we were both entering the renewed relationship as adults, and that our ripeness was preferable to the heat of youth. It took me a few months to tell him about Nathaniel. His response left me speechless. He started yelling at me, asking if I didn't think he had the right to know, and how I could do that to him, putting his career in jeopardy, everything he built so carefully."

She fell silent, and a thought ran through Elish's mind almost against his will: How monotonous are the sins of the bourgeoisie, how done to death its basic entrapment–power and vulnerable social capital. A child out of wedlock. Big deal. There are no more secrets worth hiding, no fault worth bearing in hiding. He almost smiled, but then his eyes met hers, and the sad spark in them told him, Once again, you're observing people as their brightness is dulled. So he asked, "And don't you think he had the right to know?"

"I have no doubt he had the right to know, but not the right to announce that the primary meaning of this news was the destruction of his career. The relationship between us ended just as quickly as it had begun. He didn't want to hear from me or Nathaniel.

"Then one day, last summer, three and a half months ago, Nathaniel came to see me in my office, and immediately after he left, Yehuda Menuhin walked in, smiling toxically. 'Your son?' he asked. I nodded. 'Does Gideon know you have a child?' he asked. When I said I didn't know what he meant, he laughed, then started speaking in his cold voice about the double standard of the bourgeois, who, in the name of family values, limit the freedom of anyone who chooses not to live by the same values, and secretly corrupt them constantly. Within seconds, we got into a loud argument, at the end of which he said, 'You'll approve my professorship yet.' Yehuda was a despicable man"–bitter laugh–

"who enjoyed watching others in distress, twisting and yearning for his pity. The sorrow he caused people wasn't sufficient for achieving his goals. He doubled and tripled it. He was a cruel animal who tortured his prey to death. He repeated that same scene with me five or six times that summer, and with each time he took more pleasure in watching me horrified. I didn't understand yet that all he wanted was to make me call Gideon so he could have proof. I stupidly called his cell phone, even though he'd forbidden me from doing so, and told me that if I ever needed to reach him I should leave him a message on his beeper—who knows what he was holding on to that for. Two days later—two days before Rosh Hashanah—Yehuda staked me out at the university. He walked into my office, all smiles, arrogant, and tossed over a photocopy of the transcript of the conversation I had with Gideon, saying, 'Now you can't get away. The next copy will go to your husband.'"

"So you called Gideon, who tried to get ahold of his brother and convince him to drop the issue. I can figure out the rest myself," said Elish. "Yehuda evaded his brother, but ultimately gave in and agreed to meet him the day after Yom Kippur. Yehuda never made it to their lunch date. Gideon drove to his home, found his body, and panicked. He assumed that something that Yehuda did, or said, led to his death, and that it must have something to do with the wiretap. When the police determined it was a suicide, Gideon, out of a desire to protect himself and a fear that whoever killed his brother was trying to send him a message, was not convinced, so he turned to Manny Lahav, his childhood friend, who then approached me. Indeed, Gideon likes to pull strings from the darkness of the wings."

"And what do you think?"

"I think Yehuda Menuhin killed himself," Elish lied, "and I want you to tell his brother that. I think the man committed a heinous crime and his conscience wouldn't leave him alone. The damage he planned to cause his brother only made things worse.

I think he killed himself in a rare moment of self-examination, and in the perfect time–the day after Yom Kippur."

UNTIL HE SPOKE THE WORDS HE TOLD ORA ANATOT, ELISH hadn't realized there had been a good reason he hadn't invested too much effort in investigating the circumstances of Menuhin's death. Had it not been for the web of relationships that spun around Menuhin, leading to Dalia Shushan's murder, he would have probably ended his report to Gideon in a similar fashion, out of a genuine lack of interest. Deep inside, he realized, startled, he felt Yehuda Menuhin deserved to die. What's happening to me? Who appointed me judge of all earth?

Now that the facts in Ora and Gideon's story were known, he contemplated, the solution seemed simple. He'd already eliminated Malkieli. She was greedy and had visited Dalia on that wretched evening only to pressure her into giving her a copy of the songs, but that didn't make her a murderer. She most likely had no idea who Yehuda Menuhin was. Otherwise, she wouldn't have revealed the writing on the demo she very possibly had already received from Dalia that evening, choosing to pretend it had been mailed to her in order to prevent any gossip or connections to Dalia's murder. Only later was she horrified by the power of Dalia, who had dealt with bizarre and ridiculous sorcery and ritual in her lifetime, but in death reached from beyond the grave to write a goodbye note. It was also possible that Malkieli was superstitious and found herself escaping one horror–visiting a deceased woman's home an hour and a half before her death–only to fly straight into the arms of another: a message from oblivion. That's why she cried so hard twice, out of petty fear for her own life. Levana Hacham was obsessive and vengeful, but she had no true motive to murder Dalia so monstrously and, two months later, stage the death of her bitter enemy.

It seemed that the facts–barring two or three marginal ones, which, for the sake of general, well-timed, well-oiled order, could be ignored, just like in every scientific theory–pointed to one answer: Yehuda Menuhin, an intellectual who, in an ideological battle against his own desires, murdered the woman whom he saw as their practical representation–Dalia Shushan, his lover, the recalcitrant temptress, the great whore of Babylon, the mother of all female seductions. He arranged her body in a manner illustrating his struggle–first killing wisdom, then soul; a bullet in each temple, a bullet through the heart. The hands that coveted marked with dust, the legs that enticed painted with fire, and only the flesh left to rot, the abominable stench of lust. And the goddess of fate, or the hand of randomness, leaned in his favor to prove his innocence. He escaped punishment and even received a reward. He threw out the body and its demands, and the mind came out on top: he received information that helped him win the promotion that was scorching the tips of his fingers. Then Yom Kippur appeared on the horizon, and he pored over his books, deepening his interpretation of Cain and Abel. The face of his brother, whom he was meant to meet in two days to coolly inform that nothing would stand in his way, not even the annihilation of Gideon's political career, began to haunt him. At night Dalia Shushan's voice emerged from the shadows: Look what you did to me, it's so hard to live here among the dead. He dreamed of rivers of blood, piles of chopped-off feminine parts swallowing him whole. The next morning, he wandered through his home, upset, the ice around his thoughts melting. He took a sedative, gulped down a glass of wine, but his torment persisted. Two more hours until his meeting with his brother. Dalia's voice whispered, It's cold here all alone. Remember our sweet hours. The gun is in the drawer, the power is yours. Do you not prefer the open, shimmering road to aimless wandering in airless paths through a dark forest? Come to me. Yehuda Menuhin opened the drawer and put the gun to his head.

That simple? So simple that they needed Elish Ben Zaken to come in and weave the facts together? During that dead hour when Eran Shitrit was out of the building, many things could have happened, and had happened. Elish was certain of it. Beyond the polished backdrop of the shaping story was another actor, going feral and taking the reins. A third person, he didn't yet know who, but Manny Lahav owed him an answer to his question, he thought as he watched the man's overgrown body filling the doorway to the café, his hand smoothing his hair before rising to wave at Elish.

13

So, bud, how's your mother doing?" Manny asked as he sat down. Just like last night and the previous times he'd seen him, Manny was wearing one of his endless series of baby-blue shirts. Maybe it's his own private version of a uniform, Elish thought.

"Fine. I promised her this would never happen again. I put that promise on you. I told her you were a senior police officer and that you knew who was behind the attack. That reassured her. I arranged things this morning. Now Gideon Menuhin has a real interest in putting a muzzle on Haim Sasaportas and his team of thugs."

"Odd word, 'muzzle,'" Manny said, smiling.

"Not as odd as 'bud,' trust me. But you get used to things," Elish said coldly.

"Are you finally ready to explain things to me?"

"First, you owe me an answer. Why did you want me to investigate Yehuda Menuhin's suicide? Why me, of all the private investigators in town?"

Manny rubbed his hand against his jaw, dotted with day-old stubble. "Do you really want an explanation?"

"Oh, come on."

"Under one condition. Promise me you won't think poorly of me after I explain it all."

"Why does my opinion matter to you?"

"I like you, Elish, and I don't want you detesting me."

"Okay," said Elish, thinking, This conversation isn't going as planned. "That depends on the nature of your explanation."

"Look, I've already gathered from our conversations that sometimes you think I'm an innocent fool and other times you think I'm devious and conniving. But I'm neither. I'm just a regular guy, who's aware of the limitations of his power and even more aware of the ways power acts around him. I've known Gideon Menuhin since we were young, I told you that already, and I've always known that Gideon Menuhin has no friends, only a line of servants intent on helping him conquer one goal after the other. When he approached me about this, after I'd already determined that his brother's death was a suicide, and asked me to find a reliable outside investigator to reexamine the circumstances of his brother's death, I lost it. I thought, Why is he approaching me? What does he think my special investigations team does all day? Look for easy ways out? Determine suicide to save itself the hassle? His exploitation and lack of appreciation had ascended to new levels that I hadn't known from him before. He didn't even bother to try and trick me."

"Why didn't you tell him to go to hell?"

"He's a deputy minister. He's ambitious and power hungry. He'll go far. He may not appreciate friendship, but he respects influence and acquaintances in high places. My position in the police is not the best right now. Ever since the assassination wars broke out between Tel Aviv gangs, my team, and me especially, have not been the chief of police's favorites. I had to agree. As far as I know, he could be the next minister of public safety."

"I guessed most of that myself, actually," Elish said, cutting him off. "Now you're reaching the point where I started getting suspicious. What's your interest in opening the case? If I provided him with evidence that allowed him to reopen his brother's case, you would have had to clear your office within a matter of days."

"You think that hadn't occurred to me? The advantage of his proposal was that I could pick the investigator myself. He asked to stay behind the scenes, and I could guess why. According to rumors, his brother carried quite a bit of weight on his back. I came to you because I spotted your name in Dalia Shushan's file. I read what you wrote about her. I told you already, your agency is small and has a reputation as a fair, discreet agency, which I couldn't easily say about the other investigation agencies in town."

"We'll get to the Dalia Shushan file in a minute. Why do you think Gideon wanted an investigation? What does he think actually happened?"

"He has no doubt that his brother was murdered. He didn't say why. As far as I'm concerned, there was nothing at the scene of the crime to point in that direction."

"Unless he had additional information. His brother had tried to extort Gideon's former romantic partner, Ora Anatot."

"You think Gideon suspected that Ora murdered Yehuda?" Manny asked, surprised.

"You said it yourself—Gideon is a power addict. He'll do anything to defend himself. Why would he assume others are any different? But we're getting off track from the question that is of utmost importance for this entire mystery—why me?"

"I thought you'd figured that out already," Manny said, fixing his eyes on Elish. "As far as I'm concerned, the only chance I had was to find someone to stand by my side."

"That's it? Someone to stand by your side?" Elish started to laugh. "You approached me because you thought I'd harbor trust and affection for you and empathize with your fragile status in the police force? Is that your estimation of my professional integrity, which you pointed out earlier? That isn't a good enough answer. I refuse to accept it."

Manny furrowed his brow with confusion. "What kind of answer were you expecting? I have no doubt that Yehuda Menuhin killed himself. And I thought after you'd get to know me . . ." he trailed off awkwardly.

"I'd report any new evidence to you, so you could have enough time to prepare for the consequences, or possibly stop them in time," Elish completed his thought for him.

"Yes, thank you."

"When you gave me Menuhin's file you were convinced I'd be interested in it. Why? Because of Dalia Shushan?"

"What does Dalia Shushan have to do with anything? After I heard your lecture I thought you'd be curious to investigate the suicide of a philosopher." Manny looked at him quizzically. His surprise was genuine.

Elish thought, He really doesn't know what this is about. He placed his copy of Yehuda Menuhin's file on the table and pulled out the newspaper clipping, in which the highlighted lines–"Dr. Yehuda Menuhin was so impressed with her entry exam, that he asked her to be his teaching assistant in the Philosophy Department as early as her first year"–were colored gray. "So explain this to me," he said.

The helplessness on Manny's face deepened as he looked at the clipping. He balled his right hand into a fist and leaned his cheek against it. "This is the first time I'm seeing this document."

"You didn't go over the clippings in Menuhin's archive file?" Elish demanded.

"I didn't need to. For one, it isn't my job, even though I was very involved in the Yehuda Menuhin investigation. And second, we only order newspaper archival material on rare occasions. In Shushan's case, even though we had a certain murder suspect, we had to present the appearance of an investigation, and when we open a murder investigation and put together a team, we need all necessary information, including newspaper clippings. But here it was clear this was suicide from the first time I or the head of my team laid eyes on the body."

"Oh," said Elish. Tahel floated into his mind, eyes torn open, turning her head, turning the purple puzzle piece in her hand,

and slipping it into its place on the board. "Oh," he repeated, "now almost everything is clear."

"Here we go again," Manny remarked after a brief silence. "What's the story? You assumed I was trying to pull you into this investigation for some dark reason, and that I used Dalia Shushan's name to get you intrigued?"

"That's how it seemed when you left my office that night."

"You could have asked me about that clipping a long time ago."

"I didn't trust you. That night, you waved Dalia's name around, and the next day you refused to let me meet Gideon Menuhin for questioning."

"The truth is, it doesn't matter. If you had asked me, and I'd told you I had no intention of tricking you, that I was not aware of the existence of that archive envelope in the file I gave you, would you have believed me?"

"Honestly? No."

"And if you'd have insisted, I would have told you then what I'm telling you now–the highlighted lines you just showed me don't mean a thing to me. You know how many random connections there are between people? And Tel Aviv is a small city. Someone at the special investigations team must have decided to be proactive and automatically ordered the archival materials. It's a large system, this kind of error happens all the time."

"Not in this case. Because regardless of whether or not you had any hidden intentions in adding the archival materials to Menuhin's file, you had your chance to serve truth rather than justice."

"What's the difference between the two?"

"Faith," said Elish. "That's all."

"Faith?"

"Faith. You wanted to know the distinction between truth and justice, and I'm telling you, it's faith. The truth, as dirty as it is, only needs to be borne. Justice obligates you to act. It requires faith in the idea that you're an adequate authority to intervene in the order of this world. To make judgments."

"And you," Manny examined Elish's face carefully, waiting for a twitch of the eyes, the jaw muscles, to disclose Elish's sincerity or lack of seriousness when he answered the question, "do you not have faith?"

"No," Elish said decisively, thinking, I've lost my faith like a guy dropping a coin at the market. Only the penniless and the slow-minded would duck under market stalls to look for it. Only the desperate insist that the coin they found is the one they lost.

Manny looked away, then said almost offhandedly, "Okay, whatever."

Elish knew he was simplifying things, and perhaps thus cheating Manny, because he believed that the truth, knowing the truth, was its own reward and punishment, requiring no system to translate it into the existential chaos, into the stench and hubbub of the everyday, into the kingdom of human obtuseness, of powerlessness. But he could tell the discussion was tiring Manny, so instead he smiled at him. "My turn. Let me ask you something. Esther Shushan called you and told you'd she'd gone to see Ezra Buhbut, and that she didn't believe he murdered Dalia, and you blew her off. Why?"

Manny didn't answer. He raised his hand to signal to the server. "They have such bad service here. We've been sitting at this table for twenty minutes and no one's even come over yet," he said. "Will you join me for coffee, Elish?"

Elish drummed the fingers of his left hand against the table. The familiar pain mixed in with a new distress of the arm, focusing his thinking, clarifying. "Are you going to answer me?"

"Two cappuccinos," Manny said, then turned to Elish, who added, "No foam for me."

The embarrassment fell off Manny's face, replaced by a softened expression, as he said, "The hardest thing about Shushan's file—which, by the way, was a very simple case to crack—was speaking to her parents. I spoke to them myself, rather than sending the head of the special investigations team, because of the media interest. Dalia's father had shut himself off. That I could deal with. But her mother wasn't willing to let go of the pain for a minute, as if she had to feel her daughter's death at every instant, as if Dalia would disappear if she forgot her, if she failed to mourn her for a fraction of a second."

"Don't you think she deserves to know the truth?"

"What truth? Her daughter's murderer was arrested and convicted in record time. Besides having her daughter come back to life, she couldn't have asked for anything more."

"Didn't you ask yourself why Dalia's body was positioned the way it was?"

"Of course I did. That was the first question I asked the head of the special investigations team when he caught me up on the process. You can't imagine how I felt like exploding from disgust and anger when he showed me the photographs from the murder scene. That crazy sadist. It wasn't enough to shoot her once, he had to abuse her too."

"And no one in that special team of yours had any second thoughts? No one wondered why none of Buhbut's actions matched the profile of a junkie and occasional robber?"

"What are you talking about?" Manny said, losing his cool. "Don't pull that Hollywood movie crap on me. A murderer's profile, yeah right. You never know what people are capable of. What do you think when a mother walks into her son's room and catches him looking at porn sites instead of doing his homework and stabs him to death, then sits at the kitchen table waiting for the police to arrive, is that something you can understand? Or when a man comes home one night and asks his wife why she didn't pay the phone bill and she gets mad for the first time in twenty years of marriage and says, 'I'm not your servant,' and they get into a fight, and one thing leads to another and he breaks a chair on her head, is that something you can wrap your mind around? If there's anything I've learned in all my years of police work, it's that there's always a reason, and usually it isn't sufficient. The other ninety-nine percent of the population has the same kinds of reasons, the same arguments and fights, but they never commit murder."

"Let's get back to Esther Shushan," Elish said, uncomfortable at the sight of Manny's anger. Why?

"She called me and told me the story about Buhbut and what a poor guy he is. She thinks junkies are kind souls who wouldn't hurt a fly. Her younger brother was a junkie who became religious, so it might have made her believe that there's some kind of ethical core to junkies. And generally, I think, from the way she spoke to me, that she doesn't have much faith in the Israel Police. That's a problem. From the moment you have a non-law-abiding citizen at home, nothing can make you trust the police."

Manny had no right to say what he'd said. That woman, Esther Shushan, hadn't lost her sincerity for even a moment, her strong faith in a justice system–a system that was perhaps inhuman, perhaps not in line with Elish's views, but still powerful. There was not the tiniest hint of personal interest or inclination in her faith. It was completely pure, and the insinuation that grief or an ancient abhorrence of the police force had muddled her judgment, as well as the patronizing tone Manny used, enraged Elish. He erupted, his voice rising to an atypical shout, "Maybe you're trying to say that once someone faces the brutality and roughness with which the Israel Police treats the citizens it is meant to protect, they don't have much reason to trust it again."

"Not for me," Manny said assertively. "But Sderot is a small town, and there must be some unresolved conflicts. The local cops are the kids you went to school with, the ones whose laundry you accidentally spilled your mop water on when it was hanging out to dry or whose house you threw your garbage in front of."

"This is a superfluous argument. It's obvious you're proud of your work and the privilege of serving in the police force. If that's true, I need to tell you something you aren't going to like. Shushan's murder investigation was a disgrace. You, your subordinates, and the court of law, gave in completely to the dictates of the media and public sentiment." This wasn't how Elish wanted to say these things, but he didn't regret the words once they were spoken.

Manny was astounded. "Why do you keep talking about her murder? I told you the two cases aren't connected. I'm sorry I gave you her file. I only did it because . . ." The assertiveness in Manny's voice disappeared, replaced again by embarrassment.

"Get used to saying it too." Elish finished his sentence for him. "You did it to win my affection, as a sign of trust, an emotional manipulation to help you preserve your status. I've internalized your thought patterns. I don't care. What matters here is that Ezra Buhbut didn't murder Dalia Shushan."

Manny, who had brought his mug to his lips, now lowered it sharply, leaving foam on his nose and upper lip, and looked at Elish. "What are you talking about?"

The speedy tone change of the last twenty minutes shook Elish up a little, and he burst out laughing. There was no other reason why Manny Lahav's face, covered in foamed milk, would suddenly appear so amusing. Cheap slapstick, he thought, that's what I get in return for my intense cognitive work. Cheap slapstick. He said, his voice turning shallow, emptying of all tone, "You shouldn't have asked for foamed milk. The foaming process is a German invention, the main reason for the hole in the ozone layer. It isn't about the official reason they give us, like deodorant and air pollution."

"You're nuts," Manny said, a little startled. "What proof have you got?"

"Manny, our conversation began with an air of misunderstanding and has been controlled by it ever since. But it's a good kind of misunderstanding. Because there's a limited measure of misunderstandings in the universe, and while some of it is concentrated here, an enormous layer of fog is lifting from other places."

"And in simple language?"

"In simple language, I ask you, with deference and as a gesture of good will, to check two things, the results of which I'm fairly certain of, if you would be so kind as to check them, of course. The first is whether the bullets that ended Dalia Shushan's life were shot by the same gun that Yehuda Menuhin used to kill himself. The second is how the archival materials made it into Menuhin's file."

"Then will I get a full explanation of this pandemonium?"

Pandemonium, thought Elish. The echo of the deciding blow against the deadbolts of memory. Elish heard it administered and ringing, the mechanism screeching and collapsing, the light railing and dispersing. "You have my word," he said.

14

From the first moment, Elish thought it was a bad idea, and so did his mother, though she never put her objection into words, instead overseeing the preparations lazily, barely rushing him or Yaffa to hurry up and get dressed. It was as if the morning hours were lying ahead, unfinishable, promising to stay golden forever. She sliced the bread with demonstrable slowness, smearing the vegetarian spread on the plump slices, while Yaffa, eight years old, followed her with concern from the doorway, lest she accidentally add a tomato to her sandwich or forget a double layer of sausage in Prosper's. Elish, who never showed much interest in food and subsisted, with measured chews, on anything placed before him, helped his father tie up the cooler and bring the blanket down to the car, and when they were at the car, Elish, hopping to keep the asphalt that had quickly absorbed the heat of summer from scorching his bare feet, dared to ask, "But why go to Tel Aviv? There's a beach in Ashkelon."

His father bared his teeth in a grin, eyes twinkling impishly in his bony face. "There's more eye candy in Tel Aviv. Besides, we're going to the amusement park tonight. Isn't that what you wanted?"

Of the rest of them, only Yaffa looked happy as they drove off. She loved riding in cars, even in the faltering Ford Escort they owned. She loved gluing her face to the window and watching. "I wish there were clouds," she told Elish, sitting beside her in the backseat. "We could have looked for animal shapes."

"Forget that nonsense. I brought Uno."

"Will you let me win?" Yaffa asked.

Hilton Beach was drowning with sunbathers, yards of browning and burning skin. Elish sprawled out on the blanket they'd spread underneath one of the wooden sheds. The bathers whose heads besmirched the surface of the sea took away his desire to swim. His mother was sitting on a beach chair, far away from him, near the water, her back turned to him, her hair loose, light brown, hanging on the back of the chair, carefully following his father, who wandered like an explorer among the islands of flesh flipping over on their towels. Yaffa, in a bubblegum-colored bikini, crouched down to build something in the sand. Elish returned his eyes to the book he was reading, Astrid Lindgren's *A Kalle Blomkvist Mystery: Living Dangerously*. The northern countries swallowed up the Tel Aviv beaches.

Yaffa came running up, sobbing, cracking the illusion into which he'd been pulled.

Elish closed his book. "What now?"

"Those kids," she pointed, "ruined my sand castle and kicked me too."

Elish took her hand in his. "Show me exactly who."

"So this is your brother? This twig?" one of the kids asked when they reached them. "What can *he* do to *us*?"

"Leave her alone," said Elish. "Picking on a little girl."

"Picking on a little girl like you," the other boy said, shoving Elish's shoulder. "Come on, let's see you." The other kids started laughing.

"Let's go, Yaffa, we can't reason with them." He turned around, and the boy used the opportunity to kick him. Elish stumbled onto the sand with the force of the unexpected blow. The other children cheered. One of them yelled, "We haven't seen him bleed yet!"

Elish got up and stood tall in front of the boy. "What do you think you're doing, huh?"

The boy smiled teasingly. "Let's go."

Elish drew nearer. Another, smaller boy, who'd been standing in back, somewhat concealed, unnoticed by Elish, slipped a fist between the two of them, punching Elish in the diaphragm. The sudden pain made his breath catch, and he folded over. Elish's opponent took the opportunity to slap him. The group of boys burst out laughing. Yaffa cried, "Daddy, Daddy!"

Prosper's threatening figure popped up from out of nowhere and grabbed the leader of the pack by the hair. The boy let out a scream, and his friends fled. "Get out of here," Prosper muttered, tossing the boy aside like a piece of scrap paper.

Elish couldn't contain his tears, the paralyzing pain in his stomach, narrowing his breath, or the insult of the shameful slap, which he had no doubt his father had seen. He raised his tearful face.

"Why are you crying like some pussy?" Prosper barked. "Clean your face. How many times did I tell you not to get into fights with kids you can't hit back, huh? How many times?"

"But Daddy," Yaffa defended him, "they started it."

"I don't care," he said drily. Then, to Elish, who was still sobbing, "Go back to the shed and don't leave until I give you permission, got it?"

Under the thatched roof of the wooden cabana, Elish lay on his back and stared into the sky. He could no longer concentrate on Kalle Blomkvist and his Wars of the Roses and the perils he escaped heroically.

Yaffa came back fifteen minutes later. "I'm bored," she said, "and I keep worrying those kids are going to come back. Let's play Uno."

"No," said Elish, "I've had enough." He felt a fury, having laid dormant inside of him for too long, cold and restrained, igniting. His stomach clouded his usual serenity, a white-hot dot shrinking and expanding in its center. "It's like this all the time–go to your room and don't come out, don't move until I give you permission. I'm sick of it, Yaffa, do you get it? Let's go in the water."

"But Daddy said—" she protested as Elish stood up.

"I don't care what he said." He took her arm and pulled her behind him, hard.

Prosper's sharp summoning caught them in the middle of their way to the water. "Elish, get back here. Right now."

Elish turned around and saw his father advancing over at a skipping pace, and his mother sitting up. He let go of Yaffa's hand and broke into a run. Today he would put an end to it, he told himself, it ends now. No more hitting, no more punishments. He ran to the breakwater, shoving his way between people's bodies. "Elish, just wait till I catch you . . ." he heard his father's tense voice behind him, but he'd already hopped off from the sand to the rocky path of the breakwater, realizing at the very last moment that though he'd rid himself of the heavy motion forced by the sand, he'd led himself into a dead end. His father was faster on the hard surface of the breakwater. Elish turned left, into an empty patch of rock, advanced toward the boulder belt creating a border with the water, not thinking in terms of danger, of what might happen to him, clenched his jaws, and hopped onto the boulders, which marked the pathetic end of his escape. He landed on one of them, hopping between them, until his face met a screen of sprayed water from the waves, and something within him calmed and divided. He paused and turned around to face his pursuer. His father's face was a mixture of anger, effort, and an odd giddiness of victory, like a predator about to pounce on its prey and sink its teeth into it, only three boulders away. His father raised his right foot, expanding his next skip, miscalculating the slipperiness of the seaweed-covered surface on which he was standing, which just a moment earlier had been washed over. His lithe lunge ahead became a clumsy fall backward.

Thump.

• • •

HOW IS A TEN-YEAR-OLD CHILD EXPECTED TO UNDERSTAND such a thump? Life hadn't prepared him for different kinds of thumps. There is the buzzing inside the skull, which he is familiar with, whenever he receives a slap, and there is the dull echo of the shock when someone head-butts him. But that's it, his entire thumping repertoire. He still hasn't witnessed from up close the surprise contained in the anticipation of an unusual event that evaporates when the event takes place in a revoltingly familiar fashion. He doesn't even know how banal that thump he's hearing is, how mundane the sound of a head shattering against a rock. He still can't appreciate the irony of the routine.

The light freezes around him, viscous and golden, time made of honey. A metallic cloud thickens his arteries. He knows he is meant to scream, but instead he stares at the blood attacking the boulders from the shattered head and turning the black hair into sticky mush, watching the open eyes with astonishment, fixing on an unknown point in space, at the face whose features are contorted by the pain of the blow, the face he cannot think of in conjunction with the word "Dad," and blood, more blood, streaming and showering. What does it all mean? His head is draped with a thin film of silence, a river of minutes snaking around his ankles like a swarm of ants as he looks at the blood, until Yaffa's scream forces him to prick up his ears, a dull scream from the other side of the water. His eyes are dry. He looks at her. What's she screaming about, that one? His mother comes running after her, then comes to a halt and grabs her hair, her lips opening with horrifying slowness: "No, Prosper, no." And then she raises her voice too. Why is she wearing a skirt, and a floral one, no less? They're at the beach, aren't they? Where's her bathing suit? The universe moves too slowly. Yaffa buries her small face in the skirt and trembles, people gather around, a small group of men in uniform, like fireflies, making its way toward him, tearing through the glitter of the sticky air he's breathing, full of purpose. Elish sits down on one of the boulders and watches them with wonder.

• • •

NINETEEN YEARS LATER, ELISH STOOD AT HILTON BEACH, HUMming a Blasé tune, looking directly at the powerful empire of salt and water, seaweed and seashells, under heavy clouds that darkened the afternoon. Shards of lightning danced like sparks, the gut-twisting smell of the sea finally died down. What sort of justice can be done for the dead, he'd asked Esther Shushan last Sunday. Now it was his turn to answer. What sort of justice can be done for them? They were already ensconced within absolute truth, but we, who live on this earth, still require the delusions of human memory, the deepening lies of those who've traveled to the horizon, to the depths, and returned with nothing but the shadows of fear. "I'm sorry," he said out loud, "but that's exactly what I have to do too." The water raged, as was its way. Water never stopped raging. "And I will put enmity between you and me," Elish told the sea, then laughed bitterly.

He turned around and walked back to the office, where Lilian gave him a message from Ora Anatot: "Gideon has accepted your offer. He said he'll keep a close watch," and another from Manny Lahav: "Elish, you're a genius. A perfect match. Call me. My cell is on."

He asked for an extension until that evening, and Manny—who was excited about the new findings and demanded a detailed explanation of the mystery's resolution and the connections that led from Dalia Shushan to her real murderer, Yehuda Menuhin, who later ended his own life with the same gun he used to murder her—told him he was in the midst of processing the repercussions anyway. And, by the way, the second query, Manny added, was the more complex one, but one of his investigators recalled that two days after Menuhin's suicide, when she arrived at work, she saw a messenger from the *Everything Tel Aviv* archive who was causing a scene at the lobby, saying he was supposed to personally deliver an urgent envelope from the archive to

Superintendent Binyamini. When she told him she didn't know what case this envelope related to, he excused himself, had a brief conversation over his two-way radio, then returned and said it was intended for the Yehuda Menuhin file. She thought it odd, but had the envelope filed anyway. Though he already knew the answer, Elish asked if she could describe the messenger, and Manny said he'd asked her the same thing, and that she'd said he hadn't removed his helmet or sunglasses.

Elish went downstairs to Ben Yehuda Street and hailed a cab. "Corner of Herzl and Lewinsky, please," he told the driver. When he arrived, he climbed the crumbling, urine-reeking stairs to the second floor and knocked on the door.

"Elish?" Rami Amzaleg marveled when he opened the door. "What are you doing here?"

Elish waved his recorder. "Follow-up questions for my article."

15

The door to Rami Amzaleg's apartment locked behind Elish's back as he walked into the inner room, placed the recorder on a table, and without delay, said, "Yehuda Menuhin murdered Dalia Shushan in some kind of twisted ritual. Two months later, the day he heard about the suicide of her alleged murderer, Ezra Buhbut, he was overcome by scruples, put a gun to his head, and ended his own life. What about this story doesn't add up?"

"Huh?" Rami said. "Did you go bananas?"

"Drop the act, Rami," said Elish, "I know almost everything already, and I'm tired of these evasions."

Rami turned off the recorder. "What are you talking about?"

"Seek out the motivation, uncover the power structure," Elish said coolly. "From the moment I realized Ezra Buhbut hadn't murdered Dalia Shushan, I kept asking myself the wrong question: 'Who?' If not Buhbut, then who committed the murder? It took me a while to realize that the real question is 'Why?' Why was Dalia Shushan murdered? Then I noticed an odd pattern: Nobody had a motive to murder Dalia. Malkieli wanted her songs very badly, Lior Levitan felt betrayed, you got into a fight with her the night before her death, but it was clear beyond all doubt that you loved her, that her neighbor peeped on her but nothing more. I also checked other loose ends. I even spoke to her cousin Ronnit—there was a slight chance she'd harbored a secret hatred toward Dalia. The only person to whom a possible motive could be attributed was Yehuda Menuhin, her lover, who killed himself two months later, but I was becoming convinced that his death was a murder, or at the very least a forced suicide, under coercion. Then I remembered the question you asked during my university lecture."

"Yeah?" Rami muttered, his pupils focused with suspicion.

"Yeah. I was talking about compulsiveness as the foundation of ceremony and ritual, and you asked about compulsiveness as the origin of a unique style, as an artistic thumbprint."

"I don't understand the connection between the two."

"Yehuda Menuhin's death was presented as suicide, but it wasn't. Unlike Dalia Shushan, many people around Menuhin had strong motives for murdering him. He extorted and abused people; he enjoyed humiliating others and causing misery. His brother, Ora Anatot, Haim Sasaportas, his vindictive neighbor Levana Hacham, even Debbie Malkieli or Lior Levitan, had they known him—each of these people had a motive to murder him or force him to take his own life. Then an awful thought hit me—what if, just like Menuhin's death was like a farce about suicide, Dalia Shushan's murder was also an act? What if the ritual, the open arms, the gunpowder marks, were all just spots on a camouflage net?"

"Okay," said Rami, ponderous. "You're onto something here."

"The reflection game, the sleight of hand, it all looked familiar. It reminded me of the music you wrote for Blasé. Your songs pretended to sound like one thing, but they were actually something else. When it comes to form, to structure, to flow, your talent borders on the genius."

"Thank you, but what you're saying is nothing more than an abstract idea," said Rami.

"That's of course only the cognitive framework that helped me organize the facts. In practice, from the moment I realized I was looking at the sequence of events through the wrong eyes, and that I needed to turn the image around before I could look at it properly, all sorts of tiny details started to line up. Someone was responsible for the archival materials in Menuhin's file, which connected him to Dalia Shushan. The file wasn't supposed to contain that envelope. You have a part-time job at the *Everything Tel Aviv* archive, which is where the envelope came from. Someone wanted me to show up at Dalia's tribute concert, and Nicole, your ex-girlfriend, suddenly made sure I got an invitation. Nicole–how convenient–also told me that night about the writing on Dalia's demo, which Malkieli had come over to request a copy of the night before, when she was seemingly turned down. And what's the meaning of the contradictory answers for why you didn't perform that night? Again, there's Nicole, who surprisingly left for three months in India the day after the show. That night, you told me you knew a song that, according to all testimonies, even your indirect testimony, nobody was supposed to hear before the demo appeared in Malkieli's office. I could have written all these questions off as unimportant, just little interruptions to reality preventing theories from being perfect. But I couldn't ignore the feeling that some shadow person I couldn't see was drawing me into their web, timing the performance for me."

"Well, that's because you're paranoid, but you already know that, don't you?"

Elish ignored the diagnosis. "Don't you think I've earned the right to hear the whole story?"

"You still haven't told me what you think happened."

"Oh, that," said Elish. "Dalia Shushan killed herself, and you staged it to look like murder. Two months later, you murdered Yehuda Menuhin and staged his death to look like a suicide. Then, when I began investigating, you tried to direct the course of events to make sure I reached the conclusion that Yehuda murdered Dalia and then killed himself, because he couldn't bear his pangs of conscience. I want to hear how it happened, and above all, I want to know why. Why?"

• • •

RAMI WAS PACING THE ROOM. THE RAIN THAT HAD STARTED falling as they spoke filled the silence that had landed with the roar of slamming water, which blocked out the sound of honking horns and rumbling engines from the street. The scent of wet asphalt wafted through the half-opened window, tickling his nostrils. Rami had made a decision.

"I met Dalia at the university, in Yehuda Menuhin's class. She was his teaching assistant, so she had to attend all of his classes. We got very close at the end of the first semester and started playing together. By the second semester, when I took the next part of the intro class, which Yehuda also taught, we'd already formed a duo and were writing songs. Dalia trusted me enough to tell me he was harassing her, making inappropriate proposals, constantly looking for ways to humiliate her, fixating on every little mistake she made and bringing them up constantly. He quickly recognized Dalia's difficulty with human relationships and how concerned she was about it, and would ask intrusive questions whenever he saw her speaking to anyone. He addressed every idea she had as proof of her inability to create bonds with others. I pressured her to quit her job with him, but she had trouble reaching a decision. She told me that quitting would be like admitting defeat. In the middle of the semester I walked into his office and told him to leave her alone or I would report him to the ethics committee. That dried-out son of a bitch looked at me with scorn and said, all cool, 'You'd better worry about your own affairs.' A week later I got a letter from the department, informing me that due to over-registration to Menuhin's class, they were forced to cancel my participation.

"But my efforts were not in vain. At the end of that year, Dalia decided to leave the Philosophy Department and focus on history and film. I thought it was over and now we had good times ahead. We had signed with Malkieli, and we took the summer of that year, 1998, to get the songs ready at our own pace and then record them. The album came out, and you're the last person I need to tell about all the hype around it. We both quit the university, started performing, and wrote new songs. I think it was the happiest time in Dalia's life, but it's possible she didn't know how to be happy, because one day, sometime in late '99, near the time when we were about to take a break from performing to record a second album, Menuhin came to one of our concerts and was brash enough to come see us backstage. I was seething. But he didn't talk to me. He only addressed Dalia, who asked him, 'What are you doing, Yehuda? I thought you weren't interested in music.' And he said, 'You spent an entire year listening to what I had to say. It's time I listened to what you do.' And that was it. They started chatting, and I was so mad I just packed up my equipment and left.

"Within a few months, Dalia started having those mood swings she had when I first met her at school. One day she was on the verge of tears, the next she was on cloud nine. At first I thought she was nervous about recording the second album, that she was afraid not to meet the enormous expectations built around us, and I tried to calm her down. Nothing worked. At some point, right when we were in the middle of recording the chorus for 'Like Underwater,' she started to cry."

Not everyone is worthy of love / but everyone deserves to be seen / to have another's eye linger on them / to be desired to no end for a moment in time. The words rushed through Elish's mind. "I'm hearing it a different way now," he said.

"Not me," said Rami. "I got what Dalia was trying to say right away. That was the moment I started to suspect it was about more than stress. I put two and two together and asked her if she was in touch with Yehuda. She yelled at me, saying it was none of my business, and I said nothing. I knew I'd hit the mark.

"The album came out, and was praised all around. But Dalia fell into a depression. One night, I followed her to Jaffa. She walked into some building. The next day I went to the same building to check it out. Turned out that Yehuda Menuhin lived there. I thought about ways of reaching him and forcing him to break off their relationship. I'd sit around, imagining what kind of twisted, monstrous humiliation he was putting her through. It was obvious he was the abusive type. When Dalia told me she wanted to break up the band the night we performed the new album for the first time, I couldn't keep quiet about it anymore. I confronted her. She only said I didn't understand anything. We cut off contact. Funny, now that I think about it, she called me a few months later, after your book came out, to tell me that my segment was excellent, that she didn't remember I could talk like that. I told her I'd missed her, and I was so hopeful she'd done the right thing during the months we hadn't talked. She hadn't. Her mood swings only got worse, more extreme, her depressions deeper. I watched her drowning and didn't know what to do.

"Then one day, six or eight months later, she told me they'd broken up. He dumped her and she was sick of suffering. I said nothing. She didn't even mention the name of her secret lover, though I knew who it was. Three months later, she started dating Lior Levitan. Irony of fate—if she'd told me a year earlier she wanted to date Levitan, I would have thrown up in her face, but at that point I was glad, until I realized she'd found a new and better way of torturing herself. It wasn't enough that she then went back to Yehuda's den of snakes, but she also tormented herself for betraying the trust of a man who may not have been very smart, but who loved her, adored her, and was even willing to bear her unfaithfulness."

Rami fell silent, standing up. He disappeared into the hallway and returned with three notebooks, which he handed to Elish. "She documented her relationship with Menuhin in these notebooks. He had a room in his apartment that she wasn't allowed into, and occasionally he'd lock himself in there when she came over and she had to cry and beg to be let in. He'd yell at her that she was inferior, worthless, that her songs were real garbage, but the moment he realized he'd crossed a line he'd start courting her like a teenager, telling her how much he admired her talent and what a shame it was she was wasting it on bad songs. He made sure she was always unstable. When she was happy he'd kill her good mood, and when she was depressed he made her believe in herself. He let her understand he was disgusted by her body and was doing her a favor by fucking her, that no other man would be willing to do that for her. He was twisted, and Dalia played along with it."

Elish opened the first notebook to a random page and read, "Yehuda bought me a dress that cost a fortune. He knows my size, but he still bought a dress that was two sizes too small. In the mirror I saw a monster. The silk that is meant to smooth curves actually emphasizes bulges. My breasts hovered in front of me, the flesh of the arms was puffy and swollen around the sleeves. I came to him, and he said, 'Take your guitar and sing the Blasé song that makes you feel most sensual.' I sang 'Now It's Time for the Flesh to Speak.' Yehuda laughed all through the song."

In the second notebook, his eyes fell on the following paragraph: "I talked to Yehuda about my ideas on the ending of the Book of Job. He said, 'You've got to write a paper about that, you have some original points.' I slaved over the paper for two days. It's been so long since I did any theoretical thinking, but the patterns and associations returned to me effortlessly, like an old habit. When it was finished, I left a copy in his mailbox. The next evening, when I came over, he said, 'You've got one of the dullest minds I've ever come across.' He spat on the pages, crumpled them, threw them on the floor, and locked himself in his room. Only at dawn, after hours of begging, did he open the door for me, and we went to bed. After he came, he groaned and said softly, 'Dalia, Dalia, you've got such immense intellectual potential. It's a shame you're so lazy.'"

The notebook ended with a brief entry: "Yehuda realized

that in the past week he's no longer caused me sorrow. He keeps trying, but his words and actions reach me through several cubic yards of cotton balls. I came over last night. He opened the door for me and went into his room. There was a gift on the table, with a card reading, 'To my lovely hunk of meat.' Inside I found a book. *How to Hold On to Your Man.* Yehuda came out of the room thirty minutes later. I was sitting with my hands in my lap and looked at him calmly. I hadn't bothered looking at the book. He said, 'Don't come here anymore. Our affair is over.' On my way out I felt my skin peeling, exposing my flesh to the sun again."

Elish knew how the third notebook was going to start, and fought against the expression of revulsion that crawled onto his face.

"A real son of a bitch, huh?" said Rami.

"Why did Dalia play along with it?"

"I've been asking myself the same question. The answer that seems most likely is that, like every other great artist, Dalia had a strong self-destructive urge. Other artists become addicted to drugs or alcohol; she got addicted to the man who could hurt her the most."

"That simple?"

"Yeah. What did you want to find, some awful secret she was hiding? Sometimes things are just that simple. Do you have something else in mind?"

"Maybe it was her path to redemption."

"Like those weirdos who lie on a bed of nails or starve themselves? No, no. Don't you get it yet? Maybe because you still can't admit you've been in love with her this entire time, you're missing one thing." Rami's voice broke for the first time since the conversation began. "Dalia was the fucking madwoman in the attic."

"What do you mean?" Elish rolled Rami's last statements slowly through his brain.

"When we'd just formed Blasé, I spotted Dalia at the cafeteria one day, reading a book. It was the biography of some poet who'd gone nuts and killed herself. I asked her what the book was about, and she said, 'The great cultural myth that pushes the insane into the arms of their own insanity, without realizing that even if some amazing art would come from this, it would never compare to the price they pay, the suffering it takes.' She didn't realize she was talking about herself, that she was waiting in line. At some point she discovered that her loneliness, and pain—how did she write about it in 'Before Everything'? 'Like every living thing, I'm good at wilting.' That this talent could get her love, but that no matter how much love she'd receive, it would never be enough, because her hunger for love wasn't her real damage. Her damage was someplace else. Someplace none of us could reach. But she played her part, letting the world push at her and suck the honey that dripped from her fucking wounds."

HOW ARE PEOPLE REVEALED? ELISH WONDERED. HOW DO THEY appear as they are, some glow that seeps beyond the tatter of their actions, a bright nucleus that detaches from the person and becomes its own essence, beyond judgment? For some reason, it was the image of Levana Hacham that rose before him, the remnants of bleach in her hair, the nervous gesture of the cigarette held between forefinger and middle finger, a masculine grip, her mouth that sloped downward as she talked back to the woman at the café, almost spitting the words, and her lowered, almost defeated head, as she muttered, "The day of the suicide bombing at the central bus terminal." He was skilled at observing people. So what happened? Why hadn't he seen anything more than a source in Levana Hacham? Where was her glow? Where was the revelation every human being deserved? And Rami? Where was his brightness, beyond the filth of death through which he wallowed? When Elish looked at him, what did he see? A man of twenty-eight years, skinny from years of weed smoking, the only anchor he had having abandoned him by choice.

Elish watched him fighting to escape the language he was used to, which was too meager to express what he'd done, but giving in to it for bits of sentences at a time. The stubble on his shaved head disclosed his receding hairline, which was the first stage in his body's plan of wearing out, extracting itself from Rami's control. But if Elish strained his eyes, he was able to notice something more refined. In their death, all humans take a respite from their humanity, more ludicrous than the people they once were, more magnificent. The same majesty was infused into the executioner. A thin veil, imperceptible to the naked eye, had fallen over Rami, who sat silently for a moment before continuing: "In the last month of her life—you can see it for yourself in her notebooks—after Menuhin's torture reached new levels of cruelty, Dalia decided to break off contact with all people. She broke up with Lior and Yehuda, barely spoke to me, and stayed home. That's when she wrote all her new songs. The day she died, she showed up at a coffee shop here in the neighborhood. Turns out she was waiting for me. I got there in a shitty mood, and the moment I saw her, I got angry, I don't even know why. Maybe because she hadn't talked to me for a month, was cold to me, indifferent to my efforts, then suddenly showed up, when it suited her, to demand my undivided attention.

"We talked. She told me she was leaving Tel Aviv and going back to Sderot. I got upset. I thought she'd found a new way to torture herself. We did a concert there, in Sderot, between the first and second album, at some idiotic rock festival organized by the city. As soon as we drove into town we saw that stupid sign they put up for the festival. It said 'Dalia Shushan' in the center, not 'Blasé et Sans Lumière.' Dalia lost her mind, and when we got up onstage she told me to put on a basic drum loop and play all the chord changes we usually use for our balance or warm-up. She started singing about the narrowmindedness of the people of Sderot, how primitive they were, unable to appreciate any form of art, and how hard it had been for her to grow up there. After fifteen minutes of talking shit about Sderot, and the audience booing, someone got wise and turned off the sound system. They got us offstage. After that day she was no longer welcome there.

"After that she told me she'd written twenty new songs and was going to work on them down in Sderot, and I got even madder. I should have supported her, but I felt betrayed, so I started shouting and stormed out. I couldn't calm down back at home, it was too hot, and I had to talk to her. I called her. There was no answer. I stopped back at the coffee shop, but she wasn't there anymore. I went to her apartment. It was four-thirty. I knocked on the door. She was in the middle of packing up her stuff. I offered to help her. She said it was the most nightmarish way of reminiscing, so instead we went to sit at the Meshulash coffee shop near Ben Gurion Street, which was deserted at that hour. I asked her if there was anything I could do to help, and she started spilling everything. She told me about Menuhin, what I'd already guessed, and how she was so tired and wanted to rest, and that the past month had been nothing but the pain of withdrawal.

"We sat there for a little over an hour. At six, Malkieli was supposed to come see her. She was insistent, but you're right, Dalia had no intention of caving and giving her the new songs. I went to take a walk on the beach, to clear my head and heart after what she'd told me. I got home at seven forty-five. There was a message on my machine from Dalia. She sounded hysterical. 'Rami, you have to come over, he was here, he yelled at me that I'm a whore and will fall apart in Sderot and that I deserve to go back to the hole I crawled out of. He hit me . . . Rami, Rami . . .

Please come, I can't do this anymore.' I ran downstairs and hailed a cab. I got there in fifteen minutes, but it was a minute too late. The door to her apartment was unlocked. I walked inside. From the living room, I saw her standing in the bedroom, holding a gun to her head. I didn't know where she got it. I was paralyzed. I didn't hear anything, I just saw her falling. Elish, I saw her falling, you don't know what that's like, Elish, seeing a person you love falling like that, without . . ."

"Uh-huh," said Elish.

"I'm a nervous person. Lots of things make me lose my cool. But that, what I felt there, like something was exploding inside of my chest, as if I needed fucking proof of the injustice of the world. An intense, fast anger washed over me, purifying me like disinfectant. I had three seconds to think, and all I could think was, No one saw me walking into the apartment, and immediately after that, All that Esther and Yossef Shushan will have left is a fucking piece of marble outside of the cemetery fence, where the suicides go. I imagined them standing outside of the cemetery, no headstone, no real place they could come to when they wanted to commemorate her. The thought was unbearable, and I wanted to do anything I could to fix it. I wanted to yell at Dalia's body, How dare you do that to your parents? How? Even in death you always pull apart, setting yourself outside of the group. Then I saw all of it, all the human structure of Tel Aviv, the way I see a piece of music, its clear design, like a spider's web of cause and effect, and I knew where to break it to make it sound or act like I wanted it to, and I realized what I had to do."

"You know, there was a moment in the investigation," Elish said, "when I thought it might have been a ritualistic murder. That Dalia was murdered by someone who tried to steal her intelligence and talent. You somehow seem sharper than I remembered."

"Dalia told me on more than one occasion that I was numb,

that I was intentionally numbing myself, and that she wondered what it would take to wake me up from my apathy. Why did you think that, because of Dalia's witchery stuff?"

"Yes. Because of her interest in the occult."

"Oh, it was half show. She said several times that Judaism had killed the mystery of nature and that this was her way of protesting. She called it neopaganism or some such shit. Anyway, a natural or supernatural explanation, I don't know. I only know that at that moment it was like a coil was pulled inside of me. I had three seconds and I felt like I was on fucking coke—sharp, focused. Within two seconds, I had a plan. I pulled a pair of socks from one of Dalia's suitcases, wore them on my hands like gloves. I checked her pulse. There was none. I took the gun and shot her in the other temple and through the heart. I spread her arms. I recalled from the times my father took me to the shooting range as a boy that shots leave traces of gunpowder on the side of the hand that holds the gun . . ."

"Not just that. Tissue remnants and soot dust too."

"Whatever you say. I ran the barrel of the gun over both her wrists, the center of each palm, and around her bare ankles. Then I stuffed the gun into my pants, and took the notebooks and the demo from the living room table. I wiped my fingerprints from the doorknob, smoothed my clothes, and locked the door behind me, like a normal civilian going out on his evening walk or to the café. And I left. I'd created the first step in my trap."

"Which was designed to frame Yehuda Menuhin, who had been there around the estimated time of death."

"I'd intended to follow the investigation closely, insinuate a relationship between Menuhin and Dalia to the police, in case they missed it, and plant the gun at the right time and place. I knew the notebooks would have him charged for sure, but also make a mockery of Dalia's memory. That's why I didn't expose them. I was so pleased. I'd found the perfect revenge—conviction and public humiliation. At home, I prepared the first clue: I played Dalia's new songs. What can I say, she'd outdone herself. But all the songs were about death, how life was slowly killing her, and I couldn't do it, the pain butchered my clarity. I pulled out the CD, wrote 'Menuhin' on it with a marker, and went to Malkieli's office. I left it in her mailbox. I knew Malkieli would never admit she'd been to Dalia's just a few hours before the murder, and that she would pretend that Dalia was supposed to have mailed the CD to her."

"You left Dalia's apartment around ten past eight," Elish recounted. He was creating a clear timeline in his mind and wanted to check how the facts mapped into it. "At eight fifteen, Eran Shitrit came home from his evening walk and passed through the yard to get a glimpse of Dalia before going upstairs. He saw Ezra Buhbut, who'd broken into the apartment about a minute earlier, in the living room. The next morning, the papers wrote that the murderer was caught fleeing the crime scene."

"I didn't panic when I got to my night shift at the archive and saw the news flashes on the internet. I thought any idiot would figure out immediately that it was actually a premeditated murder. So instead, I prepared Dalia's archive file. I knew the police would ask for it soon enough, so I slipped in the thick hint about how Dalia knew Yehuda."

"But then you were astounded to find that everyone—the public, the police, and especially the media—was just looking for a scapegoat, and that Buhbut had pulled the short straw," Elish completed the thought.

Rami agreed. "Exactly, and there was nothing I could do about it. Esther told me she didn't believe Buhbut had killed her daughter. I referred a journalist to her, but he thought what she said wouldn't interest anybody. Even the head of the investigations department didn't buy it. Buhbut got life in prison and I waited for my chance. I stalked Menuhin."

"Until on Yom Kippur Eve, Buhbut slit his wrists."

"I read about it online on Yom Kippur night—"

"And then you figured it out," Elish cut him off.

"Yes, that's when I figured out I had to give up the idea of publicly humiliating Menuhin and instead punish him myself. One on one."

"No," Elish said slowly. "That's when you figured out that this had to do with Dalia but wasn't necessarily *about* her. The story about punishment and revenge was between you and Menuhin."

16

You, Elish, I have no idea where you fucking pull this shit from. You can talk for hours like a normal person, then suddenly you say something that doesn't make any sense," Rami said, irritated. He was trying to tamp down his anger, Elish could tell, but the small gestures of the body revealed it—his narrowing eyes, his twitching nose, the air inhaled loudly, in chunks.

"What doesn't make sense, Rami? You learned so much, you did so much, but you're still blind to this simple fact? Why did you reach the conclusion that Menuhin had to die? Why?"

"You want to hear the rest of the story or not?"

"Only if you stop omitting important bits." Elish looked at Rami, whose stature was stretched with hostility, his lips pursed and his eyes expressionless, revealing nothing. Elish waited a few moments, in which Rami remained frozen and alert before him, persistent in his defiant silence. Then Elish said, "You know, Rami, I didn't want to tell you earlier, but Dalia was still alive when you shot her. It takes the body longer to die than we think, even after consciousness disappears. The flesh has its own mechanism. Dalia's brain may have died a fraction of a second after she shot herself, but her heart was still beating, pumping and flowing blood at a dwindling pace, her nervous system still shrank and expanded her lung muscles, slower than usual, but oxygen still reached her inner organs, her stomach and intestines digested and emptied for a moment longer, her liver filtered waste, her cells divided, her hair grew a micromillimeter longer, her skin—"

"Enough!" Rami cried. "Fucking enough." He grabbed his head in his hands. "No, Menuhin killed Dalia, murdered her, even if he wasn't the one to pull the trigger. When she did that to herself she was already an empty shell."

"Yes," said Elish. "He took her away from you long before that."

"He took everything from me." A redness spread through Rami's eyes as he raised his head to look at Elish. He recovers quickly, thought Elish. "He took everything, that son of a bitch. What was I before I met Dalia? What? Just like all those other losers recording music at home, thinking one day someone will discover the fucking masterpiece they wrote? And all because they haven't yet met the real thing. I met her. I touched it. Two months after I started working with Dalia, I could no longer listen to the songs I wrote before that. When Dalia told me that I had potential, that day I gave her my demo, she was being generous. They were shit, all those tracks I recorded on my own. Other than one playback, which she transformed into genius with her lyrics, the rest of the demo was pure shit. Twenty-four-karat shit."

"But with Dalia things were different."

"Dalia had the spark. And in its light, I could see. I could fucking see. I wasn't in love with her, just so you know. It was more than love. Such a strong connection. And when she wrote the songs for the first album, she wrote them so that I could play over them, or she wrote them over my music. I was part of her. An important part."

"Then suddenly, on the second album, when Dalia started to cry during the recording," said Elish, "you realized the songs were now being written for somebody else."

"Yes. Menuhin was the one who made her write. And then she left me, fucking left me with my dick hanging out at the debut show when she announced that Blasé was breaking up."

"She went to him. To the man who inspired her to write."

"And I couldn't rescue her. She changed my life and I couldn't lend her a hand." Rami's voice weakened. The room was dim with rain.

"But Rami," Elish remarked quietly, "you can't save anyone, ever."

"When I was a kid in Bat Yam," Rami said, and Elish wondered if Rami had heard the last thing he said, if he'd understood it, "there was one night a year when I didn't sleep in my bed. Before the beginning of each summer my dad would fumigate the house against cockroaches. My parents, my three brothers, and I would sleep in the enclosed terrace on the night of the fumigation. The terrace was super small, barely large enough for the six mattresses we fit into it. But my brothers were always psyched and started pestering my father as early as Passover, asking when he was going to fumigate. I, on the other hand, would pray every year that my father would forget. Just once, I wanted him to forget. But it was no good, he never did. It was the night I hated the most. I could never fall asleep. I'd lie on my mattress, listening to my mom talking in her sleep, my dad snoring, smelling my brothers' sweat and farts. My mouth would dry out and I couldn't even get up to get some water. You know what it's like when you're so thirsty that the back of your throat starts to hurt?"

Elish nodded encouragingly.

Rami said, "I'm not going back there. No matter what. I've been telling myself that ever since the day I left my parents' home and moved to Tel Aviv, and if I ever forget, if there's a day when I'm not careful enough, the nightmare comes to remind me. I dream I'm still on that terrace and I can't move. My body is paralyzed, like it's glued to the mattress, my throat is dry and choked, like someone filled it with sand. Whenever anything bad happened to me—if I failed a university test or missed a deadline for a paper, when I walked around concerts, trying to give musicians my demo only to have them laugh at me, every time something like that happened, the nightmare would come back." Rami laughed, a failed laugh that veered into a croak. When he calmed down, he added, "I've had that nightmare every night since I saw Dalia dying."

Elish walked to the kitchen, which he could see from the spot where he stood, pulled a glass from the cupboard and a bottle of mineral water from a six pack next to the fridge. He returned to the living room and handed Rami a glass filled to the brim. Rami downed the water in one gulp. "Why not," he told Elish. "Make yourself at home."

"I can't have you losing your ability to speak before I hear the rest of the story."

"THE NEXT DAY, I WENT TO MENUHIN'S PLACE." RAMI RETURNED to his factual tone, slipping into it skillfully, as if the recent exchanges between him and Elish had already evaporated from his memory, and the story, the course of events that he may have re-created for himself over and over since, was the only truth he could hold on to. "I rang the doorbell, put on a helmet I still had from the time Nicole owned a moped, and carried a package in my hand. I was wearing gloves. That old prune opened the door in a bathrobe. I pushed him aside and walked in. I closed the door behind me and aimed my gun at him. He looked at me, horrified, and said, 'How did you get my gun?' And I thought, I'm in luck, it's his gun. What could be more perfect? He must have left it at Dalia's place as part of one of his sick games. Or maybe Dalia stole it from him. Also, why did his gun have a silencer? What did he need that for? Who knows what he was even planning to do with it. I made him sit at his desk. In my package I had a small bottle of wine and two sedatives. I poured the wine into the glass that was on the desk and made him take the pills with the wine at gunpoint. He was trembling with fear, showing no resistance. The combination of the drugs had him out within thirty minutes.

I put the gun in his right hand, aimed at his temple, and pulled the trigger. There was no sound, but his head fell on the desk. I left the gun and the wine and went home."

"Another example of negligent police work. They didn't check whether the gun had been used in previous offenses."

"I didn't know what was going on. I spent a day and a half sitting at my computer, waiting for a news report about his suicide. When nothing happened, I prepared a clipping book about Menuhin during my shift at the archives and planted the clue from Dalia's file in it. The next day, I wore the helmet again, went to the police station, and asked for Superintendent Binyamini—I remembered he was the head of the team that investigated Dalia's murder. There was a huge mess there. The officers in the lobby didn't want to let me in, and they didn't know anything about nothing. Finally, a female officer showed up and told me she was from the investigations unit, but didn't know which file Binyamini had ordered the archival materials for. I stepped aside and pretended to talk on the radio, then came back and told her Binyamini had ordered the envelope for Yehuda Menuhin's file. She said she didn't understand what the archival materials were for, but that she'd have them filed in case someone might need them."

"Did you really think you'd get away with it?"

"You're forgetting that at that point I already had. Besides, yes, most people just wait around for someone to tell them what to think. I had to let it go, make do with my little revenge, but I couldn't, so I pulled out my last card."

"Me?"

"Uh-huh. I left an anonymous letter in Gideon Menuhin's mailbox, telling him his brother's death was not what it seemed. I was hoping that at worst he would pressure the police to reopen the investigation and at best he would request a private investigation. I included news clippings that contained your name in the letter."

"I understand. Gideon must have thought it was some sophisticated attempt at extortion. That's why he requested an investigation into the circumstances of his brother's death. He was just trying to protect himself, find out what secrets would be uncovered. You have no idea the size of the can of worms you opened when you made that move."

"What do you mean?" Rami asked, his clouding eyes disclosing the fact that he hadn't been following Elish's thread.

"Not that it matters, but why me? Why?"

"Why? You knew Dalia and Yehuda. The connection between them was natural to you. I didn't take many risks and left almost nothing to fucking chance. I sent Manny Lahav the list of the panoramic course lectures anonymously. I knew he would be interested in a lecture about serial murder, and I knew he'd finally recognize your name, which came up in Dalia's murder investigation."

"And then you showed up there yourself, to keep a close watch and make sure the fly got caught in the web."

"Yes. If you insist on presenting it that way. But I also came to pay my respects to you. Dalia always said you were the only critic who understood what Blasé was doing. There was another reason you were such an essential piece of my scheme. Dalia told me that afternoon at the Meshulash that you two met once when you were kids, and that she wasn't sure you remembered, because whenever you wrote about Blasé, or left her voice-mail messages, you spoke to her like she was a stranger."

"I worked hard for a long time not to remember. My efforts failed."

"I knew you remembered. There was some kind of obsession in your writing about Blasé that couldn't have just come out of nowhere. I knew you wouldn't rest until you found her murderer."

"Is that why you asked that question at my lecture? You were asking about obsession."

"No. Not at all. I asked that question not to expose myself, but just because that girl wouldn't stop pestering you with those dumb questions."

Elish smiled. "We're sentenced to leave tracks behind."

"That was the one element I didn't take into consideration. Not the tracks, but your thinking. I didn't realize in time what a fucking paranoid you are. After your lecture I started going home, and halfway to the gates I changed my mind. I wanted to talk to you. I went back and found you at the cafeteria, talking to Manny Lahav. I listened in. He was talking loud enough for me to deduce what you were saying too. I called your office the next morning and introduced myself as Manny's assistant. I asked if you two had already scheduled a meeting, and your secretary got pissed off, saying he'd just called a minute ago to make an appointment for that night."

Elish completed the story, "And then you started stalking me, making sure I reached the conclusion you wanted–that Yehuda Menuhin murdered Dalia Shushan and then killed himself. You indirectly got me invited to Dalia's memorial, where you incidentally ran into me, and when you heard I was writing an article you knew your plan was working. You had Nicole tell me about the demo, and you knew she was leaving for India the next morning, so you weren't afraid to lie in her name. And all throughout the investigation you kept throwing me hints–a hint about Dalia cheating on Lior Levitan, an innocent comment about Dalia's attraction to older men."

Rami averted his eyes. "What are you going to do, Elish?"

A DIFFERENT LIGHT SHINES ON THE HOPELESS THAN ON THOSE who believe they are destined to be saved. Even the tiny, nonpretentious blossoming of the Israeli coastal plain acknowledged that fact. In the crannies and the sands, the cliffs and the boulder slopes, it crouches and hunches. Even its blooming and stretching by force of wind during the hot waves of spring is nothing but a tangled web of disappearance. The sea lavender and the hispid viper, the germander and the Syrian oregano, the *Ornithogalum* and the scarlet pimpernel, the spurges and the chamomiles, the sage and the erigeron, all thriving in that other light. And Tel Aviv, which was already being gnawed on by rumors of war, with the remembered horrors of the sealed room and the stored plastic odor of the gas masks, was also becoming veiled with the ugly lighting of banishment. It seemed to Elish that in those moments when he stood on Rothschild Boulevard and let his eyes drift up, that a large animal had risen from its slumber and urgently abandoned the city, the angles of buildings sketching the tracks of its body, claw and hoof, beak and maw.

Here is the moment when you become a person, he told himself. Choose. You can look at the sky, turn to the heavens and ask, Is this your verdict? A bit of rain? A little lightning? But you are here, Elish, your eyes must rest on the ground, this is your moment of grace. Do you suppose if you eliminate every possibility of judgment you'd be able to shake off the guilt? Yaffa already told you, "It was always your fault." The stench of coffee, cigarettes, and sea will continue to haunt you. It is the only goddess of vengeance. Why did you let Rami be?

No, said Elish. Vanity of vanities, all is vanity. I, Elish, am a detective in Tel Aviv and have seen the labors at which people toil under the sun and have communed with mine own heart, What are you doing, standing here beating on the corner of Rothschild and Herzl? And you, Elish protested, tell me, my entire life I have been moving away from the body. Tell me, I am a person, I have the right to decide in the matter of the justice which I want to serve me, and here is the moment of grace in which one is made, in which one pounces from knowledge to action. Is this why you let Rami be?

Rami had asked him, "What are you going to do, Elish?" and

Elish hadn't answered. He was too absorbed in the final sections of Dalia's third notebook.

The second-to-last entry of the notebook read, "Last year on the Ninth of Av, Yehuda told me, 'Yom Kippur and the Ninth of Av are the pillars of the Jewish year, the complete opening and the complete closure of the gates of heaven.' And I thought, Dealing with theology requires a confession of one's true passions, not just toying with them. I do not need anyone to tell me about the Ninth of Av, about the pieces of the heart that shift on that day."

The last entry was dated the night before Dalia's death, a continuation of the previous one: "On the eve of the Ninth of Av, on the Jewish year 5762, I heard your words to Job from the storm, Hast thou entered into the springs of the sea? or hast thou walked in the search of the depth? Have the gates of death been opened unto thee? Or hast thou seen the doors of the shadow of death? And what do you think, that these days there is a person to whom you can address such questions in all seriousness? So you invented the behemoth. I created the monsters of the heart. Can you hear it squeaking within the flesh? Huh? And how about seeing passion wasting like a puddle of blood? Can you do that?"

Elish raised his head and said, "Nothing."

Rami kept silent for a moment, then dared: "Not that I'm trying to force you to run to the police or something. But may I ask why?"

"As far as I'm concerned, justice has been served"—thoughts of Hilton Beach flowed into his throat—"so that everything starts and ends with your answer to the question 'What is justice?' You know that certain crimes require punishment, but how does one determine the punishment's severity and the authority entitled to convict and administer such punishment? You can choose to be an individual in some society, leaving justice in the hands of a system you want to believe is impartial. This way, you remove your personal responsibility, the risk of making a mistake." He paused. He was appalled when the idea had formed itself in his mind at the beach earlier, and was appalled again now that he had to speak it. "Or you can take upon yourself the role of judge and executioner, knowing full well that there are some crimes for which the punishment itself transcends criminality." He swallowed and added, "And with regards to the method of punishment, you've discovered it yourself. It's ancient and simple—an eye for an eye, a tooth for a tooth, a measure for a measure."

Rami asked, "And what if there is a different authority?"

"And what if there is?" Elish replied. "That's your problem and its problem. If it exists, let it take care of itself."

EPILOGUE

Lying in the dark and listening to Tel Aviv rather than talking to people. His conversation with Manny had worn him out. Manny had fidgeted when Elish asked him about his intentions. Elish understood that as soon as Manny realized the scope of consequences, knew he would have to deal with Gideon Menuhin, he had decided to make the investigation go away. Elish had to say it for him: "Long story short, you have no intention of reopening either file. Buhbut is dead and there's nobody to demand his right to truth. No one but me. And now you're asking me not to do it. To make do with knowledge. True, you're right. Why would you waste your bargaining chips? Your status at the police is bad, and all of a sudden you have a chance to improve it. You can exhibit your power for Gideon Menuhin, and he will back you up in your battle with the chief of police and owe you one for choosing not to reopen his brother's file and defame him as a murderer."

"Elish, that's a little cynical."

"A little cynical?" Elish fumed. "Have you no shame? There are no other words for what you're doing. We'll talk another day," he said, ending the conversation.

Lying in the dark and listening to Tel Aviv rather than talking to people. His conversation with his mother was even more tiring, even with Tahel bleating "Eyish" into the phone. He'd called to tell her that the thugs had been taken care of. They'd been locked up, and whoever sent them would no longer dare touch him or his family. His mother begged him to quit his dangerous job, not hesitating to describe the nightmares she'd had ever since the attack—dreams of detailed, horrific deaths befalling him, Yaffa, Tahel, Bobby. He thought about her, about how her years, ever since Prosper faded with a whimper, had filled with memory. In her voice he heard her failed flower garden, finally guessing why she'd toiled so much over it—each flower was like a capsule, bearing a secret meaning that only she and his father could decipher, events from their shared past at the transit camp that they were unwilling to reveal: the games they played as children, how they discovered their bodies, fell in love, and began to learn to read the signs of the world. Yaffa's repeated pleas as a young woman were no good either, when she discovered the surprising truth—that parents do not materialize in the world as full-grown adults, hunched from hard work, but that they too, sometime in the beginning of time, had tasted a bit of the pleasure she knew. In spite of that week when she cried without end, the first time she and Bobby broke up, their mother disclosed nothing of her own love story as she tried to comfort Yaffa and soothe the agony of love, and his parents' past remained a secret, glowing and weighty. And now Elish almost asked, but realized it would take him more time to phrase the correct question, and instead promised to come over next Saturday, and asked that his mother let Yaffa know. The meteorologist predicted sunshine, and who could tell what would happen before then. The rain weakened and disappeared, the city cracking open its eyes.

Lying in the dark and listening to Tel Aviv. Elish considered how many years of his life he could waste this way, pondering the ways in which the city passed by, how each car horn forged its path in the darkness, ripping off a bit of time, the hubbub of engines piercing Tel Aviv. Though his apartment on Tel Hai Street—more alley than street, really—was enveloped in quiet in these midnights when sleep eluded him and he lay in bed, staring, turning over, had he tried hard, he would have been able to dredge up from the depths of the Tel Avivian night the rustles that composed it—the patter of high heels along the sidewalk, a cackle, a cry. His hearing expanded to engulf Dizengoff on one side and King George on the east, burning endlessly with traffic, then moved westward until it contained the sea.